OTHER
WHISPERS

OTHER WHISPERS

An Engineer's Life

A Novel

Gordon Zima

SUNSTONE
PRESS

SANTA FE

Accidental conjunctions can give big pushes into the real world. The principals of this demonstration are all fictional and no identification with real persons is intended.

Sunstone books may be purchased for educational, business, or sales promotional use. For information please write: Special Markets Department, Sunstone Press, P.O. Box 2321, Santa Fe, New Mexico 87504-2321.
Cover artwork by Paula Zima
Book design › Vicki Ahl
Body typeface › ITC Benguiat Std
Printed on acid-free paper
⊗
eBook 978-1-61139-244-9

Library of Congress Cataloging-in-Publication Data
Zima, Gordon.
  Other Whispers, an Engineer's Life : a novel / by Gordon Zima.
     pages cm
  ISBN 978-0-86534-516-4 (softcover : alk. paper)
  1. Engineers--Fiction. 2. Self-actualization (Psychology)--Fiction. 3. Pasadena (Calif.)--Fiction. I. Title.
  PS3626.I48680084 2014
  813'.6--dc23

                              2013048764

WWW.SUNSTONEPRESS.COM
SUNSTONE PRESS / POST OFFICE BOX 2321 / SANTA FE, NM 87504-2321 /USA
(505) 988-4418 / ORDERS ONLY (800) 243-5644 / FAX (505) 988-1025

To *my* ladies...P^{2}AM
and the gooblah people

"No man is an island,
Entire of itself.
Each is a piece of the continent,
A part of the main."

—John Donne, 1624 Meditation 17

1

The four engine commercial job was drifting over Cajon Pass. From his window seat, Paul Sanger could see the swift progression from the brutal wasteland of the Mojave to an astounding mosaic of citrus and grapes, beginning at the western edge of the Sierra Madres and claiming most of his view toward the Pacific. During the passage up the valley, this agriculture made occasional accommodation to urban adventure. There was a slight haze this afternoon, but not enough to hide a shining sea border, nor s ome hints of the coastal islands that garnished the panorama of Southern California.

A few weeks ago, it had been Lieutenant Paul Sanger, completing the last leg of a trans-Pacific marathon that had brought him to the formal end of his WWII military responsibility at Fort McArthur near Los Angeles. Turning away from the bright window, he closed his eyes and quickly fell into a persistent kaleidoscope of thoughts that included his military experience and pieces of his life as far back as his memory could go.

His Iowa homecoming had given him plenty of a bridge between the military and the civilian. This included a more than tacit invitation from his father to resume his role in the Sanger family farm enterprises. But he had tried to justify himself in front of his father, more in front of his sister Mary, and he hadn't backed away from his own arguments.

"Why Southern California...you could be a prince of Iowa." Mary was trying to make some order out of the random pile of her slides Paul had just created.

"While I was coming home, leaning over the edge of that baby carrier staring at that hissing foam, some of my debt to society hissed back at me...my weather officer presence on Iwo Jima didn't quite make it...square my account."

"Everybody can't be a Marine pushing that flag up on Suribachi—you found a niche, you filled it honorably for Christ's sake." They were both in swim suits. He'd pulled her out of their pool for another dive into her pictures when they'd argued over some point of history.

He had been home for several weeks. He'd tried to reenter the Sanger life via his dad and mother's doors; but his sister Mary had clapped more ligaments on him with her painting and photography and teaching, and a younger perspective which was a better stage for argument and agreement.

She'd put an arm around his neck and then pecked his cheek before picking up her question. "So?"

"Pasadena is there. Caltech is there. They've been gathering a lot of scope on a lot of things...I...I think I'd rather be a Joe there than a prince here. I want to hear some other voices...maybe *other whispers* would be better for a dedicated non-pushy type."

"When did you make *that* dedication—I wouldn't know that man." Another peck.

"Humbleness crept into me from various parts of the Pacific...let me practice a little anyway."

"Then you won't need that satchel I was knitting for you to carry your checkbook and wallet."

"Jeese...and I thought maybe you were pregnant."

"No such luck with the preliminaries."

"You liked California when you came to Stanford to see me."

"I still like it...I just don't want to see you disappear into it. That scope thing of yours—damn you, I have one, too. I can see plenty of facets on mine that don't need Hollywood—or your precious Pasadena—to sparkle."

He complicated the arm entanglement and then he kissed her, a lip business that she barely kept nonincestuous. "I'll leave my own beacons for you—you won't lose me."

As the plane maneuvered into the LA landing pattern, the harsh pile of the Sierra Madres suddenly filled his window. Briefly, he could see some of the buildings of the Mount Wilson observatory, and below this on a rugged frontal face, the clearing that Caltech boys had made into a 'T' of commendable insolence.

His knowledge of the California Institute of Technology had come largely from newspaper and magazine articles about accomplishments in physics, chemistry, and biology. Occasionally, he'd wondered about his own credentials for exposure to such a pantheon of natural science. If his Stanford momentum hadn't trickled through almost four years of the military, graduate work might be closer to reality for him. Here he was at an age when most PhDs were either taking their thesis baggage into government or commercial arenas, or they were settling into teaching and tenure. But what the hell! Men with even his modest cap were still uncommon enough and the technical explosion that *was* this time was still just that. He'd find his place...and he'd enjoy pushing around some of the young squirts in doing it.

He had no contacts in Southern California. During his Stanford days, he'd experienced the full Tournament of Roses pageant several times, and he'd helped rock the Rose Bowl with the axe yell. Two days of laryngitis had been small payment for seeing Shaughnessy's boys parade a victorious T formation in front of a hundred thousand yelling heads. He had liked the Pasadena he'd seen and the presence of Caltech was the deciding impetus for a location decision bolstered mostly by intuition.

The airport bus and cab chain eventually deposited him at the Huntington Hotel, a hostelry still wedded to the amenities an earlier, more generally opulent, Pasadena had liked. His financial situation and the Huntington weren't a good match, but he preferred to look at a new environment rather more from a top, than a bottom vantage. Furthermore, the Huntington Library and Art Gallery were close at hand.

The next day he accomplished some wardrobe improvement, and bought a second-hand Cadillac previously owned by a diminutive, venerable lady of that city...so help him God.

The Ship Room of the Huntington was a good conjunction of food, drink, music, and facilities for conversation. Paul had finished an excellent steak and settled at the bar for an inspection of the Scotch landscape. He picked a spot in the unblended malt country of the Northwest coast and was turning to inspect a ship model when his drinking arm was jostled by a passing gentleman arrayed in the splendor of the U. S. Air Corps. Checking for damage to his new suit, Paul lowered his head...but not enough. Someone took his slightly depleted drink, placed it on the bar, and then pulsed the local vocal climate with the claim, "I'll be a son of a bitch!" All of this seemed to come in the same time package.

This got Paul's attention. Close to consensus, he pulled up short at the sight of Tom Andrews, his buddy of Western Pacific locales that had included Guam, Iwo Jima, and Okinawa. "For Christ's sake!—when did *you* escape?" Both of his hands free, he grabbed back in the direction of the encyclopedic grin that was swarming on him.

"I was starting to crawl the walls of DC HQ. A good fairy plucked me off... hence, Caltech's Propulsion Analysis Group, here I come...or there I am!"

"I didn't know your aura of friendship was that comprehensive." Paul was now facing the bar and modeling a better social voice for that place.

"Take it any way you want, you bastard. I think I'm happy about it."

"How long you been out here?"

"Three days. Another guy and I came out together. Yesterday we stumbled on a hovel down in the Arroyo we're calling home for a while...but what t'hell gives with you?—this is fantastic!"

Paul's exuberance seemed to falter for a moment. "After a month on the homestead, I decided Millikan could use some help out here." Fine at the start, but it faded toward the end. Paul put his eyes on the Scotch landscape again, and then he signaled for more samples.

"No bull...you're really going to give 'em a break over there?"

"With jokers like you running around, it looks like a better idea now." He punched Tom's shoulder, went back to his Scotch, motioning to the new one that had appeared for Tom. Finally he murmured, "They haven't dug that far into the barrel...yet."

"Meaning?"

"Meaning...I'm unengaged—a good Hollywood line I think. I'll be jingling my balls in pursuit of employment...damn shortly."

"You're a technical man—why don't you give PAG a look at you?"

"Right now...with this little old bog juice quivering close to me...I'm open as hell to any constructive suggestion." A female leg was turning within his view at that moment. He improved his vantage slightly. "I would—I am—considering even an improper, unconstructive, suggestion."

Tom lowered his voice more than was necessary. "You never told me your aura reached out that far, either."

Paul pulled two cigars from his inside jacket pocket, lit his and Tom's with his old Zippo and then blew a contemplative smoke cloud.

"That the same Zippo you pulled out of that Jap bunker on Iwo?"

"Yup...wonder where they got it." Paul took his treasure away from Tom and rolled it in his hand.

"That simple little gadget will go down as one of the great achievements of our age—considering function and opportunity." Tom said, extracting his own gold plated job.

Paul placed his beat-up chromed friend next to Tom's and said quietly, "The haves...and the not quites."

"I'll drink to that," Tom said, doing it. "It's great when a guy and his place get together." The grins collided again, then Tom said, "Their personnel man, Colonel Hayes, is a good Joe. Meet me in the personnel office tomorrow and I'll give you a good screwing."

"In front of the colonel?"

"Righto."

"What red-blooded American boy wouldn't rise to *that* bait." Paul took a pad and a pencil from that same busy pocket.

Tom managed a few scratches that, with two asterisks and one footnote, tended to convey the location of the Propulsion Analysis Group. "There...with an Indian guide, you should be fat."

The Propulsion Analysis Group was one of the post-war crystallizations of the fluid of rocket talent that had flowed around the foothills of the Sierra Madres during the war, and somewhat before, under military aegis. Most of the founding fathers had been graduate students, or staff, of Caltech. From a fairly hair raising array of skeletal theory, equipment and experiments, these Argonauts had succeeded in fashioning jet thrust devices of use to the military. This success sufficed to provide collateral for the post-war continuance, or formation, of several large privately owned rocket R&D organizations, and the federally owned and sponsored Propulsion Analysis Group, administered by Caltech. The upper echelons of PAG were comprised almost entirely of Caltech alumni with unlimited campus visiting privileges, or faculty, or staff of the school on commitments to the laboratory ranging between definite and hazy.

The core of this talent derived from the Aeronautics Department of the school, simply because when venturing beyond the dramatics of the combustion chamber of a rocket, the rest of the story had better be composed by people conversant with the disciplines of aeronautics...or the rest may be silence, after a spectacular interval of less silence.

The rocket is a demanding beast, whether statically confined to a test stand, or allowed to proceed to its dynamic limit as the driving agency of a space vehicle. There are few—if any—systems of man's contriving that demand a broader scope of technical knowledge than the rocket and its ancillaries. Accordingly, the nucleus of aeronautics types was quickly supplemented by chemists, mathematicians, mechanical and chemical engineers, metallurgists, even the occasional physicist when the energy spectrums of the thing got interesting enough. The present staff of PAG reflected this technical Catholicism of the rocket. At any given time, the civilian component was spiked by a good dose of Army, Navy and Air Force people on liaison or learning assignments.

Paul parked his boat in the visitor's lot and proceeded to the temporary credentials that would let him advance to the personnel office. He inadvertently wrote *Lt. Air Force* in the 'occupation' space. A few moments earlier, he'd incorrectly told the guard that he was lieutenant so and so, and thereafter he *was* lieutenant to this particular guard.

Tom was waiting in the foyer of Personnel. He grinned and made a wry face at the wall clock.

"Not too bad for an amateur civilian, eh?" Paul countered. Hell, it *was* only 8:30 AM.

"My boy, sometime let me tell the parable of the early worm." Tom placed an arm around the shoulder of his protégé. "Joan, this handsome devil thinks he might want to work here," he said to the blond and attractive young lady. She indicated a sign-in sheet.

"Colonel Hayes will be with you shortly," she said, her look at them not entirely official.

There was a display of large colored photographs and drawings of various rocket and missile activities that had involved PAG, and Paul studied them. Tom was dispensing some running commentary when Joan announced that the time was now.

Colonel Hayes had recently retired from Army Ordnance. A short, ruddy faced, man, his shock of white hair in no way implied surrender proclivities. His bearing was confirmed by the Point ring he wore. When he greeted Paul, his voice uncovered a Southern embellishment that Paul had always found very agreeable. He motioned Paul and Tom to chairs adjoining his desk.

"Well now, young fellow, Tom's been enthusiastic about you. Tell me how much of a liar he is...and for Christ's sake, relax. Except for your possibly lucky friend here, we're just plain old civilians." These southerners knew how to blend some velvet with both smile and cuss.

Paul's discourse on his Stanford days was interrupted by the colonel's assertion, "You damn right you guys had one hell of a team. I saw that fracas in forty-one in the Bowl." Paul had a good record at Stanford, even picking up a Phi Lambda Upsilon key his junior year in chemical engineering. But he was carefully modest about his AB in view of the colonel's almost hourly contact with men to whom the AB was bare bones. The colonel reacted as a devoted listener to Paul's adventures with typhoons in the Western Pacific as an Air Force meteorologist. Tom was quiet, but Paul caught a wink, or two, between the two Point men.

"It sounds like you might find a home in our Chemistry Division." The colonel took an organization chart from his desk drawer and shoved it toward Paul. "You shouldn't have to hunt too far to find your challenges there." He looked at Paul, received no discouragement. "I'll have Joan get you a personal history form and an application. Get these back to me ASAP, then we'll see about that unemployment of yours...I'm not the last word, you know."

Paul sensed that the hurdle he'd just apparently cleared *was* important.

He felt good after he and Tom thanked the colonel and then launched a dual wink in Joan's direction as they left the office.

"Your Air Force cryptographic clearance will probably speed your clearance here," Tom said. "But get that stuff back to them today...and keep your balls tight. You'll be badged out before you know it."

"That's a splendid suggestion. I'll just go back to that empty desk in Personnel and get right on it."

"I presume you mean the forms—if I thought that young lady's honor was in any jeopardy I'd have to intervene as an officer...and gentleman?"

"Down, Galahad. By the way...even if nothing comes of this, I'm in your debt again...or is it up...?"

"Right on the first count—the second only if you don't reach my brag. Call me tonight if you want somebody to hold your hand."

His interview with several of the Chemistry people had gone okay. The formal acceptance of his job petition was received two days prior to notification of his security credentials. A mediocre Iowa farmer would have sneered at the stipend for a month of his work. But he was an apprentice now, selected for work with entrepreneurs of science in an exciting arena. Further-more, and in a strictly social sense, the crowd at the Ship Room at the Huntington seemed to be democratic.

He'd grown up along plow tracks that went into horizons with no real surprises. Now he was on the verge of other tracks where surprises were used as seeds, and horizons refused to stand still.

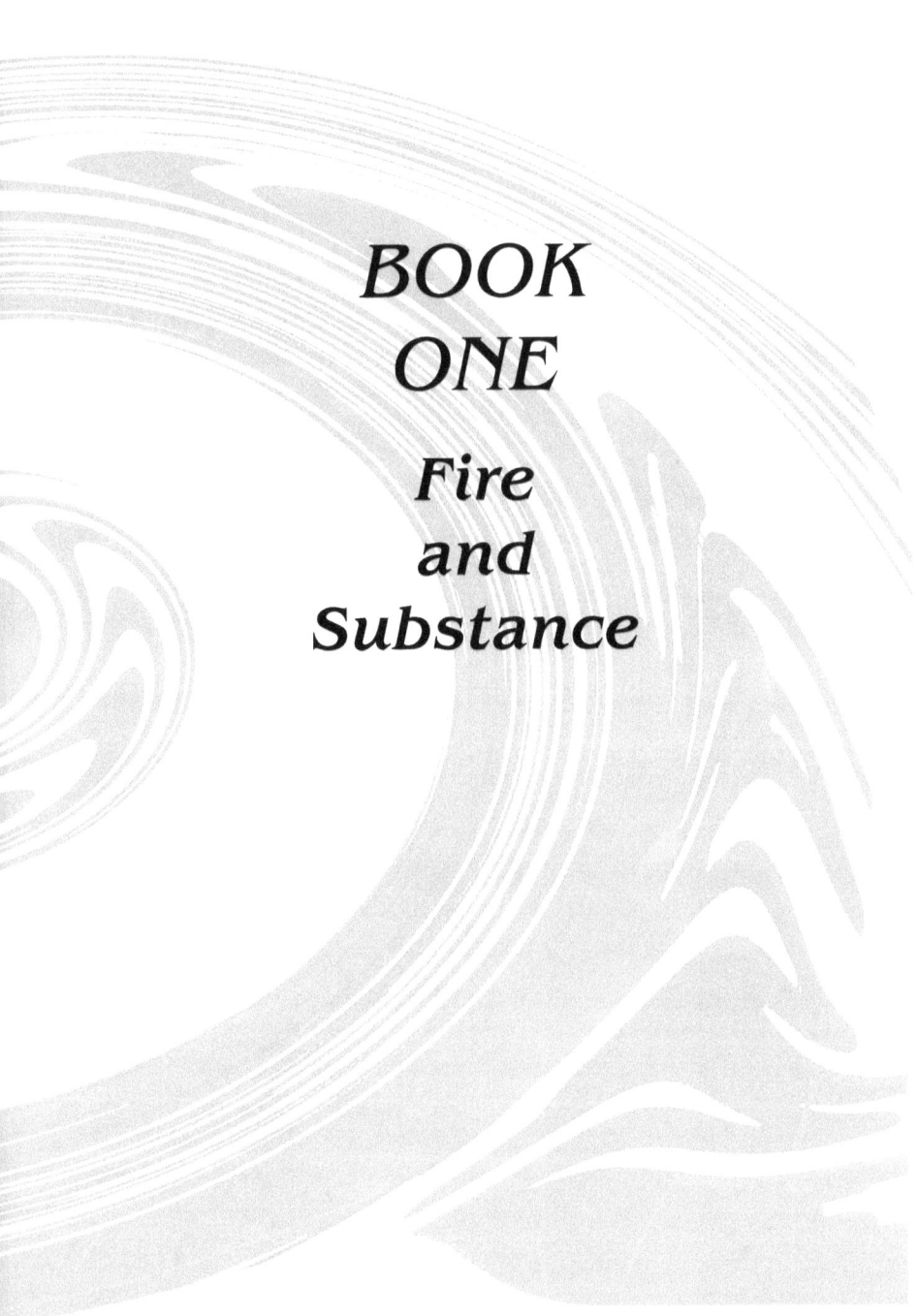

BOOK ONE

Fire and Substance

2

A tapestry of now residential Pasadena would need more coarse stuff to work into agreeable patterns of roses and oleanders than a generation ago. But the silk threads, still the essential basis of her, continued to complicate various attempts to put boundaries on her hierarchies. An aggressive one of these smooth filaments could insinuate many places and frustrate a man's honest resolve of temporary humbleness.

One of the older, large estates near the Pasadena-San Marino border had outlived the justification, but not the accommodation, for carriages, grooms, and horses. The upper level of this carriage house had been converted into an apartment.

"This is a one in a million shot...but worth a try," the realtor said, collapsing into his chair. There had been prior discussion of other alternatives among the coarser stuff.

After some confusion within a maze of streets, Paul eventually zeroed on the address. A gate, part of a wrought iron artistry that included several gargoyles, was open. The road led beneath massive live oaks for several hundred feet to a circular parking layout, part of whose arc was enveloped by the covered portico of a Tudor style house which transcended the three bedrooms, two bath category.

He saw a bronze griffin head which he reasoned was the doorbell. Three rings and the door was opened by a maid in a working costume. He'd expected at least a Beefeater with mace. He gave his name...said he would appreciate talking to the owner about a personal matter. Several minutes later, the maid returned and advised him that Mrs. Drake would see him shortly. She ushered him into an ante room.

For a few minutes, he scanned the wood paneling of the room and colored projections of a stained glass window on the parquet flooring. The variegated light also identified etchings and several small oils, a surrogate handshake from this place that tended to calm him a little. He heard heels echoing from an unseen extension of this vista and a woman entered his view. She was dressed in a yellow sun suit and carried a woven hat whose construction was similar to that favored by his mother for garden work. The gloves she was removing further supported his reminiscence...but only for a moment. Her hair seemed to be an amalgam of light brown and platinum and, as she completed her posture of reconnaissance several paces in front of him, his quick inventory included a medium height and blue eyes. Using only the criterion of some faint concessions to maturity near her eyes and mouth, he judged her to have favored some forty summers. Her facial and figure accoutrements reminded him of some of the fascinating French and English patricians he'd seen very recently in the halls and formal galleries of Henry and Arabella Huntington's Library and Art Gallery.

"I'm Martha Drake," she said. Her voice concealed particular antecedents other than perfect congruity with her surroundings.

"Paul Sanger, Mrs. Drake," and the enormity of his petition nearly choked him. "I...I've been looking for housing. One of the poor devils I've been badgering remembered that this...your estate, had a carriage house apartment that had been let by previous owners. He suggested I present my credentials... supplication...and then run like...Well it is ridiculous, isn't it." He managed a good smile despite formidable interior interference. But he prepared his face to make a graceful stand against her response to this insolent intrusion. Some of his preparation must have been evident to her, and this intuition stopped any tendency to the definitive, probably unassailable, reply that surely was in her inventory.

"You had no way of knowing our...situation," she said, her eyes still assaying the local values. "We weren't aware that there had been...tenants." He thought he saw the subtle shadings of a smile. "You've been at some pains... perhaps in the interest of historical privilege...I could show you the carriage house." Anticipating Paul's affirmative, she turned, and with a slight gesture, signaled him to follow her. They entered a foyer and traveled a hallway that eventually opened to a large veranda. During the walk, she asked him where he was from, how long he'd been in Pasadena...what his professional interest was. Among his answers was the addendum that he was a bachelor, and a veteran, placing a few details into his last credential.

They crossed a portion of the lawn and intersected the driveway. Some yards along the driveway, a fairly large structure, architecturally consonant with the main house, confronted them. It had obviously seen more exhilarating tenants than the car parked inside. Paul could see vague outlines of a still serviceable horse set-up, with stalls and feed shoots that originated in the level above and terminated in semi-spherical wrought iron sections on the back of the stalls. A stairway led upward from the side of this now sanctuary of internal combustion. Martha Drake noticed Paul's interested reconnoiter.

"I think they must have had lots more fun in those days," she said, and Paul had no trouble visualizing her as the chatelaine...with appropriate steeds and livery. She preceded him up the stairs and unlatched the door at the top.

"I must apologize for what will be a dusty and spidery place. We haven't used it for anything but some of our daughter's junk—treasure—for some time." She took a smile across the threshold.

The accommodation consisted of a fairly large living room with a fire-place, a good sized bedroom with a large walk-in closet, a full bath. A small kitchen with a dining alcove completed the principal amenities. The woodwork and flooring did no insult to the main house. The windows of the bedroom and living room opened to an aggressive combination of jasmine and wisteria. He was looking at the fireplace when Martha Drake returned from her general inspection.

"God knows when that was last cleaned...it's probably vine-choked."

"With—or without—that fireplace, this place is fascinating." It was her show. He waited for the impossible.

She escorted him along the driveway toward his car. Looking backward at the carriage house...as he did, several times, the illusion of an estate in miniature was easy to make.

"You said that the apartment had been let to a Caltech student?" They'd reached his car. He repeated his earlier assertion. "Well...there's a big space here for my husband and me to rattle around in. He may disagree about that space...but around here, Caltech traditions tend to have some imperative qual-ity." If her smile wasn't enough of a complement to the occasion, his took up the slack.

"I could resolve to uphold whatever tradition is vested in that place."

"Well...we'll have to look into that tradition a bit," she said.

After he made it to the driver's seat, she put both hands on her hips, like some top sergeants he'd seen. "You appear to be good tenant material, Mr. Sanger." Relaxing the pose, she said, "I'll see what my husband has to say and let you know. You said you're staying at the...Huntington?"

"Yes ma'am," he replied, in reflexive accord with sound Mid-Western style. He thought he detected a faint counter signal of amusement and he was damn glad he'd encumbered his courtesy with a broad smile.

His traveling biography for her had included the word, *lieutenant*. As he passed her in the driveway. she gave him a snap salute...and something else to think about as he went back to the real world.

That night, the lighted pool at the Huntington was nearly devoid of activists as he slipped into the cool green light and pulled for the far end. Four, or five, laps later he felt he'd had the cap he needed for this day. After dressing, he walked through the lobby and looked at some of the paintings, wondering if he would ever get back to his again.

By the time he reached the elevator, the paintings had lost his thoughts to PAG, the potentially good fortune of the carriage house...the lady of the carriage house. Images kept him away from sleep for a long time. *The job...wonderful opportunity. Must get some letters out tomorrow. That apartment set-up... too fantastic. Lady Fate used her benevolent hand when she tossed old Tom his way again...and what t'hell right did Madame Ligonier have butting into his affairs with her damn smile and her damn...*

Paul's first morning at PAG was spent filling out more forms for Personnel. He received a temporary badge and waited for an escort from Chemistry.

"I'm looking for Mr. Paul Sanger." This statement had issued from a head poked around a corner of the reception room. The voice, not particularly accented, had projected from a full, strong face, topped by a shock of gray-black hair that would never make a Vitalis commercial.

Paul looked up from a magazine, stood up and walked toward the head that had now joined a stocky body, several inches shorter then Paul's six feet, and wearing a lab coat over what appeared to be very casual attire.

"Guilty," Paul said, extending a hand and a grin.

"I'm Russ Kinzer. Sorry I didn't see you earlier. Our schedules didn't overlap until today." He returned Paul's grip with a strength Paul had anticipated. "It looks like I may be inflicted on you...for a while at least." Kinzer's smile was also anticipated.

"Great!" Paul had always had a thing about first impressions and this one was keeping right on track.

"Look, Paul...we don't have anything urgent at the moment. Let's take the fifty cent tour." Russ placed one hand on Paul's shoulder and indicated the door with the other.

The external aspect of PAG consisted of a motley assortment of one and two story buildings, Quonset huts, revetment-like structures and roads...the all plastered against the foothills over several hundred acres. The architectural style and color scheme was a synthesis of Later Southern Iwo Jima and Early Camp Roberts.

The administration building, with the principal conference room, enjoyed the elevation advantage. Thereafter, the laboratory flowed downward, stopping just short of a wash that was usually called dry. Pure theoreticians of various persuasions tended to the top of this gradient, sharing the invigoration of relative silence and good air with sundry overhead types who were the on-site manifestations of Caltech authority and the various guardians of the Government investment in things and people. As ideas approached the hazard of actual testing, they drifted down this gradient toward a cluster of shops, test pits and laboratories where both silence and purity of air were short transients.

At this time, PAG's experimental and theoretical thrust was more toward power plant research than the extraterrestrial management and utilization of the total vehicle that was to become the dominant justification of the laboratory. During this tour, Paul couldn't tell whether occasional clouds of multi-colored smoke—with and without bang orchestration—signaled success, or failure. Kinzer showed him the ram-jet area, with its compressor facility for supplying oxygen which the liquid and solid rockets chewed in more compact forms. One of the ramjets was eating a meal of air and liquid hydrocarbon fuel as they approached the facility. They visited the control room and here Paul got his first close-up appreciation of jet power. Although the instrumentation background was fascinating, he was mesmerized by the massive sound and the other palpable energies of the jet. Leaving the control room, Russ observed that *that* was a smooth one.

Proceeding down the slope, Kinzer gave Paul some fill-in on the ramjet principle and noted that the Germans had found a particularly nasty use for it in their buzz bombs. The Germans were picked up again when they entered a compound that served as a temporary museum of rocketry. Various components of the V2 rocket were displayed and Kinzer tried to convey some of the marvel of the engineering embodied in that weapon: the throat of the rocket large enough to pass a man, the sophistication of the feed and injection systems, the use of film cooling to protect the expansion envelope from the combustion inferno, the main propellant tanks with a structural redundancy so small that loaded integrity could be maintained only in the launch attitude, the graphite deflection vanes and the inertial guidance system. And the Providence that had denied them nuclear teeth for this awesome extrapolation of Goddard's extension of the Chinese revelation.

"Any of the Germans here?"

"Not to my knowledge. The bulk of their talent is ensconced elsewhere. If you're ready for lunch...let's go."

They pulled into a small place in La Canada and decided to evaluate the chili-burgers. Russ opened a little of his personal history. He was on a leave of absence from the Institute and had concluded about a third of his PAG allotment. His specialty was chemical kinetics...that branch of the multifaceted science of chemistry that treats of reaction rates and mechanisms. He was attempting to apply some of this knowledge to the propellant combustion problem. He lived in Westwood and admitted that—someday—either the two-way sun exposure, or the traffic would defeat his choice of residence. He was a bachelor and lived with his mother.

"Kinzer...sounds a little German...maybe a little Czech," Paul fished.

"Not bad. Actually, you're looking at a *lot* of German, a small shot of Dutch." After some more chili, Russ looked at Paul. "Let's see...Sanger could be damn near anything. I'll throw caution to the wind and say...German."

"Fair...not as good as my guess. You're looking at a lot of Czech, some Irish, a smidgeon of Pennsylvania Dutch." Paul had worked this in between chili samples.

"God...is there *no* purity left!" Russ had finished his chili, so his hands had good play.

Driving back to PAG, Russ talked a little about the makeup of Chemistry. The group leadership was rotated among four, permanent, senior professionals. The term—sentence, according to Russ, usually lasted about two years.

"What makes a senior professional?"

"The qualifications tend to the abstruse. Usually, the starting point is convincing Personnel that you belong in that great protectorate of the gooblah known as the Senior Research Engineers...or Scientists, another facet of confusion...of types."

"Protectorate of *what*?"

"The *gooblah*...spelt just like it sounds."

"I've handled the yen, peso, drachma...even a passing familiarity with some of the English coins—I guess I've missed the boat here."

"My boy, your education *has* been sketchy...hasn't it? I can see really virgin ground here for tilling with the plow of truth. I...I wouldn't begin to hazard the delicate task of your *gooblah* enlightenment under the constraints imposed by this vehicle." Russ appeared to be close to a real emotional choke, so Paul figured maybe it *was* too dangerous and he left it there for the time being.

That afternoon, Russ introduced him to those of Chemistry who were conveniently at hand. Of the hierarchy Russ had mentioned, only two were present: Harry, the thermodynamicist with experimental proclivities and Jerry, the chemical analyst with the worried look. Actually Jerry's seeming preoccupation stemmed as much from his specialty—which was a general whipping post—as from his temporary possession of the headship of the group...titular, or not. There were three lab technicians, two of them female, and three mechanical technicians who comprised the vital force of brawn and judgment on which most of the test pit adventures of Chemistry depended for a beginning, a prosecution, and an ending endowed with reasonable grace.

Within their limits, everyone appeared glad to have Paul on board. He, in turn, anticipated no difficulty in accommodating to them. In fact...with Annie, the sometimes cynical and harried secretary of the group, and what he could see of the female contingent of the technicians...there looked like opportunity for relief of any strains that might crop up. His official status was junior engineer. This entitled him to use the washroom, a desk in a cubbyhole adjoining the analytical lab, and the right to blow his damn head off if his motivation and drive transcended—or evaded—the judgment and active benevolence of his fellow workers.

He savored the evening swim. Having tested the Land of the Strangers at PAG and found it hospitable, he was more relaxed than on the previous occasion and he felt no compulsion to plow the water for relaxation. He tread this water in the deep end and he even noticed a few well supported swim suits in, and out, of the water. He was deep in old Pasadena here. The Picture Bridge, partly a useful souvenir of Switzerland, dominated his perspective and he resolved to look it over again before attending to other business that evening.

He was nuzzling his first après dinner Scotch in the Ship Room when a bellhop approached and quietly informed him he had a telephone call...and he could take it on the patio extension. The Huntington had a knack for tracking its guests, using various footprints of habit, voice and appearance.

"God help us that our rocket program should be in the hands of wastrels," a soft, definitely female voice challenged him in reply to his acknowledgement. "This is Martha Drake, Mr. Sanger." He knew this already from an excitement he hadn't denied as he approached the phone. "My husband would like to meet you...before we commit our tender little carriage house. Perhaps you'd care to finish that drink I interrupted over here? A mutual look-over would be appropriate, you know." Paul said he'd be right over if he could find her place again. She gave him explicit instruction between here and there.

He gave the griffin head its motion again and again—after only one ring this time—a maid appeared and ushered him into the softly lighted foyer, and then deeper into the senior precedents of the carriage house. Paul succeeded her into a large room where she presented him to its occupants. One of these was a man dressed in a dark business suit, slightly taller than Paul. His tan didn't suggest a sun lamp and what was underneath was handsome, and supportive of an aura of authority, if not handsomeness. He walked toward Paul and extended his right hand with a flash of gold cuff links and watch band.

"I'm John Drake."

"Very pleased to meet you, sir." Although Drake appeared to be in his early forties, the *sir* would have been appropriate under almost any circumstance of ages.

"You've met my wife," he stated, turning to the object of this fact who was standing near a large fireplace. She was wearing a dark red dress of the simple elegance that Frenchmen seem able to achieve with regularity. The active firelight had found some jewels of her necklace, and subtler targets in her hair. Both men looked at her, Paul winning the concentration contest handily. His smile was as natural an inclination as anything in his life, and he made a slight bow to her.

"Mrs. Drake was kind enough to show me the apartment...out of respect for *historical* curiosity. It's a wonderful place." At last he turned to John Drake.

"It's an anachronism...but I wish there were more of them. Well...let's drink and talk about it a little...Martha said we'd interrupted you in that respect. What particular poison *were* you taking?" Drake motioned Paul toward a sitting area near the fireplace, served by two very large, curved couches.

"Scotch is a habit I've reacquired since coming back to civilization," Paul said, waiting for Martha Drake to select a couch and then going to the other.

Drake was attending to business among some decanters off to the side of the room. Paul scanned the room. The furnishings comprised a fascinating interplay of styles. Oriental rugs textured the light transients of the fireplace. The oak-paneled walls held a number of paintings...and one in particular stopped his reconnoiter. It presented the half figure of a woman. She appeared to be wearing a riding habit. Her head, features, hair were disposed in accord with very recent exhilaration from a ride, or a chase. Her smile was definitely not one of Da Vinci's enigmas.

Paul turned to Martha Drake and then back to that painting. During these moments he knew that she was looking at him. He turned back to her. "Please excuse me...as a dauber of rank amateur status...your gallery fascinates me." But it was evident that fascination in the present context had to be more specific. It was, in fact, skewered on an axis between the real and the representational.

"My one...and hopefully *last* portrait," she said, her eyes dancing between Paul and the painting.

Paul felt that this admission justified some relief of a peculiar tension he'd felt since entering this room. He excused himself, again, and walked toward the painting. Some firelight had managed to survive the complex of reflections to catch the eyes and hair and lips of the painting in striking semblance to *her.* "This painting could complement any gallery I've seen...in fact," he added impulsively, "but for the modern habit...I'd have to bow to one of Mr. Reynolds' sharper pupils." He'd said this quietly, directly to the painting.

"Not the old boy, himself?" The soft laugh was her first for him. When he turned to her, she couldn't find any Reynolds dispute in him and somehow he'd managed a pretty fair dispassionate mask to balance himself in front of her.

Drake returned to the area of art appreciation and offered a Scotch to his wife and another to Paul. "Here's to you Scotsmen...from an honest bourbon man." He saluted them and the two Scotsmen reciprocated. For an instant of this toast, Paul also reciprocated the frank appreciation in Martha Drake's eyes.

"Well now...you're a Mr. Paul Sanger, late of his majesty's forces. An apparently personable young man and now a member of that technical fraternity that threatens to overwhelm Pasadena and surroundings." Drake paused for a draught of sustenance. "And you're now presenting a plea for occupation of the carriage house apartment," he concluded in fairly succinct summary of Paul's situation.

"I told Mrs. Drake that it was a crazy...impertinent...idea. You've been very tolerant and considerate to have gone this far with it." Paul tapped his drink and glanced at Martha Drake, who was quite content to let her eyes and the burden of the conversation fall on her husband at that time.

"This neighborhood isn't exactly zoned for..." John Drake looked for a word, "for apartments. But it's been done before...albeit discretely. With the semi-private set-up we've got here...maybe...hell, I can't come up with an objection—yet." John Drake sipped his wine, looking at his wife. "There's no car space problem. The place isn't protecting any serious privileges." He paused for more lubrication. "We don't run a monastery here ourselves, but gin bottles in the roses and full volume hi-fi isn't our cup of tea, either." He looked at his wife again for collaboration, addition, subtraction.

"I suspect that gin, roses, or hi-fi don't pose any problems with Mr. Sanger," she said, using a smile that pulled in both Paul and her husband. "I...I'd be happy to let Mr. Sanger have the apartment. I'll have to transfer some of Carla's things to another...vault. There's storage space in the lower level, I believe." John Drake's nod confirmed the resolution of that problem and it also put the tag end on Paul's big problem, too.

"What about furnishings?" she asked Paul.

"I'll see what I can find that won't disgrace your elegant appointments...or ruin me." Paul's grin didn't seem to wear out.

"God...haven't we got extra stuff in this pile?" Drake asked, spreading his arms upward and sideways.

"I wouldn't think of adding to an already massive imposition," Paul said. "If I need help, I'll try to use a soft voice."

"I have cleaning people in once a week. I can have them extend their mercy to you...if you'd like."

"Sounds great, Mrs. Drake. But these amenities might be more than I can afford now." Paul had just made his first try at confronting reality since he'd entered this house. "And speaking of luxury, what—if you'll pardon the crass word—will my rent amount to?"

Drake dismissed the inquiry with a wave of his hand, but his wife didn't side-step Paul. "I'll check with the realtor and see what the previous rent was...I don't have much feeling for these things." This announcement bisected the positions of her male attendants.

"Fair enough. Only be sure to get his factor for inflation." Paul bolstered his laugh with some eye motion. He rose and started to inspect some of the other paintings of the room. He counted a Renoir, a Matisse, and several older landscapes of the Dutch school...original in execution, and probably original, period. One large watercolor of a scene along the Thames near Tower Bridge held him. "God that's good. Oil...you can lay it on with a trowel and cover mistakes with mistakes. But watercolor...you're right the first time—or you're *never* there." He'd spoken to a painting, again.

Martha Drake was now also standing and she walked toward Paul. "You said that you are a painter?"

"My sister, Mary, and I have slopped a lot of oil and watercolor around. She's inclined to abstraction. I'm still hung up on the old fashioned, literal representational school." He was looking at another prime example of his hang-up.

"Don't deprecate yourself. I enjoy abstract work when it shows careful craftsmanship and imagination. But that dripping the theme out of a paint bucket, or putting it on with a Mohawk hairdo—backwards...and that stuff that hardly qualifies as poster art. Didn't one of the New York critics call it the biggest *put-on* in the history of art?" Her enthusiasm might have surprised him a little. But he'd been undergoing Martha Drake conditioning for some time now. She had confirmed that the art he'd been inspecting bore a more than casual proprietary link to the lady of this house.

"Here...you art critics," John Drake said, offering them fresh drinks. He glanced at his watch, which showed 10 pm. Paul followed what he thought was his cue and looked at his own watch.

Martha Drake touched Paul's arm lightly. "My husband's appetite alarm is about to go off. You wouldn't object to helping me satisfy the brute, would you?" Paul certainly had no objection to either food, or continuation of the present company.

"I'll see what Mary has left in the kitchen," she said. Her touch had been a natural...trivial...artifact of conversation...to her, but not to Mr. Paul Sanger.

Paul and John Drake settled themselves back near the fireplace, fortified with drinks that seemed to reverse the usual trend and got stronger the longer. "Where'd you go to school?" Drake asked, after some contemplation of the fire.

"Stanford...class of forty-two. I took some chemistry, some engineering. I guess that makes me *something* of a chemical engineer."

"I'll be damned. Our daughter, Carla, is a junior up there now."

"If I didn't know that Pasadena is the Southern California branch of Stanford, I'd be surprised. What's her major?"

Drake laughed. "That appears to be a well guarded secret among her, her mother, and Stanford. But she likes languages and history and..."

"Boys!" Paul's laugh was just as inconsiderate as Carla's father's.

"She's smart...independent as hell—*just* like her mother." Drake's confession doubtless had some prompting from what Paul would call the infamous empty stomach Scotch effect—its bourbon equivalent in this case.

"And in what regard, pray, is she *just* like her mother?" Martha Drake challenged from a doorway. "If you two character assassins can interrupt your pleasurable work, you'll find some humble fare in the dining room."

"That was quick," her husband said, as he and Paul followed the entrancing mistress into the room of her command. Paul adjusted Martha Drake's chair.

"We usually try to anticipate your fourth—or is it your fifth hunger pang?" she said, smiling at Paul and indicating a place for him, as her husband took his chair of prerogative.

"Now...what hunger pang did you have in mind, dear?" Drake's inflection and shading were certainly a burden on that *effect* in Paul's opinion. Even from his peripheral position, he intercepted a portion of the lady's silent censure.

There was a display of cold beef and several kinds of bread on large silver platters, and a porcelain bowl filled with the largest strawberries Paul had ever seen—and Iowa isn't bashful on that score. Paul raised a crystal glass filled with the red wine that Drake had supplied moments before. "To tolerance! My appreciation for yours." A segment of Martha Drake's glass intercepted their axis for a moment and gave him a complexly tinted tacitness about success for their zoning conspiracy. For an instant's interruption of his food devotion, Drake also seemed to support the toast.

During the meal, Paul talked about his family, some of his life in Iowa. He mentioned that he missed his fly rod adventures with salmon and steelhead in the USA and Canada.

"A fisherman, eh?" John said, his face wreathed in false dismay.

"God...here we go again," Martha said, raising her hands in support of her husband's acting.

"As soon as we can gracefully depart this board...I'll show you some things that might be of small interest to you," Drake said, glancing at the strawberries.

"Mr. Sanger...will you please start the berries' progress so he can unshackle himself." Paul watched the hostess furnish herself with some of the beauties and then he passed them to his host who, after a while, passed them back to Paul.

"We like them with powdered sugar. But we have cream, if you'd prefer," she said.

"I'll try them a la Drake," Paul said, following her lead. After some time of quiet devotion to the delicacy, Paul looked at Martha Drake, who appeared to be somewhat less occupied than her husband. "When do you think I should target my arrival?"

"Give me a couple days to have the place cleaned. This is Monday...how about Wednesday?"

"Wonderful. I'll see if I can wangle some relocation time from PAG and get a little furniture in there on Wednesday." His miracle received a smiling confirmation from Martha Drake, and a nod from her husband.

They had gone to John's study. There was no question but that this was a man's room, one to whom hunting and fishing was important sustenance. Paul noticed a large gun rack, equipped with a variety of rifles and shotguns, some of the former equipped with scopes. He walked to this rack and fingered a shining Mannlicher.

"Pick it up," Drake ordered.

Paul did, sighting it at a light fixture. "Beautiful balance," he said, returning it to the rack. There was a large cabinet containing a number of fishing rods, most of which were designed for salt water work. They ranged from lightest to the heaviest designs prescribed by the International Game Fishing Association. Paul noticed several fly rods. Disdaining the heavyweights, he picked one of the fly rods from the rack. "Hardy, Palakona," he read from the butt section. He balanced that section for a few seconds and then simulated dry casting with it for a couple cycles. "Beautiful...a bit heavy for my taste...but beautiful."

"Sir, you're talking about one of my favorites," the lady declared from a position near her husband's desk.

"*Pardonnez moi*," Paul said, with a slight bow to her. "You didn't tell me about the *second* fisherperson in this family...I would have sharpened my respect—a lot!" Paul laughed and carefully returned the Hardy to its place of rest. Adjacent to the Hardy was a fly rod of more delicate construction. Turning to Martha Drake, he asked, "May I?" As she walked toward him, she assured him that she would hazard his rough touch on that object of her affection. It was a Winston...8½ feet, about 4 ounces. "May I assemble this wonder?" he asked. She nodded, smiling. He'd heard about this famous weapon of the West Coast steelhead men, but this was the first he'd seen. After assembling it, he commanded it for a few seconds of flexing, marveling at the power he could sense down to the bottom of the hollow butt of its bamboo architecture—and the lightness of it. A piece of fly fishing like this could put the partnership of the bamboo with the back, arms and wrists and legs...the hiss of the shooting line, the flight and the settling of the fly near that last boil...into a nearly real moment and both John and Martha Drake understood the face this Iowan had put into it.

"*That*, sir, is also mine...you approve?"

Eloquence would have been justified, but he went for the bow, and was quiet about it this time. All of this interchange of the fly rod admiration society had been monitored by John Drake from his position in a leather chair near the gun rack. "I damn near made a saltwater man out of her. But she was afraid she'd get muscles in all the wrong places...that tended to dilute the purity of devotion needed for top rank performance."

"I did some of my homework, though," she said, motioning toward a wall near Paul. There appeared to be a display of broadswords against an oak panel. On closer inspection, he found that they were indeed broadswords, but lion-hearted Richard probably never saw their like. They were bills from the broadbill swordfish, probably as awesome and efficient a compact of power and cussed antipathy to man as the oceans held. Under one sword was a small silver plate with an inscription stating that a broadbill swordfish of 295 pounds had been vanquished by one Martha Drake, off Panama on a certain date. The other sword was rather larger. A similar plate proclaimed victory by one John Drake off Cabo Blanco, Peru, and that the trophy had pulled the crossbeam at 484 pounds. Adjacent to each trophy was a large photograph of the respective victor and vanquished.

"I'm in the wrong league here," Paul said, with undisguised admiration of these proofs of skill, guts, strength and determination. He was also aware that the broadbill wasn't usually sought by Joe the Wounded Butcher, unless

Joe happened to own the packing house and had outfitted a fast cruiser with a fighting chair, in addition to the partying amenities. This was generally held to be a quarry of special relevance to men and a very few women of action, of a disposition to place themselves in situations where the fisher of the pair had less than an even chance. This was still the time when game fishers disdained the use of cruiser tactics which strongly biased the odds against the fish, refusing to restructure their definition of sport.

"The quality of my saltwater battles deteriorated rapidly from there," she said, with a rueful smile, and rubbing her arms slightly. But her tendency to show payment for this kind of fish seemed to be overborne by a transient of her eyes that called back special excitement and this instant of her stuck with Paul.

"I think she was afraid of embarrassing me with her cold blooded efficiency," her husband said with a good laugh.

"A thirty pound Atlantic salmon—on the end of a six ounce bamboo wand—is the present apex of *my* sport," Paul said. "But...someday, I'd like to tackle one of those devils."

"*Devils* is a good word for them," Martha Drake said. "Up at dawn...scanning water all day that's usually very restless. If you're lucky enough, you might sight one dorsal after long hours. If your good boatman succeeds in bringing you into contact...you have the pleasure of having your arms pulled from their sockets—your back begging for mercy." She'd gone into that payment business again—but Paul was trapped in her eyes and he wasn't disappointed, again.

"Martha tends to over dramatize," Drake said, "but she's caught some of the essence. And I agree with her...it's not the sport for my kind of woman...I think."

"I'd still like a crack at 'em some day," Paul maintained, looking at the bills and photographs...particularly the one of Martha Drake. She didn't look at all unhappy.

"We occasionally get some marlin activity off Catalina. Maybe we can cook up a little something for you," Drake said.

"Wonderful," Paul said. "My God...it's after midnight...I'm sorry."

"We've enjoyed it, I guess you two have the sordid details worked out. Don't play the landlady too hard, Martha—we may have a marlin man here."

That night, Madame Ligonier graced part of both the preliminaries and his actual sleep. For the unconscious segment, that Englishman had put some subtleties into both her background and her eyes that could be construed as piscatorial...definitely piscatorial.

Russ Kinzer piled some stuff on Paul's desk and suggested he look it over the next few days. He also correctly reasoned that Paul would need a couple days respite from the technical fray and he reminded him that PAG might be many things...but a time clock wasn't one of them.

Paul cut out at noon on Tuesday, taking a few unclassified tomes on the science of propulsion for homework. His brief exposure to PAG had shown him glimpses of a technical world that was virtually foreign to him. Before, and during the war, real cognizance over rocket development was had by few laymen and relatively few professionals conversant with the applicable disciplines. Knowing of ancient ingenuity and the proliferation of it through pictures and words was one thing. But he had looked into the throat of a power that could add an awesome dimension to mankind. He'd found the professional challenge for which he had forsaken the comfortable prosperity of the Sanger Enterprises. He had lucked into a close association with a Caltech scientist...and a hell of a good guy, to boot. These, and the other images now in his perspective, didn't let any ambiguity creep into the vistas in front of him.

But a funny thing happened on the way home from the rockets. He had barely entered the little grove of oaks near the entrance to the laboratory, when he passed a man carrying a small pack, striding in a non-hitchhiking mode in the direction of Paul's travel. The hiker was bearded. His general aspect would have suited any trail, of any land, where the reason for legs hadn't been forgotten. This almost impudent indifference to assistance inspired Paul to stop. When the hiker reached the car, he pushed his beard into the open window on the passenger side.

"May I be of assistance?" he asked. The voice was soft, a vestige of New England about it. It could have been more than three quarters of a century old. But the eyes—and what face the beard allowed—didn't speak of age. The question was rather impudent, too, but a smile came along that caused an equal reaction from Paul.

"Well...you stole *my* question," Paul replied.

"Then...I must honor myself with your presence for a little while," the walker said. He quickly assumed the front passenger seat. He was going south, and then east into the Sierra Madres for some time of communion. Paul took him as far as Arcadia, and during the trip he talked about the technology that was a glory of man and the principal part of his own excitement. His passenger did most of the listening. When they reached a logical parting point, he thanked Paul for his kindness. Then he asked, "What is *your* escape velocity from earthbound problems?" Before Paul could chew on that one, he was waved at...and then the voice was gone.

Doubling back to Pasadena, Paul made some smiles when he thought about the smile with the beard. The unanswered question didn't trouble him. But that voice...like the impudent insistence of a young wind that used a whisper...had deposited it to his account.

3

For some time, the verbal content of the room had been words of a code that should have been useful to a defense lab like PAG. They conveyed strength, weakness, strategy, counter-strategy, and gave the various tinctures of conviction to all of this. But two successive *passes* had just occurred. This had caused the classical masks to fall away, and now there was no pretense of anything joined to a defense issue.

"What'n hell did you double on...we got you clean," Harry said, making adjustments to what he represented as a formidable holding.

"Play 'em," George challenged quietly.

There was some hesitation before the steamroller gathered its advertised momentum and then there was silence, broken only by the slaps of Harry's successive victories.

"You should watch these bastards very carefully," Myron said, turning to Paul who was kibitzing the game. Myron was the one senior member Paul had not met earlier. A slender, handsome Jewish man, Myron was the embodiment of the local scientific renascence—in his opinion. "That would be a good use of your apprentice time," he added, while servicing Harry's steamroller on the losing end.

"That's as good a compliment as I've had all day." Harry used an exaggerated wrist action in putting the finishing touches on the tricks that flowed toward him.

"I'm not talking about your alleged technical prowess...I had your bridge tactics in mind," Myron said, glancing at the score pad, and then at the wall clock.

"Ah...notice the sly peek at the pad—and then the clock. Next there'll be disclosure of urgencies in his agenda. How *is* that redheaded urgency up in Electronics coming along?" Harry persisted. Myron was a bachelor. He was very communicative about everything except his sex life, and this facet of him was under virtually constant harassment by his associates.

"By God!—I should have a hot little item up in Electronics," Jerry, the winning partner said.

"When our pillar of sobriety starts responding to the heavenly vibrations... we *are* going to hell," Harry declared.

"I'm talking about that God damn automatic spectrum analyzer—you peckerhead!" Jerry exploded in an untitularheadlike way.

This was as good a signal as any for the termination of the game and they started to drift out of the large office...officially listed on the PAG engineering drawings as a conference room. But these particular walls were as plastered with hearts and spades as they were with implications of asymmetry of molecular structure to spontaneous ignition of rocket propellants.

These guys were a revelation to Paul. They all held the PhD. And if the mutterings of Annie were any criterion, their contributions to a broad spectrum of journals and conferences were weighty and frequent. When the substance of these dissertations required multidiscipline support—which was about always—there was much overt consultation among these worthies. Another scenario had covert consultation between two of them who doubted the intellectual capacity of the others. Occasionally one hero would hold off a pack of erstwhile collaborators and consultants. Somehow, each of them maneuvered himself through this labyrinth of technical prerogative in his own way and the wounds appeared to be reasonably equitably scattered. In the few instances Paul had overheard the birth pains of an idea, or a paper, he had retired with a growing respect for the power—and the frustration—of the scientific method.

Myron was only two years his senior. He'd taken his degree at Columbia and had worked on the Manhattan Project during the war at Columbia, and later at Chicago. Paul was yet to know about the awesome scope and drive of that project. But he knew enough to envy Myron the education it must have afforded. Of the others, only George had experienced the inspiring influence of direct military involvement. He'd entered the Army Chemical Warfare Service from a teaching post at Illinois, and had seen only the somewhat restricted panorama usually given to officers on Stateside liaison with industry.

The principal mission of PAG Chemistry was the identification of liquid and solid propellants that could bring smiles to the faces of the mission planners. This task was multifaceted. Harry, George, and Myron were expected to carry their candles into the Stygian dark and eventually stumble forth with promising scrapings. Very rarely did these explorers find major values that had been overlooked by prior expeditions, most of whom had a fondness for liverwurst. Occasionally, our boys would materialize something that under more comprehensive analysis, or the illumination of better data, would cause some modest excitement at the base camp. As Annie would be happy to testify, these intrepids could, however, find more than enough interest in the scenery to—and from—the cave of frustration to keep theoreticians and experimentalists happy indefinitely.

Myron's forte was the theoretical prediction of thermodynamic properties. In the course of his occasional forays into systems of some practical interest, his revelations had various effects on his associates: Studied indifference, signifying that the data they were using was reasonably well supported by Myron's work. True indifference, signifying that Myron's data didn't apply to any of the components they were sweating over at that time. Varying degrees and superpositions of truculence and contriteness, signifying that Myron's data did not support data they were using, or that they had submitted a paper that was so handicapped, or that such a paper had already enjoyed publication. As his understanding of these things matured, Paul could see that the disposition of these people to horseplay was a vitality of sanity.

Russ' role in this identification was the theoretical and experimental analysis of the propensity of the propellant components to get down to business. And in this business, the experimental tended to precede and inform the theoretical. On the basis of purely theoretical reasoning, which used the present-ultimate tracks of quantum mechanics, it was not even possible to predict whether, or not, A and B would react spontaneously. There was still substantial ignorance about the effect of environmental conditions...temperature, pressure, chemistry of the ambient atmosphere...on the reaction propensities and the subsequent combustion history. When third, or higher order, components were involved, the complexity became delightful...a persistent fount of inspiration for physical chemists. Here also, an observant traveler could find plenty of report material on his journey to practical application. Russ was as observant as any of them.

This dependence on experiment was the chief justification for Paul's presence in Chemistry. In accordance with his maturity, Russ was expecting him to take certain interesting propellants into the next qualification course beyond the laboratory and the desk calculator, and the staring at the ceiling. This appraisal of certain physical chemical attributes was to be done by small scale rocket motors. If the feed rates, the chamber pressure, and the thrust were measured carefully enough, a rocket of 50 pounds thrust could develop data of fairly immediate significance to the missile men, whose power plants exceeded this thrust level by a factor of 1,000, and eventually 100,000.

Part of Paul's equipment for these adventures would consist of a test facility, comprising a control room, and two test stands...the whole enveloped on five sides by reinforced concrete and penetrated by armored glass observation ports. Also, Paul had his crew chief, Luke, and Eddy and Art, to provide a major part of the brawn, a lot of the three AM kind of guts, and the skills and judgment with chemicals and machines he didn't have at that time.

In the satisfaction of the private amenities, he had done nobly...rather he'd stumbled into an accident of tolerance that should have relieved a man of problems in that respect if anything could. He had tapped his resources to the extent of a double bed, a roll top desk, a few wicker chairs and a card table set for the dining alcove. The first morning he had come to the carriage house as a tenant, he'd found it cleaned and polished. There was a large bouquet of iris on the mantelpiece. An envelope near the flowers had a note, stating simply, *Welcome, M. D.*

His exciting contention with the new world at PAG had compressed the last few weeks into an illusion of a few days. The accommodation to the carriage house had, as John Drake had predicted, fulfilled the requirement of mutual privacy, broken only by natural opportunities for communion. This had consisted of a few conversations and a miscellany of manual and verbal signals of recognition during travel transients that had overlapped.

His struggle for some professional identity should have dominated his agenda for serious thoughts, and his off-job circumstances should have provided a near optimum climate for them. But ex-laboratory, Martha Drake would abide no such exclusion. Particularly in the night, when the forces of wakefulness and sleep were contending, a multitude of images of her...still life, and with various degrees of vitality with various non-carnal couplings to him... weighed the side against sleep. And this phenomenon was not diminishing.

He didn't mind the kitchen combat. His appetite was usually poor in the morning. His lunch was usually an away from home affair. Dinner could be as leisurely a compromise between simplicity and gourmandizing as he cared to make it. This Friday, he'd tipped toward the gourmand and purchased a filet mignon. Martha Drake had supplied him with an array of utensils for cooking and eating, and he was in the act of laying his table when the knocker on his door fulfilled its destiny. He opened on a grinning ape named Tom Andrews.

"You must have smelled the raw steak...you bastard."

"Is that any way to greet a bottle of Pinchbottle and two glasses?"

"Friend...how long *has* it been"

"Your directions were okay. I just lined up Polaris, turned twenty degrees west and bumped into your damn gargoyles."

"That gate *is* something, ain't it."

"This whole set-up is fantastic. What'n hell did you do to deserve this?"

"It's a beautiful story...like a fairy tale, complete with a princess...or a queen." Paul used his slow smile this time, and he hadn't looked at his visitor.

"What's the catch?" Tom had ignored the dramatics and reached for the bottom line, as Paul had first done a few weeks before, and in subsequent private reviews of increasing frequency.

"Bring your damned bottle and glasses in here...we'll talk about it." Paul led the way to the alcove. Over Scotches, he gave a rough summary of his housing adventures. Other than saying that the Drakes were damn fine people, he didn't move into any local particulars qualifying that statement.

"What've you done about dinner tonight?" Paul asked.

"Thought we could go on the town, if you're not engaged...as they say in carriage houses."

"I've got no serious objection. You might like a ride in a good heap for a change."

"That broken down Cadillac still operational?"

"You bet, you got wheels yet?"

"If you take the trouble to peek into the bowels of your damned mansion here, you'll see a sweet little old invention by a guy named Ferdinand Porsche."

"No shit?"

"Better not be at *that* price."

"By God, you continually amaze me with your coupling to life's better facets. Give me some clean-up time and we'll hit it."

They took the inland route to Capistrano and then headed north along the coast highway. It was a clear, cool evening and the Porsche relished it. Eventually, they saw the masts and lagoons of the Balboa-Newport area. Near the inner harbor, they found a small place that showed prospects for food and drink. Paul wheeled the Porsche under an entranceway into the waiting arms of an attendant.

"Mind the paint, lad. My friend doesn't want his new toy scratched," Paul ordered, and then he and Tom unscrambled and strode toward the inner sanctum.

"Damn...that's a sweet little job. One of these centuries I intend to take that particular plunge," Paul said as they moved onward.

"Your coupling is maturing nicely," Tom said, as they entered a dimly lit foyer, coincident with the concluding bars of *Amor* by an unseen pianist.

"Dinner, gentlemen?" This question was posed by a statuesque brunette receptionist who'd emerged from the shadows.

"Snort first?" Tom asked.

"Look, buddy, you took me away from food a *long* time ago."

"Okay. My friend is still a growing boy and needs his nourishment," Tom said to the brunette bomber. "Take us to your chef."

They had decided that some ablution was in order. They were emerging from the second door of the small vestibule that separated the boy's room from the foyer. Paul was leading, and Tom noticed that Paul was taking some pains to open the door for him and also that Paul had a paper towel in his door hand. When exit had been achieved for both of them—a feat requiring manual dexterity from Paul—Paul walked over to the reception desk and dropped the wadded paper towel in a waste basket before rejoining his friend. Handy, discreet, waste baskets improved the insouciance of this maneuver. This time it came out okay.

"What'n hell was *that* for?" Tom asked, after they'd negotiated the dark passage to their table and chairs. Paul reached for his menu without looking at Tom, and with no overt attention to Tom's impertinent intrusion of a ritual he'd maintained as one of his private little protestations to the terrors of this world.

"Like I said, *lieutenant*...what'n hell was *that* for" Tom repeated, practicing a rank being pulled over friendship maneuver he hadn't used for a while.

"*That* is a technical opportunity," Paul replied quietly, without interrupting his study of the menu.

"*That* looked liked you were going to end up on your ass—with a paper towel in your mouth." For that, Tom had tailored his voice and face with a quality of amusement that was provocative. He reached for his menu.

Tom had just shown something of a gauntlet, so Paul decided to deny his friend the menu sanctuary...and also the last word on a subject that wasn't trivial to him. He set his own menu aside and then favored Tom with the full compliment of his attention.

"Do you mean to imply ignorance of the Sanger theory of Prick Proliferation?" He'd carefully tailored his voice to a place between their surroundings and Tom's attention.

"For a second, I thought you said *prick*," Tom said, his voice still tempered by some quality of humor. He reached for his ice water, his menu concentration still unperturbed.

"I did." Paul used the same voice. That overture stopped the ice water travel and tended to set a good mutuality of interest at that table.

"I have a very uncomfortable feeling—already. But go ahead," Tom said, giving up all resistance to education impromptu.

"It's really very simple. In the course of your perambulations through the restaurants, bars and whorehouses of this world, have you acquired any perspective on the toilet habits of your fellow slobs?"

"Only that there are certainly a lot of obnoxious sons of bitches."

"I'll go along with that. And I'll amend it by saying that there are a lot of *dirty* obnoxious sons of bitches." After a few seconds, Paul persisted, noting what he thought was the nucleus for a bead of sweat on Tom's forehead. "I'd judge that something less than 30% of the hands that have fondled pricks, been sprayed with urine, wiped asses—with varying degrees of success—ever see a washbowl prior to leaving the doors of what we euphemistically call a *wash* room."

"Jesus...I *knew* I shouldn't have encouraged you—before dinner," Tom muttered, in the grips of fascination and disgust.

"To the noble thirty percent we can allude with gratitude," Paul continued. "It's the seventy percent who return to their—read that *your*—environment... people, furniture, food, books, et cetera, with hands that would make a sewer plant worker blush, that my theory addresses."

"Is this trip *really* necessary?" Tom started to reach for a sour dough roll...and then stopped when Paul's axis with him, mainly the eyes, answered his question.

"Consider what these bastards do: Disdaining the wash bowl—even a token visit in most cases—they may, or may not, rub their hands through their hair while they see Cary Grant in the mirror. Then they leave. Up to this point, they haven't interacted with their fellow men...we'll take this assumption anyway, under the press of simplicity. As soon as they touch the door, the fascinating phenomenon I mentioned earlier, in all modesty, begins. Usually, the door requires activating some kind of handle with one—or both—hands. There is one, sometimes two, such impediments to the extra-toilet world which our hero has to overcome before he's free to touch your bread." Tom's resolve toward the sour dough had not been resurrected.

"The first handle that he touches, depending on the vagaries of his technique, receives the major dose of his negligence. The second door, a lesser share of the wealth. Thereafter, *anything* that SOB touches—your food, your lady—receives some part of the diminishing dividend of his toilet. If you're statistically inclined, you can come up with some impressive chains of influence."

"I think my imagination is equal to that task," Tom said, with only a glance at his menu, and now genuinely thankful for Paul's pas de deux with the paper towel.

"And the sad part of it," Paul continued, "the poor devil in the 30% bracket who doesn't protect himself—as I tried to do—is made a party to the

whole unsavory business. His own, surrogate, contribution can be significant...
he becomes a deficient angel, even if he *does* see a halo in that mirror."

"You bastard! You've opened a whole world to me that I don't like. I can
see *miles* of paper towels...various delaying tactics in opening doors, suspicion
of dinner companions and waiters—no damn end to it!" After he'd calmed
down, Tom asked, "What'n hell do you do about it?"

"The designers of the toilet lay-outs could spend less time on the decor
and more time figuring out a way for a man to extricate himself from a toilet
area without hand contact. At least that would protect us thirty percenters from
the first stage penetration—now *that's* a good old Air Force ending for you."

"What about that *extra*-toilet world you've just laid on my head—and that
dirty seventy percent?"

"Not a damn thing you can do about it...short of becoming a pariah by
refusing all contact with your fellow men and women. Practically, we can only
trust in our choice of friends, and waiters and the gradual enlightenment—and
education—of our fellow travelers to oblivion." The Right Reverend Paul Sanger
was going into his menu...again.

"I guess there *is* technical opportunity here," Tom said, uncheerfully.

"Outside our present little arena there're plenty of dirty backwaters
that've been overlooked in pushing the show for Madison Avenue. I got a nasty
feeling we may be walking in some of them up to our ass someday. *Involuntary
involvement in somebody else's shit* is the phrase I've just implied and it can
strut confidently to a broader stage than toilets—let's order."

"Let's *pray*," acolyte Tom said, almost forcing himself to pick up the large
recitation of culinary delights.

Later, and safely in the drinking phase again, they stood at the railing of
the restaurant veranda which had lagoon viewing privileges of a special kind.
Directly across from them, the lights from Lido Island played catch with a forest
of masts. The water ripple compounded the degrees of freedom of the beauty,
and a breeze was in the right direction to replicate faint laughter and music
from a hundred sources.

"When you've got a place on that island, a floating bedroom, and a place
in Beverly Hills...I guess you could say you just about had it made," Tom observed quietly.

"You substitute the better reaches of San Marino, or Pasadena, for your
fleshpots to the west, I'll go along with you," Paul said. There were no words for
several minutes. Then Paul pulled at the conversation threads again. "I believe
the Drakes might have something close to your semi-paradise. The maid mentioned that they were at Balboa the first time the realtor called them." For some

damn reason, he had a sudden vision of a laughing Martha Drake contributing to the firefly dance of light and sound across from them and he didn't like the gut twinge this prompted. *Jesus*...she was old enough to be his mother...well, a precocious mother.

Tom looked at Paul for a few seconds and then returned to the marinescape. "You mentioned a...a queen in connection with your apartment. Care to tell me anything about it?" He'd used his best soft voice, sensing that something—or someone—had stolen his friend for the moment.

Paul's eyes continued to scan the masts and hulls silhouetted against the natural and augmented light of the scene. At that moment, it was transmitting an almost excruciating composite of invigoration and enervation to him. " Martha Drake," he finally said, almost in a whisper, more to himself than to Tom. Then, after a few seconds, he went to a better social volume, but still bound to the ambiguous panorama. "I was getting pretty anxious to find a place. Then... this joker reaches into his memory bag for that damn carriage house. I don't know why in hell they let me in—but they *did*. You saw the set-up...those gates, the grounds, that house. Christ! I don't come from a family of slobs...but that place would impress damn near anybody."

"All but maybe a tenth of a percent of the population," Tom said, tapping his drink lightly. "I...I must take it that your Mrs. Drake doesn't satisfy your criteria for a typical landlady." Tom carefully placed his look on the lagoon.

"The gods have conspired against me," Paul said, with just the amount of smile needed to bring a whiff of relief to both of them. "Have you been to the Huntington Library?"

"No...in San Marino, isn't it?"

"I'll have to pick up the burden of your education again."

"For Christ's sake—you've already ruined my life tonight."

"Henry Huntington, abetted by Arabella, parlayed a talent for railroad design and administration into a capacity to collect on a monumental scale— art, books. Fortunately he happened to like San Marino. His treasures there include one of the best collections of 17-18th century paintings in the world, including fascinating studies of French and English aristocracy." Tom made the rash assumption that certain females of that class were on Paul's immediate agenda. "Beautiful, proud, haughty...some looking like they'd just had it from a lackey behind the lilacs...some like they were anticipating the same. But generally evocative of a life style that left out damn little."

"I must submit that you've read a little more into some of these portraits than the adoring painter intended...or Henry and Arabella would allow, publicly...although I think I've heard that Arabella had a sense of humor that could handle that."

"Maybe. But I saw *her* in one of them when she came into that foyer with her damn yellow dress and...mouth and eyes..."

"Steady boy!" Tom admonished, something less than half in fun. "And this paragon of womanhood is happily married...has a daughter at Stanford," Tom summarized quietly and succinctly from earlier information. "I...I think you'd better reconcile yourself to the delights of platonic love...amid the more open reaches of her estate, *far* from that carriage house. Remember what Lawrence said about *those*—or was it barns?"

This very good advice didn't penetrate more than the skin of Paul's consciousness. "She's an art lover of my own persuasion...a fisherman with impressive credentials—she's got better fly rods than I have... and she's tangled with *broadbills*, for Christ's sake! An equestrian..."

"How long have you known her?" Tom interrupted with a wicked grin. "And I hope I'm not conveying any of the Old Testament here."

"I really spent only one evening with her...and her husband," Paul said, still lagoon ward, and Tom had given up trying to analyze the nuances of Paul's voice.

"Well...you'd better get rested up for that *second* evening." Tom placed an arm around Paul's shoulder and tended them both in the direction of the Porsche.

They took the coast highway north and eventually found their way to Pasadena. They had talked about PAG, about trying some shots at yellowtail and albacore when their season came around there, of trying the beach at Malibu and San Clemente. They didn't talk about Martha Drake.

Tom pulled up at the gate about midnight. Paul got out and was solving the latch work puzzle when he and the Porsche were illuminated by another pair of headlights from a car that had stopped in an approach attitude behind them. Paul concluded the opening and motioned Tom, and then his successor, through the portal with an elaborate bow. Tom pulled up a few feet, and Paul closed the gate behind the second car. As he approached the driver side of the sport Continental, he was hailed by John Drake.

"Now isn't *this* a hell of a time for a young scientist to be dragging in?"

"Good evening, Mr. Drake." And then he could see that further salutation was in order. "Good evening, Mrs. Drake," he said, bending his head for a better vantage of the passenger's side.

"Having a gatekeeper is the very essence of luxury...indolence," she said, with a small laugh. She was wearing a fur coat with a hood partially retracted and, from the gate light, Paul caught a signature of jeweled earrings, and subtler signals from lips and eyes. "Please introduce us to your friend," she said, turning toward the Porsche. Tom had received some of the aftermath of this chat and he'd left the car and was approaching the passenger side of the Lincoln.

"Mr. and Mrs. Drake, my friend Tom Andrews...*Major* Tom Andrews if it pleases you."

There was a short conversation among the gate conjunctioneers. John Drake offered a nightcap which Paul and Tom declined with as much grace as they could muster. Then the Porsche followed the track to the carriage house, and John Drake chose the entrance circle.

"God have mercy on you," was all Tom said, as he left Paul close to his portal.

Saturday, Paul bedded down with reports, some collateral text book reading, and tried to make a dent in his correspondence. The principal facts of his job and housing situation were easy enough to assemble for his mother and father, and their letter came off easily. He saved Mary's letter for the evening, possibly the next day. There had always been telepathy between them and he would need more cool than he could find now if his letter to her was to come out right. Tom's parting benediction had bothered him and, with varying intensity, it was still interfering with anything he tried to do. Martha had broadcast a powerful transient of her essence last night. And Tom's receiver hadn't been screened. He'd opened up too much to Tom in Balboa, and his friend had apprehended a situation that could be despair and joy—but from Tom's last remark, he seemed to hold the joy as a fragile interloper in aggressive darkness. The bastard was probably jealous as hell...but damn that long face in that Porsche.

He wanted to sketch the carriage house for Mary. He picked up some drawing pencils and a large sketch pad from Vroman's. Later, he discovered the good food at the old Constance Hotel, took in a lousy movie, and was glad to sack out. He was tired—but work didn't have anything to do with it.

At mid-morning the next day, he took one of his collapsible chairs and art equipment to the shade of a large oak that projected a partial image of itself on the front surfaces of the carriage house. He'd achieved a few basic lines of his sketch and was studying his next refinement when he was informed that it was quite good. He turned in his chair, and then stood up when he saw Martha Drake.

"I hope I didn't startle you," she said. She was wearing a light beach robe, bound at the waist by a red sash. Her hair was quite free to respond to the light breeze. "My husband has often said that I'd make a good Indian...and on this grass, these slippers don't help my considerate image."

Paul managed to look as far down as her slippers and saw that she was indeed equipped with creations of white and gold leather which the word *slipper* didn't quite fit, but the Venetian had called them that when he sold them to her.

"It *is* very good. Please don't let me interrupt." She seated herself on a wooden bench that girded part of the base of the oak, then she adjusted to a position that gave her an oblique view of the proceedings. Paul guided himself back to his chair, with a quick vision of perfect legs being assigned a less active role. She appeared to be wearing a bathing suit and Paul's wonder at this was answered almost as soon as he resumed the sketch.

"Somebody has to attend to constitutionals on a day like this. The only way I could get John into the pool on a regular basis would be to stock it." Her head was against the oak, and she was looking at an artist who was trying to concentrate on the perspective that had been there before she came.

"The treasures of this place continue to amaze me," he said, without looking up from his work. "I've peeked...that pool *is* a beauty."

"Oh...we haven't given you the complete guided tour yet, have we." She used that soft laughter he'd heard before.

Paul piled more lead onto the paper with fairly rapid strokes, pausing to scan some detail near the eaves. He worked for about five minutes under a quiet gaze he could sense, but which he avoided under a legitimate excuse.

"I'd like to see some of your oil work, sometime," she finally said, without altering any feature of her relaxation.

"Flattery just might get you a horrible shock, Mrs. Drake. From your remarks the evening I met your husband, I suspect I'm way out of my depth in art *and* fishing." The lines continued, but less frequently. Finally, they stopped. He laid the pad on the grass and adjusted his position to face her.

"I've no talent whatsoever in originating art. I flatter myself that I am a good art appreciator. My parents guided me through every public gallery they could find, here and abroad, and a lot of the private ones. Some of that has to rub off on you unless you're a complete idiot...but when I say that I became quite a student, before my feet got tired, I may be assuming unwarranted stature." She tucked those feet under her. "There's a lot of art worth seeing in Southern California, but you have to know where to look. If you can inveigle your sister Mary out here sometime—we'll give her the works!" Paul joined the laughter this time. She and Mary *would* make a pair that could give him, or anybody, the works.

"As a matter of fact this masterpiece is intended for my little Irish sister."

"Sanger sounds *much* too serious to be Irish."

"That's right—it is. Me faither is full blooded Czech, but me maither is half Irish and half German...and it's the Irish part that counts with Mary." He hadn't worked his brogue for a long time, and it seemed to tip its hat to this lady.

"She sounds perfectly delightful—now I *know* you'll have to entice her out here." She stood up and glanced at Paul's prostrate sketch. "If you don't think that it'll place your creative drive in too much jeopardy...perhaps you'd enjoy a swimming break." At this time, Paul was also standing.

"Gad, m'lady...is there no end to your largesse," he said, making what he thought was a passable leg to her. With one foot slightly advanced, her head attitude like the perfect chatelaine's, her smile was an apparent confirmation of his opinion.

"I'll wait for you here." Her smile was persistent and it propelled him up the stairs to one of the quickest exchanges between clothes and swimming trunks he'd ever made.

As they strolled toward the tall hedge that was a false terminus to the rear grounds, he was careful to give his physical equipment as much of a break as he could, and damn glad that he hadn't gone ape over his mother's pastry which had showed up from time to time while he was overseas and even on his present ground.

In her low heeled slippers, he noticed that the top of her head just came to his shoulders. He had some difficulty concentrating on her comments about the gardening problems for a place of this size, and the fact that they had given up trying to make it all look like the Huntington gardens. He was quite conscious of legs and other curved places which the robe hadn't been designed to conceal.

They reached an opening in the hedge that was hidden from most vantage points of the house. Beyond this opening, the grass sloped downward for a few yards and stopped at the flagstone border of a pool that had been designed for serious swimmers. Possibly 40 by 80 feet, of rectangular shape, it had the inevitable diving board, not quite so inevitable plated gold touches on the ladders, a definitely not inevitable dressing facility that suggested a playhouse for Chinese aristocrats, The pool itself was a pale blue mass of sparkling crystal, a quality that only expert attention to purification, and other related matters, can accomplish.

Paul stopped a few feet beyond the hedge, his appreciation of the scene obvious to his partner, who'd also stopped a little beyond him and was looking at him.

"It *is* a bit much, isn't it," she said. "Thank God, for the Acme Pool Service, and my husband's obsession with clean water." She walked toward the diving end of the pool and prepared for action by removing her robe, donning a bathing cap and kicking off her slippers. She disappeared for a minute into the pavilion and emerged a shining water nymph. She looked at Paul for just a second, then she moved her arms and legs in a quick gathering of momentum and made a good, clean dive into the crystal.

Paul watched this progressive revelation of beauty from the shallow end of the pool. When she surfaced near the opposite end, and side, she turned to him and raised her arm to encourage that which needed no encouragement. He found a shower, used it, and then not trusting his rusty diving form, he lowered himself into the deep end. She had one arm resting on the apron and had not changed her original position. He started toward the shallow end, managed a fair speed reversal, and then returned to the deep end with almost as much vigor as he'd left it. She had watched all of it, and she patted her free hand against the apron in gentle acclaim of his performance. He swam toward her, stopping several yards short of her.

"I detect a youth not entirely spent in pool halls," she said.

"Wonderful water...my congratulations to your husband's careful concern—and the Acme Pool Service." He tried to arrest a stream that flowed from sources in his hair.

She pushed off and moved efficiently with a crawl stroke toward the shallow end, on an oblique trajectory. Even with pouring on the coal, he barely overcame her advantage in time when they reached the shallows. Then she turned and started back. Halfway back, he felt that he had achieved a reasonable, relaxed, speed match and they made a non-competitive tableau back to the deep end.

They both laughed with the exhilaration of the business. Then, she pulled herself up and out of the pool with the assistance of one of the shining ladders. Removing her cap, she shook her hair and then lay face upwards in total—if not wanton—surrender to the sun. Paul assumed a similarly disposed, but carefully distant position.

The water, which persisted in replenishing itself in his eyes, and the bright sunlight, combined to furnish him with a colored fantasy like others he'd experienced in the Western Pacific under similar conditions of nature. He thought about this and of the difference in the circumstances of these displays, as he felt the unequal contest between the sun and the vestiges of the pool on his body.

"You shouldn't have done this, Mrs. Drake," he finally said, without turning away from the sun spectacle. She did turn her head toward him and from a distance of several yards he heard the soft laugh again, and a quiet protestation, "Of what, sir, am I accused?"

"I'm supposed by my family and friends to be a hardworking engineer... temperate in taste and action—as befits this station."

"And?"

"You've brought me...allowed me to come...to this place where there's been a most grave seduction to unknown splendor."

"That's charming...but I've confidence in your resistance, young man." As she said this, Paul turned to her, and the exchange of their eyes was not handicapped by the separation and it gave Paul no confidence at all in his resistance.

"Feeling a powerful urge to change the subject," the smile he'd been using maturing to a full grin, "may I ask what Mr. Drake does?"

"I'll excuse your ignorance on the basis of your late coming to Pasadena." Her smile had also managed to absorb some of the dimensions of a grin. "I'm the proud wife, of the proud owner, of the Drake Instrument Corporation."

"That does sound impressive. I...I wasn't aware that your husband had overcome the handicap of a technical type education." He'd assumed a belly down position and was now looking at her with his chin supported by hands that were against the tile.

"Oh...he hasn't, he didn't...I mean, he didn't have to. Apparently, what the Harvard Business School didn't teach him...he doesn't need." She'd assumed a similar position, except that her eyes were higher than his because of a chin that was supported by a bipod of her arms and hands. "John has never had much difficulty in finding competent technical people. His forte is the get up and go!" Her eyes had drifted toward the pool with that statement.

"And *that*, madam, is the story of most technical professionals. Always there when you need them...depending on the Harvard Business School—or equivalent—to activate, inspire them to anything really exciting." Paul's eyes had followed her lead to the pool before the end of that declaration, whose last part was a diminuendo, but accessible to her.

"Such formality—and your deprecation is preposterous," she said, nailing him with her eyes again. "I think you will build your *own* inspirations, Paul Sanger."

This remark was, possibly, made in perfect sincerity, no conspiracy with a spark that Paul had been striving to keep inside the harmless corral. She couldn't have known of the strength with which the composite force of her present person, his growing appreciation of her, and her final remark had struck him. But suddenly he obliterated their separation, warped her torso into contact with his, then the heads, and then he was kissing her. The program for the pressure against their lips was his at first, unilateral. But there was a gradual disengagement that had more of her design...away from violence. When she had completed the kiss, she stood up, looking down at him. She might have upheld some conversation even then, but he wasn't receptive. He just stared at her. Finally, still under her eyes, he lowered his head and she barely heard his, "Please...forgive me."

No words were spoken during the walk back. He avoided her eyes, which he knew had probed his in unknown humor...several times. When they reached the tree of his art project, she stopped, waited until he was looking at her, and then she said, "You must finish that sketch." Beyond that...nothing. Possibly an absence of anger, some understanding. He did finish that sketch, but Mary's letter had to wait a week for it.

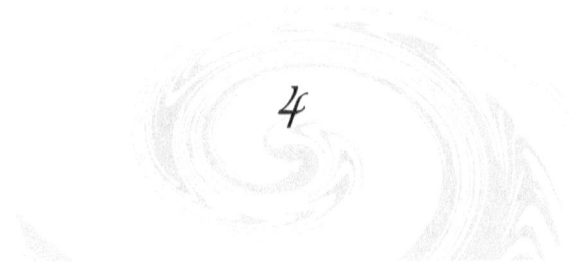

4

"The three principal parts of a rocket motor are the injector, the chamber, and the nozzle...and there are manifold problems with each of them." Russ Kinzer was standing at the blackboard in his office. All of the offices at PAG, except Paul's cubbyhole, were so endowed and PAG would have foundered within hours of the chalk supply petering out. Paul was sitting on Russ' desk, intent on this discourse. After a month, or so, he was being led into a confrontation with a beast of the pit.

"The function of the injector is to effect as efficient a wedding of the fuel and the oxidizer as possible...and I refer to both the spatial and chemical efficiency. We know damn little about the actual combustion dynamics in even the simplest systems...less about the precise mechanics of getting the most from a given reaction." Russ paused to light a churchwarden pipe he occasionally used under the stress and exhilaration of instruction. "When both the propellants are liquid, and have disparate physical properties, the problem is toughest. We get some break in the preliminaries when a gaseous fuel, or oxidizer, is used...but you can generally forget that except for test stand work."

"Meaning?"

"Meaning, the missile boys don't like to carry tanks of high pressure gas on their precious structures...too much weight for the energy value." Russ paused for a couple long drags. "The liquid stuff has been injected in solid linear streams, swirled by arrays of injectors which impart a helical action to the stream, been broken into sprays of various fineness. This has all been done forward and backward, and these games have been played with both components, fuel and oxidizer., singly and together."

"Forward and backward?"

"The symmetry vector of the injection pattern having a forward, or a rearward component of direction with respect to the nozzle." Russ explained, using a sketch.

"What's the best?"

"Damn you, boy! Don't ask such impertinent questions. As I've tried to tell you, the only really impressive aspect of this business is our ignorance. Oh… with a specific system we can get some variation in the characteristic velocity and specific impulse by varying the injection. But this is *strictly* an empirical affair. For all their vaunted sophistication, the combustion theorists are only too happy to latch onto an experimentally inclined lad, whose imagination admits neither prejudice, nor inhibition." Russ sketched a few more injector types, and then paused to remove some imaginary and some very real chalk dust from his shirt and pants. He sat down, one leg on top of his desk, the churchwarden glowing.

"The various configurations of the simple spray injector are usually as good a starting point as any." Russ was staring at a ceiling spot that had been used before.

"Forward…or rearward?" Paul asked with a grin, showing that not all of Russ' exposition had been wasted.

"Forward—I've seen some lovely burn-outs by looking backward."

"Burn-outs?"

"You will—I predict with due somberness and regard for your laundry-man—experience a burn-out quite soon in your career here." Russ' grin owed some of its Mephistophelean cast to a smoke tendril trickling from the corner of his mouth. "Consider that the temperatures—theoretically—at the core of a hot propellant system may well exceed 5000 degrees on Herr Farenheit's scale. The melting point of the practicable containment materials is…say, 3000 degrees—the structural significance limit a lot lower. Unless some benignity interposes itself, hell is bound to break out…and I mean that quite literally."

"The fact that the Chinese had pretty fair rockets would seem to be a testament to this…benignity, as you call it."

"Yeah…two, three thousand years ago." Russ pulled at the churchwarden and picked up the ceiling spot again. "The gods of natural science have granted us this in the gas film." He paused for a few seconds. "This obtains from the very happy fact that the gas phase species near the wall of the combustion chamber are not well disposed to convect, or conduct heat…and this happy inclination increases the closer to the wall they get."

"This factor tends to grant us an entrance somewhat akin to that which certain movie stars are said to enjoy," Paul observed, in paraphrase of a more compact expression, and also with some finality in his voice.

"If we're careful not to interfere with the formation and stability of this gas film," Russ said, inconsiderately untracking Paul's thought train that was just starting to roll.

"What, pray, does this deed?"

"Improper injection patterns that lead to wall impingement of unreacted propellants; injection and feed instabilities that bring vibrations into play within the chamber cavity, discouraging the formation of a stable film; an injection system that generates an asymmetrical flame structure with respect to the chamber geometry; an injection..."

"Christ! It sounds as if *injection* is all of it."

"It...and a combustion chamber of a size and shape appropriate to the feed and energy load...*is* about all of it." Russ's churchwarden made another contribution to the colloidal particle burden of that room.

"What about the solid rockets? The Chinese started them, and I've seen pictures of some big Roman candles that we've been messing with. You're dissertation..."

"Will leave you essentially blank there. You've heard some of our Roman candles huffing and puffing here in the arroyo. The solid boys can get intimate mixtures of fuel and oxidizer and can design propellant grains that purr beautifully. But to get their tractable solid form they're limited to compounds that generally carry more dead weight than liquid propellants. And I like to see more separation between my prenuptialed fuel and oxidizer than they can get with a couple tons of solid propellant all ready to bang. The big candles can help in that first shove away from gravity, but their heroics are constrained to those invigorating few seconds by the nature of the solid beast that says 'use all of me while you can—or you'll be sorry'. Please let me leave it there...I still have a couple friends in the solid group."

"It sounds as if profundities are being propounded herein." George had poked his head into the office. "Don't let *my* ignorance interrupt." He parked himself in one of Russ' chairs. He had barely done this, when Annie walked by, muttering and carrying a stack of papers.

"Looks like somebody's augmenting his pile of gooblahs," Russ observed.

"Myron's got her sweating over his tome to the Army Ordnance Review Council in DC," George said. "I've eye dropped on at least three fascinating thermodynamic milestones that he's threatening to stick into our humble landscape."

"Russ...some time ago, you mentioned this *gooblah* business...and didn't feel compelled to explain it at the time," Paul said.

"Do we feel so compelled...now?" Russ asked George.

"I think this young man's progress would be seriously handicapped without some tutoring in the discipline of the gooblah." George straightened himself in the chair, preparing for more awesome discourse. "May I?" he asked Russ. Russ graciously deferred to his colleague by a nod.

"My boy...when you leave this office...before you leave this office...what do you see?"

"Well...I see...a blackboard plastered with techniques of rocketry. I see...a window, a desk, a..."

"Yes, yes," George prompted. "Please skip the trivia."

"I see...two distinguished scientists devoted to this very science of rocketry."

"Go on," George commanded. "Some people might say that you're still laboring in the trivia...but go on, go on."

"Well...by God, not being privy to more of your philosophies and inclinations than I am now...I'm at a loss for words." Paul scratched his head.

"Damn good thing, too," Russ muttered.

"I doubt that you'll ever be at a loss for words, my boy. But with regard for your ignorance of our foibles, what else do you see here?"

"Two guys wearing shirts, no ties, reasonably presentable slacks, quite casual shoes...one of whose number, by the way, would enjoy a trip to the boot maker." Paul glanced at one of George's prominently displayed shoes.

"You're getting a little closer to the core," George announced. "Don't stop now. What's your opinion of our apparel?"

"Jesus. Well...you guys will never have to worry about being discovered at Schwab's drug store."

"What n'hell is *that* insulting remark supposed to mean?" George challenged.

"Well...you guys dress okay, as I implied...not elegantly...but okay."

"Actually, *quite* modestly, right?" George asserted.

"*Very.*"

"Would you say too damn modestly for men who are clambering perilously close to the...peak...of their careers?" George's voice came close to a crack on that one.

"I must presume that you have a little something at home for emergencies. But now that you've forced candor on me...yes, God damn it, the modesty of your apparel appalls the hell out of me!"

"Ah," Russ said, after Paul had finally torn away the shell and was starting to reach for the meat.

"Just what'n hell this mysterious...*gooblah*...has to do with all this crap is not evident to me at this slap-happy juncture." Paul sensed that he wasn't going to like the connection.

"Do we appear unhappy to you? Do you see many dejected faces in your frequent—very frequent, I might add—passages to and from this emporium of unnatural science?" George's smile was not a product of natural inclination.

"As a matter of fact, you characters are about the slap-happiest bunch I've ever seen...except for some guys at the bachelor officers' quarters at Hickam Field...I..."

"Spare us your disgusting memories." Russ could go to a good pontifical shading.

"To answer your question then...no, I haven't seen much depression hereabouts."

"To what do you attribute this happy condition?" George asked.

"Oh...satisfaction with your work...the excitement of being on a frontier of science...the..."

"God, this boy positively *exudes* inspiration, doesn't he, Russ."

"It *is* a little close in here." Russ stood up, walked to his window, and opened it, slightly.

"Nothing else?" George persisted.

"I feel that I've shot my wad."

"Well...permit us to give you more wadding. You haven't been around here very long. But surely you've noticed the wicked little grin that Myron, or Harry, or Russ...even I, occasionally sport."

"I've noticed an occasional expression...reminiscent of a cat eating sh...a canary," Paul replied.

"Any explanation?" George asked.

"I must presume that you've accomplished some minor diabolism against your fellow man—maybe that's too strong, but I'll let it ride."

"We have—in fact—accomplished the acquisition of one, or more, gooblahs as a result of the revelation of a technical achievement of some weight to a superior; or the acceptance of a paper by a conference; or the publication of a paper in a journal of stature."

"Preferably with a large lay audience," Russ muttered again.

"This...*gooblah*...is a certificate of merit?"

"Oh...it's nothing so crass as a material object...such as money...which is a very transient thing. This is a unit of...*prestige*. A unit of undefined magnitude, but a unit, none the less. Fortified with a few gooblahs, men such as Russ and myself...men of quite modest attainments as you've so graciously observed... can stride into a lunchroom filled with their peers...into an auditorium similarly loaded, even..."

"I've seen some awesome displays of gooblah power in rest rooms," Russ added reflectively.

"Even into the inner sanctums of the *Institute*," George made a proper obeisance with that, "with the proud demeanor which belies their poor exteriors."

"Then this *gooblah* does have certain of the characteristics of money?"

"Ah," George said.

"Ah," Russ said, with the realization that Paul was chewing on the meat, and his process of digestion was starting.

"With a satchel of gooblahs—albeit an immaterial bag and contents—we tend to look at our bank accounts through the glass of roses," Russ said. "In fact, there's no question in our minds that the gooblah is weighted heavily in our salary negotiations...that the management is quite cognizant of the inspirational value of this semi-unit, this..."

"Ducat of frustration," George said.

"This symbol of a grateful country," Russ said.

"This symbol of the technical man's bondage to proud penury," George said.

"This culmination of professional achievement," Russ said.

"This God damn link in a chain of exploitation that couldn't get you one-way passage to a broken down shit house in Coney Island," George cried in his culmination.

"Now George! Is *this* inspiration for our young aspirant?" Russ declared.

"Forgive me, my friend. I tend to wax a little eloquent on the subject of gooblahs." George laid a paternal hand on Paul's knee and gave it a little squeeze.

"I'll be God damned," Paul said.

"Perish the thought!" Russ cried, hands and eyes turned heavenward.

"May your bounty of gooblahs be substantial...and persistent." With that supplication, George made his devotion to supernal authority and then he left Russ and Paul to their own thoughts, which happened to be considerable at that moment.

"Tom, you'd better caution your charges to remain where they are until I give the all clear." Paul was trying to keep his voice volume high, inside a three-sided revetment that was used for demonstrations of spontaneous and delayed reactions of propellant components. Tom was escorting a group of Army and Navy officers of various ranks. Some of these gentlemen had a casualness to catastrophe that bothered Paul, and Tom too, somewhat.

"Look you guys, you may need your balls...and then, on closer look, maybe not. But stay put until our mentor gives the high sign. I just had this uniform cleaned and they charge extra for blood and guts." A group of about

20 officers was clustered around observation windows on the sides of the revetment.

"First, I'll try a spontaneous reaction. I'll put some hydrazine in the lower cup and hydrogen peroxide in the upper one. When I yank the pull wire, they'll mix and should bang right now, like good spontaneous propellants." Paul completed his preparations, checked the pull wire that ran through a port to the outside. When he was outside the revetment, he said, "Everybody ready?" Hearing no protests, he pulled the wire activating the tipping mechanism and an explosion resulted almost simultaneously with his action. He let them see that very little was left of the beakers, and that the aromas of hydrazine and hydrazine residues have a cloying sweetness. "The Germans claim that hydrazine has certain aphrodisiacal powers," Paul said to no one in particular.

"Better bottle me a couple quarts of the stuff," Tom said. "And I know some guys who could use a gallon, or two...couldn't you, Colonel?" he said to one of his superiors in rank.

"Now we'll try an exercise in delayed reaction," Paul said, back inside the revetment. "We'll use fuel A of your notes, and our old friend, hydrogen peroxide. As I showed you before, A and peroxide don't like each other to the extent of banging right now. So...we'll coax 'em with a few drops of catalyst. This, we place in fuel A. If you put it in the peroxide, you'd blow hell out of it...as I also showed you before. When the catalyst-loaded fuel is dumped into the peroxide nothing happens for a few seconds...then we should get a good detonation. For Christ's sake, stay put. The delay time on these things is indefinite as hell—at least the way I do it. Don't poke your beans into the revetment until I say so." Paul retreated to his control position. After assuring himself of a clear area, he pulled the trip wire. The more observant noticed the formation of an appetizing sparkling concoction. This persisted for about five seconds, with only a slight increase in the effervescence. After several more seconds, some murmuring started among the observers of this excitement and several of them started to drift away from the revetment—when it happened. It was a detonation of real laundry significance, and it brought tears to the eyes of those affected by the miscellany of reaction products and residues.

"Goddamn! What do you do for an encore?" Tom asked, wiping his face with his handkerchief.

"Never saw one take so damn long before," Paul said to the impressed multitude. And that concluded *that* exercise in delayed reaction.

Paul and Tom had finished their lunch and were nuzzling their second cup of coffee in a lunch spot in La Canada.

"That bit today should teach those jokers to keep their ears open around PAG," Tom said. "I don't mind shooting the stuff from a control room, but I'll never feel comfortable around fifty gallon drums of high test peroxide, or anhydrous hydrazine," he confessed to a smiling Paul.

"Your apprehensions are well founded. Last weekend, one of your fifty gallon drums of peroxide detonated at the lab. Damn lucky it was in a storage revetment...on a weekend. They found the imprint of a wrench in a concrete fragment...and you could read the serial numbers."

"Any explanation for the bang?"

"The analytical boys found traces of lead oxide on fragments of the bung hole...and *that*, is all she wrote."

"Lead is a catalyst for peroxide decomposition, isn't it?"

"One of the best. That stuff will get mad at damn near anything. Get the concentration above 98%—you *can't* be too careful around our temperamental friend."

"All those blond bombers walking around...if they only knew what power they held in their little bottles," Tom said, like Russ, reflectively.

"You are—of course—still talking about peroxide."

"*Mais oui, mais certainment.* But, no bull, does that hydrazine really have certain exotic powers?"

"Our perceptive German friends did report that—but I never made a literature search there...my German technical vocabulary probably couldn't do it justice."

"Man...the thought of those big, blond, rocket experts frothing at the mouth tends to bring the gooseflesh up, doesn't it, my friend."

"It has a certain exhilaration to it...I have to admit."

"Not to change the subject...but how's everything going?" Tom managed to find a target for his eyes in his coffee.

"Well...lab wise...it's a real education in things technical and not so technical...a real bunch of characters, stimulating as hell. If I don't blow my head off...I should do okay there."

"And otherwise?" It was coffee time for Tom, again.

Paul looked at Tom for a second and then he turned his head to the window. When he came back, he aimed at Tom over the rim of his coffee cup, "If I don't blow my head off...I might do okay there, too."

When Paul returned to his office area, the badminton game was still in progress in front of Chemistry. Ruth and Karen, the lab technicians were battling with Horace, the other technician, and Annie. Eddy and Art were holding up a corner of the building, watching this spectacle. Art had just commented that Ruth had an interesting butt, and Eddy had responded that Art could have Ruth, but that Karen sure did crazy things when she went for a high one. They were both good married men, but not *dead* married men.

As Paul passed Russ' office, he noticed that Russ was talking on the phone, and that he didn't appear to be projecting conviviality. He'd recently returned from part of his annual cycle of conventions and review meetings. Such trips had a big potential for generating shock waves whose vestiges could trail into the heads of the participants for weeks afterward. The senior staff at Chemistry upheld that tradition, and Paul suspected that Russ was in the throes of a vestige.

Later that afternoon, as Paul was trying in a purely physical way to put unread papers and reports in a less intimidating posture on, or near, his desk, Russ walked by his door on the way to the parking lot. He gave a terse "Hi" to Paul. Paul overhauled him at the outside door. He held the door for Russ, and made the unnecessary comment that this had to be a good day because it was Friday. Russ grunted in agreement, and they walked together toward their cars.

"You made a pretty good bang out there today," Russ said, in reference to the delayed reaction bit.

"Yeah...must've slipped up there a little with the amounts," Paul replied, with a quick glance at Russ.

"You keep making noises, boy—maybe *you'll* get some appreciation, some day."

"What's the trouble, Russ?" Paul felt that the friendship was solid enough now for that question.

Russ threw his briefcase into the back seat of his old Buick and turned to face Paul. "Oh...just some personal crap. There's *got* to be some of that, or I'd get spoiled with all the fun and games." He spread his arms apart to pull more of the fun toward him.

"Got anything to do with gooblahs?"

"As a matter of fact..." Russ was trying to build a smile for Paul. He was also confirming Paul's worst suspicion. Russ didn't feel like conversation, but he didn't relish that jungle between PAG and Westwood, either.

"We neglected a vital corollary in your gooblah indoctrination...maybe several." Russ leaned against his car, accepting whatever invigoration he could get from instruction. "We're tending perilously close to paranoia here. Maybe *defensive awareness* is a better emphasis...yes, defensive awareness hides the paranoia nicely."

"I don't know if my fee covers the second semester on gooblahs."

"I'll advance you a little credit." Russ didn't have to work at feigning seriousness. "My boy, neither a snooper, nor a sniper, be. And now shut up for some definition. Snoopers are self-explanatory. These ones have a large component of inquisitiveness in their professional drive. This is a good attribute in any man. But the gentlemen in question are motivated more by reaction to what their fellow men are doing, or thinking, than by honest search for their own fulfillment...for original targets for their own energy. There are degrees of snooperism, but we'll skip the subtler parts for now. They range from ball faced theft of another's work—by deliberate confusion of precedence, to map stealing."

"*Map* stealing?"

"If you can find a well enough annotated map to an objective, you can divorce yourself from a lot of dirty ground-searching and be a twinkle toes among the lilacs when the other poor slobs stagger from the underbrush."

"You mentioned another type that tends to wiggle your whiskers."

"Snipers." Russ took another short journey into the memory of his recent trip.

"I'm still speechless."

"Stay that way! This character is no less reprehensible. His influence can be sadly pervasive...he's like a bucket of liquid shit tossed into a spring pool. He tends to false sympathetic extroversion. He's very solicitous of your welfare... very appreciative of your accomplishments, and very converse with respect to the other people of the moment. And he plays this game with everyone. He attracts brown-nosed incompetents and sycophants to him and—like a comet— the bigger he is, the bigger his tail. Yes...liquid shit is a good simile, very good. End of lesson. Now remember, we never refer to this as paranoia...it's *defensive awareness*." That got a grin on him. "Now you've seen my feet of clay." Then he left Paul, and by the time Russ had started to gun the Buick out of the lot, his smile was well developed.

Those feet of clay had been leaving exhilarating tracks, but they took some unexpected detours.

5

Paul had just parked his car and was climbing the stairs to his aerie when another car—the Continental—pulled into the carriage house space. Usually, the Drakes used the parking and garage facilities adjoining the main house. Occasionally, just to keep in practice, and bowing to Martha's historical privilege, John wheeled into the ample space he'd just chosen.

"Hey fellah...how's about some unwind?" John shouted.

"Sounds great, Mr. Drake. Let me crawl into something that doesn't smell like hydrazine." He took his last steps in one bound.

"Mrs. Drake reminded me to be properly respectful of the Drake Instrument Corporation," Paul said, followed by a sip of the massive Scotch his host had just provided.

"Uh...she tipped you off, did she." John laughed, and then tapped his equally impressive bourbon.

"She also mentioned the Harvard Business School—that really impressed me."

"The word *logarithm* has always made me run toward the dictionary. That should indicate my scientific prowess. My dad was in banking in New York. My apprenticeship therein was just enough to keep me from adding to the supply of dumb bankers. So, I decided to join another branch of the unscrupulous businessmen instead." John took another slug.

"Like I said...I'm impressed, having usually done the dictionary bit myself when something like *amortization* comes up."

"It sounds more impressive than it is. Every discipline—I believe you fellows call them—has its own mystique...and works hell out of it."

"Guilty as hell, too," Paul said, the Scotch starting to unbridle his tongue. "I've just enough math, and just enough scientific vocabulary, to know that you can hide a really impressive ignorance if you've got the edge on the other guy in math or vocabulary...preferably math *and* vocabulary—they can be a wicked little synergism in the right hands."

"Now...don't tell me all your secrets...I like a little mystery."

They concentrated on their drinks for a while and on the restful panorama of the posterior portion of the Drake estate. Paul didn't mention that he'd gone beyond the hedge row and experienced the hidden delights of the blue crystal. The totality of that experience he certainly held privately. Since that day, his concourse with the lady of this house had consisted of one exchange of hand waves as he passed her car in the driveway. She hadn't shown any encouragement for a resumption of their artistic camaraderie...nor had she shown any reprisal for his massive impudence. She could have told him to get t'hell out. This was an appreciated compassion. But Paul couldn't really savor the soft cushion of the lounge chair, despite his host's frank hospitality. His discomfiture wasn't relieved by the sound of high heels approaching on the flagstone.

"And speaking of mystery...awful and wonderful mystery," John Drake said, rising and turning toward his wife. Paul didn't need prompting to do his honors.

"Mysticism...so early in the evening?" she asked, as she seated herself on a chair bounded by her admirers...one quite overt in this office, the other much less so. She was wearing a cheongsam of dark blue silk. With jade pendants at her ears, an upward swirl to her hair, and a complement of dark red lips ready for conspiracy with her eyes...she was the strongest possible support for John's charge of mysticism. As she accommodated to her chair, the uninhibited slit of her dress did just what its designer intended, and she asked no constraint of it.

"What's your pleasure, my dear?" her husband asked the acolyte of mysticism.

"Someone had better keep sober here," she said, glancing at the bourbon and Scotch reservoirs on the low table in front of them. "Just a smallish Scotch on rocks, please John."

John Drake retired to a corner of the veranda and worked with one of his decanter sets.

"Did you finish that sketch, Mr. Sanger?" Her eyes were now some of the blue crystal they'd both shared recently...but her smile, this time, would have pleased Senor Da Vinci.

"I finally threw something together that I thought gave some of the place to Mary." He didn't avoid her eyes. "But I *shall* return!" His McArthur caricature rewarded him with a franker smile. "...Although formal artistic concentration is subject to serious perturbations hereabouts." She accepted his *perturbation* without more response than a subtle collaboration between her eyes and smile that a more sophisticated man than himself would have to translate.

"Light Scotch...*avec les roches*," John said, presenting the glass to her. "Paul and I have been exchanging confidences."

"Oh?" She'd given that just the tiniest rising inflection. Her eyes, now focused on John, also responded with a barely perceptible enlargement.

"We've been discussing the hoodwink techniques of business and science, respectively." John's smile had no particular target.

"And which do you gentlemen deem the most reprehensible?" This time, she had enough smile to give a portion to each of her attendants.

"There appears to be enough dastardly content to keep both camps quite happy." Paul's laugh also flowed around well. "In an effort to quickly render our respective images more palatable...may I ask where your business is located, Mr. Drake?"

"We have a research and manufacturing...complex, I like to call it...out on Foothill in Pasadena. You might have seen it, but didn't identify it—I don't like to be too forward."

"Sounds like you've been forward, indeed...but don't make the sign people happy." Paul sipped his reservoir. "What type of instruments?—we're coming close to some of my own passions here."

"We spread ourselves around fairly broadly: Stuff for the chemical and oil industries...detecting, monitoring, control instrumentation. Some for aerospace...multi- channel oscillographs, pressure transducers, strain monitors. Some auxiliaries for the camera and optical people. And occasional action with some of the Hollywood people for their various special effects wonderlands." He glanced at his wife, back at Paul, and then John Drake obviously enjoyed a slowly fed charge of bourbon and small ice.

"And you have a little something back in Washington DC," Martha Drake added.

"Yes, a little something in DC...we call it a listening post. Some people call it lobbying."

"If I didn't know that you're courting the bourbon equivalent of what Mr. Sanger has called the *infamous empty stomach Scotch effect*, I'd be inclined to let this Drake advertisement continue. May I suggest we consider the sensible alternative of dinner?" Martha Drake set her drink down and stood up.

"Capital, my dear, capital," John said, as he and Paul surrendered their drinks to the table and arranged themselves in accordance with the lady's command. "He that proposeth...shall suggesteth," Drake challenged, his tongue on a remarkably short leash.

"Once again...I impose," Paul said.

"Silence!" John ordered, looking at his wife for the expected suggestion.

"Do you think you could find Perino's in your present precarious condition?"

"With Paul in command...you as his co-pilot...the night holds no terror for me."

"Perino's doesn't sound like hamburgers and chili....I'm afraid my wardrobe may be unequal to this venture."

"You *do* have a dark suit...I've seen it," the lady stated.

"That...and a tie which harboreth not neon lights...should do nicely." John clamped a hand on Paul's shoulder.

Half an hour later, Paul entered the house through the veranda, as ordered, and walked into the room of his first meeting with the master of the house. This time, no firelight. John joined him a few minutes later, and then shortly, Martha Drake completed the company. In the interest of expediting the venture, she was carrying a sable coat. She was wearing a creation of a color similar to her earlier gown, but which now bore that Frenchman's artistry in a cocktail style. Dark stockings, black pumps, and a rope of pearls completed a picture that needed no service from firelight. Paul assisted her with her coat and was rewarded with a smile that was frank enough now.

"Paul, will you haul forth the chariot," John said, tossing Paul the keys to the Continental. "We'll intersect you at the front."

"The carriage house part of this night holds no terror for me," the lady declared. And with the smile that dazzles, she led her escorts onto the veranda... and thence to the place of execution underneath the inspirational panoply of oaks.

John Drake had been resolute in his insistence that the navigator should be in close conjunction with the pilot, so he forced himself into the luxury of the back seat. After securing the door of his seatmate, Paul journeyed to the front of the vehicle and eventually assumed the command center. Drakes' logic didn't depress him at all.

He found the Pasadena freeway by himself, with only one minor inadvertence near Orange Grove. He accelerated the powerful machine to a velocity that seemed to be a fair compromise between the traffic and the vestige of the Scotch. He glanced into the rearview mirror. "This *is* a fine hunk of wheels, Mr. Drake."

"For Christ's sake, Paul! You hit me with my age every time you call me *mister*. I'm taking your money as a tenant. You're a good tenant...and potential marlin material...and you work for one of my customers. Those credentials, God damn it, entitle you to a more flattering familiarity." John was loud, jovial.

"Okay, John. You've got a fine hunk of wheels here."

"That's better. My wife will have to make her own arrangements," John said with a close chuckle. For a second, the pilot and the navigator exchanged glances that suggested some negotiation had already started.

Martha showed Paul a little maneuver that saved some time getting to Wilshire. Before long, they were on that artery of Los Angeles and hamlets to the west.

"I must show you some of the galleries around here, Paul," Martha said, in effortless transition to the familiarity her husband had encouraged. "Between here and the coast, you can see really quite a lot of the good and the...well." Paul stole another glance in time for some of her smile.

"God, Martha...I just remembered...this is Friday night. Our influence might not do the job at Perino's."

"Fortunately, someone had the foresight to make a reservation."

"Two guesses?"

"Flatterer," she said, turning a small laugh toward the back seat.

"Good evening Mr. Drake...Mrs. Drake," the mâitre d' said to two who were not strangers.

John still enjoyed enough faculties to order a meal that met with general approval, except for a minor dissention from Martha. She also enforced a discipline of no further alcoholic stimulation until some food had crossed their lips. This stoicism was relieved shortly by a Beaujolais that well represented French treasure. Eventually, John upheld the dessert tradition with a creation of cherries, flaming brandy and ice cream to which both Martha and Paul made laughing, unsuccessful protest. Over coffee, they were talking about the growth of Los Angeles, its pleasant and unpleasant dividends, when an exit bound couple passed their table.

"Martha...John...how nice!" the woman said without pretense. She was wearing a formal gown with an orchid corsage. Possibly in her early fifties, of medium height, very pleasantly proportioned. She was a raven haired Jewess of quiet beauty and there was nothing about her that argued against tasteful elegance. Her companion was a short, plump man with a facial structure that was frank in its statement of antecedents.

"John, old man," he said, and he grabbed John's outstretched paw.

"Hetty and Jake Sternglas, may I present Paul Sanger," John said, turning to Paul.

"Please...sit down...very pleased to meet you, Paul. We're on the tag end of the private part of a little anniversary party," Jake Sternglas said, smiling at his wife.

"Congratulations you two," Martha said. "Let's see...ten years, isn't it?"

"My dear, you should've been in the diplomatic corps. I thought that *thirty* years deserved a quiet little party, as this brute has said." Hetty Sternglas reciprocated her husband's smile.

"My God...you two could pass for newlyweds," John said. His laugh was almost as good as Jake's.

"Please don't let us interrupt. Hetty and I would be honored if you'd join us at our place for a toast—or ten," Jake declared, his hand on John's shoulder. John looked at Martha, Martha looked at Hetty, Hetty looked at everyone, and that was that.

Jake's house was deep in the trackless wilderness called Bel Air. A butler had taken Martha's coat and as John and Paul escorted her to the room of principal gathering, Paul knew that he'd just stumbled up another step of the Temple of Affluence.

John had diffused to the bar in the game room, responding to the forces of new and old friends, and the memory of an exhilaration that dinner had perturbed some. Paul was sitting with Martha on a massive couch in front of a fireplace that could have served Charlemagne. Their companions in conversation were Hetty and three couples...the all disposed on thick carpets, or pillows or furniture well within the glamour zone of the fire.

While he chatted with one of the men about the football situation at Stanford, and on the coast in general, Paul couldn't avoid other broadcasts of the opera season, a new couturier in Beverly Hills, the gross on a Warner's epic...and why'n hell hadn't they let Oscar handle that one?...the problems of getting that building, or that shopping center *just* right, some of the merits of diamond purchase from the Amsterdammers as opposed to the New York houses. The fireplace drew him many times, and after sampling some of the fiscal atmosphere, Paul felt that the crystal in his hand *had* served fiercer eyes than any he could see in that room.

"Martha tells me that you're an artist, Paul," Hetty said, leaning slightly forward from her position on the couch beside Martha.

"Mrs. Sternglas..."

"Hetty...please!"

"Hetty...Martha is a very kind lady." Paul tried to return Hetty's smile, but he was overmatched by the little flashes she could make in her dark eyes.

"Martha, *dear*...you never mentioned your charming protégé before." Both the face and voice of Hetty's reconnaissance caused Martha and Paul to laugh.

"You've far exceeded my potential, Hetty," Paul said. "John and Martha were kind enough to give housing to a homeless waif with a slide rule in his pack." Paul had to alternate his look between Martha and Hetty, and he couldn't begin to analyze the complexions he picked up on *that* trip.

"*Ach so...du bist einer slippenstikker, nicht wahr?*" Paul turned to the rear of the couch and met the smiling face of his host, who'd been enjoying the fire for a few rare moments of passive contemplation.

"Boys and girls...may I say that I would like to make a toast to my bride." Pursuant to that objective, Jake's butler was approaching the area with a large cart, loaded with grand necessities for Jake's proposal. After everyone had been equipped with the essential substance, Jake raised his glass to his wife, "To my Hetty...*all* my best love." Many glasses supported that simple statement of love and devotion. Apparently, Jake had appraised the situation in the game room and given it up as hopeless for his present purposes. Afterwards, Jake joined the membership of the fireplace club more conspicuously.

"A *technical* man." Jake made that statement sitting in a chair close to Paul and the ladies, and looking at Paul. He'd intercepted some of the byplay among Paul and his companions and he felt that his assessment of this young man might not due him full justice.

"Guilty, sir," Paul replied.

"Jake, young man, Jake...please."

"Paul is trying to blow his head off at Caltech's Propulsion Analysis Group," Martha said, with a slight raising of hands and eyes heavenward.

"Rockets! God grant that you—and your fellow workers—can keep them friendly." Jake gave a slight smile to Paul with that. "That damn bomb...the *rockets* now. What we have seen, Hetty!"

"Jake...please don't excite yourself. Have some champagne." Hetty caressed him with a smile that was a fair return of his toast. Jake returned a reflective gaze to Paul.

"You said *slip-stick*, Jake," Paul said, after a few seconds under the beam of the Sternglas eye power. The quality of his voice invited the attention of close ears, and then he gradually picked up most of the others in the room. "Sometimes I think...*slippery* stick might be better." Jake's expression of slight melancholy warped partly to his version of a shrewd student.

"In what respect?" Jake's voice was quiet, slightly accented, and various versions of it, or its surrogates, weighted conversations and communications with most of the significant pulses of the world's economy."I think it's a matter of repayment for graces of enlightenment...*technical* in this case. I think enlightenment entails responsibility...whose neglect could ruin what progress we've made." He finished with a small smile, still looking into the dark eyes fixed on him. At that moment, the eyes and the whispers of the old voyageur of the grove outside PAG came to him...unbidden, and he knew that some part of him *had* been thinking about that question that had stuck to him. "With respect to present company which puts the 'go for it' into the technical ideas—and I'd better swipe my last glass of champagne," he did it, "I think that responsibility's been looking too much like exploitation. " Jake had to wait for him, and when Paul's train started again, his voice was softer, tailored more for a muse than an entrepreneur. "We pile chemicals on the land, into our animals, to push production, yet the implications of much of this stuff—to us—are damn poorly known, or largely ignored if there *is* knowledge...and there's no real pressure to force understanding...or compliance with understanding." Jake's eyes still had him skewered. Paul couldn't read anything behind the eyes, but he could still qualify for young impetuosity, so he milked it some more with a bigger voice. "We're pushing technical processes for creating everything from petrochemical hamburgers to rhodium plated condoms...throwing out slip-streams of miscellaneous crap for the poor bastard downstream of us who doesn't give a *damn* about a lot of it...maybe just the condoms. This guy just wants a quiet afternoon with his wife and kids...tapping his share of the *good* earth."

"Christ! Those rhodium plated condoms sound uncomfortable as hell." Jake used his first grin in some time. "Have some more champagne, Paul." Jake followed his own advice, then he said, "but some people call that progress, my boy."

"Oh...I don't deny that. Unless we get a better handle on that responsibility—better appreciation of John Donne's other bells that we're clanging—we'll progress right into a quicksand where emergency ropes may not be long enough to reach us. And, by the way, the guys over at Caltech aren't too happy about the living costs on the *other* planets we know about—or this one either, if we let 'em get out of hand." Paul sipped his drink and then set it down on the big coffee table fronting him. There was still some eye lock left with Jake, and Paul used it. "We're constantly trying to pick Nature's brains for our own advantage. We'd also damn well study some of her strategies for protecting herself against our mistakes—because she'll *always* be some jumps ahead of us."

There was no conversation. Martha finally whispered to him that they'd better collect John and make their departure. Actually, some time before, John had drifted into that room and had overheard most of Paul's seminar from a rear vantage. He'd achieved an alcoholic euphoria that transcended his earlier one, but his acuity had been trained to work under handicaps.

"Damn you boy...you'll ruin me with your ideals." John's voice was a tad too loud for the fireplace club.

"Don't discourage him, John. He's definitely not kosher. But he's got some of our prophets in him." Jake's voice had soft edges now and it carried as far as he wanted it to go.

"Hetty...Jake...our congratulations again. May we help you celebrate your *next* thirty years," Martha declared at the door.

"God forbid that we—or you—should last *that* long," Hetty replied.

"I want to see more of our prophet," Jake said, turning to Paul.

"Oh...Martha and I have artistic plans for him...*haven't* we Martha." Hetty's leer hadn't lost a thing.

"I've told him that there may be some enlightenment in these here now hills of Beverly." Martha also used a smile that an imaginative one could've credited with facets that complemented Hetty's.

John had been more than happy to resume his rear seat domain and to take advantage of the no conversation sanctuary of it. Actually, he slept most of the way back to Pasadena. When they reached the Pasadena freeway, Martha had finally overcome most of her resistance to letting Paul hold her hand. Her head was back against the seat and she savored the rare absence of smog in the air of this night.

"You have some fascinating friends, Martha," Paul said. "Jake is obviously a man of many parts."

"Indeed. There aren't many parts of our time he hasn't touched...he's a dear." She made just the slightest attempt to disengage the hand coupling. The rest of the trip was silence, except for the lovely purr of Mr. Ford's mechanism.

When they reached the house entrance, Paul escorted Martha to the door, and then he assisted her slightly slap-happy husband to the foyer.

"All right, now?" he asked her.

"Thanks, Paul...I can manage the brute from here."

"G'night, Paul...thanks for piloting," John said and then, as he turned to the nether regions, Paul thanked him for the evening.

"I...I'd like to take advantage of your pool once more, Martha. I think a little unwinding is in order...before I embrace the sleep goddess."

"Well, a midnight swim isn't unknown around here...but you *must* be careful of those goddesses, you know." With that, she gave him the full force of her eyes and she left him standing in the foyer.

About a half hour later, Paul had completed his second traverse of the cool wonder of the pool. He'd pulled himself up to the tile apron and was lying belly down, feeling the slight breeze augment the pool effect, studying the mirrored image of a full moon. He hadn't been in this attitude for more than five minutes, when he saw a whiteness appear near the far end of the pool and stop near its edge. The whiteness suddenly contracted and fell downward. From its former space, he saw a silhouette test the water and then slip into it. Every sense of his being told him that he was now imperiled by a goddess. He didn't move. The pattern of moonlight on the water was being perturbed by an advancing superposition of wavelets that warned him his peril was imminent. The agency of this concern suddenly appeared about a yard to his left, and downward.

"I fear that two of us needed a little unwinding...as you say," she said to him from the water. He stood, extended his right hand to her and then he pulled her to standing at his side. She slipped a little and he placed his free hand around her waist to steady her. After the rescue, he removed both his hands from her and stepped away from her.

She moved away from the pool, ran her fingers through her hair, which hadn't been protected, and then left her hands on her cheeks. And she held this position, head slightly back, studying him. She and the lambent moonlight sculpting her made him think of some non-passive, contemplation the Greeks had put into a few of their marbled women when they were surfeited with the untouchable, frustrating nuances of temple decoration.

Paul couldn't speak. He only looked at her eyes...a marvelous trap for the moon light. After a few seconds—years to him—neither had surrendered the ligament of their eyes. He knew that this was the confrontation with a situation he hadn't denied. His excitement with Martha's response to him, her challenge to him now, denied him any refuge of irrelevant speech...and any action that could be construed as honoring John Drake.

"Christ, Martha...I'm *not* made of iron." His voice was as soft as the tendrils of moonlight caressing her.

They were about four feet apart. It was her initiative that shortened this space and when she was close enough to use a whisper, she said, "Oh?—then perhaps I'd better toss you back." And with that, damned if she didn't push him into the pool...and follow him shortly afterwards.

When he surfaced, the moon told on a nearby ladder and also eyes and lips that were near it. He made directly for the primary target. He put one hand on the ladder, the other around her waist. Then he repeated his first days ago kiss triggered by her compliment...with the variation of more bilaterally inspired contact pressure, variously applied, and absolutely no disengagement, or calming, effort from Martha. He brought his torso into a conjunction with hers that defined new parts of her for him, and also some extra details of her submission. After a few seconds, he made the commendable maneuver of mounting the ladder with her cradled on mostly one arm. He laid her on the apron, her head perilously close to the abyss, her waist smarting from his pressure. Then, he repeated his kiss of only instants precedence, except that now he started to use both of his hands to clarify possible vestiges of her resistance in the area around, on, her breasts.

"Paul," she whispered. "I need breath...and I'm awfully close to the edge." He was close enough to her face to pick up the tiniest signals of her eyes. "There is more sensible space for...conversation."

He looked toward the place that needed no more of her direction. Then he picked her up—a proper cushion of both arms this time—and strode toward the Chinese fantasy. Inside, there were enough vectors of moonlight to identify some furniture, and some walking space. He saw a number of chairs of a substantial, elegant, oriental mode, and at least one couch that could handle single, or crowded two person, exuberant lounging. But a heroic futon, mounted on a teakwood frame that raised it about a foot from the floor, providing undoubted scope for uninhibited two body conversation, was his major discovery and terminus. He went there. She had nibbled his right ear and whispered the word braggart while he was making his progress to the pavilion. And then, while he was making his prospect of the interior amenities, his passenger had nibbled his left ear, without comment, although he was strongly pressed to read the words in her eyes.

The day of their first communion by the pool, she'd worn a one piece bathing suit of white, modestly revealing. This night, she was wearing a two piece suit that touched the brazen limits of the bikini style. It was of black silk and even dry it couldn't burden his imagination. Now, it was wet and it seemed like a reluctant barrier to her revelation resolve of that night. He stood her on her feet next to the futon. And then he kissed her again, working his hands against her back and buttocks. He fumbled with the fastener of her upper garment and succeeded in releasing it. Her breasts had already started to respond to his ardor and during several short respites from his kiss—their kiss—there was enough light for him to enjoy a symmetry and texture and sculpting that defied calendar age. He took his lips on a downward trip that included stops at her throat and neck, and at the V of her bosom...before he came to the tips of her breasts. At that point, he had two targets for what was now his kiss and he alternated his attention, seeming to hear breath emanations from her... sounding like words. He had one hand around her waist and the other was starting to work on the lower part of her costume. It was a step-in design and when his hand—the rover that had insinuated to the upper part of her mons Veneris—discovered this complication, he lifted her off the ground. Then he, they, succeeded in removing the tiny lower part of her modesty.

She stood straight, legs together, her hands trying to do something about errant strands of wet hair. She left them in this upward position, head slightly back, like at the apron by the pool. Only now, the full revelation of her...the interstices of moonlight granting him portions of a still moistened body which perfectly complemented his other, limited, visions of her in his memory...tried to take away his words. As a result, she beat him to the first intelligent conversation—excepting the pool play—since their false goodnight an hour ago.

"And *now* what?" she asked. The emotional content of that moment was enough to pull almost any response from it. She could've been close to laughter, or disdain, or some synthesis of compliment or outrageous provocation—any or all of this befitting a night goddess. She still had her hands parked near the top of her head. And her eyes, during these instants when he came around to that part of her, didn't afford him unambiguous incentive for his next action. But this—he knew—was a well known characteristic for a goddess of this kind.

"This unilateral nakedness has *got* to stop." he said, testing her neutrality by closing on her mouth again, and bending her backwards with attentions he brought to her breasts and buttocks almost simultaneously.

He removed his trunks. She hadn't altered hardly any aspect of her surveillance, except for several slight displacements lingering from his last embrace. The giant pulse of his excitement now had an obvious focal point. He stood in front of her, close to her, no parts of them touching. But she had reason to know that this transient of respite was about to be obliterated. He picked her up and placed her on the futon, in a position that gave him a useful annulus of space around her. As he came to her mouth and breasts again, she worked her hands in his hair and along his back. Their sets of legs had also discovered each other and she enticed their entanglements and started to reciprocate his lip work that had become progressively attentive. When his hands started to explore the inside of her upper thighs, and then the silky portal of her vaginal zone, he heard her say his name. And then the pilot-navigator couple of them was reborn as she led him toward the culmination of her. Her voice wouldn't serve her. But—as he entered her—she found enough reserve of breath and muscular discipline to say, "Paul...I..." and then she gave herself up to what Paul had once called the *gentle rage*—but he'd never really known about it until that moment.

The pavilion became very quiet after a while. This was finally broken by her complaint that she was tired...she was wet...she was cold. He conceded these points to her, and finally relented.

They stood near the sketching oak, as she had called it. She had firmly resisted his suggestion that he had more artwork in his rooms that might interest her. And then she kissed him...and left him standing in a dream.

The next morning, she called him and commanded his presence at her first introduction to Wilshire art. An hour later, he joined her and John on the veranda and shared their morning coffee.

"I'm taking your wife on a Beverly Hills art tour today, John," he said, in a direct—but totally irrelevant—effort at confrontation with the situation of Martha Drake and him.

"Good," John said. "There're a couple jokers at Annandale who've been asking to have their ears tacked down...I aim to oblige 'em today. You golf, Paul?"

"I've contributed my share to the frustrations of the greens keepers."

"We'll have to look into that one day. Have fun, you two...I must pick up the burden of instruction." And then he left them.

She was wearing a kind of bolero costume, with high thin leather boots that couldn't conceal the curves of her legs. She looked absolutely smashing... he told her so. She adjusted his tie and, after pressing a finger gently to his lips, suggested they depart.

When they had lunch at the Beverly Hills Derby, she seemed pleased to have this man beside her. This place was a significant repository of auras...but except for their own, neither of them noticed any.

6

"Art...check that vent valve?" Paul turned from his control panel toward his technician.

"I think it'll hold this time...got to give it a working over after this test." Art wiped a hand across his face, picking up some sweat.

"Oxidizer up." Paul glanced at the pressure gage registering 550 pounds per square inch, and made adjustments to the regulator that fed helium pressurizer to the 98% hydrogen peroxide, H_2O_2.

"Fuel's up," he said a minute later, looking at the gage showing a comparable pressure over the anhydrous hydrazine, N_2H_4.

"Instrumentation okay, Luke?" he asked his crew chief and compatriot in pyrotechnics.

"Chamber pressure doing okay; thrust sensor steady...flow sensors zero on the button. Your thermocouple array looks like it might make it this time, too." Luke also wiped some sweat away.

"Cooling water?" Paul persisted.

"Like the Colorado river," Luke answered.

"Christ...I hope not." Paul concentrated on the display of gages in front of him, looked down at the switch console that would bring fire to the mouth of the little beast a few feet away. He glanced at a mirror set to reflect the motor to his position, and then activated the firing circuit with a key. "I'll fire on three...one and two and three," and he flipped the switch that started the peroxide and hydrazine to their wedding. There was a second's delay, a cough, a burst of random flame and smoke from the nozzle...and then the combustion approached the equilibrium that the nozzle design, the feed pressure, and the kinetics and thermodynamics of the propellants would allow. The exhaust built into a steady roar and the brilliant, translucent pattern of shockwaves represented an orange and yellow flag of success for test 13: N_2H_4-H_2O_2.

"Lovely...lovely," was all Paul could say, skimming over his recorders and looking at the mirror. He'd seen his first rocket exhaust in another pit a long time ago. His own technical adventures had matured to the point where he now furnished most of his own excitement. And if he saw a hundred—a thousand—such displays of the conversion of chemical potential into thermal and kinetic energy, he could never deny the thrill of it. The progeny of each propellant system left their own signature as they entered the world in a usually controlled explosion.

Russ Kinzer had started his experimental indoctrination with tests of liquid oxygen stability against various lubricants and valve packing materials. Paul had rigged up a simple drop-weight tester that managed to impart enough activation energy to a few cubic centimeters of the pale blue stuff to blow hell out of damn near anything he put in the test cavity. Almost anything bearing carbon would blow...the materials recommendations of the Air Force and Ordnance departments notwithstanding. On more occasions than the occupants of Chemistry cared to remember, Paul's rig would produce a low order detonation that reflected off the walls of the small revetment where he did this work and transferred some of its momentum to the walls and windows of the chemistry building. Just for kicks one day, he tried Ivory Soap chips. He got one of his best bangs.

Hydrogen peroxide is a very convenient gas generator, converting itself to steam and oxygen with just the slightest inspiration from a catalyst. He'd spent many fifty gallon drums of the high test stuff in an analysis of gas generation parameters, and an attempt to optimize the flow capacity/bed volume ratio. These were not particularly exciting tests unless the flow meter, or the feed lines, or the main tank, or the valve system happened to be less than virginal with respect to contaminants that aggravated peroxide. Then, a number of fascinating manifestations of the energy of decomposition could be realized. One flowmeter had exploded seconds after it had received a full peroxide presence at 700psi. The armored glass front of the meter, and the metal casing, were distributed in random array afterwards. Eddy, whose head had been the last to clear the pit before the test, had an extra cup of coffee that morning.

With the somewhat more spectacular peroxide-hydrazine system, they were accumulating a fairly satisfactory array of data points in their analysis of the effect of mixture ratio(fuel flow/oxidizer flow) on the characteristic velocity(c^*) and specific impulse(Isp). The former parameter reflects the ability of the propellants to develop chamber pressure for a given nozzle throat diameter, per unit of total propellant flow rate. The latter parameter, the ability to develop thrust for given nozzle characteristics, also with respect to unit propellant flow rate. Paul's partial delineation of the characteristic curves on the c^*-ratio and Isp-ratio grids was pleasing Harry and George, and Russ. Some time before, they'd included this propellant system in their endless calculations, and Paul was supporting their professional integrity in part...and it didn't take much of a part to keep smiles persistent thereabouts.

During the time that combustion products are making their energy exchanges within the converging and diverging portions of the nozzle, did the elements, compounds, radicals, ions, respond to the temperature and pressure changes and array themselves into species typical of these state conditions? Or, were they better mannered, and refused to depart from the identity they had *just* before they left the warm hospitality of the combustion chamber for their ride through the nozzle? *Equilibrium*, or *frozen* flow they called this business. Some of Paul's data were illuminating a tiny corner of this problem of chemical kinetics.

In the course of his travels through the confusion of empirical and theoretical devotion that was Chemistry at PAG, Paul had heard the word, *fluorine*, mentioned with increasing frequency. He knew that this was one of the breed called halogens by the chemists. He knew that of these halogens, fluorine was unique in its ability to grab electrons from weaker neighbors. *Oxidation* they called it. And that was about all Paul knew about fluorine. Harry and Russ and George and Myron knew a lot more about it. They knew, or anticipated on good bases, that a wedding of fluorine with a bride—such as gentle hydrogen—would be productive of a very precocious progeny of energy, and probably with a minimum of parental substance. To the knowledge of these men, and a few of the visionaries on the upper slopes of PAG, even the Liverwurst Ones hadn't enforced *this* marriage in reality...probably more a result of the exigencies of war, than ignorance. This was a pure system. It combined pure elements and produced pure hell—anhydrous hydrofluoric acid. Many at PAG were quite anxious to open this particular box of Pandora.

This Friday evening, the smog had teared Paul's eyes as he drove along the rim of the Arroyo and attempted to find the course to Arden Road. There'd been some of this stuff in the early days of the war, but it had now built in substance until there were few days—in *any* season—whose atmosphere resembled the Southern California of the padres. *Valley of the Smokes*, the Indians had called the land between the Sierra Madres and the coastal hills, proving a natural inclination of this land to cooperate with people given to atmospheric clutter. Smoke, hell! This was dilute *acid*...with the extra stimulation of a few oxides and peroxides. Many thousands cursed it—and endured it. He looked like he'd lost a good friend when he finally pulled into the Drake grounds and found his sanctuary. The shower helped, but his eyes were still puffed and red when he poured himself a good slug of Scotch and collapsed on his bed. *Earthbound* problems, old man? We got 'em—in spades.

He hadn't seen John, except briefly, for a few days. Martha had interrupted their art instruction for a trip to Palo Alto to console Carla over something, or other. Their instruction had been platonic, virtually so, at her insistence. She'd allowed him the liberty of a few kisses when the situation was propitious...and on her ground, her criteria applied. Paul was well into his drink, when the phone interrupted this surcease from the smog. John invited him over, with the advice to save his Scotch for emergencies that would surely come.

How's about a little golf action tomorrow?" John asked, over the pools of bourbon and Scotch.

"Sounds great! Annandale?" Paul had driven past this club many times and had noted what appeared to be an interesting layout. "Jeese...I don't have any tools."

"That's the least of your worries. Shoes?"

"Ditto."

"I'll get you a pair at the pro shop. Let's call it a small token of appreciation for helping to keep Martha's smile a little more persistent, lately." John had said this with a true grin. Paul's smile was less than truth, and he felt a sharp twinge of guilt added to a reservoir that had been filling for some time.

Paul had a date with Tom for dinner that night. When Tom gunned the Porsche into the driveway near the carriage house, Paul and John hailed him from the veranda.

"Good to see you, Major Tom," John said. And he quickly overcame Tom's disadvantage in bourbon, over Tom's vigorous protests, of course.

"Unless you guys have something more exhilarating cooked up for tonight, I could suggest a good steakhouse up on Lake that just might let us in." They had nothing in conflict with that plan.

The steak *was* good, and before, and after it, the talk had bounced around. Some of it about John's business, a lot about hunting and fishing, sports they all shared. From prior conversation, Paul knew that John had a foursome set up for their game, or John would've asked Tom to join them. When Tom left Paul's apartment after a long session of reminiscence, about the last thing he said was that John certainly was a good Joe—old Tom really had a talent for leaving raw nerves ascending.

"Come on you bastard...you trying to make me look bad?" John called to Paul, who was on the practice range, limbering up. The clubs he'd borrowed from the pro shop were good, if not quite tailored to his address, About every other shot with the woods was fair. His remembrance of the long irons was better. And when he worked his way up the iron ladder, damn that little old number five felt good!

They joined their companions of the links on the first tee. One of these gentlemen was an insurance broker; the other was a pillar in the Technicolor Corporation. John and Paul were teamed and there was an arrangement for a fiscal accounting after the match that wouldn't embarrass a young engineer who was an infinity away from a golden parachute. They questioned Paul briefly about his game. After the opposition had assigned him a handicap, and made some cutting remarks about his poor showing on the practice tee, they took to the arena. Paul knew that his handicap would give his team trouble.

On the ninth, which greened out back of the clubhouse, John made a good explosion shot from the sand that landed about four feet from the cup. Paul had hit his approach shot well, and it had preceded John's to that place of smoothness, if not flatness. The opposition hadn't done so well on that hole. But, some time before, they knew that their problems that day were small ones. Paul holed his long one, and John his shorter one. Following some grumbling from the other side, the four of them crossed the parking lot and prepared for battle on the back nine, after a shot of Coke. Later, in the nineteenth hole of the men's lounge, they shook those damnable cubes under the partial inspiration of the second round of drinks. John introduced Paul to several members who happened by and all in all it was a typical, very pleasant, very relaxing afternoon in the land of Annandale...where there was sufferance for neither snow, nor boastful winds of care.

"Really enjoyed that one, John," Paul said to the driver of the Continental.

"They took us...but not by much, by God." John laughed, and slapped the wheel.

"Considering you had a stupid and damn inept partner."

"Not a bit of it, lad. For your first game in four years, you held your share of the honors." Paul didn't argue with that. It *had* been a fine—and needed— outing for him.

John had enticed him into his den with the promise of showing Paul a new salt water reel.

"Big...beautiful," Paul said, as he handled the Fin-Nor 12/0. "This is definitely *not* for brook trout."

"I've a hankering to improve that broadbill trophy one of these years." John glanced at the bill display Paul had seen before.

"My head is still bowed." Paul's voice, demeanor, and usual vivacity around fishing matters, were not coming together at this time.

After some talk about the golf game, broadbills, both men settled in John's big leather chairs and gave a good imitation of relaxation. John's part of this was better, truer, than Paul's, including the assault on his reservoir, the one that had the bourbon.

Paul's maturing guilt feeling, suddenly augmented the previous night, hadn't dissipated from the golf exercise and he wasn't an expert at dissembling...he could protect himself under some circumstances, but they weren't here. His love, infatuation...obsession for the lady of this house...the flow of this man's friendship and hospitality...were two forces on him, and they were rapidly coming to his point of critical compression.

John and Paul had been together under enough complexions of sobriety for them to spot persistent upsets to perceived norms. Paul had gotten no upset signals from John, and this was an element of the compression. John was a better actor. But he was, in fact, now tending to a compression situation tailored for him and it was on the verge of tipping a wake-up call to Paul.

"John...I...I." Paul tried to take the first step toward some kind of declaration that could start to move the mask off his face—but he couldn't, and he looked away from John.

John Drake wasn't a stupid man. He had his transcripts from Princeton and Harvard in support of this. He'd achieved a spectacular success as an entrepreneur in a very tough racket, and this tended to lesson his burden of proof. Also, he hadn't been as drunk on the night of Jake's party as Martha and Paul had thought. By the barest chance, during a late night passage to his bathroom, he happened to glance out of a window and he saw two figures walking toward the carriage house from the direction of the pool...two who showed absolutely no discord. He'd seen enough to know that a casual teacher-pupil compact had been passed sometime before.

And John Drake had given good lip service to a flexible tolerance for both the shared, and the private, adventures that are indispensables for a solid married relationship...under *his* definition. At the time of their marriage, Martha had recognized this attitude as one aspect of an *avant-garde* nature she admired in John and she accepted the general structure of it without much consideration of troublesome corollaries. On several occasions during their marriage, John had given this structure severe endurance tests. After her time of introspection, Martha hadn't worn the cap of hypocrisy in the continuation of the marriage. She had never, to John's knowledge, exercised her maximum prerogative under this, his, tolerance, had never—until now—given him a crucible to test the quality of *his* belief.

Under the constraints of a regimen that had finally shown its teeth to him, John had few options of response. He could continue to ignore the relationship, hoping that graceless parts of it would have minimal exposure. He could make some display of that knowledge of his—but this resort could cost him virtual destruction of a philosophy that had already served him...and it had lots of potential rubbing spots, promising damn little ease to anybody. And he operated under another constraint—he liked Paul, another aberration that wouldn't overcrowd the philosophy he'd paraded in front of Martha. Whatever the precedence, the situation hadn't developed any strong counter-vectors to an admiration that had been building since they'd opened the carriage house to him. A single word—a glance of appropriate construction from Martha—would've made a quick end to the business...but these hadn't come and Martha's considerate ordering of the affair now challenged him. He preferred his first option. And under the grace of the last few minutes of two actors' performances he'd decided to take that path.

But Paul was making a complication. He obviously wasn't enjoying any of the equanimity John could summon. He had few of the defenses of maturity. He was damn near ready to explode with contrition.

John pushed himself away from the soft leather throne and started a slow walk around the den, his drink a passenger. A large pheasant tail feather, a vestige of a fly tying exercise, lay on a cabinet and eventually he picked it up as a walking crutch, a surrogate for words that wouldn't come. He finally stopped in front of a large oil of Joseph of the Nez Percé. The eyes of this man who'd fought at the interface of two worlds had drawn John many times before, and he sought some communion now. After gross silence had permeated the room, he spoke directly to the painting, almost in a private voice. "A great people... we saw only an edge of them...a complicated society with ten thousand years precedence." Then, after he'd put more silence into that room, John slipped off his reasonable path into a thicket of thorns. "Some of the compliments of friendship among some of these people must've taken a good man to handle them...God damn it!—it *still* takes a good man!" He'd destroyed the almost private voice, and he compounded his inadvertent new strategy by turning toward a sector that happened to include Paul, the pheasant feather almost an axis between them.

If some of this unilateral conversation hadn't penetrated Paul's own communion, the last of it had both the subject matter—and the props—to trigger his response. His knowledge of *compliments of friendship* was good enough for this occasion. He stood up, not taking his eyes off John, who now stood near his desk. Paul's expression gave no camouflage to the effect of the revelation that John had most certainly known about him and Martha.

"What *is* this" Paul took several steps toward John. "I...I...we have *compliments* here?" He came closer to John, stopping his progress with a hand on the edge of the desk, staring at John.

"Right now...I can't come up with any other words I can handle." John tried to use the kind of voice that wouldn't build an irreversible path between him and Paul, although he'd just taken a couple steps in that direction. Silence might have been a better response, but Paul had already taken this conversation outside reasonable strategy...and John had put down some map for him.

The contrition vise wouldn't relax on Paul. He moved closer to John, his face warped by a storm of emotion. "I...I think I'd seam a bastard like me up the belly with that Mannlicher." His hoarse voice made a diminuendo proceeding from bold challenge to almost a whispered groan. Wildness flooded his eyes... he didn't pull back from John.

He'd just thrown an ancient gauntlet and John picked it up. He flicked his eyes to a chair backing Paul and then he shot a straight left to Paul's chin. The blow had most of his objectives, but it drifted closer to Paul's mouth than he'd intended. Paul's head snapped back and the rest of his body followed. He slammed into the chair. With this generous gift of momentum, the chair took him over backwards with it.

Paul staggered to his feet, rubbing his chin, a small stream of blood coming from his mouth.

"Feel better?" John had carefully tailored his voice to address the present state of the balance scale they'd just been chatting about.

"I...I don't know," Paul mumbled, rubbing a hand across his mouth. He sat down, head in hands.

John kept himself busy for several minutes, puttering with his equipment. He fixed the new reel to a heavy rod, and then tested the whole in an action of imagination. Finally, Paul stood up and started to walk out of the room. When he reached the door, he half-turned to John, "I'll get t'hell out of here—soon as I can." John could barely hear him. In his travel to the door of the room, Paul had rubbed the bloody hand against a white table runner, a fact not imprinted on his consciousness.

"Wait a minute, Paul." John walked over to him and waited until their eyes had come together. "This one...we'll play it by ear...for a little while" The eye tension held for another second, then Paul turned and continued his walk. In trying to pull Paul away from an irreversible path, John had just handed him the pommel end of a double-edged sword that had the mark of his own forge.

The next morning, Paul was jarred awake by his phone. Martha had returned the previous evening and she asked Paul to join her and John on the veranda for breakfast. Her voice signaled no discontinuity. It was probably one of the few catalysts capable of defeating his inclination to return to the mood of his most recent visit to John's den. He accepted her invitation and then tried to build a more palatable form of himself. The last of this work consisted of fixing a small Band-Aid on his mouth. Eventually, he made his appearance in an open-throated shirt, wearing the same slacks he'd used for golf the previous day. As he walked toward the veranda, Martha waved to him, and John muttered something behind his newspaper.

"Good to see you, Paul," she said, and that damn cut started to hurt again. His powers of observation weren't up to his usual standards, but he couldn't fail to notice another cheongsam, this time of dark red silk. And his debilitation didn't prevent his absorption of some of its effect.

"Please sit down...have some coffee." Martha barely noticed the Band-Aid. "Mary will expand the provender shortly."

"Thank you." Paul accepted the coffee, grateful for the warm sustenance, and its instant sanctuary.

"John...please move that paper so I can insert some coffee under that concentration."

John finally moved his paper. In fact, he tossed it to the flagstone. Paul was looking into the depths of his coffee and then he tried a quick glance at John...and then he *really* looked at John. Around his left eye was the prettiest shiner Paul had seen for a long time. He tried not to stare, but not successfully.

"What'n hell happened?"

"Martha saw the damn runner," John mumbled.

Mary was pushing a server toward them and Martha ignored the small drama and turned to Mary. "Here will be fine, Mary. Thank you." And then Martha was busy, solicitous of the men, both of whom were trying to ignore her...one, under the drive of curiosity, the other, embarrassment.

"And you had to open your big mouth."

"My boy...there are women in this world to whom a *closed* mouth is the greatest challenge." John touched a finger gently to his sensitive eyebrow.

"Cream, Paul?" Martha asked.

"No thank you, Ma'am," he answered inadvertently, massively inadvertently. With that sweet little reply, Martha took a better look at Paul's Band-Aid, and then at John's shiner. The men looked at the wounds facing them, and then they both looked at Martha.

The trigger for the next part of this breakfast meeting is hard to ascribe.

It might have been Martha continuing to alternate her look at the men—her face, mostly the eyes, bringing no particular censure to that congregation. It could have been John, or Paul, both of whom stared at opposing wounds and at Martha, also with no baggage of particular censure. These passive postures made unconscionable opportunity for an outrageous summation. It came to Martha first, she got in a sound like the first pulse of soft laughter and this was the impetus for John and Paul's overtures to an avalanche of laughter that almost made a shambles of Mary's fine breakfast. Some solid Pasadenans would have been appalled. But neither in the actual moments, nor in the later memories, was Paul able to hold up his end of decent abatement of it.

In the middle of the following week, Martha told Paul that John was going to Washington for a few days and that she'd told John she would be spending some time at their Balboa place. John's eye was coming along well, and he was disposed to keep it that way. Martha suggested to Paul that they could review their art progress under the stimulating beneficence of sea exposure. Paul also had no argument with her.

They took Martha's Cadillac and Paul drove. She'd told him the seminar might last for several days and to equip himself accordingly. He had a fair feeling for the roads to the coast by now and he got them on the Coast highway without any problems, other than a vague apprehension about his capacity for absorbing the full scope of her seminar.

Somewhere near Huntington Beach, Martha broke the relaxed silence that had prevailed for some time.

"Please, darling...hold it down."

"Hold *what* down?" He wondered how she knew.

"Silly...the speed. A couple gendarmes along here seem to have a special affinity for this car."

"That's easy to believe...and I don't blame them." He reached for an accessible hand that was hers. "I would stop this car—if it had a certain woman in it...*any* time I saw it."

"For what purpose, sir?"

"Well, if the flora along here afforded more privacy...I'd show you. But it doesn't, so I'll only say that my planned invasion of your privacy wouldn't be practical."

"This would appear to be only an academic exercise—I won't hold you to practicalities." Blue eyes were laughing at him.

"Your persistence shall be rewarded m'lady. I'd explore a number of the exotic variations with you—after satisfying myself with the basic primitives."

"Mr. Sanger!—I'd *never* believed you capable of such excess." Those eyes still had him targeted and he nearly hit the road's shoulder during a simple turn.

"Try me."

"That *is* a challenge to my endurance—and your ingenuity...isn't it."

"It is—and it *will* be, my perceptive art teacher." There were no constraints between them now and she returned his hand squeeze in kind.

They reached the Newport-Balboa area and she showed him how to get to Lido Island. Finally, they stopped at a gate that was the only break in a high wall of ivy. He opened it with a key she'd given him and then he drove to a large carport, instead of approaching the other option of a triple garage set into her little cottage of four double bedrooms and five bathrooms, and such other amenities as one of the better, more precocious architects in Pasadena could provide. She handed him another key and he opened a large door that led from the carport into the lower level of the house.

"Woooo...it's cold in here."

"I can think of several ways to warm it up," he said.

Ignoring his suggestion, she walked to the main floor and adjusted a thermostat that cooperated with a heating and cooling system to keep the place in very good humor.

"That'll simplify your suggestions." She reached for him. Following a kiss that had several interesting tongue embellishments, she broke off the engagement and gave him a partial tour of the house.

There was a large living room, with a sunken fireplace surrounded by alpaca rugs laid on oak parquetry. This room had a waterside exposure over its entire length, with glass doors leading to a large sun deck. A drape system could give the room any degree of privacy. There was a large dining room, with similar lagoon exposure. Paul looked out of this glass wall and studied the opposite shore. He couldn't identify the restaurant of many weeks ago, but he knew it was there. Her image that night had been too strong to be less than truth.

"See someone you know?" She'd exercised her Indian talents again and come close enough to him to use her whisper.

"I *did* see someone I know...but my look was reversed at the time." He hadn't changed his stance, or his view, but suddenly her living image had come into the glass...an almost unsettling overlay of his images at that moment.

"That sounds dramatic. Tell me about it...if it's any of my business." Her whisper had come close enough to touch her lips to his closest ear.

"It *is* your business." He turned to her. "Tom and I were having dinner at some place across the bay." He described it briefly, she knew of it. "Afterwards, we looked across this lagoon—I saw you in every damn light dancing on the water...in the sounds, too." He had turned toward her before the last of that, and then both of them erased the space between them

"My darling...I didn't know I'd affected you that way." There was no shading of tease in her softest voice. His hands captured both of her hands.

"I think you knew from the day I stammered the purpose of my visit." He used his hands so that her arms ended up behind her. He kissed her, maneuvering her so that her breasts had to put impudent pressures against his chest.

"Paul...we must have something to eat."

"You *are* my sustenance." It was whispered, but she was close enough to use that service.

"You know about energy, and such things. You'll need *real* sustenance." They couldn't have made a better coupling of the eyes, and he had seen her like this, very prematurely, in real dreams.

"I don't want to go out tonight."

"Perhaps we won't have to. Let's canvass the refrigerator situation." She left him, with some lingering finger entanglement.

She led him into the kitchen on the lower level. The service umbilical to the dining room consisted of an electrically operated dumbwaiter. The kitchen, size and equipment, was appropriate to the servicing of a large party. There was a large wine closet; a large, upright freezer, with a matching refrigerator. She opened the latter and, after a short inspection, made the sad announcement that all she could furnish on such notice was steak.

She sat at a large central table and watched him barbecue the steaks over a built-in charcoal grill. He was unnecessarily flamboyant in his various ministrations and she laughingly cautioned him on several occasions. She prepared a simple salad, and with some wine Paul had selected from the closet, they were ready for one hunger. Paul placed the repast on the dumbwaiter, and pushed the button for it. Then he grabbed her and they raced upstairs to see if the thing really worked. She knew it would, so did he, but the finding out was all. It beat them to the dining room and its contents had to wait while Martha put minimal equipment on the table. She managed to do this despite serious interference.

After they'd killed the one bottle of wine she had insisted was their limit at that time, she admonished him that exercise too soon after eating wasn't considered wise.

But they weren't wise at that moment. She hadn't shown him the bedroom area and she was doing so now, her arms around his neck, under his power. Paul looked into the first bedroom. "Charming...but the bed is too *long*." He strode farther. "Charming...but the bed is too *wide*."

"Darling," she whispered, "there *are* just so many variations on the basic theme of beds."

The third bedroom they entered—it happened to be the smallest he'd seen—was where he stopped. "Remember what Brigham Young said at the Point of Darien?"

She'd taken her lips to the regions very near to both of his ears during this most recent trip in his arms...no nibbles now, a soft caress of lips against these places which she moved downward to the edges of his mouth...but not so close as to hamper his duties as pilot. "I think you're going to have to get *senhor* Balboa in there someplace—but I'm afraid I get your point." She'd said this with fairly good continuity, only a short sojourn to his left cheek...just before Balboa.

They had come to Lido Island dressed for a late fall day that had some blessed snap, and the surcease from smog had improved the closer they got to their target. She'd worn a dark brown vicuna car coat over a navy suit, shear black hose and maroon pumps. After removing her coat, he'd seen the white silk blouse layer of her. His soft navy blazer, gray slacks and white cotton turtleneck shirt held fewer surprises. Under the actions of preparing and eating their dinner, they were now down to the final bastions of *strict* modesty under their present circumstances...blouse-skirt-stockings-pumps and slacks-turtleneck-cordovan loafers. They were, therefore, at a more complicated junction of passion than they'd faced in the pavilion of her pool. Now there were two, possibly more, layers of them to frustrate his dictum of no unilateral nakedness...with a minimum of lag time.

Once again, he stood her on her feet alongside an action field of his choice. He kissed her, bringing himself close enough under his—their—impetus to cause a mutual revelation of a number of parts of them. Then, she stood away from him, one hand on a hip, almost a good neutral face studying him.

"Don't say it," he said.

"*What*, Paul?" Her lips and eyes and the unsettled regime of her hair seemed to call for more intimate address...but this was *his* play...let him find his own way out of it.

"'And *now* what?'" he said, reminding her of her past prelude in the pool pavilion, in the moonlight, at the doorway to another universe. He didn't dare touch her. He hadn't yet identified *his* prelude and the wrong kind of touch could limit his plans.

"You had me at some disadvantage...I didn't know my next...turn." She could hold a pose like some he'd seen in Athens, and down in the Peloponnesus, on marbled goddesses...she had collaborated with the moonlight at the edge of the pool to bring such a woman closer to him, to his satisfaction, and now she was doing it again against the handicap of full clothing. "I...I was *justified.*"

"I suggest some cooperation...to avoid a repetition of your...disadvantage."

"I've tried to be cooperative with you—*now* what do you have in mind?" She'd come very close to their other moment of the pavilion, his objection there, but she'd tailored it a little for this one.

"You...and then I..." he suggested.

"I've already subscribed to things that sound like that." She made a slight adjustment of her legs that almost pulled him off-sides.

"Our apparel...one for one, as much as possible...down to whatever complications we find."

"You mean...like this?" and she reached for his shirt. The turtleneck of it required some of his help, but she removed it, and scored first points.

"And this..." he said, unbuttoning her blouse and using very little of her help in removing it. She wore a revealing brassiere.

Then she did the unbuckling, unbuttoning, and unzipping which were prerequisite to an orderly removal of his slacks. They came away easily...with some more of his help. He did her skirt, and then her silky half-slip.

"You jumped me a step," she protested, standing before him in her panties companion to the brassiere...her garter belt, hose and pumps still intact and in her present pose she made the most of them.

He was down to his boxer shorts, shoes and socks. A major adjustment of her complaint would ruin his modesty. She made him sit on the bed while she removed his shoes and socks. He stood up, and then he made the good observation that she had too many parts left to restore any balance to their endeavor.

"That's your problem," she said. But any surcease she might have anticipated from this remark was short-lived. He removed her brassiere and then her panties. For the latter, he used a one-handed lift which caused her admiration, as it had that night by the moonlighted ladder of the pool.

"Trade you these...for those," she said, indicating first her residuals—garter belt, stockings and pumps, and then his—his shorts. He did his part. When she started to remove his shorts, some interior structure interfered with shocking persistence and presence. After she had exposed him, she hesitated a moment before proceeding with the complication of snaking of his shorts over his ankles. He swept her up and toward the bed, his lips locked on her mouth. After settling her, his hands started a more comprehensive caress...the breasts, then the outer thighs, and then the other opportunities of her for his hands, his mouth. But she refused a virtual passive captive role, and when his expedition looked to be gathering for a triumphant main gate entrance, she grabbed his principal expedition asset and adjusted her position for its close inspection. "This is remarkable," she remarked. "But I wonder if we're looking at *full* potential here." She started to use her hands to test this quality and this activity was soon supplemented by an action of her lips and mouth that definitely put the seniority here on her side. Her sudden Amazon put him on his back and made a shambles of his plans. Finally satisfied with the increments she'd put into him, she slid to where she could kiss him and then, reassuming her position that had been close to the just previous apex of his expedition, she silently invited him to do his best. At her pavilion, she'd found enough resources to make some token words when he entered her. But now, as they strove for their utmost union—under a cooperation that was, and had been, bolstered by their strongest mutuality—no speech was token.

Paul found the wood closet and built a fire in the fire pit. He opened the doors and drapes to the lagoon and the night breeze and they lay together on the rugs...words redundant. Finally, he asked her to tell him something about the parts of her that were still a mystery...her life in New York, her likes, dislikes. When he became burdensome, she found enough energy to silence him—each and every time—with a kiss, and usually the word *uncle* came from him.

That night, they slept on rugs moved to the sundeck, whose privacy had permitted Martha's approval of such audacity. Several times that night she called to him to warm her when the light covering she'd provided hadn't been enough. Several times that night her words...the ones that tumbled between speech and silence...also covered part of him. And once, when she had been a comprehensive aggressor, he'd had a short-breathed fusion of a real goddess with some of the Greek fantasies that coursed the black vault above them.

Paul lay on his back on the deck and hadn't dispelled the sleep that had finally come to him. His subconscious started to dream of oceans and rainbows...and then his conscious part ascended and he truly saw the sun and rainbows through a mist of water. He didn't move, and then he saw her in the colors and brightness. Before she could spill any more water on him, he grabbed her and pulled her down to his rugs, spilling her glass of torment. After a long kiss that lacked no imagination, she gasped, "Your breakfast, sire, such as it is, awaits you."

They didn't use a table, but spread her repast of oranges and crumpets and marmalade over the rugs and ate like Bedouins. After most of the oranges had fulfilled their destiny, they both lay back, absorbed in the light blue infinity that Paul knew very well. Finally she said, "Paul, darling...I'm not—as you *know*—insensitive to your awesome manhood...but I do think you'd be rather more comfortable with some apparel." He hadn't noticed this deficiency and, but for the limitations it might place on their less private agendas, he was content to persist in his original state. He conceded to her, however, and left to don slacks and a polo shirt. Shoes were superfluous and he refused them...as did she, who wore only a white cotton sheath and a band, like Saint Laurent's, in her hair.

They descended to the lower deck and then went toward the lagoon. Snugged against their dock was a cabin cruiser of some fifty-five feet in length, and about the best system that the Chris Craft people could put together at that time. It had the name We're Here II inscribed on her stern plate. Paul knew about the Bluenose schooner that had borne part of that name, and also about the man of this cruiser who would be quite comfortable on the Grand Banks.

"Beautiful," was all he could say, as they approached the gleaming white hull and the teakwood and glass and steel superstructure. Martha preceded him aboard and led him to the command cabin.

"I'm not qualified to captain this monster," she said, placing her hands on the wheel. Actually, she'd performed that office very well when John had succumbed to the sirens of sea, sea air, and a soft lounge chair.

Paul looked at the instruments and controls and played his hands over them in imagined action. "Beautiful," he persisted in saying. "When—God forbid—paint is scratched hereon, I want John to be in *full* command."

She showed him the saloon and galley and the state rooms which, though small, had every amenity for comfortable sea transit. They finally stood on the foredeck, scanning the miscellany of sails and powered hulls in the lagoon. Then they walked to the stern and there Paul noticed that, among other provisions of the deck, there were brackets for two fighting chairs. He leaned over and touched one of them.

"I see potential here for aching muscles," he said, looking up at her.

"Indeed, sir, indeed." She sat in a deck chair. "John has covered quite a lot of Southern California and Mexican water in quest of his foe...not too successfully I have to admit."

"And the object of this relentless search, I must presume, is the billed one with the eye of malevolence." Some of the grin that had showed during his first time in John's den was back again.

"Right again. The swordfish holding of these waters is not as spectacular as it used to be in Zane Grey's day, and the travel agenda of what's left hasn't meshed with ours very well." She'd just confessed being a collaborator.

Paul assumed a chair on the other side of the deck, facing her. They looked at each other for a long time, reliving some of the adventure they had shared. Finally, Paul said, "I'm jealous of your time with the swordfish...I'm jealous of your time with all the rest I've missed." The grin had gone, and his face was a good stage for his words.

After a time that was unnaturally long for him, she said, "My darling... don't look into *our* wine...too closely." Her smile was as gentle as she could make it. But Paul received a gut shot of maturity with it that gave him some of the pain he had felt in his second trip to John's den...but she'd also triggered an inane fusion of ancient worlds with opportunities lost that had dogged him before her. The pulse of sadness made him turn away from her. She sensed more of this than he could know. She came to him, and joined their hands. "Let's see what the beach at La Jolla is like about now." Then she kissed him and ran from the boat. Her words, her kiss, her run, were just what he needed.

One of Martha's friends had given them access to a private beach near La Jolla. They had tried the surf and then he chased her back to their nest of towels. It culminated in a wild wrestle that he stopped with a kiss.

"I love you." His eyes were so close to hers that he could see the pool of the pavilion.

"You're interested in me...*very actively* interested in me." She made no attempt to uncouple their eyes.

"I love you," he repeated, and then he rolled over on his back. The fair weather cumulous clouds were the principal parts of his scene, but he didn't really see them.

"Too much seriousness here. Let me divert this stream by asking you what you've learned in the Land of Wilshire."

When he came back to reality, he said, "I've seen much good, some bad...like someone I know said I would." He hadn't changed any part of his posture, or the direction of his eyes.

"Excellent...but please be more specific."

"Some of the abstract stuff I found extremely interesting...not the electronically inspired and mathematically precise work...but the free images of form and color that conjure partial worlds for you."

"I must congratulate myself." She gave him a soft laugh. Her head was now elevated above his by the device she'd used at the pool...the day of her first assault on this helpless heap of man. "And?" she prompted.

"And I took a long look at some of the Dutchmen's...that small one by Rembrandt, particularly."

"You feel that Mr. Rembrandt may have possibilities...do you?"

"One of the glories of man's span on this mess of matter that the sun tolerates."

"Would you say the supreme glory...artistically speaking, of course."

"I would say that if Rembrandt sits in that chair, there should be room for at least one more—if we're just staying with painters here."

"Some of the others?" She had to wait a while because he had to attend to pushing her presence away long enough to track some ancient memory.

"A few years ago, Mary and I talked our parents into letting us go to Europe for the summer. In the land of the Dutchmen...the Haarlem revelation came to me."

"That sounds like something out of Conan Doyle." Her blue eyes probed his face at very close range.

"We entered a drab brownstone in the village of Haarlem and found ourselves in a house of the seventeenth century. In that place...I saw figures of men...women...single and whole *rooms* full, that were—to me—an epiphany in trapping the human soul with paint and canvas...and I haven't had much chance to use that 'e' word—on anything."

"And the doer of these deeds?" *His* answer was what she was after.

"Franz Hals."

After a few seconds, he continued his answer. "I think we put too much into splashing around the dark in portraiture. Mere darkness doesn't open up the soul any more than a kid waving a flashlight. The *total* rendition is all." He turned and assumed a position similar to hers that brought their faces close together, but his look was out to sea. "Hals could do this with light...with dark too, if he wanted. But, mostly, he did it with light...and he's made the hackles on my neck tingle more than any artist I've seen—and I've seen a few." They worked silently on the same panorama for a little while. Then he finished his answer for her. "If I had to decide on a single sight of art that would be the last I would ever see...I'd have a hell of a contention between Michelangelo's real *David* in Florence's Academia and some of Hals' flat glimpses of his world."

"My darling...you've surpassed the teacher...our instruction may be coming to an end." She forced his face to confront her, then she kissed him.

This casual remark about the scope of his artistic appreciation brought him back to the stream of depression she'd almost diverted. He stood up, took her hand and pulled her to him.

"On the boat...you mentioned a...a wine. How many bottles have we got left?" She tried to turn her head away, but he enforced her steadiness with a gentle pressure of his hand.

"I...I haven't looked into the closet lately," she lied.

"I think you took a peek when we were on the boat."

"I think we may both be surfacing to a little of the real world." She'd said this with a little smile that cut him like a knife at that instant. Then she turned away from him.

"I haven't had both of my feet in the *real* world—as you call it—since I stared at those damn gargoyles on your gate." Finally he released her, and reached for their towels.

"Did you say that Mary is coming out for Christmas?" They were climbing the stairs to the level of her car, and her question had broken a long silence.

When they reached the car, he said, "I talked the little rascal into coming out a few days before Christmas...and she'll stay the following week." He assisted her entrance to the car, stowed the towels in the trunk, assumed technical command, and then pointed them in the direction of the Coast Highway.

That night, they found a place near Laguna Beach that afforded some food and some soft music with provision for active enjoyment thereof. On the small dance floor, he held her close to him as they responded to the slow foxtrot. Occasionally, she looked up at him, and the music would fade for him then. Mostly, she would rest her head on his shoulder. Once, she murmured that he was holding her too tightly.

They chose another bedroom that night and they didn't leave it...except once to take a big drink of the night. Before sleep finally claimed them, they'd made another inroad on a store of wine of very elusive capacity.

The several weeks before Christmas was the time of the report for Paul. He had yet to submit a formal treatise on his adventures in the test pits and the revetments and now he had sufficient excuse for it. Russ had mentioned that Management had been complaining about the lack of in-house reports. Graphs, and most of the words, come easily with good data. It'd been Paul's fortune to have a crew, some subjects, and some luck, that could all crowd under that *good* word. He was beginning to understand that this combination was the sesame for success in the technical world—or *any* world, for that matter.

When he left PAG the night he was to meet Mary at the airport, he dropped two tomes on Russ' desk, with the announcement that one of them—not the smaller one—should qualify him for a gooblah.

"You damn young whippersnapper!—what makes you think *you* can aspire to our mysteries?"

"You did."

"Oh...I must've slipped up there...a little." Returning Paul's wicked grin, Russ wished Paul a safe, sane and sober Yuletide—and told him to have a couple for him.

7

He saw her through the crowd of passengers looking for their luggage on the merry-go round. He ran to her and their clinch, and the kiss, didn't seem to be handicapped by their relationship. Mary wore a dark blue plaid suit. With a matching tam that barely constrained lustrous dark brown hair, eyes and lips in perfect consonance with the Celtic challenge she chose to make this day, she was an export of Iowa's best bounty.

"You look *terrific*, Tiger." His eyes devoured her.

"You look like you've been dissipating your modest substance on the beach...probably with wine and women." Her eyes did a good job on him, too.

"Oh, occasionally I hit the beach when the pressure of work gets to me." He guided her to the labyrinth that eventually led to the parking lot if you took all the right turns. By the time they reached their part of the lot, Mary had gotten her first good shot of the invigoration that poured from a few hundred thousand tailpipes and a few thousand stacks.

"God!" was all she could say.

"God damn is permissible here. Also, there are such pleasantries as, 'It's not as bad as yesterday...I can see my feet,' or 'Dad, can I use the gas mask tonight?'Or..."

"Stop it!" Her eyes were already making their salute to Southern California. Paul's had preceded hers by at least an hour.

"My...aren't we the young aristocrat," she said, when they reached his car.

"It's nothing. Just seventy-two dollars and nineteen cents a month for eighty years...and it's all mine."

He activated the mechanical object of his affection and pulled them into the traffic jam.

"Where, sir, are you taking me?" she asked, after they'd cleared the night-mare around the airport and were headed toward the Sierra Madres.

"To a den we call The Huntington."

"Is it a good place for young, inexperienced, Mid-Western girls?"

"It's a good place for you, my darling," he said, leaving it on an insulting edge, and she told him so.

She registered and then they went up to her room. Paul had asked for a court room for her because of outside botanical embellishments, and they had obliged.

After Mary had settled down a little, they talked about the family, about the crops, about Mary's love life.

"You're too damn impertinent—I don't pry into *your* affairs." This had given Irish eyes plenty of action scope.

"Like hell you don't." He walked closer to her and captured one of her hands. "Mary, me darlin', I have friends who have to meet you. They wanted you for dinner tonight...but I told them it would take you too long to fix your face... what with the tight arrival time, and a' that." He barely ducked a left hook that belied the face and figure of its perpetrator.

After he'd exposed her to his Ship Room, and enforced a regimen of only one glass of wine during their meal, with the information that he wanted her in presentable shape, they took the course to Arden road.

The griffin head was easy now, and the maid said, "Good evening, Mr. Sanger," and they entered the place of the Drakes.

Martha had more than enough poinsettias and mistletoe, plus subtler accessories, to convey the general idea of the season. The maid conducted them to the room of the big fireplace. It was doing its job beautifully. John was seated on a couch, reading a magazine, when they entered. He rose quickly when he saw his guests and walked toward them, spending most of his look on Mary.

"John, may I present my sister, Mary...called the Irish one by those who can duck fast enough. Mary...this is my friend, John Drake."

"I'm pleased to meet you, Mary. Your brother has mentioned you...briefly." John's grin and his eyes gathered in the smiling beauty in front of him.

"My brother has the sin of gross exaggeration...among *many* others," she replied, ignoring Paul. Her hand was received by John with an almost too firm clasp.

John escorted them to the couches facing the fireplace and guided Mary to her seat. Mary was bracketed by the men and, between John's questions about her trip, she tried to see some of the room. The Lady of the Hunt arrested her glance as it had her brother's. Then she had to respond to more of John's questions.

Several minutes later, Martha entered from the direction of the dining room. She wore a yellow dress of as much simplicity as that Frenchman would permit. A necklace of pearls and small pendant gold earrings did what they could to compete with the rest of her...an ensemble that brought an immediate signal of significance to Mary and a much stronger one to her brother. The three conversationalists rose to the occasion.

"Martha...may I present my sister, Mary."

"Mary, dear, I've so wanted to meet you." Martha's smile was one of her best. Mary tried to reciprocate the greeting.

"That painting," Mary said, turning to *the* painting, "it *is* of you, isn't it?" She looked at Martha, and glanced quickly at her brother, who was starting to worry about his dissembling.

"I'm afraid so." Martha took a seat near the fireplace and motioned for the others to follow suit. "This brother of yours will make art experts of us mortals yet. He's attributed a certain Reynoldsian slant to it—I can't refuse that." She continued her smile, and had opened the first page of a book where distortion of certain facts was unconstrained.

"He's told me of your expertise in that area, Mrs. Drake," Mary's intuition of a more than simple involvement here rising with every second in this house.

"Perhaps he's also told you that my area of expertise lies mostly in appreciation—not execution." This statement continued the principal prerogative of that book, a part both men present could support, strongly.

"May I refresh your glasses?" John asked.

"We haven't any glasses, you brute," Martha declared.

"Did ever a man hear a better invitation for excusing himself?" John looked at the two beauties...the younger, the longer. "Mary, what's your pleasure? The habits of your companions are, alas, only too well known to me." John meant that entirely with respect to the present moment. Paul took it that way. Martha almost that way. And Mary had less than a full acceptance of its specificity.

She leveled her own smile at John, nevertheless. "My brother has been stuck in a Scottish bog for ever so long...I prefer the humble richness of our native bourbon."

"My dear, you do know how to dazzle a man, don't you." John's remark was consistent with most of the conversation so far in that he'd shown only the tip of a berg, too...in this instance his appraisal of Mary Sanger.

"John, please...none of your reservoirs," Martha cautioned.

"Let my lady speak her own mind on this." John turned from one of the decanter sets that seemed to enjoy ubiquity in this house. "Mary...would you prefer a tiny portion of the brew of the elves—of a size for elves—or would you like to pleasure yourself as befits a queen of the forest?"

"That's a trap if I ever heard one." Mary's laughter was like a forest queen's, and John got the message.

Martha was trying to show Paul some of the basics of the game of kings. It was a drama being played on a large board, over which a Florentine craftsman had labored for many days. Knights, bishops, kings, queens, and men...four to six inches high, were now fighting a one-sided battle.

"Paul...you *must* try to visualize the scope of action of certain pieces," she admonished softly.

"I have an excellent appreciation for the scope of action of certain pieces." He looked up from the field and into her eyes with an impertinent smile coming along. This play was permitted by the fact of John and Mary's presence in John's den, which the chess players could see from their vantage. The former two were sitting on a couch in that room and were obviously engaged in an equally one-sided story that required the frequent use of John's hands, and sometimes his legs. Mary's delighted laughter didn't discourage him.

"John's found another victim for his Munchausen." Martha glanced toward the den. "She's absolutely delightful, Paul. We must make some plans for her while she's here."

"If you mean that, I'll make a forward, and specific, suggestion." He gave up the frustrating battlefield in front of him.

"I've found some of your suggestions to be...not unrewarding." Her smile of Leonardo again, and she also rattled bottles in that ambiguous closet of theirs.

"Mary would be thrilled with your boat. Would it be possible..."

"Of course! After Christmas, perhaps, would be better...but we'll do it! I'll ask John—and he'll do it!"

"May I assign a general kind of nautical adventure to your *it*?" He'd used his own version of Leonardo here.

"Tu es très impertinent ce soir, ma chéri."

"Je vous demande pardon...mais..ce soir...la lumière...mes yieux. Je ne peux pas trouver ma politesse." It was poor, but it tumbled out.

"La lumière?"

"Oui...tu es ma lumière, mon amour." With that fervent declaration, he tried to get more playful and reached for her hand. She avoided his grasp and gave him a small slap on that hand for his pains. Martha turned toward the story in the den again. It was now reaching them with increasing frequency and volume.

After Martha had served a late supper and shown Mary more of the paintings of the house, they all strolled to the veranda. There was enough skylight and garden lighting to show some of the beauty of the grounds. Mary begged for a short tour. She was obviously exhilarated...slightly by the stuff of the elves, more by the company, and one could possibly be more specific than that.

Paul called for Mary at a respectable hour the next day and took her to Mount Wilson. The smog had relented enough to reveal much of the valley to them. But Catalina was not allowed one of her very infrequent appearances. They hiked around the observatory grounds, saw the publicly accessible equipment, and had a snack on the mountain.

"They're getting ready for the big one, down at Palomar." He described what little he knew about the great eye that was under final polishing at Caltech. He told her that the smog was now choking some of Mount Wilson's power, and might even threaten the unborn wonder some day.

Coming down the mountain, they were very quiet. In fact, they'd been very quiet with each other since Paul had scooped her up at The Huntington that morning. When they were almost down to La Canada, Paul, with careful casualness, asked her how she liked the Drakes.

"She's the most beautiful landlady I've ever seen...possibly the most beautiful woman." Mary's head was resting against the seat, her eyes scanning nothing in particular outside. Paul said nothing for several minutes, but he thought about her and Martha. Perhaps Reynolds would have disdained her for more haughty beauty...but Lawrence had some of her in his *Pinky*, and he'd seen more of her in Leonardo's Mary at the Louvre, and some of the faces at the Uffizi in Florence which fused various beauty with various strengths.

"John's quite a guy, too," he said.

Feeling he needed some answer, Mary said, "Yes...he's quite a guy." She didn't change her position, or the direction of her eyes. Paul took some of the gold that is silence.

That night, he took her to the Beverly Hills Hotel for dinner, using the Wilshire track as far as he could go. She enjoyed the dinner she let Paul orchestrate, and later they danced, but she was still very quiet with him. He played finger wrestle with her on the way home, but her usual viciousness wasn't in her. He left her at her door after kissing her goodnight. She'd told him that two days of hospitality had left her a little tired, and part of her smile for him confirmed this. Just before sleep got him that night, a woman other than Martha dominated his thoughts...he was concerned about her...but he couldn't give this much definition.

Two days before Christmas, Mary made Paul take her back to Wilshire and, specifically, Bullock's Wilshire. He'd made the mistake, while passing that emporium earlier, of noting that it was one of the better joints for quick exchange of monetary and material resources.

Their parents had given them both their presents in the nicely compact form of checks. Mary was now threatening a wanton exercise of her gift-giving prerogatives as she dragged Paul along the section of Wilshire that included Bullock's and a dozen other shops of particular intrigue. In a small bookstore, she found beautifully bound and printed copies of Zane Grey's *Tales of the Angler's Eldorado—New Zealand*, and its freshwater counterpart, not restricted to New Zealand. She bought them, while Paul was contemplating a Melville. In Bullock's, she battled the problem of what to give a woman such as Martha Drake. She finally found a cluster of bluebirds, wrought by Royal Copenhagen, for her. To round out her gift of the book for Paul, she chose a set of gold cufflinks, bearing a suspicious resemblance to ones that John had worn on the night of her introduction.

On their way back to Pasadena, she showed some of the real Mary. "You're not going to make me wait until Christmas...are you?"

"Damned right—maybe Christmas day, if you don't behave yourself." She got one of his fingers he'd carelessly left by her side, minding its own business, and she applied pressure to it that argued its construction.

"Ouch—you devil!—wait 'til I get you home."

"You're not taking me to see your etchings—*are* you?"

"Indeed. It's high time you saw where your brother serves God...but no Mammon." He lied like a...well, he lied.

"Is it *really* a carriage house?"

"As much as any we saw in Merry Olde."

"They don't have such things over here...certainly not *Pasadena*."

"That's what you think, my little Irish Einstein." He swung up the Orange Grove off ramp and started one of his many variations of the road to Arden.

He went past the gargoyles and pulled up outside the carriage house, which had not been on Mary's agenda the previous visit. He opened his door, rushed around to her side, flung open her door, scooped her up in his arms with her screams and laughter, and ran with her up to the place of horses and sanctuary. He hadn't seen John and Martha, nor another one, who were on the veranda, but they had all seen this little play of nonsense.

"Why...this is charming," she exclaimed, as she ran through his rooms. "And a fireplace, yet...and this wood!" Mary caressed the paneling and looked at the random oak flooring.

"It's nothing," he said, giving that line a second outing. "Just what any conscientiously applied, red-blooded, Pasadena boy would have."

She sat in one of his very modest chairs, while he looked at her from a position of utter indolence on his bed. He'd protested—without effect—this invasion of his privacy while changing to sportier attire.

"You've recovered from your slight indisposition, madam." He could taste the recovered exhilaration of her, but he tried not to be too obvious.

"This is all so wonderful...you don't deserve it, you know." Her smile and her rebuke went right to the target of him.

He looked at her for several seconds, through fingers displayed in a crazy pattern across his face. He removed the fingers and assumed a more seemly position on the bed. In fact, he swung his feet over the side and sat on the edge, his head turned enough to give their eyes a collision course.

"What'n hell is *that* supposed to mean?" But he hadn't forgotten the telepathy that had also been one of the special bonds between them and she was about to nail him...again.

"You know very well what I *mean*."

"If you persist in this game of abuse and evasion, I'll take you hence and ply you with various coercions...that your tongue may pick up more respect for your own blood." He stood up and walked toward her, hands extended. She accepted them and let him pull her into a close clinch, and the kiss she also permitted was a stronger example of the one at the airport.

"I do need some fresh air...your pipe has left this place with less than its original aroma." She maneuvered him toward the door. "Do you think the Drakes would shoot us if you showed me more of their grounds?"

"Not a bit of it. John hasn't plinked a poacher in over a fortnight...and the yuletide season should add some compassion to him." They descended to the place of her desire.

As they came forth into the sunlight and Paul pulled her toward a rose garden, they were stopped by a challenge from the veranda.

"Unhand that maiden—or hear the sounds of combat!" said a voice like John Drake's. That he'd promoted the semi-Elizabethan flavor Paul had already started was also a noteworthy flavor of that moment.

Paul and Mary stopped and turned toward the sound of the voice. They saw its source...and also the two ladies who were attending it. One of them, Paul would know from a distance like the breadth of the lagoon at Balboa, the other, he didn't know. As they approached the veranda, one of the ladies spoke to them.

"Paul...from our vantage...it *did* appear as if your companion was in some jeopardy of honor—particularly in the manner of your entrance to your cave."

"If that were truly the case, Martha, I assure you that John's black eye would have to take a minor place among the history of the local wounds." As soon as he said that, Paul wished that a torn tongue could have been added to that list.

"What black eye, Daddy?" the other lady asked her daddy, and then, tacitly, her mother.

"Paul was showing your father some tricks he learned in jungle training and one—or both—slipped a bit." Martha's explanation to the young lady beside her caused two people, both males, to let out some breath.

"Paul, Mary, may I present our daughter, Carla. Carla, this is Mary and Paul Sanger."

Paul had glanced at a photograph of Carla in John's den, but his remembrance of it did no justice to her now. She was a little taller than her mother, on equal heels. Her hair was about shoulder length...of a blackness that pulled in some of the peripheral light and emboldened it with slight movements of her head. The composite of facial features might have been closer to John. But any such assignment would deny some of the uniqueness that she *was*. She obviously could accommodate the subtle facial placements into pleasure... and heavy laughter, too, he suspected. But, as an introspective man himself, it was her equipment for the nuances of somberness, thoughtfulness, that also registered on him. She was beautiful. She lacked some of her mother's voluptuousness, but from what he could see of her, time would adjust that grace very well for her. Her eyes, like another's of this family, were blue, and they gave a splendid residence to the soft flux of veranda light. He also noticed that these eyes could differentiate that light, making scintillations from it that suggested a man would have to careful with his foibles around her...also his declarations. She wore a tan, silk, suit that signaled a perfect stage for inherited touches.

"Carla...I'm very glad to meet you." Paul bowed slightly to her, and then he stepped forward to accept the hand she'd offered him.

"I'm pleased to meet you both." Carla's smile had elements that Paul already knew very well.

Paul turned slightly for a bigger audience. "Ignoring your insults, I'll say that I was about to show Mary some more of your grounds. Before accepting my offices, she wondered if you shoot interlopers on such a day." Near the last, Paul had finally physically acknowledged John.

"Only if they don't let the master of the house perform his own offices—damn you." With that, John took Mary's hand and led her to such splendors as he could show her at that time.

"It's difficult to argue with that...I must relinquish my sister." Then Paul joined the ladies of the veranda. "Carla, your parents tell me that we may have Stanford in common."

"If I can manage to squeeze through my senior year." Her smile spread to both her admirers.

"I've no doubt of it. At the risk of impertinence...may I ask what your major interest is...at this critical juncture of your long life?"

"That *is* impertinent, sir," she said, with a little laugh. "But should you press me, I'd have to admit to an interest in languages...French, Spanish, Italian...and that great ball of nothing in particular they call the *social sciences*. That, sir, is my forte," she concluded, showing some vision of perfect teeth. "You are...I believe my mother has said...a scientist?"

"Your mother has the gift of compliment." That torn tongue wish almost surfaced again, as he deflected some of his look toward Martha. Carla's mother took more of the dimensions of that remark than were intended for her daughter, but there was no print of this on her relaxation. "I labor—sometimes quite frustratingly—at the place of sound and fury they call The Propulsion Analysis Group...a child of Caltech and Uncle Sam."

"That *does* sound fascinating." Carla was qualified to put various shades on that, but she had fashioned a true compliment for him.

They chatted about many things, for a long time. Carla had made several trips to Europe and the Orient with her parents, and this patrimony plus her independent acquisitions at Stanford, and elsewhere, carried her very well on a number of subjects of interest to Martha and Paul. Martha's genuine relaxation distributed itself in nearly equal shares between Carla and Paul.

Finally, the veranda ones heard other voices. Two voyageurs were returning from the direction of the pool. Martha and Paul shared the briefest exchange of eyes when they saw this. Just prior to passing through the hedge that screened the pool from the house, the two had obviously shared an invigoration whose vestiges still trailed them. Carla saw nothing more in this than the overt hospitality that was a characteristic of her father.

"It's just wonderful," Mary said, for at least the second time in the past hour, as John escorted her to the veranda.

"I know it's a bit early, dear, but...couldn't we?"

"Get on with it...oh slave of habit."

With the exception of John and Carla, the company had begun a round of Scotch, and a bourbon for Mary. For some unyuletidelike reason, Carla had insisted on a gin and tonic, and her father had made a big show of rushing into the house for the quinine water required. While there, he had occasion to answer Mr. Bell's invention. He was back soon.

"It was Jake...he wants us over there...tonight."

"*Tonight?*" Martha's eyebrows came into play.

"You know Jake and Hetty. Each of them expected the other to call us weeks ago. And Jake made the insulting remark that if we didn't have, quote, black-tie embellishment, unquote, his butler could dig something up for us." John wiped a hand across his face, still looking at Martha.

"This is short notice. You told him—I presume not—that we have guests?"

"He said we'd better bring 'em, or else—Jake's *elses* tend to have scope."

"Mary...I must presume that you're slightly unprepared for such ostentation." This was smilingly confirmed by Mary.

"You and Carla are of a size...I wonder."

"Mother! Let's take her and try to drape her in the rags of Carla!" Carla took Mary's hand and then the three ladies disappeared into the house, transporting laughter.

"She's absolutely charming, Paul...absolutely charming." John relaxed in his chair, leaving no doubt about his subject.

"Welcome to *my* club." The eye union was good when Paul said that. But just afterward, their drinks...no reservoirs now, but enough surface on them for a useful target for the eyes, served both of them. During the time away from their drinks—the silent instants of contact—Mary's local admirers built part of an encyclopedia around her.

"How about you, old man...how's the tux situation?"

"Oh God! I forgot all about it." Paul did the hand on face bit himself.

"That could be a problem this late in the drinking season. Let me call a guy I know and see if we can get some threads for you." With that, John left Paul on the veranda, with thoughts that included the tux as a minor topic. Several minutes later, John returned.

"Let's grab the Lincoln and get t'hell down to Green Street. One conscientious man has apparently resisted the call of the season—so far." He clapped Paul on the back and propelled him toward the Lincoln near the front of the house.

Several hours later, the Lincoln returned, its occupants successful in convincing the tailor that there were glory and bucks in expediting Paul's plumage. John glanced at his watch. "Let's see...seven o'clockish. We'd better array ourselves in some compliment to the ladies—and be damn quick about it." Paul copied his host and ran toward *his* diggings.

By eight thirty, Paul and John were sitting near the central fireplace that happened to be resting. No drinks. They'd talked about fishing, but not much. From the laughter and talk echoing from a paneling with increasing volume, they had a right to assume that certain disciples of the Goddess of Beauty were approaching.

Carla made the first appearance, and she clearly had her mother's flare for style and subtle beauty in dress. She wore a long gown of pale yellow, a French braid claimed her black hair, and this was only one part of her that made her accolades a crowded challenge for her admirers. Next, Martha entered, looking slightly over her shoulder as she did so. She wore a gown of a color very like the one Paul had seen when he first entered this room. Her hair had been swept upward by an expertise that complimented Carla and Mary, and their exploitation of Martha's natural equipment. Her diamond necklace and earrings were only fair condiments for a feast of her that hit Paul between the eyes, and her husband only a little less so. And the flourish had to be sustained as Mary entered the room. Between the treasures of Carla and Martha, and Mary's own equipment, they'd created an Irish beauty who could have easily taken a place beside Martha in her painting. Paul could hear Reynolds muttering something off in the shadows.

The effect of Mary on John was instant and powerful. From the corner of his eye, Paul noticed John put his hand on the coffee table as he stood up, and he seemed to have some difficulty with this simple action. When the two men finally gave up their passive commitment to the scene, and started their approach to the ladies, they faced respective problems of service to the protocols of beauty...Paul's almost as formidable as John's.

John piloted the Continental that night to Jake's. Paul was beside him and the lights of Wilshire, then Beverly Hills, were resident many times in three pairs of eyes in the rear seat that kept Paul on a busy program of assimilation and John, less comprehensively, through his rear-view mirror. Paul had to caution him—several times—to get back to his driving or they'd all be the worse for it.

Jake's house was arrayed in subtle consonance with the season. There were about twenty couples circulating among the less private rooms of Hetty and Jake's establishment. There was an envelopment of soft music. In the game room, several couples danced to less classically biased sound. As the butler and a maid were assuming the coats of John's party, Jake and Hetty entered the large foyer.

"Ah...I see my butler's other services won't be needed after all," Jake said, walking toward them.

"It only took a few minutes to get the smell of camphor out of our things." Martha said, planting a kiss and a smile on Jake he didn't deserve. She and Hetty exchanged careful kisses. Mary was introduced. Carla was very well known to Jake and Hetty, and Jake was careful himself in putting his mug close to Carla's.

"Please come in and try to take your rightful places at the bar, dance floor, or bed rooms."

"Careful, Jake...the party's not *that* old." John bounced a glance off the ladies who were tangled in animated conversation with Hetty.

"And I see we have our philosopher with us again...welcome, Paul. I'm glad to see you again...we got a couple loose ends."

"Same here Jake on the seeing...and I'll try to pick up those loose ends whenever you toss 'em." Paul and Jake made an eye axis that had more grin on Paul's side, more reconnaissance on Jake's.

The three men waited for the ladies to disengage somewhat and then they escorted them into the room of Jake's main fireplace that Paul had encountered before. This one was very much occupied in spreading its flattering aura over a large area. After a few more introductions by Jake and Hetty, the Drake party gradually diffused itself throughout that room, and the game room. Carla was quickly grabbed up by several younger types who looked familiar with the Dow Jones index, and she was holding her own very well.

John and Martha found some of their friends from San Marino and others from Santa Barbara, and they were gradually joined by others who, at fitting times, also called Cap D'Antibes and Rome and Paris home. Paul knew he'd be in some water over his head there, so he was in no hurry to order his walk with Mary in that direction. In the course of the path they did choose, they chatted with an insurance executive and his wife from Beverly Hills; a gentleman who seemed to know his way around the Hollywood studios and a young lady of careful beauty who seemed to value this connection; several other ladies and gentlemen who, in the most natural way possible, conveyed their opinions that Paris was lovely about now, Stockholm was too...if you were an Eskimo. And that, generally, the world was something of their oyster. At the end of a random walk affected by many collisions with bodies of significance and genuine interest to Mary and Paul, he held her in a slow fox trot in the game room. She could compete very well with any woman in this house and Paul was aware of this, as were other eyes of the male. His reverie was finally jolted by a hand on his shoulder, and the accusation that he was monopolizing her. He had to defer the remainder of the dance to John.

Paul saw Martha in a group near the entrance to the game room. He walked toward her, and then led her to the dance floor after a minimal disentangling repartee...started by Paul, finished by Martha. He did his best to tailor his grip of her to their circumstances. But she was required—on several occasions—to use some strength in keeping the semblance of casual, mutual enjoyment for this particular rhythmic exercise. She whispered her protests, and mentioned the good music and he whispered back that there was *other* music he'd prefer to enjoy at that moment. They traded dances with several other couples, but despite the obvious charms of his other partners, he couldn't take his eyes off her for long. And once, from quite a distance, she reciprocated his look in a way that made his shoes a little tighter at the front. Gradually, the dancing was sustained only by a young couple newly come to the state of matrimony and they had no intention of wasting their glances on others.

Martha had out-maneuvered him and achieved a fireplace aura situation within a group of conversationalists that definitely included Hetty. Paul had resigned the chase and now stood close to one of the medieval andirons that bracketed Jake's great fire pit. Some of its antique iron reminded him of Celtic pagan-religious fusions he and Mary had seen in Northern Ireland, and a thought of her flashed to him when some of Jake's firelight found an intriguing path through the ironwork. This firelight was still playing games with his eyes when he felt Jake's hand on his shoulder. When he turned to his host, this light was resolute in sustaining—improving—the reconnaissance mode that Paul had seen earlier on Jake, and it put enough luminescence into his own eyes to improve the game for Jake, too.

Jake had seen some drops of Drake wine tonight. He was an expert on wine. He had one of the best cellars in Bel Air...*the* best he claimed. He knew that some spillage is inevitable to its savoring, even toward the bottom of the glass. And in the rarified circles he frequented, extrapolations of the province of wine...John and Martha's or any others'...were commonplace, even to esoteric situations John had never contemplated.

"*Ach so...wieder es gibt der slippenstikker.*" Jake's fractured Deutsch pulled their local climate into a special synthesis of their own. Paul kept one hand on a barely comfortable extremity of an andiron, while Jake played his look around Paul's face...Paul's eyes always the main ground, however.

"*Ja wohl*, Jake." Paul could feel the radiation from the fireplace on one side of him, and from Jake on the other side. "But let's keep away from that *slippery stick* gibberish tonight—I made a damn fool of myself last time." As he looked away from Jake, his eyes picked up a special transient of firelight that had some projection into Martha's group...and *she* saw it, maybe Hetty, too, because the men of this pair—so close to the fire—was a logical focus of that room.

"This aspect of responsibility...who must share it with your technical man?" Jake had just stepped on Paul's humble pie, and pulled Paul's eyes back to him again. Jake hadn't lost a beat of their earlier conversation, and he'd come in crowding the apex of it that this young engineer had spilled over some of the territory of Jake's own paradise.

Maybe the duality of radiation pressing both sides of him again, allied with Jake's flavorful hospitality, was the incentive Paul needed to satisfy Jake. When he answered Jake, he was looking into the fire, the scintillations of it working his face like a biblical philosopher's responding to a fire placed on *his* altar conducive to truth. Jake caught this second image.

"Too many people have been looking away from the reaction side of our technical masterpieces...those positive and negative tears of accomplishment are tied too damn close to the profit buck—not enough to the *reaction* buck."

"This means?" Firelight scintillations, whatever their special auras, were old hat to Jake. He was now ignoring all of the local ones except Paul's—bolstered by some biblical inference Jake would never admit.

"This means that people like you, Jake...people who swim in the profit dividends of the ventures...are in it—up to *here!*" Paul had removed his hand from the andiron and shoved it up as high as he could make it go, above the two-faced iron that the fire had just garnished with extra presence, a duality of credentials in that iron for dealing with opportunities—devilish exploitation or responsible cultivation—giving it a ligament to the thesis that Paul had just stuck into Jake. It was a move of some drama, close coupled as it was to the master of the house, and everyone in that room had seen it.

"Throw the bum out!" Jake cried. And then he stepped away from the hot zone he and Paul had shared. "Boys and girls, if Hetty wasn't lying to me, there should be some pickles and hamburgers in the dining room." There were, but two of the best caterers in Beverly Hills would've been unhappy with Jake's description of the bounty they'd accomplished.

With the contributions from Jake and Hetty and nearly everyone at the massive table—including Mary's outrageous use of her Irish brogue—any gloom that had walked into that room had a hard time getting out.

It was getting late. Paul had said that he was very interested in seeing a first class Bel Air garden. Jake advised him that he'd come to the right place and that Martha was the best guide he could think of. For a few minutes, they strolled through the best that a staff of gardeners could do for Hetty and Jake. When she could keep him behaving, Martha *was* a good guide.

They were just turning into a lane that led to the big pool at the rear of the grounds, when they stopped...rather, Paul stopped them. He'd been the first to see a couple engaged in a kiss that lacked no passion. It was John and Mary.

He couldn't keep Martha from seeing them. She looked at them for a time that didn't include the end of the kiss, then she took Paul's hand and they started back to Jake's house. Approaching the broadcast of music and laughter, they didn't talk, and Paul certainly behaved.

She still held his hand, and he tried to make the right face when he finally turned to her. He had come, stumbled, into the Drakes' lives. If what he had had with Martha was part of a bad spirit that had hitched a ride with him, then what they had just seen could easily be added to the forked tail of that same spirit. He'd brought Mary into its scope. She could cope with her own demons — but he was supposed to *protect* her, not put another one on her. That damn ambiguous, fire bloated, hot iron posed between him and Jake had poked its nose into their talk. Now it, a conceivable warp of that spirit, was leering at him as he tried to accommodate, excuse — justify whatever he had brought into the Drakes. Never mind Drake collusions, it was *his* part that was on his back now... but before he could get to any words, she partly saved him.

"I think that any questions I might've had were answered — rather explicitly — by John's response to Mary earlier this evening." She hadn't looked at him, but then she upset her own regimen and she stopped them and then she kissed him. "It seems that our wine isn't so exclusive." Her whisper had touched his cheek, just before it came around to his lips again.

Mary had found a compact of special beauty and efficiency at one of the shops at The Huntington and Carla was delighted with it, and Martha, with her gift of the bluebirds, had to kiss Mary for it. Mary had wrapped the two Zane Grey books in gold paper and at this moment the men were absorbed in rending Mary's careful work, saltwater for John, fresh for Paul.

John saw his first. He looked at Mary, and then back at the book. "My story wasn't *that* good, Mary...but thanks for this beauty. It's the best edition I've ever seen."

When Paul finally got to the meat of Mary's cuff links, he flashed a wink at her, and then he flashed the present so John knew he had some competition in that department.

Paul had nothing of real value to give to Martha. He handed her a large, flat package wrapped in silver paper, with a gold ribbon.

"I'll apologize now for what I deem to be a *gross* inadequacy." His small smile didn't bother with any local complications.

"I...sir...shall be the judge of that...very shortly." And then she saw his Lady of the Pavilion and she gasped. Paul had begged a picture of her and she had finally given him a small one that he could hide deep in his wallet.

The picture caught enough of her so that, with his memory, he finally did a likeness of her in pastels that pleased him. The lady of the sketch showed only part of her shoulders. He'd suggested a scarf about her throat, and she was disposed like one who'd found the closest past moments...hours of life to be a pleasure, and those in her anticipation, no less so. Martha finally had to show it to the others, and from it, Carla came to know of her mother...and Paul Sanger. Mary was hard pressed to keep her outward response to the sketch within the academics and the kidding of the critic and the sister, respectively.

Paul gave John an attaché case and they had appropriate banter with that.

John added to Martha's extensive jewelry collection with a necklace and earrings of jade and gold that had traveled centuries to find her. When she modeled them, Paul's sometimes obsession with antique worlds got restless again.

To Paul, John and Martha gave a Winston fly rod, of a size for steelhead and salmon. He flipped over it, and threatened to assemble it. Martha over-ruled him in the interest of her vases.

Her parents gave Carla a gold pen and pencil set, and they added some pieces to her modest jewelry collection which brought squeals of delight from the young beauty.

John turned to Mary. "You've troubled us, my dear...only in the gift category, of course. Perhaps, though, this little token of our appreciation for your presence will please you." When Mary opened the package, and saw the necklace of pearls that the woman on Rodeo Drive had supported with the statement that she would personally kill any woman who didn't like them, she stared in disbelief, looking up at Martha and John, and then back to the pearls. Her parents had been good to this one, but this was a new dimension in gifts for her. She looked at Paul, back at the beauties, and then she started to cry. Carla came to her. And Martha, with her hand resting lightly on Mary's shoulder, told her that she couldn't deny the rest of them such beauty. After daubing at her eyes with a bit of lace Carla had provided, she donned the treasure of the humble oyster, and raised her head. With the firelight conspiring with eyes that still were moistened, she threw a picture at them that perturbed all of the rhythms of breath around her. Her brother came to her.

"I'm glad I caught you in a weak moment, Tiger." When she saw the photograph that one of the better Pasadena lens men had wrought of him, she started to cry again. But Paul quickly kissed this inclination away, and she managed a grin at her sappy brother.

"Carla, only humble books for you," Paul said. Among these was some of Benet's prose and poetry. Carla made him promise to read some of Benet's evocation of Americans to them before the evening was done. Carla gave Paul books...of poetry, of Donne and Shakespeare, and one of old French poems. Mary's own artistic bent was challenged by Carla in the form of a beautifully compact water color set, designed for wide-ranging travelers.

Paul excused himself after the first pulse of gift excitement had subsided. When he returned, Mary was standing near the fireplace with Martha, and Carla was seated near them reading one of her new books. John was standing some distance away from the ladies, absorbed in his renewal with Zane Grey. Paul's acting ability still needed improvement. When he walked into the room, he was stiffer than he'd intended. And he was also less clever in concealing a toma-hawk he carried in the hand farthest from the ladies. It was a harmless enough thing...the best he could do on a sudden, crazy, impulse...made from a piece of cardboard and a few feet of red ribbon for color and texture. He'd made it too long and part of it, the business end, peeked at the ladies as he walked by them. Martha saw it first, then Mary. Their little vocalizations of surprise attracted Carla's attention and finally, even John's. Everyone was now privy to an act that Paul had designed as a quiet little piece of business between John and himself. He couldn't stop now, so he kept walking toward John, who was now fascinated by the spectacle of Paul's approach with something that looked dangerous at that distance. Paul stopped right in front of him. With the best attempt at a straight face he'd ever made, he said, "And now, welcome to *my* lodge, brother," as he handed the tomahawk to John.

John's mouth was still partially open when Paul turned and walked back toward the ladies. He garnished his performance with a wink and started to build a grin that was well developed when he reached them. John hadn't moved. He still held the tomahawk in one hand, Zane Grey in the other.

Paul picked up Carla's Benet and started to read. He started on Crazy Horse. His voice carried well—especially to John. Soon, the man of the Sioux had intruded most of the thoughts of that room, but it didn't preempt a lot of them. Mary and Martha held their positions. Carla was resting her head against the couch, listening to Paul's recital of Benet talking about original America... about the scope of a man. Martha and Mary let their eyes...each on her own agenda...alternate between Paul and John. And each achieved her own com-munion with these men. Carla had absolutely no idea of what the Indian drama had been about. Mary was less certain of noninvolvement and Martha's senior inventory of her husband's responses whispered that Paul's mouth wound had just found some reciprocation in that room.

Two days after the fine Christmas day that Martha had helped to provide, the entire company was aboard the WE'RE HERE II headed for Catalina. The channel crossing was rough and the men had to caution Mary and Carla not to be so free with themselves on the foredeck. It was a happy, windblown, sea sprayed group that finally pulled into Catalina harbor and dropped the hook. They could see Zane Grey's adobe house on a hill, and John told them a little about this man of the pen and the heavy rods and the big sails. Both Carla and Mary wanted to feel more substantial substance under them for a while, so John offered to escort them on a walk around the harbor.

Martha dived from the boat, staying underwater for most of a minute in a fine imitation of a mermaid. Paul followed her a few seconds after she'd entered the water. He saw her through the light and dark patterns of greenness and while she was still submerged, and in mid-stroke, he encircled her waist with his arms and his kiss finally forced them to the surface, laughing, and sputtering the Pacific.

After he'd helped her up the ladder, they paused for breath. And then he chased her around the deck in a laughing, screaming pursuit. She hid behind a deck chair which afforded her no protection, and she knew it. From a distance of a few feet, he pretended a tiger stalk of her. At the last of it, he rushed around the chair at her. This was fine sport, and it would have ended grandly...except that there was no good coefficient of friction between the moist deck and his wet feet. He slipped in his turn, and banged his head against a bulkhead. It wasn't really bad, but it was enough to justify laying himself out in front of her in a simulated agony. She ministered to him, cuddling his head in her lap. And then, two wet faces came together in what has been called a kiss of lasting duration.

He had showered and then, growing impatient of her, he stepped from his cabin and entered the open door of the master suite, He hadn't thought about the courtesy of clothing and when he saw her, she was fresh from her shower, sitting on the bed, adding slippers to an ensemble consisting of a light beach robe and a red band of silk for her hair. Her action and posture left little concealed of perfect legs and thighs. When she acknowledged his presence with a smile, she added some of the sound that is sometimes used for children when they've been naughty.

How is impulse analyzed? It's made of a thousand things, from ten thousand years. Perhaps it was the sudden flux of some of her essence to him. Perhaps it was his memory of her implication--stronger than that—that there would be an end to their wine. Perhaps it was some vestige of the bump on his head. Whatever it was, it was enough to bring her into his arms with a sudden action that had none of her design. No playful obeisance now to his dictum of no unilateral nakedness. He thrust aside her robe and had the equipment to take her as she was...changing her surprise to shock, and then almost to fear. They'd done this vertical business before...but the preliminaries had put a strong mutuality of interest and urgency into it that wasn't there now.

He forced her into a sort of grotesque *pas de deux* that finally her senses made her respond to in kind, and then she started to give him as good as she got from him. Their path around the stateroom was then made by action and reaction that was a fusion of *them*, not rhythmic or random him then her, but *them*—a state of affairs that had been part of the culmination of the design of their love. But, although they had good precedence for it, there was no, actual, conversation here...the eyes and mouths seemed on the verge of conversation, but they never got there and they continued their work on spikes of memories of friendlier passion...where there had been words. This last state of affairs might apply to people hell bent toward Martha's *real* world, and wasting no time on the graceful parts of it.

They reached their respective peaks of this wild climb almost together, and then they collapsed against a wall, his head in her lap which her robe had accidentally covered. This lap was soon shaking with his sobs and wetted by his tears. She heard him beg her to forgive him and she replied with a soft application of her hands to his head and neck...then she made him look at her.

"We got awfully close to the dregs that time...didn't we, my darling."

When John and Mary and Carla returned to the boat a little later, Paul had enough of a headache to be confined to his cabin. And Martha pleaded enough indisposition from sun and sea exposure to request private respite also. They *just* wanted to be left alone. But the three crazy devils who had returned from the island wouldn't let them be. Between their own fun and games, they made frequent solicitations of the welfare of the distressed ones. Once, Mary and Carla ducked a book thrown from Paul's cabin. And there was John narrowly escaping an orange that smashed into a bulkhead behind him. Compared to Paul's trajectory, the one of the orange lacked some power, but not resolution.

8

Part of the conversation would have pleased the Inquisition brethren. Jake's eyes weren't there this time, but there were others as perceptive as Jake's. There were four pairs of eyes, coming back to Paul on their own agenda with increasing frequency as the chat developed.

Myron commented that his physical equipment wasn't bad...if you didn't mind an asymmetrically dimpled chin, a slightly aquiline nose, tousled blond hair, and a tantalizing sprig of hair showing above the V of his sport shirt.

George commented that his morals might prove to be a detriment for a project requiring purity of devotion.

Harry noted that he'd already dirtied his hands with practical applications and that—despite this—he'd had the gall to mention the sacred gooblah.

Russ observed that while most of his steps had had a depressing faltering quality, a few *had* been in the direction of the Temple. This admission prompted other questions whose resultant touched the supplicant's qualities for advancing so far as to the steps of the Temple, perhaps even to the point of approaching the High Priestess and...

"Goosing her," Myron said.

"Screwing her," George said.

"I...I think our lad gets the general idea," Russ said, finally turning what could be construed as a friendly face, unimpaired by playful hypocrisy, in Paul's direction.

And so, Paul Sanger, late of the U. S. Air Force, came to some priests of the Temple and bowed in acceptance of the Goddess' first real trial. And it was a beauty. It was fluorine.

In the course of more sober conversation, Russ told Paul that they'd hit this one together and Paul was glad for the company. Under conditions where fluorine is allowed to frisk about under only the constraints of the low pressure gas phase, it will snap viciously at anything that would crowd its play. If you make it more cantankerous by pushing it into a liquid state, and hugging it with a pressure of upwards of a thousand pounds per square inch, it has a remorseless tendency to seek farther afield for fun. Should you be impetuous enough to supply a bride, such as gentle hydrogen, for this raptor then the rape must be confined cunningly if havoc isn't to come of it.

They were planning to do just this violence and Paul listened very carefully as Russ and George and Harry and Myron described the happy characteristics of fluorine, and the energy possibilities of a wedding with hydrogen.

At first, they were content with a small wedding, in a chapel appropriate to about fifty pounds of connubial thrust. And they weren't content with just the problems of the wedding. They decided to incorporate the birth of fluorine into proceedings that were rapidly running out of caterers. The fluorine would be born in an electrolytic cell that fed on sweet hydrofluoric acid. Under the stimulus of electric potential, this cell would give birth to fluorine, and its intended bride, hydrogen. This particular hydrogen wasn't destined for the wedding. They were delegating this office to a maiden of high pressure who'd been made by others.

In the course of planning this controlled holocaust, Paul journeyed to engineering drafting rooms, to electronic and hydraulic laboratories of PAG where such wedding necessities as flow- meters, pressure sensors, thermocouples, valves, storage tanks, feed lines, purifiers and condensers were developed and despaired over, not necessarily in that order.

In trying to select materials of construction for such of these things as would feel the direct breath of fluorine, Paul had much excuse to talk with the Dutchman, Gruif. He was a tall, thin man of rather formal mien, with a shock of gray-black hair that he usually managed to keep out of his electron microscope, metallographs, X-ray machines and the hoard of other equipment he used to probe the solid state. Paul received his first real dose of indoctrination in the devotion required of a true man of science from Gruif and Russ.

These men didn't appear to be suffering. In their presence, it was easy to get swept up in honest enthusiasm for subjects outside the immediate scope of the Wall Street Journal. They didn't recognize formal working hours...an idea, a problem, usually related, would come to them at any hour of the day, or night, and any day of the week. And they would respond with thought, or action. They weren't ashamed of their bank balances. But the personal finances of such men, with a few exceptions, would never satisfy a Journal man for more than a very short career transient.

On this particular sunny morning, Paul and his crew and a few electronikers were engaged in calibrating a flowmeter of a type that showed some promise for their temperamental friend. It consisted of an entrance section that imparted a regulated swirl to the incoming fluid, a small ball that was constrained to a circular track perpendicular to the flow axis, an electromagnetic sensor that told on the ball every time it passed within its scope, and an exit section that tried to get rid of the fluid with as much hydrodynamic grace as possible. The impulses of excitement sent to the sensor by the little ball were forwarded to various black boxes, which converted these signals into more palatable form for the oscillographs and recording potentiometers. To provide an environment for fluorine that would minimize its nervousness, the whole of the meter had to be enveloped in a liquid nitrogen jacket, then a vacuum jacket to keep the nitrogen happy. A layer of solid insulation completed the design for keeping the curious and relatively more excited molecules of the ambient atmosphere from imparting too much excitement to the proceedings within the meter.

The characteristics of this meter had been under study for some time by Paul and a dozen, or so, others at Hydraulics and Electronics. They had run it with gas, and it proved to be a fine instrument with gas, responding to flow transients in surprisingly good fashion. They'd tried it with water, and it was splendid in every way. Everything with water usually was, although some of the people in Hydraulics would argue that one. Now, they were trying it with liquid nitrogen.

The test rig consisted of an insulated tank, with a capacity for several hundred pounds of the cold stuff. Insulation was provided by a vacuum shell, and a second shell filled with solid insulation. For rough flow measurement, the whole assembly was mounted on a heavy cast iron balance designed to minister to sides of beef. Liquid nitrogen was supplied to the inner tank through a temporary connection to a mobile dolly, and a vent valve allowed the nitrogen to escape in gaseous form during the cooling down transient when the nitrogen was coaxed into liking the liquid phase in the inner tank. If this vent valve was closed prematurely after the inner tank had been locked off, a dangerous over-pressure could develop in the inner tank from gasification of the liquid nitrogen. A stand-pipe led from the liquid nitrogen tank to the flow line that traversed the meter. The meter discharged its cold drink into a vented drainage system. The driving force for the liquid nitrogen was provided by helium that pressurized the liquid nitrogen via tubing that penetrated the inner tank.

They had been in the cooling down transient when what passed for the noon klaxon was heard. After some adjustments to the equipment, the crew dispersed to their lunches, which all happened to be at some distance from the test revetment.

After lunch, Paul was the vanguard of a scattered group of people return-ing to the calibration. He'd just entered the passage leading to the interior of the revetment, when there was an explosion. The primary pressure wave used this passage as its principal escape route. Paul was about at the focus of its strength and it slammed him against a wall of the passage. He got a good enough bump on the head to render him unconscious. Several other crew members got a lesser share of the wave.

Tom heard of the accident by the grapevine that seems to travel with sonic velocity at places like PAG. Paul's name had been mentioned and he lost no time in seeing what he could do for his friend. Medical had called the only emergency number Paul had given them...the Drakes. The maid told Martha, and Martha called John. There really wasn't need for that much excitement. Paul regained consciousness after he arrived at Medical. He tried to get off the cot, the nurse said no. When John arrived, the presiding MD told him that all Paul needed was a couple days rest. Tom offered to drive him home, but John said that—as a taxpayer—he resented Tom taking time off for such trivia, so he took Paul home, telling Tom to get over there for a drink as soon as he could sneak away.

Over Paul's protests that his apartment was plenty good enough for the occasion, Martha and John escorted him to one of their guest bedrooms. They undressed him with no concern for his modesty, cased him in a set of John's pajamas and tucked him into bed. His disclaimers notwithstanding, he went back into a deep sleep almost immediately.

It didn't take Jules Verne's imagination to appreciate what would have happened if the explosion had waited for company. During the test, eight versions of the fragile envelope that is man would have been close to the test rig. The post-accident analysis determined that the cause of the explosion had three consecutive parts: During its history, a copper tubing had been installed at the bottom of the high pressure storage tank. It traversed the vacuum and insulation shells and terminated in a small valve that was covered by the wrapping on the exterior of the insulation shell. The copper had been corroded by exposure to chemicals which further degraded the structural integrity. This design anomaly where nonredundant copper shared containment responsibility within a heavy steel complex, coupled with inattention to corrosion, qualified for part one. Paul had borrowed the test rig from another crew and assumed that it was sound enough for the nitrogen testing. This assumption completed part two. Part three was achieved when the vent valve had been inadvertently closed just before the crew left for lunch under the condition of a large mass of unstable liquid nitrogen still growling in the inner tank. When the evaporating nitrogen built up pressure against the closed vent, the corroded copper line burst at its section in the vacuum tank, allowing a large mass of liquid nitrogen to enter the evacuated space. The vaporization of this charge built up enough pressure fast enough to blow the lid assembly off the tank system. The resulting thrust force shattered the beam balance into pieces no larger than a grapefruit, and various size pieces of shrapnel from it and other material affected by the general disintegration were projected around the test area. It had been a drama of negligence and Death had been denied a good day by only seconds. When he was in better fettle, Paul thanked God for more of his mercy.

That night, Martha brought him his supper herself. Over his protests, she fed him mostly stuff that only a baby could like...to the accompaniment of John's frank, and vocal, amusement. After the scene had quieted a little, Martha read to him from John's new Zane Grey, over John's protests that he hadn't finished it yet. Once, when they were alone, she stopped her tale of successful and unsuccessful pursuit of the great game fish and kissed him... too tenderly he complained, but she was quicker than he at this time of his indisposition. And then he slept again, and he dreamed of swordfish, and of a solicitous goddess who knew well of swordfish.

Martha had him planted in one of her veranda chairs the next morning. He was enjoying the respite from his battle with fluorine...and the solicitation. She read more to him about New Zealand, and of the black and striped variet- ies of the billed one. She supplemented this with several stories of her own adventures with these fish off South America. Although Paul tried to improve the kisses she dispensed from time to time, she didn't respond with vigor... certainly not her vigor.

"I've done all I can to apologize for what I did on the boat," he said, feel- ing that a vestige of that unpleasant incident was responsible for her reserve. Shortly after they had returned from Catalina, on successive days he'd brought her several large bouquets of white chrysanthemums—her rose holding was too vast to make any impression with them—each of them bolstered with a note that tried to supplement the passion of the flowers and define his contrition unambiguously for her eyes only.

"Paul..." she put Zane Grey on the flagstone, "you're working on a sched- ule at PAQ, aren't you?" He'd told her all he could about his work.

"And how!" A sudden recollection of his substantial responsibilities hit him at that moment. "But...I...I don't see what that has to do with us." Since the time of first blood in John's den, they'd all played their tune by ear. Neither John, nor Martha, had shown a disposition to perturb whatever quality of equilibrium existed. John had been particularly disinclined since Christmas. There had been no extension of the Paul and Martha adventure beyond the boat incident. Paul had been on the verge of unilateral termination of his tenancy—several times—but he hadn't found enough steel for this yet. And flashes of a dream world continued to blind him.

"I...I think that you and I had better discuss schedules."

"I'm all for it...anything you say."

"Your impetuosity may get you into trouble one day, my lad." Her smile had familiar qualities.

"My impetuosity has brought me more than I could've stuffed into my dreams by myself." His look probably could have carried him without the words.

"I think we should close our...closet." For that instant, Zane Grey seemed a better target for her eyes, and that course did give them a quick privacy.

He should have been prepared for this occasion. He'd had plenty of leads for gracious endings, which could run between a kiss on the lips, her hands... both without the clutter of words; or it could be nothing but silence and only the flux they could build with their eyes. These would probably have been acceptable to her...but there never seemed to be enough energy, or resolve, to steer him in the right direction.

"Is that all you can say about *us*?" At least he tried to discipline his face like a man should.

"Oh...I can say much more about us. You say I've given you something... you've more than matched me." She turned away from him. And now what had been moisture...a special supplement of eyes...was tears. He came to her, but the role of comforter would've been hard to distinguish here. After a moment, she dabbed her eyes with a handkerchief, and looked at him. "I think I'm entitled to *my* relief valve—you damn engineers seem to have plenty of them." And then, when he tried to kiss away a tiny part of her valve, she pushed him away, firmly.

"You'll have to practice your resistance. I fully intend to hold up my end of the devastating attractiveness around here—you and John have no monopoly on *that*." Now, she had made a little tease, and some flash of eyes, from ingredients that had some pain in them. "And I also intend to hold up my end of our friendship." Her softest voice had now come into it...and this caused her eyes to focus better than his.

"Hey, you two! You're deafening me with your laughter." This had come from the doorway leading to the veranda. And it was far enough away that they could gain composure before John descended on them. But this was a man of some compassion. He could detect tears even at that distance and he made no intrusion. "How's about a little unwind?" He hadn't moved from his greeting stance. They didn't object. John was unusually long in his preparations, and they turned out to be modest by his standards.

"Jeese...what a day," John said, relaxing into his chair and carefully avoiding looking at either of his companions.

"More travel coming up, dear?" Martha's face had picked up remarkable composure.

"Afraid so. I've got to go to Chicago again. Leave tonight...be gone about three days."

Paul had also recovered well, although any nosey observer could notice that the smog hadn't been *that* bad. He'd also recovered enough to hear a faint bell when John mentioned Chicago. In her last letter, his mother said that Mary was doing quite a lot of traveling lately...Chicago had even been mentioned. Paul managed to look at John, who still didn't feel any compulsion for an eye-to-eye confrontation with anybody, and he was starting to understand John's posture as a tentative, reluctant, host.

Paul stayed at the manor house one more day. He could feel the fluorine job pressing on him...but this was being done by matters here, too. His preoccupation had been noticed by Martha at the dinner table, and more so when they were seated by the fireplace after John had left. They were trying the game of kings again, and again Paul's appreciation of the scope of action was locally deficient. Finally, Martha broke off contact and made them go to the more comfortable reaches of a couch.

"Paul...it wouldn't take one of John's sensors to tell that something is troubling you...and I don't feel that I can take all the blame for it." She reached for, and captured, one of his hands.

He didn't know how much Martha knew about John's involvement with Mary. She was, in fact, very well informed about some of it. On one of their trysts, the lovers had chosen New York City on a crazy impulse. And even crazier, and John should have known better, they chose the Pierre, where one of Martha's friends saw them.

"I *know* about John and Mary," the softest voice still in action, "and I think that's the big part of the answer to my question."

"My God!—how can you be so calm about it?" He tried to put real excitement into it, but now he had some knowledge of her and he hadn't been surprised by either her revelation, or her presentation. That sprite, spirit, hadn't left them yet. It had devised some new twists for the skein that had been a class project—and let them try to get it untangled before it choked all of them!

"My capacity for...calmness as you say, has been sorely tested hereabouts." Her grip on him at that moment could have been taken from either the pavilion, or near a lagoon. "I certainly can't claim any right to censure John *or* Mary." This was a succinct summary of a situation of enough complexity that it gave Paul no real leads for a response. She still held his hand, and then he made it a bigger stack of hands.

"That word...*largesse*...it keeps coming at me around here."

"There's none of that. If there's guilt...then there's plenty to share. But I admit none...and you shouldn't either with all the provocation I gave you."

"What provocation?"

"Ah...your word again...I guess it *won't* go away." She allowed a short time for a kiss.

Later, when he petitioned her to let him show her that he hadn't forgotten his capacity for tender love, she forbade him this. They'd passed many deadlines for better behavior. But the present one, Martha...and finally Paul... couldn't deny.

"Those triple-walled lines are going to be damn tricky to build," the draftsman said, looking up at Paul from a schematic of the fluorine system that was gradually assuming more palpable shape from Paul and Russ' sketches. "It'll take damn good welding—and better inspection," he continued. The object of their immediate attention was the main fluorine tank. It had incorporated a capacitance level indicator, and all of the details needed to help an aggressive bridegroom flow toward a destiny with hydrogen.

"Yeah...we'll have to watch all of that. Those nickel alloys can take punishment, but they need help...and we'll give it to 'em" Paul said, scanning the lines showing parts of the fluorine and hydrogen systems that would bring a fire such as PAG had never seen to the beastly focal point of the whole business.

The test pit itself had been sited in a remote corner of PAG, on a hill behind the ramjet facility. Some constituents of Fluorine Test Pit No. 1 were now taking more substantial form than lines on paper. The formidable exhaust of anhydrous hydrofluoric acid would fly forth at thousands of feet per second. The chemical scrubber for this wedding derivative was taking shape on the hillside. The electrolytic cell and its generator were pre-fabricated and these parents of a child of awesome tendencies were already installed in the in-law quarters, where they waited in sullen silence while preparations were made to receive their child. The cell product had to be scrubbed and filtered before it reached the first stage condenser. Some of this prerequisite was also in evidence, as well as some of the lines leading to the main fluorine tank, and the mounting for that sepulcher itself.

Vacuum and liquid nitrogen jackets that enveloped *every* part of the liquid fluorine circuit, had to be serviced by a battery of vacuum pumps and a liquid nitrogen supply system. Part of the vent circuit for the fluorine tank was now installed. Redundancy was the word here. If anything prevented the release of the helium driving pressure—that might go to a thousand pounds per square inch—over a full charge of fluorine, the potential events spectrum wasn't pleasantly attractive.

The hydrogen for the wedding would be supplied from a simpler system, a manifold of high pressure cylinders. It would enter the test cell through ports in the revetment that opposed the fluorine line entrance. Paul had insisted on as complete a separation of the bride and groom as possible...right up to the chapel.

These components, and the water cooling system for the combustion chamber, the safety ducts in the pit complex, and a dozen, or so, other subsidiary circuits, required a tubing and wiring maze that had Art and Eddy and Luke and a few other assorted guys mumbling for weeks. And that was just the test pit side of it. The pit had to be coupled to the control room, and that linkage contributed to the mumbling, if not the groaning.

The control room was downhill from the test pit and through its armored glass ports one could see the motor with the help of a large mirror. Paul had wanted a pure electric coupling to the control room for the pressurization circuits to the fluorine tank. This equipment would have required substantial development time. Already, Administration was being careful to advise Russ and Paul that they would *see this thing through*, implying a magnanimous patience and forbearance for the foibles of the test pit men. The hardest thing some of those jokers had to see through was their cigar smoke. Oh...they *did* sweat over their budgets, and Russ and Paul appreciated this. So...they accepted the gas lines into the control room.

The critical test cell instrumentation—chamber pressure, flow rates of fluorine, hydrogen and cooling water, cooling water temperature sensors, thrust sensors—was fed to a new, centrally located instrumentation center, hundreds of yards from the test site. This system had been tested at other pits and it seemed to be satisfactory. But it was still damn nice to see your own stuff coming off the charts in front of you. Hell...you were adding the competence of a dozen, or so, other men to that of the test crew, a competence that could make or break a test and you really didn't have much control over it.

During these preliminaries, the boys had their hackles raised a little when the time came to pay some attention to the electrolytic cell. This beauty was about the size of a sarcophagus for a minor noble. To function, it needed periodic infusions of anhydrous hydrofluoric acid. This chemical has some interesting effects on human tissue. It runs a close second to fluorine for cussedness and a mistake with it can cause painful and very slow healing burns, if they heal at all. It's bad enough in the usual dilute laboratory version. Anhydrous—it spits and grabs at you, a properly devilish handmaiden of fluorine—and they were also going to make it a child of fluorine and hydrogen in the bedroom that was called the rocket motor cell.

Once, Paul had been careless with the dilute stuff in a chemistry lab at Stanford. He'd left a vestige of acid on the lip of the wax HF bottle that he managed to transfer to a finger nail. About halfway to Pasadena that night on the Southern Pacific, that finger started to hurt. For the next few hours he waged a losing battle with acid penetration under his finger nail. When he got to Burbank the next morning, he had a hunk of black swelling where his nail should have been. He saw the Rose Bowl game with a vial of oil taped to that finger. That was the *dilute* stuff.

They ordered what was then probably most of the U.S. supply of Teflon to make two complete suits, head to toe, of this fluorcarbon to protect them during loading of the cell. The acid came in big tanks, that required a thermostated water bath to drive the acid into the cell. When they finished their first loading, Paul and his crew had another long cup of coffee in the service trailer.

It was getting close to the moment of truth...as close as Administration could make it. The Director had escorted a number of people through the facility at various times. Paul met Von Karman there, and he talked with this high priest of aeronautics through a speaking tube. He met the younger Millikan, the aerodynamicist, and a number of others famous in science and engineering. These included Simon Ramo, who one day would found one of the major aerospace companies, and several compatriots of his who would provide the backbone for the US effort to the moon, and beyond. Paul hadn't yet proved himself to his satisfaction, or that of many others. But the steps he'd taken in that direction were promising. As much as he could, within security, he tried to convey some of his excitement to his parents, and Mary and Martha and John. He didn't see Carla very often, but she didn't escape all of this, either.

This business moved fast. The knowledge of today quickly became the burden of the libraries tomorrow. But he had the feeling that some part of his work might someday ride on the big ones that would take his countrymen beyond the clutch of Earth's gravity. Fluorine didn't make many people smile. Even the rabid theoreticians probably thought that *this* one would always require more respect than could be carved out of the monolithic drive for the moon and the stages beyond it. Most people with some real knowledge of this matter of fluorine, probably hoped that it would *never* come to a large scale confrontation with this stuff of wanton destruction. But this element was chiseled into Mendeleev's symphony of periodicity—it was a crux point of it and the data it made couldn't be denied. And they would have to be proved in the fire before they became an interesting alternative.

"How're you guys reading me?" Paul asked over the intercom to Instrumention Central.

"Too loud...obnoxiously clear." Some of those jokers didn't share the tension in the control room.

"Cooling water to motor?" Paul asked.

"Reading steady on limit marks."

"Pump on for the exhaust scrubber?"

"It is *now*." Paul and Russ hoped that that slip-up wasn't contagious.

"All motor instrumentation reading okay?"

"All okay. A little instability with one pressure sensor...but we're redundant there...should be okay. Water flowmeters to nozzle and chamber sections steady and ready."

"How about the fluorine and hydrogen flowmeters?"

" Also steady and ready—like sin."

"Keep your damn private lives to yourself!" Russ barked.

"You sure you opened *all* those bottles on the hydrogen manifold, Luke?" Paul asked his crew chief.

"Yup. Pressure two thousand two hundred psi on the manifold sucking ten bottles."

"Okay," Paul said. He turned to his sweating friend near him at the control console. "I'm afraid I can't hold 'em much longer, Russ."

"Let's climb these steps together," Russ said, placing a hand on Paul's shoulder.

"Ok, we climb," Paul said to one and all, and this time the crew at IC got some of the tension creeping down the wires...so did the Director, and a few visitors from the Institute who were at IC.

"I'm taking the hydrogen up now. Call it out to me at one hundred pound intervals, Russ. We'll stop at one thousand."

"Six, seven, eight, nine...you stop at *one thousand*," Russ intoned in a monotone, broken by the limit call.

"I'm taking the fluorine up now. I've got my baby blues on this one." After a few seconds of Paul feeding the helium pressurizer to the fluorine tank, "Fluorine at full pressure...eight fifty...*now*." The knowledge that a good slug of the liquid phase of that stuff was under that confinement sent a chill into more than one of the knowledgeable people in the control room and at IC.

"Oxidizer and fuel both up. Instrumentation still okay?" Paul asked, with a small sigh.

"Still okay." This time there wasn't a smidgeon of fun in the soft voice from IC.

As he fitted the key to the firing circuit, Paul looked at Russ. "*Your* honors, Russ."

"I wouldn't think of interfering with your gooblah, my boy." Russ' grin was sustenance at that moment of confrontation that put crucial muscle and impulse into Paul's ligaments going to the firing key.

He couldn't wait any longer. Paul took a deep breath, let some of it out, then most of it. "I'll fire on three...one and two and three."

Everyone stared at the big mirror, heads and bodies being moved into various vantages within the crowded control room.

There were a few wisps of vapor as soon as Paul fired...a cough...a puff of disordered white smoke and flame...and then they saw it. It started out as a small pencil of whitest white and then it built into the brightest, most brilliant shock-wave pattern anyone at PAG—or in the whole world of propulsion—had ever seen. It had some of the rainbow, in that all the spectral colors could be seen in the exhaust plume. The roar was lovely, too, for such a small motor. And when he could tear his eyes away from the motor, Paul could see great clouds of steam belching from their exhaust scrubber. They'd gone for a full charge of fluorine, and the run lasted for about ninety-six seconds. When it finally died, with a sort of reverse of the starting sequence, there was absolute quiet in the control room. Then suddenly there was shouting and clapping...hands against hands, against backs, even faces. And damn if that Kinzer guy wasn't lousing up his eyes, just like the rest of them.

Russ finally turned to Paul and said simply, "That just might get you a gooblah—*first class*." The eyes filled out a lot between these two, and Paul silently accepted the mantle of a *gooblah man*.

The people at IC had nursed their charges along well, too, and Paul and Russ had some good data to show the Director and a few dozen other people around the world of propulsion.

There were other tests, some with different brides for fluorine. On one of these, a small leak developed in the liquid fluorine circuit. *Wisps* of fluorine vapor drifted to some asbestos insulation nearby. The reaction made cracks like a bullwhip...and if that doesn't make good gooseflesh, nothing will. In some quarters, asbestos is held to be a last ditch bulwark against the perils of this world. Here...it was just a convenient and tasty snack for an aggressive eater. On another one, Paul smelled fluorine just after he'd taken the fluorine tank to firing pressure. There wasn't anything he could do about that damn gas coupling to the control room, so he took it, and that was the first good shot to his nose, courtesy fluorine. A liquid fluorine line gasket failed on another test. Before Paul could give up his emergency action at the control console, a cloud of fluorine had drifted over the control room. Paul shouted at the crew to get out. Before he got out, the inside of his nose was coated with bloody mucous, and his odor perception had dropped a couple notches forever.

That was about it. He and Russ collaborated on several meaty reports on the program, and they held a few more gooblahs in their satchels. But his moment had come when he saw that pencil of white turn into a rainbow for the first time and heard that rainbow evolve that steady roar that pulled up the hackles on his neck. The rest was anticlimax. He'd had much to do with the realization of a chemical fury—and beauty—no other pair of chemicals on Mendelyeev's Table of Periodicity could match. He sensed that his God usually granted only one peak like this to a man...and he would move the proof along on that one.

9

Some of the guys in Chemistry had rubbed off on him...a lot had rubbed off on him during his sojourn in that crazy house that was PAG, and Chemistry was the padded cell for the more violent cases. As a bloke named Sabatini had said, they'd given him the gift of laughter...shown him the utility of the light—sometimes outrageous—heart even in the arenas of science. They'd also given him the incentive for the credentials that Russ had said were absolutely essential for the serious acquisition of gooblahs, namely, the PhD. There had been more of the horseplay about Paul's decision. And he'd told them to stick it up their butts if they didn't like it and it wasn't any of their damn business. But it *was* their business. They'd partly activated this mature child of ambition, although acknowledgement on both sides of this effect was obscured by the peculiar language that serviced it.

He'd been accepted for fall entrance at Caltech in the Graduate School. This gave him permission to start a climb that, if he survived it, would bring him to some vistas a PhD shares with no one...the Journal ones included.

He decided to take a little breather and pick up some of his painting and photography again. The past few months had been something of a meat grinder and he felt he deserved some respite. Russ and the other guys had been fighting it a lot longer, but they had responsibilities he didn't have, and he was going to milk that some.

Mary was through her high school teaching chores for that school year. She had received a rather mysterious letter from Martha, asking her to be in Pasadena on a day near the middle of the month. John and Paul had been told to adjust their affairs to accommodate a specific date for a small social occasion. Two days before this date, Mary arrived and Martha hid her at The Huntington. This was her party and she controlled the drama for it. She had also told everyone to wear formal attire. Mary complied with this request with the help of a Huntington shop and Martha's own resources.

On the evening of the party, Martha told Paul that one of her guests was staying at The Huntington and asked him to escort her to the house. Mary hadn't been mentioned, but this request with merely a room number, and the old telepathy, about did it for him. He wasn't surprised to see the Irish beauty who confronted him at the door of her room.

"God help me darlin'...if you ain't the sight to dazzle these eyes."

"And you, sir, I must confess...don't anger me either." He pulled her to him with as much vigor as her formal image could sustain and he tried to kiss her within these constraints. The eyes also tried to work out the complications of this last time apart...a flux that satisfied Paul, and almost Mary. Mary carried a heavier passport to Southern California this time and her now credentials for criticizing this guy in front of her were not as strong as before. Most of this flowed between them for the seconds that their telepathy was working out the proper postures for them...and this work was mostly silent, and the culminating smiles of this exchange seemed to be about equal in weight...just before Mary permitted a copy of his last kiss.

When the maid ushered Paul and Mary into the room of the central fire-place, Martha was already there and she pretended a great show of greeting Mary. Actually, she'd ministered to Mary earlier that evening at the hotel.

Tangled in the various respects of beauty, any man would've had trouble trying to choose between these ladies. John was still fighting his shirt studs and hadn't appeared. When he did, and he saw Mary, Martha was—for an instant— truly sorry that she'd made this surprise for him. John gave something of the reaction to Mary that Paul had seen on the night of Jake's Christmas party...and then he recovered, according to a man who can't compete in his jungle without that talent.

"Mary," John's smile had had some tailoring in that room before, by the same stimulus, "I...I'm awfully glad to see you." He kissed her hand, and Martha made a prayer that she would be able to bring the evening off as she'd intended.

They talked about everything, even, in various combinations, drifting into John's den taking words about legitimate sporting subjects.

Eventually, Martha's Mary appeared with a set of crystal glasses and a magnum of a champagne some Frenchmen had been sorry to see leave France. She maneuvered the butler's cart to a large coffee table near the fireplace which was working beautifully again.

"I must propose a toast." Martha's assumption of the focal point of the room had been quick, graceful, although some of the priors had let it be antici- pated. With a slight hand motion, she established an axis between John and the impatient magnum. The filling offices done, Martha picked up her glass.

Had her company a better perspective of her, they would've seen a complicated collaboration between slightly moistened eyes and almost aggressive firelight. What they couldn't see was an encyclopedia—whose present authors happened to be in that room. She kept this flux of unplanned, largely unseen, emotion to the briefest possible span—a victory over this encyclopedia. When she turned to them, smile and eyes now unfettered, she was ready for them.

"Here's to *us!*"

Sometime before that evening, Mary had made John accept some of the logic Martha had forced on Paul. Martha had sensed Mary's work with the same intuition she'd always used to discover what was keeping John from enjoying his bourbon, or the big strawberries.

"And to assure that this evening will not deteriorate into less than we have—right now, I have several specific suggestions: For one, I propose that Mary and I use the coming summer to improve our knowledge of whatever pleases us in Europe." Both John and Paul knew that such a curriculum could have awesome scope. "For the other, I propose that you two brutes do take yourselves to the places of the billed ones...and proceed to such execution as you are men enough to do—for as long as you can stand it." The final suggestion hit the men right between the eyes...both the subject matter, and the shock values Martha had put into it.

If Paul's bad spirit, sprite, had also visited Martha, this lady would have suffered none of its intimidation, and she'd just given it its *coup de grâce* as far as this congregation was concerned. Her communion that night...with its resulting fission into two ostensibly unisexual adventures...might have been another aberration of conventional behavior, but it also protected a precious remainder of friendship, and good vantage points for comprehensive steps into the future—let the conservatives tangle with that as they please.

Panama had been too slow to hold them for long. Eventually, they came to the town of Cabo Blanco on the Peruvian coast...a coast washed by the great upwelling of the Pacific that brings food for fish, that are food for fish that are for kings...the swordfish of the broadbill.

After settling themselves in modest diggings, they looked up a gentleman named Francisco Gomez. Señor Gomez was a fisherman. He was the kind of fisherman to whom men from New York and London and Paris and Madrid often looked to for help in bringing them to the one with the broadbill...a request that frequently left them incapable of enjoying the full panorama of their clubs for a few days after Señor Gomez had rendered his services. He did this whenever he felt that a little play on the water wouldn't compromise his other agendas, that included some commercial fishing, a little guiding of the more adventuresome tourists, and some work in the cantinas up and down the coast that helped them realize just enough profit to keep them smiling.

"Señor Drake...I am happy to see you."

"Francisco...it's been too damn long." John exchanged grips that gave him a wince he was barely able to keep inward.

"Francisco...this is my friend, Paul Sanger. He's made the mistake—several times—of saying that he likes to eat swordfish." John's grin swept over both Paul and Francisco. Paul also found that grip needed all he could put into it.

"To eat it...one must perform the little office of *catching* it." He'd answered John, but he looked at Paul. "He looks like he might be capable of a good chair dance." No one explained that remark.

Paul studied this man. He was almost as tall as John, but his muscular development was more extensive. His face bore much sun intensification of a naturally dark complexion. A drooping, black moustache, thickly structured eyebrows, were complemented by a mouth and eyes that gave Paul the funny feeling that he was looking into the face of another Francisco, the one they called Pizarro. Those eyes told that they could bring joy to a woman and fear to a man—probably in quick succession on propitious occasions.

"You are accommodated?"

"We've found humble quarters," John replied, his hand resting on Francisco's shoulder.

"Good. Now let us talk of swordfish and tequila...not necessarily in that order." He led them into a recess, a dark transition from strong sunlight and eventually it opened to a barroom with a few tables, some sleepy customers and bottles to match.

"It is not the good season, compadre...it has been slow...as you say. But we will try." The word *compadre* didn't come easily to this man. And if you didn't hear it after you had been on the water with him for a few hours, you were in some trouble...that is, your capacity for coming to grips with the billed ones was seriously diminished. Francisco turned toward the bar and commanded a large bottle of tequila and three glasses.

After several rounds of the unsubtle flame that is tequila, they were talking about fishing adventures that included John's hereabouts, and some of Paul's definitely not hereabouts, more modest accomplishments. This man's appraisal of the young one was carefully casual. Apparently he saw some of what it would take if they came to the pass of trial.

"Give me a couple days to make some preparations," Francisco said to them after they'd left the cantina. John knew that these preliminaries would include a careful overhaul of such boat equipment as needed it, and a thorough checking and refurbishing of weapons that were the barest essentials for combat.

They used this respite in hiking around the country, poking into ruins, and ogling the señoritas and señoras who weren't too bashful around these handsome gringos.

Finally, Francisco came to them and told them that they would take a little ride and to meet him at his boat at dawn.

They took a little ride. They took little rides every day for seven days, rides that pulled them thirty miles into the Pacific and which, in aggregate, burned them almost as dark as Francisco. They'd seen a few tails and dorsals, but Francisco—over John's protests—had refused them. Paul had been seasick the first two days, but now he felt he could take anything Mother Pacific could hand him.

That night in the cantina, they had been very quiet over the drinks. Even a guitar buried in shadows couldn't do much for them. Finally, Francisco decided that his friends' eyes had burned enough holes in the knife-scarred table in front of them.

"Tomorrow is a feast day, compadres." His voice didn't do much for John, or Paul, either. "It is the feast of Santa Teressa."

"Never heard of her," John mumbled, but he managed to lift his eyes for a quick look at his disgustingly cheerful friend.

"She is a...*local* saint." Some quality of Francisco's voice did it. John and Paul both looked at him, not with eyes a sparkle, but they looked at him. That grin, unveiling white teeth, told them that this Teressa might be a saint to some men, but the local padres would argue about that.

"I think we've seen your...saint," John said to him. He used a small grin that pulled some of Paul into it.

"We often invoke her...aid...in times of some stress and...urgency." There was no question about this business now. "I will pray to her...that we may come to the one we seek."

"When?" John asked. Paul's unspoken same word piggybacked on John's.

"Tonight." Both John and Paul knew that a strong invocation on their behalf would be offered up that night.

They had driven for four hours over the blue hills. Both John and Paul were lying on their backs, trying to shade their eyes. Francisco was driving as usual and he continually scanned the hills for signs many men couldn't see if they traveled this way for a lifetime with a telescope.

John was turning onto his belly, and Paul was thinking about another cold Carte Blanca. Francisco's voice came to them both...perhaps a little stronger to John. It was timbre, not volume, that caused both men to rise...and with that sense that is sometimes born among companions their eyes found the same spot on the blue, slightly whited surface of their highway.

"*Madre de Dios,*" Francisco said again, "that tail...that dorsal."

They could see it. About two hundred yards off the quarter of their stern, they saw two black objects slowly moving through what appeared to be a small cloud of sea birds playing on the water. The birds were playing at the serious game of scooping up small fish that jumped and skimmed over the water in frank terror. The two objects were the dorsal and tail of a fish that seemed to give a great span between these pieces of equipment. These fins would occasionally move more swiftly in various directions, but they didn't appear to be excited by the ballet of the birds and the fish.

"My God, Francisco—the *size* of him!" John cried.

"That...my young compadre...is the *one* we seek." Francisco's quick look at Paul's face furnished the rest of the response he needed for the strength and courage he'd just assigned to his boat.

They dropped a teaser back on one line. This large wooden fish replica was structured and maneuvered to do a tantalizing dance a few yards away from a large bait fish. The attachment to the bait consisted of a hook of formidable size, affixed to the bait with an artistry of Francisco's that made the bait move in some semblance to a living, wounded, counterpart of the teaser. The hook was secured to a double-stranded wire leader of some twenty feet in length. This leader was attached to a heavy linen line that eventually ran over roller guides of a heavy rod to a Fin-Nor reel. The rod rested in a quick release bracket. Before the line could take an ocean swim, it was forced to detour to an outrigger that held it fifteen, or twenty feet above the water, and about the same distance away from the boat. The outrigger could release the line on command from man, or fish.

Francisco had made some maneuvers that brought the teaser to a near collision course with the present track of the billed one. The chair was ready for a guest. Paul bowed slightly, and moved his hand in an arc that connected John and the chair. John hesitated—just a moment—and then with a leg that La Pompadour would have accepted, oriented between Paul and the chair, he said, "Let's see what *you* can do—bully boy." Over Paul's sincere protests, they strapped him into the chair.

"He comes! He comes!" Francisco cried. And he *did* come. Passing the teaser insolently, he struck the bait with his great sword that Paul now saw for the first time.

"Give him slack now, Paul," someone said to him, very quietly and deliberately, and Paul moved the clutch lever that threw the complicated reel mechanism into free spool.

They waited for seconds whose length had originality for Paul. It was so quiet that a sudden pulse of sound from the sea birds almost deafened them. And then this arrogance, this power, decided that one more little snack might just round out his morning of gourmandizing, and he took the bait. The outrigger snapped, and Paul felt the first handshake of the tension.

"Hit him! Por Dios, hit him...with *all* the strength in you!" Francisco cried. And Paul hit him. Throwing the drag lever, he heaved once, twice, three times... with all he had, and at that time it was pretty good.

There was nothing for a few seconds. Christ, this was just like hooking one of those big catfish in the Iowa sloughs. Nothing. Then the thought occurred to one of the participants that there was some insolence here to be disposed of quickly and he shook his head...once, twice, three times, four times...swinging his sword in an arc that Bayard would have envied. And then he came out of the water in a leap that showed his full length to the men of the boat. His body was an undulation of silvery power for the second before he exploded a big piece of the Pacific.

Then he decided that a little stroll with the insolence might be good. He took great chunks of line from the reel with a speed that frightened Paul, and that *is* the right word here. He took one hundred, two hundred, three hundred yards of the precious stuff and then he decided that some depth would be fine and he made the first of the sounds that would put good teeth into the trial.

For two hours, Paul, worked with his friend...the most thrilling contact of his life. He could see the broadbill trophy...even a photograph. And then his friend decided that simple pulling at depths that ranged from the surface to five hundred feet wasn't enough exercise so he started to jump again...great leaps that four, or five in succession could claim over a hundred yards of travel.

"Drop your tip! Drop your tip! Try to anticipate his jumps!" someone cautioned. Anticipate his jumps? Hell, he was just along for the ride. He couldn't anticipate his friend any more than he could Etna, or Krakatoa. His friend had pulled his arms and back and legs so that they were now calling on resources they'd never used. But it was just a beginning for this young whippersnapper who had affronted one. And this one would tease him a little more before getting down to business.

Paul was tired. He complained to them, and they laughed at him.

"Our little baby needs milk, Francisco," John said to the man of the chair and to the one in control of the boat—but he was closer with his words to the chair man who would soon need sustenance he could pull from anywhere. John had dipped into some of what was just beginning here, but from his looks at what was on the other end of Paul's line he knew his bow to Pompadour, and to Paul, conveyed more then any of his precedence could handle.

"I will see if I can find some...also I will look for rattles." At that time, Francisco wouldn't have left either his controls, or his quick reconnoiters of the chair situation, for the most beautiful señorita who ever wagged her butt at him in Lima.

"God...I...I can't hold him." Paul's words had come through clenched teeth and with eyes that were starting to show some of the sweetness of distress. They laughed at him and he cursed them and the fish and himself. Mostly, it must be said, the curses curled back on himself. And their taunts continued to dredge up resource for him.

But this was an ungrateful guest in the chair. He really had nothing to complain about. Besides the abuse they were feeding him, his thoughtful hosts also'd had the foresight to provide two kinds of drink for him. One of these was a dilute wine that, with a bota, John—sometimes Francisco—would try to feed to the moving target of his mouth, mostly without conspicuous success. The other was water, by the bucketful, that they dumped on him to cool him and his reel. These amenities he'd rather enjoyed in the early stages. The water had given him some resuscitation, and the baby wine he could tolerate. Now...he cursed the wine and he also tried to push away the water that was bringing him the bitterness of salt more frequently from sources on his head and elsewhere. The slaver that streamed from the corner of his mouth was now showing flecks of blood from local battles his lips and gums were losing to his teeth. He was a very unappreciative guest.

There were another two hours...hours sustained for him by less rabid insults, but there were still frequent aspersions about his manhood, his way with women, the delicate beauty of his woman's mouth and eyes. These eyes were now showing only pure desperation. He'd called on his arms and legs and back and they'd answered him in the way the pillars answer the overburdening mass of Notre Dame.

And then, almost five hours after his former friend had decided to play, there were some signs, very slight, that the end of the coupling that was only pain—the end opposite Paul—was showing some real concern. Paul didn't know them, but John and Francisco did. In the past several hours, Paul had used both external and internal supplications to keep him a man in front of these two.

Long after it became as dark as that latitude and season would permit, they saw the double leader in the light that John held. It was still, perhaps, fifty yards away, but it was there, and the two faces of this company that were still outward bound looked at it in the way good men have always looked when some opportunity struts inside a thin slice of time.

Paul was in a state of near collapse, his head on his chest. He was just trying to hold a position he'd despaired of many times in the last minutes. He had worked the billed one close to the boat. This had required an effort he could *never* recognize as his own.

"Can you get to the tail?" John yelled hoarsely at Francisco.

"I will try." John knew that if an effort *could* be made, this man would do it.

And then the billed one called on *his* God. With a great heave and twist of his body—and eyes that seemed to look at everyone on that boat—he worked his sword between the boat and the leader and he broke the torment he'd shared with Paul.

Francisco stood transfixed with disbelief, and John supported him in this. Francisco held the broken strand in his hands, staring at it. And then he held the end of the game in such a way as a supplicant might have presented beads to a passing priest of Incas. He came to Paul's collapsed form in the chair and down on his knees he put an arm around Paul.

"You *beat* him, compadre...as the good God is witness to me—you *beat* him."

And then this damn fool, this sun blackened, sea drenched, Pizzaro face was crying. And if tears were good enough for Don Francisco Gomez at that time, they were plenty good enough for John and Paul. When the moon finally broke out of its shroud of scud clouds, there wasn't a scene on the Pacific more deserving of tears...or laughter. But a lot of men would've tended to tears.

They told Francisco that they would rest for a little while before traveling on the blue hills again. He laughed at them and called them babies who couldn't take a little exercise without total collapse. But he understood and his eyes argued with his words.

When they did come to the hills again, this time, after two hours of search, John assumed the chair of torment. And he called on others many times himself before, three hours later, they boated a broadbill that pulled the beam at 690 pounds.

"It's a nice *minnow*," Francisco said. His best grin was on him and he was looking up at some twelve, or thirteen feet of broadbill. They took pictures that got everybody in the act.

Just before getting on the bus that would start their steps away from Cabo Blanco, Francisco came to them, carrying a long package under one arm.

They made him open it. It was a very well carved, and painted, replica of a broadbill's sword. And it was as close to the look and size of Paul's tormentor's as Francisco could remember. He'd had it made by a local craftsman who had labored under ball peril if it wasn't right...and on time.

"You children must have your toys," he said to Paul. Paul held it up like a lance, gripping it near the middle of its length. John grabbed it near Paul's hand...then Francisco's joined them. D'Artagnan would have understood this.

They went to Argentina for landlocked salmon, and then on to Tierra Del Fuego for sea-run browns. After some battles with various salt water species off Brazil, they were ready to come home. There'd been none of Paul's design in this piscatorial odyssey. Martha had recognized its potential for adding fishing line to the threads of the tapestry she was resolved to weave between the Drakes and the Sangers. John and Francisco had been her co-conspirators in this and Providence had placed the great billed one in Paul's path in such a way as to leave durable threads in this tapestry between John and himself.

Martha and Mary had preceded them by a week. These ladies had fulfilled John and Paul's most concerned speculation about itinerary. Mary couldn't decide which ensemble she would wear for any number of fascinating occasions. Martha had done very well in this department, too. This component of their adventure had brought joy to couturiers from London to Milan to Madrid.

When the gladiators finally staggered in with their load of gear and trophies, there was some very free kissing all around. These two characters looked liked Francisco's more affluent brothers. They both sported moustaches, for a while. The ladies had liked them until they had a better feeling for their secondary effects. Paul would leave his sideburns a little longer and there was consensus that they did do a little something for him. He knew they did more than that, and he saw Francisco in his mirror for a long time afterwards.

That night before the fireplace, the men enacted some of their combats. Paul held them for a long time with his description of his great battle...as much as he could remember of it, and John filled in the rest. There was laughter, and then some tears came again at the end of it. They showed the sword of Francisco and after it had been passed around, it was taken to John's den—at Paul's insistence—and placed alongside the other swordfish trophies. For some reason, John wouldn't place his latest acquisition there, but he would sneak it in later. Looking at Paul's sword, it didn't take anyone's bragging to know that this was an unnatural, but acceptable, vestige of senior combat.

The ladies had gifts for the men, and these were properly admired. In their turn, the ladies enthused over the shawls and native jewelry the men had brought from South America. Fortunately, they'd had the foresight to use the airport shops in Miami to good advantage. John had secured sets of tortoise shell combs with silver and gold embellishment. Paul had come up with some good French perfume. The ladies insisted he smell it. He made a good show of it although, thanks to his old friend fluorine, he had to use some of his actor.

This company had managed to find paths that had given fairly equitable shares in the totality of the adventure. Mary would find the confines of Mason City a little too restrictive for her now, and John and Martha were sensitive to this. They made suggestions to her, and she listened. By the strangest coincidence, John found that one of the better private schools in Manhattan needed a teacher with just Mary's competence. She was delighted with the opportunity. After John and Martha and Paul had assured her that they would be bothering her in New York, and points west, they let her go.

Paul decided that his coming trials at Caltech would require more resources for concentration than he could find at the carriage house. He located a small apartment near the school that appeared to be adequate for what would be a near monastic devotion for—at least—three years. John and Martha understood this logic and helped him make the change with a minimum of strain for all concerned.

When he left the carriage house for the last time, he couldn't identify any particular thought, emotion. It had been a dream of travel through brightness and some shadows. The shadows hadn't claimed him. Nor did he feel that...on balance...he'd been diminished by them. But he owed his traveling companions a deep bow.

BOOK TWO

Into the Dreams

10

In the fifties decade, The California Institute of Technology was a quiet place. One would have to look a little to find much ivy, and the total holding of that stuff wouldn't have impressed many Eastern schools. Generally, the buildings didn't make gasps from foreign, or local, architects who happened, on one pretext or another, to venture into the grounds. It was, in short, a very modest assembly of buildings devoted to classrooms, laboratories, seminars, and administration. And these amenities were, and are, held in about that order of importance. It was modest. But it was enough to draw physicists, chemists, biologists and engineers from all the world to this humble cluster. Quite a few of these people had given the Nobel Foundation an excuse for a ceremony it holds annually...an affair whose fruit Russ had referred to as the *ultimate gooblah*—with embellishment.

It didn't take Paul long to get into it. The necessary forms had been ac-complished quickly. They, and he, had decided that his background in physics and chemistry wasn't sufficient to allow him to regard either of these disciplines as his major target...targets yes, but not his major one. The wonderfully varie-gated world of mechanical engineering appeared to beckon most strongly to him and he didn't resist this call, or the advice of his CIT authorities.

The PhD isn't dangled in front of a student upon stepping into Graduate School. There is, at least in the halls Paul frequented, a presumption of enough intelligence, ambition and fortitude to persevere to the Master's. If there aren't enough of these things in him, it will be found out before even this milestone is reached. If there *is* a reasonable basket of these things, and it doesn't bring too many frowns to too many faces that covertly and quite overtly scan his action, then the program leading to the PhD may assume more palpable shape. *Program* implies nothing more than continued surveillance, continued posing of drive and motivation and progress before virtually the same set of eyes and ears.

Paul was one of the older ones now, perilously close to the end of his twenties. That this circumstance never really bothered him could be attributed to several factors: the scattering of fellow veterans who were also using the GI Bill, the presumably more serious mien of post WWII Graduate School, and his auditing of the course in instant insanity conducted by Herr Professors Myron, George, Harry and Russ at PAG which held him up on those occasions where some frivolity was irresistible.

It had been six years since he'd engaged a formal regimen of classrooms, laboratories and homework. It took him some time to get the hang of it again. Russ had a few more months to go at PAG. When he came back to the campus, it would be to Chemistry. Gruif also would shortly abandon the smoke and fire of PAG in favor of more gentile situations at Mechanical Engineering. This was fortunate for Paul. These men, many more like them, would give him the occasional goose he needed to keep going. They would scare him—but they would keep him going.

He took a few papers to his apartment on San Pasqual of a night. Sometimes, near one, or two, in the morning, when that vibrations problem Hudson had said was a matter of minutes was still staring at him, he thought he'd never seen a paper mountain so big. And when it wasn't vibrations, it was physical chemistry, or statistics, or metal science, or metallurgy lab, or some economics. He never aspired to penetrate very far into the latter mystery. But once, when his econ professor told him that he'd damn near thrown caution to the winds and given him a B, instead of the C he got, he felt that this close brush with compassion reflected favorably on that discipline.

He enjoyed the mechanical engineering laboratory. One of the men who presided over this area had a Greek name, and the Greek talent for inspiration. Kyropolous was tall, thin, with a shock of black hair that resisted any tendency to order. He was ubiquitous. He would pop up over a double orifice system Paul and his lab partner were studying, with eyes and a few concise questions that tended to intensify concentration. He liked his infernal combustion machines and he would run them at top speed to challenge them to reveal their secrets to him. This noise kept some of the boys up the wall, but you knew where Kyropolous was...possibly. He was clever in handling the boys. On more than one occasion, a relaxation inspired by the roar of machinery would be shattered by a quick flash of that face. Eventually, he succumbed to the lure of one of the automobile companies, who—in this instance, at least—knew a damn good thing when they saw it, to the detriment of CIT and the students.

The father of this young disciplinarian, the senior Kyropolous, as a Research Associate was rounding out a career that had seen Berlin University and Göttingen. He'd known Planck and Born and Prandtl and Tiejtens and Von

Karman and his stories about some of these men spilled plenty of respect, and laughter, on Paul. From these talks, he found that other men had subscribed to the technique of a light heart interwoven with purpose—and apparently some of these guys could've shown Paul and Tom how a seduction *should* be handled. The profile of a genuine top man—scientist, engineer, entrepreneur... for examples, seemed to keep close to the *well rounded* man according to Kyropolous and Paul's own indoctrination so far.

Once, when Paul was studying for his German exam, he was sitting across a table from the senior Kyropolous in the chemistry library. After studying a passage of the wonder that is technical German, he succumbed to the lure of the German expert within easy grab. Paul pushed the book across the table, with the request for some clarification of a passage. After this man—who'd heard Born and Planck lecture at Göttingen and Berlin, and made some noises himself at these places—had given the passage a good look, he pushed it back on a quicker return trip, saying, "I *think* it means this..." That made Paul feel better, if not more confident about the German exam.

There were many good men in Mechanical Engineering, none, in fact, that any university in the world wouldn't have been happy to grab. One of these was a short, no nonsense gentleman who, besides being called Professor, was also called *Doc* by the boys. Doc's technique for reducing a snotty freshman to more palatable stuff was something to behold. Paul was damn glad his trajectory hadn't crossed Doc's until now. He would plaster his blackboards with phase diagrams...two and three dimensional. When the fury tended to subside toward the end of the hour, more than an average number of his students in physical metallurgy had more than an average idea of what Doc had been talking about. God help the unfortunate who left one of Doc's metallographs in less than mint condition, or his dark rooms sloppy. Paul damn near cut off the tip of a finger with a large paper cutter in a darkroom. It wasn't Doc's fault, he wasn't even in the building at the time. But Paul had been brooding—for a millisecond, or two—about a cutting remark Doc had made about Paul's ability to keep a metallograph in proper humor.

And there was a gentleman who usually turned his head if someone shouted *Cubb!* Paul was privileged to come to this man early in his sojourn in Mechanical Engineering. He was from Boston, had taken his degree at MIT, and was a top man in the broad classical respects of the PhD, and the layman. Cubb knew about metal physics, diffusion, and he tried on many formal—and informal—times to hammer some of this into Paul. He also subscribed to the philosophy of laughter. He told Paul a story about rolling down the steps of the castle at Heidelberg, after some fluid mechanics experiments that used wine instead of water, that tended to confirm Paul's suspicion. One of Cubb's hobbies was gardening. He had his place in the hills above La Canada so plastered with stuff of green and aromas and spines and general tentacles that you were lucky to get to his door without something grabbing you. And Cubb liked Paris.

Another who liked Paris, was Gruif. When he finally decided the noise at PAG was too much, he came to Mechanical Engineering. By virtue of an experience that comprehended an astonishing interest and accomplishment in materials science—metallic and nonmetallic—and a devotion to these things that could be awesome if the problem happened to be interesting enough, he was the senior member of the group that would be the focal point for Paul's work at CIT. He'd worked with Gruif a little at PAG. One of their collaborations resulted in the first demonstration that hydrogen, fed through a porous metal combustion chamber, or nozzle, was an excellent coolant for high performance rockets. They hadn't given this concept the challenge of fluorine, but neither Gruif, nor Paul, had doubted that it would've worked. Gruif's competence was the attraction for men who came from Washington, and other citadels of power to see him. And sometimes he reciprocated the pleasure: to Rome, London, Vienna...and Paris.

These were a few of the men Paul was to confront many a time and oft during his CIT days. He often thought about that time coming into the valley when he saw the T on the mountain above Pasadena. That he'd actually attained this place still needed some sinking in...attained in the sense of a kid with a horn being allowed into Carnegie Hall with the advice that some of the musicians might give him a little time...if he showed enough precocity and stamina.

The new apartment wasn't bad. It was tolerable. All he really needed was a bed and a desk and a bathroom, and he seemed to use the desk more than the other facilities. His military service had entitled him to a graduate education at Government expense, and a very modest living allowance. This wasn't enough to cover him, but he had resources to sustain him for about a year. Then...he might have to write his parents a business letter.

He saw Tom fairly frequently. This character was up to his ears in missiles now. He and Paul had many long talks about the military philosophy and the military commitment and what—to Paul, at least—was the military preoccupation of the country. The days of twang the bowstrings and work the siege engines, and then retreat for drinks and do it again the next morning if the weather was okay, had been over for a long time. Paul had looked into the throat of the V2, and he knew as much about nuclear weapons as any reasonably intelligent layman could know. The two made a very unpleasant conjunction. And now they were building carriers that dwarfed the V2 in size and sophistication, and not without the help of some of the fathers of the V2. There was *this* fact, and the one of the commitment to the principle that—until somebody came up with a good deterrent—the more the better as regards nuclear teeth for these carriers. There were many at CIT who had contributed to this arsenal and to the only application of the nuclear power of it near the end of WWII. This had been a wartime enterprise and action that would be argued until Armageddon, or its alternatives. Paul couldn't condemn any participant in this arena. He'd been ready to go into Japan for the final battle. From what Allied observers and intelligence could construct from the evidence of defense preparations all over Japan…and from the temper of the Japanese stamped on American graveyards all over the Pacific—above and below it—it was possible that Americans would have died by the hundreds of thousands if the invasion alternative had been chosen. The memorials of Hiroshima and Nagasaki notwith-standing, there was no living man who could claim he held the unequivocal answer to these bombs at *that* time. There were some, whose careers had been brought to fullest luster by the Manhattan Project, who decried the decision that was made. This atti-tude was quite safe now, and it tended to popularity in lay circles that had never looked into Japanese armament—and resolve—at ranges that were closing. There were no constraints now such as two million men can bring.

But this was history. Paul's questioning of the technical emphasis of the day got an infusion of vitality every time the smog burden of his air made some new arrogance of intrusion. From what he'd seen at Stanford, and from his Caltech vantage, there seemed to be a technology capable of coming to grips with this insult to humanity…a gentleman over in Bel Air also had some new perspective on this subject.

11

"Weeee!" she said. The non-integral parts of her were a vision of the best that Abercrombie & Fitch could provide. She wore a vest and shirt and pants and waders and wading shoes...the all having just the barest patina of respectable use. She was using a Winston rod, about 4.5 ounces, 8.5 feet. This was attached to a torpedo head, sinking line, a tapered nylon leader of some ten feet in length, and thence to a number 8 Allcock hook arrayed in the splendor called Royal Coachman by certain people of a fraternity not famous for honesty.

The inspiration for this unladylike behavior was a sizeable female steelhead that had just made the sometimes fatal mistake of gourmandizing on exotic fare in a riffle at the head of a long pool. The tantalizing waters called Trinity was where it was happening. The lady in the water had just made another of her jumps and the sunlight caught the faint redness along her broad sides. Martha had been enjoying this stimulation for only several minutes. Fifteen minutes later, she was showing some sweat under that cute hat, and she was also showing some impatience at the efforts of her male companions to help her.

"Hell...I wouldn't interfere in this for all the swordfish off Cabo Blanco," John said, from a very relaxed, supine position a few yards upstream from Martha.

"I'm inclined to support you in this particular matter," Paul announced from his position of almost equal indolence, not far from John. Actually, he was watching the course of Martha's line rather carefully and hoping that the other lady wouldn't decide to take some invigoration in the fast water downstream of Martha.

Her Hardy reel screamed its raucous song. Paul had always found this *song of the reel* to be damn annoying—Hardy advertisements and hundreds of sportswriters to the contrary. He'd removed the drag from his Zenith and substituted a Teflon element that gave him a very light drag—and *no* noise. He also found that his percentage of caught steelhead and salmon went up when he used this virtually drag-free reel. You had to watch the overrunning, but with practice and an agile finger against the spool flange, this was no handicap, and it had saved him many times when a run erupted with a powerful fish in charge.

"Martha...keep your tip up...try to put a little more pressure on her," Paul called.

"I can't...do a thing...with this *her*—as you call this beast!" She almost stumbled with a backward maneuver. Her had taken all of Martha's fly line and was now taking big bites of her backing as well. There is no such person as a *jaded*, shore-walking, steelhead flyfisher. The shocking obstacles to success a good river can put into the game along with the power and talent of a healthy, sizeable, steelhead, don't permit such a person.

"You're doing beautifully," John finally shouted, in decent encouragement. "You *must* tell us how it comes out...we'll be down at Douglas City having a drink." That did sound like a damn good idea.

"You'd do it too—wouldn't you," Martha just barely said, as her got more inventive and combined an interesting tail action with a leap that could've broken Martha's leader if she hadn't dropped her tip. Finally, after many more minutes that saw a good measure of Martha's expert handling, a surfeit of advice, and the measure of the pure luck that always attends the capture—via classical fly rod technique—of any fresh run steelhead by a shore-mounted angler, Martha led her to a sand bar that, mercifully, was reasonably flat and unobstructed.

"For Christ's sake—walk back and keep the angle of your line flatter!" John didn't show any emotion.

"That's better...keep the pressure on her—not too much, for God's sake!" Paul yelled, not showing any emotion, either. "Thaaat's it...and now...I'll get behind her—*got* her!" Paul tailed the beautiful fish and held it up for all the world to see. With the sun doing its bit, the natural qualities of the steelhead, it *was* a sight no one should miss.

Martha walked over to Paul, pushing her nosey husband out of the way, and held her own fish.

"Not bad," Paul said, looking at the steelhead, then at John. "Whaaaadah ya say...about five pounds?"

"God man—you do have a tendency for exaggeration, don't you. I...I couldn't go a pound over *nine*, myself." With that slowly developed accolade, Martha had to kiss them...first John, then a peck for Paul.

"Want t'keep her?" Paul asked the beautiful disciple of Nimrod. He'd never seen her in action against the billed ones, but the exhilarated, sun-filled, complexion of a classic victory mode on her for this instance filled out a lot of this absence for him.

"With the two you characters stole out of that fish truck...that would make one too many." With that, Martha brought the other lady back to her environment...moving her back and forth until she showed good recovery, and then released her. Paul had been active with his camera throughout most of this.

That called for some rest for Martha. Actually, the men had about had it for that day, too. They'd covered more yards of water, mud and rocks than they cared to remember before John, and then Paul, struck the gold that is steelhead. It had been a better than average day and everyone was pooped... very pleased with themselves, but pooped, as befits an honest steelheader.

John pulled a silver flask from one of his many pockets and offered it to Paul. About halfway in its journey, the flask was intercepted, and the hand and arm attached to it started to do justice to it through lips that were dry, and down a throat that needed lubrication.

"For Christ's sake don't kill it—there're *other* critical cases here." John's polite request prolonged Martha's sampling.

After the excitement had simmered down, John looked at Paul. "How goes the battle of the student?"

"This expedition was needed sustenance...believe me." Paul rubbed his chin and played his eyes across the source of some of the voices of the Trinity.

"How'n hell are you going to hold out for at least two more years?"

"John...that's none of your business." Martha removed her hat, and shook her hair into a less confined array.

"I'm used to his damn insolence." Paul grinned at John, threw his hat next to Martha's and settled back on the greensward. "Uncle Sam takes care of the schooling, a little of the rest...I can hold out for another year."

"And?" John persisted.

"That'll be history, some day."

"I'm interested in the future."

"I don't know...exactly, right about now." He rubbed his arm against an oak, plucked a piece of wild grass and stuck it in his mouth. Martha made him give her a straw like it, then John followed suit—and if that wasn't a bunch of hay seeds *avec les fly rods*. No one said anything, they just watched the ballet between the light and the Trinity, and listened to the infinite voices of a great river.

"You guys don't want to give any more battle—*do* you," Paul finally said.

"This boy has had it," John admitted.

"This girl—if you'll pardon the flattery—has also had it."

"This is...disgusting." But Paul was the van on the way to the Continental on the bluff behind them.

After they'd cleared the pass from Weaverville and were past Redding, headed for places like Pasadena, they gradually assumed more serious conversation...like...did Martha put *all* her gear in the car. Her Winston rod, and its ancillaries, was critical baggage.

"Coast, or inland, Martha?" the pilot asked the navigator. Paul was piloting again.

"Let's pick up the coast as *soon* as possible." No argument there. Except for the charming hamlets, of course, there is no more dismal stretch of California than that between Sacramento and the Ridge Route if you go right down the middle.

"Want to stay in San Fran?" John asked the navigator.

"That always costs you too much money." Martha's laugh was the kind a successful steelheader is prone to use.

"Please help with the specifics," the pilot asked.

"The Inn at Paso Robles is a good specific. Let's shoot for that and stay the night...I think I once heard Paderewski's ghost playing the piano in the old dining hall." Martha had nailed that specific down.

In the small amount of serious conversation that squeezed into the mostly unserious quality of that day, John once mentioned, very casually, the possibility of Paul's pulling some part-time work at Drake Instruments. Paul had thought about this more than the subsequent talk suggested.

Martha's insistence on feeding her companions when they arrived at Arden road had to be pushed back on the schedule. They had stopped at Santa Barbara for a short conference with one of John's business associates. Actually, he wanted to rub some salt into a fellow steelheader. Martha successfully fended off more of their friends' hospitality and they eventually pointed toward Pasadena again.

Paul was ministering to several large steaks over Martha's grill in her kitchen, under the glow of John's insults and Martha's laughter. This occasion was at some variance with another one when only Martha and Paul could smell the magic born of good meat and charcoal. Paul thought about this, several times, while doing his offices. And a nosey intruder of Martha's thoughts would have found that her banter wasn't a true reflection of all of her in those moments, either.

After they'd devoured the steaks, and Martha had furnished them giant strawberries to complete their gorge, they settled back on the couches before the big fireplace and sipped cognac and let the conversation ball bounce where it would.

"Carla coming down for Thanksgiving, Martha?" Paul asked.

"I don't know. She's been very busy—she says. And this *is* her senior year."

"And she'll do very well, I'm sure...right up to that diploma." The fireplace wasn't active, but Paul managed to find some targets for his eyes within its shadows. Finally, he said, "She's a wonderful girl. You and John can't overwork your pride in her...only..." His brandy was a local target for that moment.

"Only *what*?" Martha challenged him, her own glass stopping in mid-passage to her lips.

Paul took some more time, and when he spoke, his voice was softer than before and it tended toward his crystal snifter. "Only she'll need encouragement to make the opposition to convention that's in her."

Now that was a strange remark for anyone to make...certainly someone who—as far as they knew—didn't know their daughter very well. Paul wouldn't have agreed with them.

"You will amplify that remark, sir—more than somewhat," Martha ordered.

Paul tried to obey...somewhat. "She has a feeling for certain limitations of our present approach to poverty and ignorance and some of the things caused by these deficiencies that goes rather beyond her years...her experience."

"I didn't know her waters ran that deeply," Martha replied. She had to make a small smile come along, too. But she *did* know of this in the thousand ways of a woman, and sometimes it had troubled her that Carla should have this maturity, this intrusion of a life at a time that wasn't appropriate for it.

"Paul...what do you think about that little business I mentioned up on the highway?" John had quite a full appreciation of that daughter of his, too, including some perception of an extracurricular depth to her. But he had serviced Carla's part of this conversation with only a smile.

"John...I appreciate your suggestion. I sure as hell could use the money—whatever you pay for legitimate, honest sweat, that is."

"Of course, there'll be no lapse of legitimacy here." John's grin had been getting a lot of practice around Paul that weekend.

"The work at CIT is starting to build. I'll get past the Master's okay...but that's just the preliminary for the main show. I...I don't know how I'm going to make out on that one." He caressed the planes of the crystal with his chin and moved the snifter downward to tap its interior qualities. Then he took a small smile from Martha to John. "I wouldn't want anything to add to my jeopardy." The lower register he'd put in at the last *was* effective.

"Appreciated. But let me tell you what's in my craw on this. You have perspective—you'll have more...of new ideas, new problems, applications. It's difficult to find these things in the rat race for the buck. If you could squeeze in some time for me on this...away from that jeopardy, I'd appreciate it. God damn it!—you *do* owe me something for saving that big brown for you off Tierra Del Fuego."

Paul did owe John a little something...for that big brown, for instance. Before he left that night, he said to John, "I'll give your petition the benefit of what passes for thought here." He tapped his cranium. With that he shot a short left hook to John's belly that stopped short enough. John grimaced and clutched his belly.

"I'll accept that," he said.

Paul thanked Martha and John for the fishing and the rest of the hospitality, and then he said that he'd be seeing them...they said he'd better, and they let him go.

12

Then there was the final scramble up the little hill to the Master's. When he returned from a short Christmas vacation in Iowa, he plunged once more into the math and metallurgy and applied mechanics and the laboratories. The five unit courses wouldn't allow a man much time to dally in the flesh pots that were Pasadena. But he could handle them. It was the damn *two* unit courses that nearly killed him. He never worked, sweated, more over a two unit course than Hudson's on vibrations. He finally surmounted the obstacle presented by that almost cherubic face, but just barely. Thereafter, he was more careful in selecting the smaller unit increments to his knowledge.

Doc had finally despaired of teaching him his standard of deportment in all things. But Paul had picked up some pointers from that man that would stick to his ribs the rest of his life.

Cubb would occasionally murmur something about looking toward the doctorate program...but Paul was too busy worrying about his present program to appreciate the subtle compliment in the way of a Bostonian.

He finally finished several laboratory programs that were the last hurdle to the Master's. He wrote these up. And when the last of them had got its conclusion, he allowed himself a good sigh. Mr. Paul Sanger had achieved a pinnacle that might cause a wink, or two, from some of his authorities. He decided not to attend the ceremonies of formal recognition. He knew he would be uncomfortable among the crowd of much younger faces. He would come to another ceremony one day, if he were man enough to furnish the prerequisites.

Paul took the job at Drake Instruments, telling John, implying to John, that they would play this one by ear, too. After John had introduced him to staff people who would be interacting with him, John and Martha left for New York. While in that hamlet, they visited Mary. And several of the better bistros of that city echoed to a laughter that tended to perturb the local words...but New Yorkers have always had a high tolerance for beautiful women. Mary told them that she loved her teaching job, and it was also evident that at least one poor slob was enduring the agony that is another component of a beautiful woman with some of the devil in her.

Drake's company was interesting to Paul. There was as good a manufacturing facility for instruments as the technology of the day could provide. There was much advertising and sales effort, and there was some research and development dedicated to improving John Drake's posture in the marketplace. That marketplace was still patronized by men of the chemical and petroleum industries, but the aerospace and defense contracts were rapidly becoming the principal sustenance for Drake Instruments. The missiles and weapons systems and nuclear carriers and submarines were gulping great hunks of electronic and optical gear and John Drake, as virtually every man in a comparable situation, wasn't closing his eyes to this federally fed cornucopia. It was assuming the aspects of an explosion of technology, beautiful in some respects, terribly significant in others. But it tended to interfere with the man in the field getting a good look at his plow...or the course of his plow tracks.

Paul worked with some of the people who were most concerned with the chemical industry. The new apparatus for gas analysis was fascinating to him. The gas chromatographs, the rapid firing analyzers of many types that could sample a gas stream and tell on its secrets of carbon monoxide and ozone and the halogens—even his old friend, fluorine. All of this was a close relative of what he'd been talking about with Jake.

Carla graduated from Stanford that June, to no one's surprise. Paul couldn't attend the ceremony, but he was certainly aware of that particular pageant. Before Martha and John left for another venture in the East, and before Carla started out on a European jaunt that was her parents' token of appreciation for services rendered Stanford, and herself, she and Paul had occasion for another talk.

"And now," Paul asked her by the pool, in a question just like the one his father had asked him an age before.

"And now," she said, rolling over on her back and letting the sun have another vantage of her, "I'm going to Europe and flirt outrageously with Englishmen, Frenchmen, Italians..."

"Whooooah! You didn't tell your parents of these base motives. In my ear dropping, I thought you said that you were going over there to improve your mind...to savor some of the inspiration of Rheims and Chartres. By the way, *do* spend some time at Chartres. In that place I felt some of what hit me when I really saw Franz Hals for the first time, in Haarlem." He stopped his tease of her for a few seconds, and then picked it up. "And you were to study many other parts of what is man's glory—too damn seldom." It was easy for his smile to envelope her, and he was aware that this one would tax the fortitude and ingenuity of many of his kind before she was done with them.

"Oh...I'll try to look into some of *that*, too." A laugh rippled at him toward the end of that commitment and then she jumped into the pool and challenged him to beat her to the other end—and back. Later, as they approached the house, Martha saw them from the veranda. Carla said something to him, and he replied with a butt slap and then he ran toward the house, yelling for help.

"Be careful, Paul," Martha said, after Carla had retired to the house to dress, and he had collapsed in a chair near her. "we Drake women don't take provocation lightly." Outwardly, he took this play with the lightness that might have been intended. Privately, from the totality of it, he also took the first signals of a warning.

And then he came to a world whose vistas are somewhat beyond the Master's. It was populated by men with names like Planck, Einstein, Gibbs, Maxwell and Dirac and Brillouin and Bateman and Schrödinger and Tolman and Pauling. He came to Pauling's den in his fall quarter. Unfortunately, he hadn't studied the prerequisites for the course closely enough. But, despite his near failure of it, he never regretted it. Pauling was a great scientist. He was also a great teacher of those with proper credentials. And he was a good actor. That mane would fly about during his lectures, and when the fury and carefully circumscribed laughter of it were over, his *boys* knew that they had seen good drama, and much better exposition of molecular orbitals and bond theory and some other things that had merited one of his ultimate gooblahs.

He came to Verner Schomaker's place, too. This guy, on occasions that usually coincided with the best skiing at Mammoth, or Big Bear, or wherever he went, could be seen hobbling around the campus, sometimes with a crutch. Paul's introduction to the fascinating madness that is statistical mechanics came from him. And from Schomaker he came to know much more about Gibbs, and the wonderful calculus of the saddle-point integration of Fowler and Gugenheim. Schomaker had been known to drag himself up a flight of stairs to bring some poor wretch to a critical peak of competence during a final oral exam. One didn't tend to forget Verner Schomaker.

And there was the math. Paul had always liked this play with paper and pencil. He'd had some exposure to differential equations at Stanford—but this was ridiculous. Those teaching assistants over in Aeronautics never knew when to quit. They'd fill their blackboards several times during an hour and then they had the foresight to provide just enough problems and reading to keep the boys busy during such trivia as occupied them between math classes. This enough reading and problems usually was a major contributor to any redness in Paul's eyes. Why did those mathematicians have such beautiful names...LaPlace, Fourier, LeGendre, D'Lambert...when they brought so much misery? But they also brought enlightenment and beauty to those with eyes to see and the stamina to stand up to them long enough for understanding. He was entranced by the way functions could be approximated and coaxed—even tricked—into behaving themselves so that the complexities of mechanical stability, of elasticity, vibrations, of the continuums of macrostructure, and the periodic wonders of the micro-world that led to the atoms and nuclear particles themselves, could be made more tractable. It was all very beautiful. And in some important respects, it was also something of a little snow job.

One day in operational math, a bright eyed young instructor devoted an entire hour, and most of the next, to an analysis of a vacuum tube circuit. The complexities of this circuit would have made a high school radio buff sneer with disdain. But even the partial analysis of its steady state and transient characteristics required this time. And a fair share of the modern engineer's mathematical apparatus had been invoked during this analysis. When it was done, the instructor *apologized* for not giving a more complete grasp of the thing. If electronics hadn't gone worlds beyond that circuit, the crystal set would still be awesome. It is...but only in nostalgia, thank god.

Paul had had occasion to witness some of this analytical limitation at PAG, thanks to the talk, and sometimes the shouting, of Myron, George, Harry, and even Russ got into it when it was interesting, frustrating enough. He'd known very little about those limits then. Now, some of the real anguish of those sessions was coming to him.

He'd never deny the importance of this edifice of analysis that had been building for millenniums. But with its present ability to portray the *real* world—the transient, nonequilibrium, nonlinear, multibody, multiconstrained, multicomponent *real* world, that awe had some bounds. He'd seen statements attributed to some of the great mathematicians of our age...such as Hardy, which would have us believe that they decried the entrance of men of their caliber into the theatre of practical applications. If truly their opinion, then this is a very great loss to mankind. It will take men like Hardy—and a thousand fold more—before man can look fearlessly into the infinities and infinitesimals that God has wrought without tragedy to himself and his fellow men. While waiting for better knowledge and equipment, men at the perimeters of applied mathematics were bending toward numerical techniques to approach non-linear problems with multiple constraints. Where their increments into the unknown—the differences between solutions of their equations for specific values of the variables and the various dependent derivatives, integrals, and other characteristics of their equations—were small, and the tracks of their solutions managed to avoid the sink-holes of unpredictable instability that litter the *terra incognita* surrounding their largely linear equipment, the numerical tip-toeing could be useful. But, in the main, it was like trying to realize an image of the Mona Lisa from the interference patterns of pebbles tossed into a mill pond of the non-linear real world.

He valued and used much of what he learned from the mathematicians, but his horizon was expanding. One day, he laid a simple sketch on the desk of one of his instructors. It consisted of a metal-sheathed thermocouple inserted into a chamber that was enjoying the affection of a gaseous atmosphere hot enough to require the fourth power radiation transfer law, plus the more prosaic conduction and convection mechanisms, in description of the heat transfer conditions. Paul asked the instructor how Messrs. LaPlace, or Gauss, or LeGendre, or Fourier, or Poisson would have handled the elucidation of the temperature correction for that thermocouple. The look of disgust—or frustration—he got from that instructor he never forgot. What he had posed had been a practical engineering situation close to the borders of simplicity...but it had been of the *real* world.

This limitation has other, more comprehensive implications. If the ability to come to grips with the inconsiderate complexity of reality is so limited, how could the great refineries, the airplanes, the skyscrapers, the bridges, the electric generators, the transmission networks for power have been built with this handicap? They were most certainly there...and so were other examples of man's ability to think and to do...the nuclear reactors, the nuclear bombs, the ICBM's, the agrochemicals, the medicinal chemicals, and all the rest of it. He could never know more than a tiny fraction of the disciplines involved in these creations. But he *would* know that they were built from a synthesis of theory and experiment and almost pure—and pure—intuition which good men, and some men who should never have participated, had brought to the problem. He would know that the major part of it was experiment and that fact posed the biggest barrier to absolute standards by which to measure the correctness of a decision. Complacent release of chemicals inimical to the biosphere, structural failure due to design and-or maintenance deficiency, agro or medicinal chemical insertion that triggers negative effects beyond the original concept sphere of the agent...these are manifestations of errors in theory, or in the application of the theory, or in the interpretation of the experiments that inspired, or were born of the theory. Or the component of intuition—which has a very great span of competence—was too strong. Or Reality had laughed at the simple assumptions or limited conscience that man had called to mesmerize himself into thinking he knew what he was doing. When the dollar intruded this analysis, the slice of good men could get thinner and that laughter heavier. He'd pushed some of this into Jake's face when he'd had insinuating fire and provocative iron for props.

He spoke about some of these things with Russ, who had come over to Chemistry from PAG that fall. At first, Russ covered his real self with smiles and insulting reference to Paul's inability to savor the intricacy of the tile work around the Temple fountains and patios. But gradually, he gave up this facade and they were coming to better mutual ground.

"Understanding comes very slowly, Paul. That mathematics you've complained about has taken thousands of years to get to you—don't be too deprecating of it." Paul had trapped Russ one day in Russ' office at Chemistry.

"Have you been to the Parthenon, Russ?"

"You insult my capacity to stay on the goddamn job—my nose to the fucking grindstone." This was the first time Paul had heard Russ fall back on that crutch of Anglosaxendom, and he was shocked...as any good Air Force man would have been.

"*Pardonnez moi, monsieur*...I'd forgotten that devotion."

"You had a slight mental lapse about the condition of what I laughingly call my estate. But no, God damn it, I haven't glimpsed that edifice...except via television, magazines, et cetera."

"I hope you can see it someday...I'd like to be with you when you see it."

"Goosing me up the steps, no doubt."

"If that's what it takes to force a dose of true art and a souvenir of true greatness on your stubborn hide."

"*Souvenir* of greatness? Why should I cherish souvenirs when I have direct objects of greatness *all* about me?" Russ moved his hands in expansive play and with eyes and a general face that didn't support veracity.

"How feel you about the Greeks...the Greeks of the Parthenon?"

"My bag of knowledge there isn't big." Russ' grunting laugh made Paul suspicious. "I know that...in respect of art, particularly sculpture, they've never been surpassed. In respect of bringing generalities and subtleties of architecture into an agreeable aesthetic whole, ditto. In respect of what it takes to order a man so he can savor the fullness of life, I'd like to use my *ditto* again."

"For Christ's sake, you just scooped a lecture out of that humble pie."

"This is high school stuff—maybe grammar school," Russ snorted. "Very occasionally I peek into a book on the subject you've had the temerity to raise."

"That last bit...about the *ordering* of a man...I guess it boils down to how much do you think we've progressed in the twenty-five hundred odd years since then?...how much of the good parts of their *blue prints for man* have stuck to us?"

Russ started to fill one of his briars. His churchwarden was on a short sabbatical. Paul followed Russ' lead and loaded his own furnace.

"We've learned of ways to slaughter our fellowmen with greater efficiency of time and effort, unless you count the background work that goes into the preparation of our little toys...that would raise that *effort*—exponentially."

"Give me some of the *glory* that's ours—the fulfillment realized since then. I tend to depression easily."

"I'll try to uncover something for you. We've learned a few things about making life more comfortable for a larger number of people...even the upper classes, if you only look at the amenities the local pharmacy and the medical profession—some of it—can provide. Some of the life styles in ancient times would make the greatest opulence in ours look like shanty town."

"Agreed...but nothing else besides an improvement in combating the worms and ticks of man's bedevilment?—my depression is starting to feed on you."

"What a hell of a prospect for your depression. I'll try...harder. We've made the work of our fellowmen easier by various mechanisms and gadgets and fertilizers, and by the diversion of radio and television and..." Russ struggled to keep his cavalcade rolling.

"You might at least mention books and magazines and newspapers, crediting man with improvement in knowing his world...the ability to dream a little more."

"True. He can dream, perhaps with greater scope—but sometimes this is dangerous." Russ also had a faculty for quick dips into sobriety.

"Oh?"

"If he has access to books, sometimes he'll find a history book—*ancient* history. He might discover that man hasn't gone forth from the admirable, in some respects, starting point of a few of the ancients on a path that's led to much improvement over those years of yours."

"What about the toothpaste, radio, television...movies—stop me!"

"The toothpaste, I'm sure, had ancient counterparts just as effective. Radio...a *true* jewel of man's accomplishment. Although it exploits only one sense, this sense is precious to the lonely man, woman, for whom music, talk, laughter, debate are purest sustenance. And for the not so lonely, looking only for some respite from the rat race...with minimum involvement. I'm forced to concede you a damn good point there. Television has provided some true entertainment and enlightenment. It's also provided more incentive for indolence with respect to that *ordering* than any gadget of man's contriving...the movies shall remain silent."

"Some guys over on Sunset will argue with you."

"I fear not their slings just so they sling a little money my way."

"You'll never fall away from the sacred gooblah."

"I may have to, my boy—from hunger."

"Let me divert this stream. What else can you say about man's clambering through the ages?"

"He's increased his ability at intercourse." This had come between puffs.

"Hold that phone. I think certain of the ancients—*very* ancients—would argue that one. There were certain temple rites in Crete and Babylon such as would make each particular hair to stand on end...as another sad man once said."

"I see I'm wasting my precious few words on ears tuned only to the baser qualities of our man—qualities by the way that, in the generality, haven't changed *one iota* in ten thousand years despite the persistent and insistent caresses of all our inventions of religion and philosophy. But I'll persevere, ignoring my handicap of reception here." Russ took a few long drags on his briar. "By intercourse—damn you—I speak of the exchange between, among men and women...of words, ideas, facial nuances, agreements, arguments leading to agreements...of *everything* that makes it possible to distinguish a recluse in an absolute wilderness from a statistically normal man in Manhattan."

"Ah...you must admit that *this* is an accomplishment, even on your scale."

"I think we're tending to the crux of our discourse," Russ admitted with as much pontification as he could get in the absence of his churchwarden.

"Please—the suspense!"

"Intercourse—damn that word—mental exchange among humans, with its various ancillaries, is the agency for education, assuming that one of the participants is smarter than the other(s) in something and that's almost a statistical certainty." Russ came close to carving a smoke ring with a sudden puff from his pipe. "I think we've stumbled on our pivotal word...education."

"We've increased our capacity to educate!"

"We've increased our capacity to educate those favorably disposed as to location and situation. This group *has* tended to increase in the last few thousand years, if we must continue to refer to your damn time frame. This must be counted as another accomplishment. The quality of this education may be exceedingly variable, but, on average, it *has* improved."

"What've we done for the not so favorably disposed?" There was a long pause then, and during that time the two pipes made that room a delight for aerosol and colloid specialists.

"If the size of one fraction of the world's population has increased, then I'm trapped into admitting that the size of the remainder fraction has decreased."

"Can't we pause here...in sober appreciation?"

"You may dally as long as you like." Russ sent another smoke pulse upward, no artistry this time.

"And you will not, I assume from your insulting implication."

"I'm moved forward at my usual faltering pace by certain considerations."

"Ah...drama again. I can wait now, my feet are getting tired."

"The *decreased* fraction comprises a very substantial number of people. It doesn't take much of a percentage of a few billion people to make a big number...but I'll spare you your hated math. Let's just agree that this number of people *is* substantial—the underprivileged as far as participating in the modern world—the poor sons a bitches who haven't got a prayer of improving their relative lot much above that of a beggar in ancient Babylon—better make that London...those table scraps in Babylon must have been quite tasty."

"The Queen will hate you for that. But I'm frowning again, and you had me on a peak—*several* of them."

"Let me augment your depression a little...it's good for the bowels sometimes. This considerable group—and you don't need safari equipment from your beloved Abercrombie to find them, a token, even a short walk will often do it—constitutes a real and present threat to our complacency, my friend. It's quite capable of erasing whatever progress we've made over your damn time span...and I think we now agree that *that* is a fragile thing."

"I could pull *ominous* out of here someplace."

"I think the capacity for violence—premeditated or inadvertent—is very thinly sheathed in what we've tried to call *civilization* in the last few minutes. Here I define *capacity* as inclination plus implementation power—a prop we've improved over your time span to where we can now damn near carry literal hell in a briefcase. I think this capacity—right now—is far greater than that of any mob that ever howled through Rome, or Paris, or places that have left us hardly any whispers...and that it needs no more to trigger it now than it did then. You can color the havoc yourself—my supply of red crayons is too small for *this* job."

"You're suggesting that some heads may roll in the clean streets of our modern cities?"

"The heads of anyone this mob feels has anything to do with keeping their noses in the *general* crap in, or outside, our *modern* cities."

"May I suggest that *our* heads might be included in this picnic?"

"We, as technical people, do have some responsibility here."

"I said something like that to a guy over in Bel Air. I hope you can meet him sometime, Russ."

"My boy, I hope I can meet *anybody* from Bel Air...sometime."

"Well...I'm afraid I get your point. I also think that others have spoken to these things many times before."

"Some of those ones have a tendency to diarrhea of the pen."

"And the mouth."

"My words exactly, my boy. Now we leave this discussion right where we started—close to shit on the temple steps. You must hurry back to your studies...your grades can always use improvement."

"How'n hell do you know what my grades are?—I haven't bragged to you yet."

"That's one discussion whose frequency and excitement will never perturb or incite my sleep, or envy, respectively."

"See you later, your exalted eminence." Paul started to leave the smoke filled room and the Mephistophelean grin that cut right through it. But he stopped at the door.

"Where are we—*now*?"

"We're on our own spots on the continuum between the infinite and the infinitesimal—the astrophysicists looking one way, the particle boys the other. And I expect to see some unambiguously useful movement of *your* spot, my boy—now get out of here."

13

The year following the Master's went by quicker than any he'd ever known. He was always under the gun of a problem assignment, class notes to unscramble before the frequent tests, lectures to make more notes. Those tests were real cute. He saw very few of them where the class average was more than 50 out of 100. A little beauty that Yost had given in physical chemistry went for 35. One never tended to get arrogant around the halls of Chemistry and Mechanical Engineering. He took his required courses and the few electives he could afford. He regretted that this careful allotment never took him to certain quarters with some claim to preeminence at that school. That would be Physics. Once, he'd considered a meat grinder that Anderson ran on three days of the week. But he had more obligatory meat grinders and he couldn't indulge the luxury of Nobel Laureat Anderson's. He'd always had a fondness for the basic, general approach of the physicists. And if he hadn't successfully resisted an impulse before the start of his sophomore year at Stanford, he might be one of them now.

He finished his required courses by the end of his second year. The rest of the class work was fairly well up to him. This was a wonderful freedom that the impending thesis trial wouldn't let him enjoy too wantonly. He'd managed enough social activity during his vacations and weekends to keep him from venturing too close to the precipice of nervousness that had claimed some... possibly not at CIT, but elsewhere. John and Martha and Russ and Tom had helped him there. And Carla and Mary and the rest of his family had dispensed enough grace of personal contacts and letters to add sustenance to him.

The summer following his Master's he'd spent at Drake Instruments. And he would spend most of the next summer there. Such time in between these summers as he'd been able to squeeze in, he also spent at John's place, as Martha called it. His recompense from John for his services was not in logical proportion to his worth, but he didn't complain. And on the occasions when he'd been close to the verge of it, the Scotch and bourbon reservoirs wouldn't allow it.

The language exams in French and German were now behind him. The German had been tough enough. He'd been lucky that some reading he was doing for his thesis preparation coincided enough in vocabulary to satisfy the examiners. The French had been easier. He'd become fascinated with Brillouin's discourse on tensors and he'd translated many pages from Les Tenseurs; a circumstance that gave him almost frictionless passage through the exam. Once in a while it *has* to be easy, for Christ's sake.

He faced his final orals in the fall of his third year. The oral exam for the PhD is a fascinating thing. No supplicant to the Temple who comes to it had better show less than proper respect for either the Temple, or the set of priests who happen to be presiding, if he expects to leave it with smiles. When he comes to this room, he has satisfied the priests that he has acceptable credentials for further steps into the sanctuary...the mental attitude, the accomplishment of classroom and laboratory disciplines, the will to succeed. His capacity for original research is largely untested, but if he has the credentials to pass his oral, this gate will admit him to this trial. Most of the examiners at this time will enjoy seeing some of his sweat, even one of his tears, that they may know he truly cares about the procession he's making. But without the stimulus of extreme provocation—and the activation energy for provocation does vary from priest to priest—if he uses proper humility and, at the instant of a question, his mind responds with some alacrity, and some correctness, then he shouldn't fear the oral. But they *do* fear it, and Paul feared it. Fortunately, his set of priests had all had good breakfasts that morning.

With his orals and language exams and the formal regimen of class and laboratory work behind him, Paul would spend most of his last year in the thesis foyer that leads to the final room for the supplicants. This is a large area and it's easy to get lost in it. If one chooses a subject that requires too much development of equipment, is too inconstant to a given subject, or doesn't persevere strongly enough in the face of obstacles that nature, possibly some men, have conspired to place in this room, then he could be frustrated, and the priests might cast him out. Very few find the strength to come that way again.

Paul talked to Cubb and Gruif and Schomaker about this room. He finally decided that some exploration of the oxidation of metal at high temperature would suit him, and it might satisfy the criteria for a reasonably short stay in the foyer. The only real friction he ever had with Gruif was over the choice of thesis topic. But, in the end, Paul wasn't ashamed of it. Cubb and Schomaker weren't ashamed of it. And Gruif admitted that it wasn't a bad piece of work.

By April of his third year, he'd completed his experimental work on oxidation. He had succeeded in defining, in somewhat greater detail than had been done before, the destruction of nickel and chromium alloys by pure oxygen at high temperature. He'd developed and analyzed enough X-ray film to plaster a hunk of Colorado Boulevard...well, maybe a few large paving stones. He'd seen those lines, that those atoms put on that film, in his sleep. His discussion of it had a very minimum of mathematics, but he made no apology for this lack of ostentation. The mathematicians continued to awe him...but that small, private, smile just wouldn't go away.

At that time, graduation exercises at CIT were held in the temporary splendor that could be wrought in the parking lot adjoining the Athenaeum. After a lot of really young squirts were taken care of, quite a few Master's candidates came toward the rostrum. A few Engineering degrees were awarded, and then a larger body of people came to receive their final accreditation as priests of the Temple. Paul was standing about two-thirds of the way down this line because of the S his family had given him. There were older ones in that line, but not many. Paul remembered looking at the spectators, He didn't see his dad, or his mother, who were there. Mary was there and so were Carla and Martha and John. Not together, but they were there, someplace. He thought about them in various combinations and permutations of memory.

And then he was alone on the platform. Du Bridge placed the PhD's mantle on him. He heard this man's quiet voice say, "Congratulations, *doctor.*" And then he got down from there with reasonable grace—for a PhD.

He'd come to this place as a wild eyed supplicant. The priests had shown him sternness...but they'd had a greater capacity for mercy.

14

Paul had been sitting in a small conference room at Drake Instruments for the past hour. Some of the bits and pieces of the conversation that were his weren't wrapped in his usual exuberance. The talk was about major instruments and control systems and subsidiaries that would render the speech of the detectors and analyzers more palatable to observers, engineers and technicians of the chemical and oil industries. There were two engineers besides Paul, a representative of the sales department, and the manager of Paul's department, called Chemical Instruments. The span of ages represented here put plus ten minus five around him. In the matter of age he felt no discomfort. In the matter of the application of some of these instruments he wasn't keeping his annoyance in bounds.

"For Christ's sake, Paul. Don't worry so damn much about what goes on outside these plants. Worry about the inside...that's where our sustenance comes from—the *inside*." The manager delivered this speech, and he wiped an executive type smile over all of them.

"You mean to tell me that those big babies down in Pedro and those other paradises don't use detectors on any of those stacks, those goddamn stacks that are giving the air conditioning of this building a hard time *right now*?" Paul's expression was less parochial than the manager's.

"They must have something that tells what they're putting out. But this is trivial. God damn it—let the bullshitters in Congress handle the messages."

"I'm not striving to take the bread from John Drake's table. And don't give me that ivory tower crap. I've seen as much mud, smoke and shit as any of you people. I'm only suggesting that we slant some of our product toward the pollution side—not much, just enough to let some people know that *somebody*—God damn it—is thinking about them. This thing may not have immediate dollar value. I predict it'll have a hell of a return in the near future. The outfit that gets some precedence here will have a good seat for the main show." He pulled out a pipe and tried to calm himself with loading and firing it.

"You talk to some of 'em and they don't believe that they *have* a pollution problem," the advertising man said.

"I have tears of appreciation for that one." Paul wiped his eyes with his handkerchief. "I've heard nasty rumors that when the County inspectors come down there, some—or all—of the lines just happen to be down for maintenance. I've been in a boat, a plane, and a car in the early morning down there and I've seen some of that non-pollution wrapping their citadels of purity—it's like a translation of those stinking fumaroles in Yellowstone to Pedro, only here it's not a *natural* wonder." Paul blew a smoke ring at the amused manager.

"We'll try to get you a certificate from the Chamber of Commerce for your concern, Paul. What were you saying about that spectrometer, Joe?"

The voices kept in the vein the manager had defined as the mother lode for Drake Instruments. Paul heard them, occasionally tried to put in something sensible. But the full compliment of his attention wasn't there anymore. He'd had these talks before, and they never amounted to much more than humorous diversion from a perspective of markets and profits that didn't have as much of him in it as a well paid engineer under John's auspices should have had.

Following graduation, Paul had assumed a more spacious apartment on Orange Grove, near the Arroyo. Tom had wanted him to come down into that vale of greenery, but Paul resisted an impulse that had never been strong. Right now, he was dispensing Scotch and bourbon to Russ and Tom from a kitchen vantage of his new sanctuary.

"By God...those eyes that have glimpsed the full form of the Goddess *do* look a little red," Russ said, between slugs of Bourbon.

"Goddess, hell! That fucking invigoration the Chamber calls *air* is what's doing it."

"Oh...that word. Didn't we warn you about using it in the sacred precincts?"

Tom supported Russ, muttering something about the fucking state of the local grammar.

"Why yes, you did. You also said, as I recall, she might get the idea I was there for fun and accommodate me."

"She does have a tendency to snatch at unwary priests, especially the younger ones." Russ was still finding pieces of mirth in his bourbon.

"You *are* stripping the mask of devotion off me, aren't you—short, sharp jerks. I'll tell you about your Goddess—*our* Goddess, damn you—she needs all the help she can get."

"I've harbored similar thoughts in *very* private moments." Russ' slow smile ripened into a full grin of appreciation for this youngish priest. He knew that Paul would bounce the ball again, so he waited for it.

"My friend, John Drake, like a few others in his position, is riding an explosion of technology...and you can see more volcano there than sunrise."

"Volcanoes sometimes can regenerate, renew a stale landscape—but you're not inclined to that long view?"

"I'm not inclined to a few poppies on top of a sea of lava, Russ. I don't like the time-scale of your damn regeneration. All that physical chemistry of yours needs a better workshop than lava and eons of whisking fertilizer toward it."

"Leave me out of it," Russ stated.

"Me too...you damn idealist." Tom had interrupted the Scotch contest he was having with Paul, and winning handily.

"You jokers are in *it*—right up to your damn crotches, maybe your mouths."

"That *does* sound stimulating." Russ actually twitched a corner of his mouth, not necessarily joyfully.

"Strawberry...chocolate?" Tom asked.

"You've been tasting it. I think it'll get stronger. I'll soon be able to give you plenty of sulfur, some of the piquant peroxides, definitely some chlorine. And—if you're *really* lucky—maybe a smidgeon of fluorine for you."

"Somebody's slapped him down at Drake's," Tom said.

"Somebody's tromped on his Temple shoes and gotten 'em all dirty," Russ added.

"I'll plead guilty on both counts you perceptive bastards."

"That's no way to address your professor."

"You're drinking my bourbon. You're insulting my convictions and morals—again."

"Well...if you put it *that* way."

"I've made the mistake, several times, of suggesting that we divert a *little* bit of our energy to looking out from those plants of accomplishment toward the people who're keeping the owners smiling, and their yachts at Pedro and Balboa sleek and big."

"And your sterling perception was diffused into nothingness by gross economics."

"That's a snappy and insulting way of putting it. Yes, it floated out the window, as I'm sure you knew it would, Herr Professor."

"One of the characteristics of a good priest is perseverance under adversity." Russ had been tempted to preen, but he didn't. "I've never found you wanting too much in that area before."

"If I can find a way to bring some scraps to my table—I'll fight my discouragement." Paul polished the heroic timbre with a grin, a fist pushed into the air like during his time with Jake in front of Jake's ambiguous andirons, and then he slugged some Scotch.

"Bravo!" Tom cried. "By God, you weren't kidding about that Prick Proliferation Theory stuff—were you! You're pushing it *way* beyond ruining the dinner of your innocent companions. Incidentally, I'm a convert—want to see my paper towel burns?"

"That's a theory that apparently has escaped me—am I fortunate?"

"Don't call it, Russ. It's made a damn bathroom paper sculptor, and ballet dancer at the toilet exits, out of me...let it rest. But I'll trickle a mite of its substance for you, to wit, *involuntary involvement in somebody else's shit.* That piece of it seems to roll right along with our pleasant little chat here—but that's as far as I'll take it." Tom barely looked at Paul as he resumed the Scotch contest.

"I think I'm afraid I'm privy to this theory. Let me borrow your 'Bravo!' Tom, and then we'll hurry along." Russ had just tipped his bourbon glass toward Paul, and then he said, "But those table scraps can become quite scarce, my boy—*caution* in your heresy is the word for you here."

"You could find yourself on the wrong end of a very unpleasant screwing," Tom put in.

"You're not suggesting that sodomy is rampant in the Temple?" The face that Paul held out to Tom seemed to be straight, but it slipped off toward Russ, who answered him.

"We have...occasional...trouble with some apes who scale the walls and drop into the gardens...very near to some of the fountain groves used for contemplative reclining."

"You don't have to go so far as the Temple to find apes." Paul said, quietly.

"But be careful of them. Some of the larger ones aren't famous for weakness—or mercy." Russ had stepped away from the playground again.

"Yeah, those white hunters have said that you got to stand your ground in the face of a gorilla charge or balls may fly—not theirs, by the way." Tom stared into private panoramas swimming in his Scotch.

"Indeed, Paul. You're an educated man, in some respects. Brush up on your dissembling, and subtle attack, if you're going to persist in a rebellion that has been—will be—the best exercise ground you could find for such talents in you."

"That sounds like an assignment." A venerable eye axis between Paul and Russ sparked again.

"This is an extra credit...thing." For a target, Russ chose the less complicated surface of his bourbon over Paul's eyes.

"I don't want to aggravate John...you guys know something of my debt to him." That was true, Tom a bit more than Russ. "But I don't think my train can travel on his tracks much longer."

"Everyone has constraints, Paul," Tom said, supporting the suddenly serious mood with surprising incisiveness, considering his very relaxed mode.

"True," Russ added. "Perhaps he's got more sympathy for the puffs of your engine on his tracks than you credit him with...but I'd like to grapple with some of his constraints just for a little while." Russ' thoughts took a quick, solo trip, his eyes cooperating.

"You'd get dangerously distracted with such opulence," Paul muttered.

"Perhaps I *would* run like hell after it!"

"Ah...here's inspiration to make your fellow priests cry in frustration."

"That cry is no stranger to our halls, Paul...those tears have scrapped plenty of good designs on ancient surfaces."

"Pardon my crude subservience to such scraps as anyone might throw *our* way—may I suggest we take this philosophy into the presence of food?" The talk had stripped away a lot of the veneer Paul's Scotch had laid on Tom.

"I would entertain such a motion," Paul said.

"I would kick your butt out of that chair, if you didn't," Russ said.

"Let's take a peek at the Ship Room," Tom suggested, again.

"Ship Room!" Russ cried.

"They're accommodating as hell over there," Paul stated.

They did go there and damned if Russ didn't see one of his friends, hovering very near the bar as a matter of fact.

Tom was pleading a headache. Actually—as they found after not too patient probing—he had a new girl friend. It looked like the old warrior was now on the receiving end of a good pair of hooks. With suitable solemnity and commiseration, they finally let him go from the bar into which they'd stumbled after a substantial, good dinner. Tom would be returning to DC soon, looking for more walls to climb. But he'd have a bird colonel's wings to help him climb, and soon a bride for extra impetus. This one would never get away from Paul, if Paul had anything to say about it.

"I think that you and I are of a mind on some of these things," Russ said, slowly doing his bourbon some justice again. "But there're forces here that no one man can confront for long. To use the simile of our old fluorine friend."

"I get your point, Russ." Paul looked into his glass while talking. Russ had just corroborated the joy of company on significant excursions into the unknown.

"I would also remind you that some of the men who've entered that arena have either not left it, or have been scarred for life...I think I've advised caution here." Russ' soft voice spilled some into his glass, too.

"Yeah...I appreciate everything you've said. We've never worked over Don Quixote together, but I think you're trying to conjure windmills for me and a threadbare crusader poking at the air between those revolving slats." Russ was thinking about a denial, but then Paul gave him more to work with. "I've complained about some smokescreens that I thought were laid down in the math classes. I've been thinking about this some more. I think I've just come from a school where a man is given the best kick in the butt he could get for doing something about what he thinks is wrong—about the math, or whatever is the major stick in his craw. Newton said he could see farther because he stood on the heads of giants. Caltech gave me a flock of heads to stand on. Du Bridge called me *doctor*—that's one peak I'd like to stand on a little longer."

"You're determined that you might be one of the knights who can make a successful sally of unpleasant portals?"

"I'm toying with the thought that I may be one of the bastards who can leave that arena with some part of his balls intact. Half a ball is...you know."

"I've heard of this wisdom."

"I'll just bet you have. You didn't seem too unfamiliar with some of those temple rites."

"Now which particular rites did you have in mind? There was a minor fertility thing during the Second Egyptian dynasty that had a certain extra inspiration for concupiscence."

"You mean the one where, on the night of the third day of continence, when the young priestesses would..."

"The very one, my boy. You *have* been neglecting your statistical mechanics—haven't you?."

Carla had traveled a lot after her graduation. In addition to her graduation odyssey, she'd made two more trips to various parts of the world since then. She *had* flirted with many of the targets she'd mentioned to Paul. And she had also taken a good look at Rheims and Chartres and the Louvre. She'd even gone to Haarlem.

"And after your eyes became accustomed to the gloom of the place," Paul prodded in mock solemnity one day on the veranda of the Drake house.

"Then...I saw it."

"Saw *what*? A hot dog stand, a Mickey Mouse watch some American tourist had dropped on the stones, a..."

"Stop it, you beast! I saw the columns...reaching higher than any I'd ever seen before and flowing into arches whose beauty was also original to me." Carla's eyes and her words were a match.

"And then you sneezed—shattering the significant quiet of the place."

"And then...I walked around very slowly and I felt some of what you said I'd feel—and I don't like being told what I'll *feel*."

"I'm glad I contributed in a small way to the modest educational component of your adventures." Paul used some of the grin from Russ' own cabinet.

And after Chartres, she told him about Michelangelo in Florence, and the Rijksmuseum in Amsterdam. He let her rave about Rembrandt, Vermeer...and Hals. Paul did almost all of the listening to this young one with the extracurricular dimensions.

"My, it sounds as if our investment wasn't entirely squandered," Martha said to them as she approached from the house. She was wearing a cheongsam after an abstinence of several years, and its architect still would have smiled. "I've asked Mary to bring us something cold," she said, after joining them.

"Ice?" Paul winked at Carla.

"Ice—you degenerate, with some dilution by quinine water and gin."

"Capital, though we must be careful not to encourage dissipation around this young one—but she may already have had irreversible European tutoring." Paul just barely ducked Carla's swipe that had Martha precedents.

"I've had excellent tutors." Carla had turned her eyes demurely downward. Paul and Martha exchanged glances that signaled more care around Carla.

"Let that remark rest quietly...it may find quick expiration," Paul said, feeling some resurrection of almost forgotten tension.

"Yes, Carla, you must be careful in giving credit for your education." Martha's smile might have had some quality of strain in it too, but that was small payment for mercifully deferred revelation.

"Let's let it die, then," Carla said, making a quick stomp of her foot against the flagstone. Actually, at that moment, everyone wished that the damn subjects of stones and fragile glass hadn't surfaced.

"Hah...contributing to the delinquency of our young one, are you." John's voice said from a doorway. The veranda three could have killed him for his innocent salutation. Somehow, each of them got to a proper smile and greeting.

After John had caught up with them in the drink department, they were managing to keep the conversation within better bounds.

"Haven't seen much of you lately, Paul. I guess you're still on the payroll," John said to his fishing compadre and employee.

"I've tried to keep your conscience clear regarding my pay check. And—by the way—I've been meaning to talk to you about that," Paul countered with a small smile.

John was damn near ready to say something about hospitality and advantage, but he caught himself just in time. Instead he said, "I've noticed an occasional memo you've sent to some of my managers...suggesting we pay more attention to our *indirect* customers." John's smile here was a little rueful.

"What shade of pink *do* you use on your goodbye slips?"

"Not a bit of it, lad. I like to see some of those characters shaken up—not too much, mind you. Sometimes we tend to get hypnotized by our prosperity and I'd be the last to admit that we're not prospering." John's smile this time wasn't rueful, and it brushed Martha and Carla.

"I must assume that you don't support all of this prosperity, Paul," Carla said. Her eyes made a quick trip to her mother's before they came back to Paul. He had predicted some facets of her when he first saw her on this veranda and she had just proved some of him.

"Carla, dear, perhaps we'd better adjourn to the house...there *must* be some soap for your impertinence." But Marta's bulwark for her husband didn't sound rock hard.

Paul saluted Carla with a small smile and a tip of his glass before he sampled more of John's hospitality. Finally, he looked at John, as he pushed away a long silence.

"John...I...I've got to get some of this off what passes for my chest. I feel strongly about this pollution bit. You have on-the shelf equipment that can do something about it. I feel—I know damn well—my attitude isn't shared by most of your guys. They've heard of smog. And they've got as much talent for lip-service as anybody—now let's talk about severance pay instead of raises."

"Whoooah," John ordered. "You're suggesting that I divert some streams that are putting that quinine in your glass...by the way, Martha, *please* stay with Schweppes...that I sacrifice some of this for noble purposes?" John laughed, but it was a solo.

"My compadre of Cabo Blanco...I'm suggesting *just* that." There was only a trace of his grin and his eyes tried to track the elusive target that John was getting to be. "I'm suggesting that you'll pick up other streams from other sources. I'm suggesting that when your eyes tear from those trickles from your present streams, it'll be some solace for you to know that you—God damn it—are trying to do *something* about it." Paul leaned back in his chair, but there wasn't any relaxation there. He'd gone away from the agreeable posture of Carla's artistic mentor to something close to the wild-eyed windmill fanatic—in only seconds. And he'd done this in front of a man who'd worked with the threads of Martha's design for friendship that had included him, Dr. Paul Sanger, in a big way.

"I *knew* I shouldn't have come home so early," John said to Martha. After trying to straighten a face that suggested Paul had plucked a couple more strings on his harp, he came back to Paul. "Once, you admitted to me that you didn't care for the rat race—the inspiration, God help me—that's business. That's okay. It would get too damn crowded if some of you guys didn't feel that way. But let me bore you with a couple facts. I own Drake Instruments...somewhat. I have investors who expect me to furnish a few niceties like dividends and profit—junk like that. Believe me, some of them can get nasty if I don't deliver. Jake isn't one of them by some accident of Providence. But you've seen Jake in action. If a man like that feels his investment is in any jeopardy, he can be formidable...and I'm thinking now about those mako sharks we saw off Panama—but didn't tangle with." It was lubrication time for John.

"I know you've got constraints," Paul said, echoing Tom's remark of a few days before. "When you've finally latched hold of a good market, and you don't study the local alleyways too closely, nobody can blame you—that's the old self preservation bit, eh?" Paul's voice trailed off and he took some Scotch lubrication.

"Your consideration impels me to ask you when you want to go fishing again."

"Ah...that *was* a low one." Paul managed to pull out something of a smile, but it had a short life. "I've stuck my foot in my mouth and I can't seem to get it out. I...I really feel that my presence at your place will embarrass you." John raised his hand, but Paul's train had passed that signal. "I don't know what one SOB can do about it, but I think I'm going to take a look." His small smile took a short trip to the ladies with that.

"Let's talk about dinner," Martha said, in an attempt to find some diversion here.

"Thank you, Martha, I've other plans tonight. Let me have one of my very rare rain checks. I want to leave this thing where I'd like to leave it—but damned if I can think of anything." Paul stood up, and John joined him, his hand on Paul's shoulder.

"This thing...we can talk about it, a lot. I should be able to dredge up something inspirational now, too—damned if I can, either. Are you *sure* you won't join us for dinner?"

"Let me have my rare rain check, compadre." Paul looked at Martha, Carla, then he left the veranda.

John tried to call Paul at his home and made several attempts to catch

him at the plant. But Paul was elusive. After a couple days, he submitted his res-
ignation, without the courtesy of the few days' notice that usually attends these
happy affairs. There weren't too many long faces around Drake Instruments,
maybe a couple of the secretaries paid him a few seconds homage. One of
Martha's calls finally reached him at home. She told him that their house at Lido
Island was at his disposal. He thanked her, and declined. Christ...that place
would *really* nail him. He'd felt sadness there under better circumstances than
he had now and he certainly didn't feel like giving Fate a better shot at him.

He drove to Tijuana and took in a bull fight. He stayed a couple days near
San Diego and played beach boy. This exposure to the ocean helped him a little.
He thought about Francisco. His path would cross that devil's some day again.
He thought about the battle with the great billed one that almost killed him. He
thought about CIT and PAG, and his battles at those places. He thought about
the night on Iwo when a grenade dropped close to his tent and took out one of
his buddies. He thought about the time he tried to cut a pilot out of a burning
P51 with an ax and didn't quite make it in time. He thought about the Old One
of the grove who'd challenged him to look in *all* directions. He was feeling too
damn sorry for himself and resolved to give Russ' ear a bend.

"You *did* it." Russ was poised over his coffee, in his office in Chemistry.
"Yup."
"Now what?" Russ' words continued to dog him.
"That's what I hoped you could untangle for me."
"Damn you boy. You *do* know how to touch right in the family jewels —
don't you."
"Yup."
"You try me. I presume you're waiting for me to inspire you...activate you.
If this moronic display continues, I'll have to toss you out of these premises of
learning." Russ' rising inflection at the last got Paul going, a little.
"Russ...if you were to make a symbol, a gesture of the technical man's
concern, his thought of helping out a little in just one critical part of the civilian
arena, what would you do and where would you put it?"
"Oh...off the top of what hair I have left, I'd have to pick up the smog as
one of your critical areas. See, you've gained tremendous insight already and
you haven't been here five minutes yet. And I would say, as the physical chemist
I am, I would consider a little something along a physical chemical, or chemical
engineering line in the way of a...symbol. As for where to put it — that question
tends to greatness." Russ paused to contemplate the stream of inspiration he'd

just released. "Maybe we can find an abandoned pickle factory. We could always boil the barrel staves for sustenance."

Gross economics is a powerful temperer of enthusiasm and it did some of its work now. Russ tried some tempering of his own. "There now, see how quickly we've reached the point of imbecility—next case."

"I agree we've reached a point. Let me call it challenge, my friend. What's that old Greek stuff about putting up, or..."

"Shutting up."

"I wish I'd said that. Let's let the pickle factory rest a while—what about the symbol?"

"You're determined to involve me in your madness?"

"You were a big hand pushing me toward the Temple. It's time for you to crawl into some of that put up, or shut up."

"*So be it* is another phrase I hate to see pop up now. But you've tended to nail me to a Temple privy. I've tried to run away from you—but I'm too old for this play now...this refuge of the..."

"Chicken hearted?"

"Couldn't we make it a nice plump bird? *J'ai faim.*"

They did just that. They had a plump one at a place in Monrovia that bragged about its chicken. And they talked about the symbol, the gesture of concern.

"I've been immersed in detectors and controllers and display equip-ment for months," Paul said, between sips of coffee. "Maybe there's something there...a detector..."

"With a very impressive array of recording instruments and lots of lights and bells and warning horns and..." Russ could roll with an occasion.

"You're overacting, but you're pulling up the hackles on my neck—keep on with it."

"Well, according to you, your friend Drake has off-the-shelf equipment that could serve some of these purposes, maybe all of them, with some imaginative ministrations from us, of course." Russ continued his fantasy. "We might select a few of the more obnoxious gases favoring us...sulfur, nitrogen and carbon oxides, possibly one, or two of the halogens. We ought to throw in a sweet little organic peroxide, or two. We could pick such equipment of Drake's as would give us a handle on these beauties, equip ourselves with that ostentatious bank of recorders and indicators—bells, horns." Russ might have been overacting, but a transient of his version of one of the joys marked his face.

"And might I suggest that we put the inlets of our nosy bits of science and technology on top of a tower of suitable location, height and functional design, and..." Paul wasn't fighting the fantasy, either.

"And we call it the Sanger Tower," Russ said. He'd finally managed to trap Paul's eyes.

"Kinzer Tower...Kinzer-Sanger...Sanger-Kinzer..."

"I like my first suggestion best. It has the ring of solid Mid-Western America to it—don't underestimate that attribute, my boy."

And so, the crazy idea of the Sanger Tower was born in an office of Chemistry one day...with inspirations flavored by good chicken and apple pie *a la mode.*

"Carla...it *is* good to see you," Paul said to the smiling beauty who had just assaulted his doorbell. After he escorted her to what passed for his drawing room, he motioned her to a chair with a bow that hadn't had much practice lately. "Your presence is more than enough excuse. But...perhaps there's a little something else to which I can give thanks." He *was* very glad to see her. This was the day after his talk with Russ about the tower and he'd been fighting the soldiers that General Unresolved had been sending against him since that time.

"You're a bad boy, you know." Great, serious eyes came at him. She was wearing a navy suit, similar to some he'd seen her mother wear. But she had many touches about her that were pure Carla.

"Before we get into that...may I offer you something cold, or hot?"

"Coffee *would* be good. I haven't had any breakfast and Mother has been very uncooperative lately." She shook her hair a little and settled back in the chair, crossing legs Martha had been very generous in sharing with her.

After Paul had put some boiling water and powdered coffee together and brought it to the small table fronting them, he also relaxed into a chair...he made an effort in that direction.

"I'll not say...*and now*. Those damn words have been haunting me for years—if I never hear them again, it'll be okay."

"I could say them to you. But out of consideration for your haunting burden, I'll not. I *will* say that my father and mother have said very few words to me—or to each other—since you left us on that damn veranda." She sipped her coffee, and her eyes roamed the steamy panorama of *that* caldron just before she came back to him. Her mother was a virtuoso in placing a face into panoramas that challenged him. This was another inheritance that had just walked through his door.

"I was crude—and abrupt—that evening. I'm sorry if this has caused you, or your parents, unpleasantness." He tried to smile, but it wouldn't come out right. He also tried to handle his end of their eye axis, but she continued to hold most of that unfinished structure...ready and able to accommodate both the subject and emotion of him.

"*Unpleasantness* isn't quite the word...let's see if we can find another. *Unhappiness* might do for a start...*dismay* has some ring to it that could crowd in here, perhaps." Under her prompting he finally managed to make a decent reciprocation of the eyes.

"Carla, you're looking at a jerk. The priests and occasional visitors don't like people kicking over Temple vases. I could lose my credit card for it—I might even find it hard to pick my way along the alleys *behind* the damn place."

"Paul Sanger, you *are* something of a jerk." She set her coffee down and swept him with the same model radar he'd once felt in a foyer as gardening gloves were taken off. "You're also something that's made my mother cry since you left. She's been careful to hide it...but I saw it. And you're also something that's made my father very irritable lately—I can hardly get a civil word out of him. What *are* you, Paul Sanger?" If she wore a smile, it was a subtle master-piece that would tax a conscientious traveler in the halls of Huntington's gallery to find a counterpart among those almost living aristocrats.

Paul felt no compulsion to pick up the conversation ball. The vestiges of mutual adventure had been handled well by Martha and John. They'd given him a gift of friendship he had accepted and handled with reasonable maturity. But he hadn't been aggressive enough in disaffiliating himself from the House of Drake. A prime derivative of this negligence now confronted him and he couldn't deny that he'd had prior warning of it. He'd pulled too much of his life in front of Carla, and she had more than usual capacity to respond to some of the stimuli it carried. John had once told him that they'd play *their* tune by ear for a while. If he had developed any virtuosity in that respect, he would need all of it now and any claim he could make for manhood would be tested by this guest sitting right in front of him.

Finally, after their axis had cycled through made and broken many times under a complicated thick silence, she said to him, "Your sketch of Mother...her reception of it were *quite* explicit. And as long as we're kicking this extramarital diversion around a bit, I'll say that my father and Mary didn't show any serious discord, either." Carla had placed a smile and complementary voice around her statements, with a particular softness for Mary.

Paul rose and walked to her, and coupled her right hand to his hands.

"Carla...you've had your little game finding words for me. But—see now—you've left me with only one word for you...*wonderful*." it was structured almost as a whisper. One soft smile preceded his speech, another was made by it. Then she gently uncoupled their hands and she straightened herself in the chair a little, head slightly back, looking at him.

"And...and...I *can't* keep myself from those hateful words! What *are* your plans...if you'd care to tell me?" She was ready for an unsubtle smile now.

"I'll tell you as much as I know about them." He sat down again. "You haven't met Russ Kinzer, Professor Russ Kinzer of CIT. We've had some words about my hang up. We've evolved a little nonsense that could prove distracting to a few people." He paused, longer than necessary, a smile trying to decide where to land on his face.

"You're teasing me."

"We tried to find a symbol...a token gesture, to show some of the people that they aren't the lowest rung on every man's totem pole."

"I believe you've found this...symbol, as you call it," the perceptive one said.

"We've decided that a tower, devoted to sampling and telling on the air pollutants might be somewhat appropriate, using some of our best gadgets— probably some your daddy's best gadgets. And we would try to give them as good a show as we can on what we pull out of the Los Angeles air. It's sort of a put up—or shut up as far as I'm concerned...the *first* step beyond the words that are running out for me."

"Where will you put this erection of science?" If Carla had felt any of Paul's torn tongue wish, she certainly didn't show it.

"Don't know yet. This thing is in the preliminary—*extreme* preliminary —stage."

Between her European trips, Carla had worked for the LA County Welfare Department. Over several years, she had seen much, but really done very little beyond the humble offices assigned to her. She *had* thought much about what the greatest, richest country on the face of the globe was doing for all those fortunate enough to be her citizens. This symbol business of Paul's hit her right between those eyes and she covered none of it.

"Paul, I...I would consider a chance to participate...in *some* way...a very great favor, a great opportunity for me."

Opportunity! Much of the world's treasure was open to her and she could easily slip into any society where a license for caring very ostentatiously about these things went with the territory. Carla's attitude preempted swift reply. He looked at her with a carefully neutral face for a long time, while considering his response options.

"Carla...I'd suspected that beneath that Cardin suit there might be an extra heartbeat for others—but this is ridiculous! Assuming we get this thing off the ground—and there's a teeny little hold-down called *money*—your parents would never let me involve you in this...business." He'd tried to speak softly, pushing some reasonableness into the words, but he'd failed all around, he knew it, and now he was pacing the room making some buffer of space around her.

"It's *not* ridiculous—as you call it! For some time now, I've also felt your damn call to *put up, or shut up.* You—and your precious Kinzer—haven't any monopoly on *that!*" She remained seated, but she followed him with challenging eyes that had come close to flooding, several times, in the last few seconds. Huntington's artists might not have captured these respects of her on any of their canvases...which generally were peaks of relaxed contentment, or hauteur, or well-served sensuality some steps beyond misted eyes. But she was close to dangerous potential that was implicit in most depictions of those aristocrats.

Finally, he *had* to stop his walking. He looked away from her, almost afraid to try his voice in speech that could easily become irreversible. She was complicating his process of disengagement—but he could blame no one but himself for triggering a conscience very much like his own. When he thought he had some control of himself, he said, "We'll talk about it. I'll try to submit a petition to your parents—and I'll bring my track shoes when I do it."

This man was different from any she'd ever known. One can't talk about Leonardo and Hals and Chartres, and many other values, as they had done, without *much* communication. And he had coupled tease and provocation with an understanding of her. If there were other dimensions to their acquaintance-ship, then she had tried to keep them in proper perspective, constrained by the memory of the axis between him and her mother. She was tempting fate to cruelty if she mishandled her emotions. But she had gained this maturity of conception. And she had confidence in her discipline. When the time came for backs to be turned, *she* would damn well make that decision—and that was that!

"You will talk to my parents then—at your *earliest* opportunity."

She had risen, and this young one could have just stepped away from Gainsborough's canvas with consummate credentials of the aristocrat—that potential, that razor's edge between satisfaction and anger unsheathed now. Paul couldn't stop a grin of appreciation. "I...I believe the good form is *convenience*," he dared to say, compounding the grin she and Gainsborough had just put on him.

"I *said* opportunity—I *meant* opportunity!" She hadn't changed a whit away from the challenged, and challenging, aristocrat. Then, still in this mode, she strode to his front door and it got slammed just after her exit.

15

For several weeks, Paul and Russ worked on their plans for the tower. They decided to detect just about the same array of gases they had catalogued in their first session that had only teetered on seriousness. There were many more, more complex, species that made their contribution to the Southern California invigoration. But these would do for the gesture. With the help of catalogues Paul had retained from Drake Instruments, their plans gradually evolved. They would place their inlets near the top of a tower about a hundred feet tall. One room of the associated building would house the display of their information. Prospects for considerable drama in that room looked promising.

"And now," Russ said, in innocent violation of Paul's wish, and Carla's consideration, "how'n hell are we going to pay for it?" He dragged a heavy hand across a face that knew some sweat.

"I've been kicking that around some, myself. Give me a couple days to show my ignorance—and impetuosity."

"Good luck," Russ called, as Paul left the office. Privately, he'd already chalked this one up to a stimulating exercise in futility.

Paul *had* been thinking about this little prick of reality that has a strong affinity for balloons. He'd considered going to a bank. And then he remembered that a bank was where you went when you didn't really need money, and you'd better not show too much prophecy for future needs for it, either. He'd thought about the great charitable groups...Ford, Rockefeller. These might have been possibilities. But laying the extensive groundwork for a proposal posed a depressing time obstacle. He'd thought about a gentleman over in Bel Air who had once listened to him. Jake just might be good for a few laughs and a constructive suggestion.

"Mr. Sternglas will see you now...please follow me," the butler said. Paul followed this worthy along a long hall, across several rooms he hadn't seen before. Eventually, they came to a room that could qualify as a study. No swordfish trophies...hundreds of books covering a broad scope of subjects, a few big red leather chairs and several matching couches. A large modern globe mounted on a stand with antique accessories that could have heard Borgia laughter. A teletype, a large wall-mounted map case and a leather-embossed rosewood desk whose playground could handle any executive exuberance, filled out the landscape here. Jake's collection of etchings and watercolors in this room was another extension of this man into certain privacies that didn't perturb the useful specter of an international investment tiger.

"My boy...I'm glad to see you. Please sit down and grab a cigar and a drink, in your own order." Jake availed himself of the same privilege, cigar first. "I hear I must call you *doctor* now." Those eyes did their work again and Jake's smile didn't dispute some pride in this young squirt who'd had the effrontery to challenge him under his own roof.

"Guilty, Jake. That was about a hundred years ago. *Stinky* will still do me okay." He sipped his Scotch from Jake's big hunk of crystal.

"Have *you* come any closer to grips with that responsibility you made me think about?" Jake's grin was now resting on hands whose elbows were supported by the arms of his chair.

"Funny you should mention that, Jake. As a matter of fact I...I've come to ask your advice about a little piece of that responsibility...and what a friend and I are trying to do about it."

Jake wasn't sitting in that chair, surrounded by that executive parapher-nalia, because he had no talent for reading motives. But he let Paul rave away anyway. Paul told him about the symbol he and Russ had cooked up. Paul took a sketch—several of them—from his jacket to fill out his verbal presentation. They had these sketches laid out on Jake's desk for a long time. Jake's ques-tions about the *stunt*, and about Paul, and Russ, reflected his usual stupidity in matters of substance, very probably his substance. After they'd found the chairs again, Jake studied the opposing face for a few seconds. His memory could also call hot andirons and an impetuous fist punched into the air right next to his face.

"What do you think this little ploy might cost?" Paul hadn't even men-tioned money, but using tremendous prescience Jake had anticipated him.

"With the complete set-up...tower, instrumentation, display stuff, maybe a hundred thousand, plus a little piece of land without too much crap on it." Paul sent this off with a prayer carrying a wince.

"Christ!—if you'll pardon the word—you guys have expensive con-sciences." Jake's eyes did some roving around the visible symbols of his empire. "You didn't tell me where you're going to put this erection."

"Don't know—first things tend to come first."

"You guys ain't going to pick up anything with this stunt," Jake grunted.

"Maybe some publicity, Jake."

"You can make a living with *that*? Your legs don't look like Betty Grable's."

"Everybody's been giving this pollution bit nothing but lip-service. Except for a few lonely voices in a few labs, the guys who *can* get a handle on some of it have been looking the other way." He left the soft leather and started to walk, trying for casualness by inspecting Jake's big library. "They've been diddling with this thing for years in the LA basin—arguing over who's doing what to whom. Well, the stuff for getting a quantitative handle on where its coming from, how it responds to weather factors, dissipation and retention factors, et cetera, is on the shelves *right now*—or damn close to it."

"You jokers are going to do *all* that with that one little prick you're sticking up?"

"Our prick might show some people what *could* be done. It might start to feel uncomfortable as hell up the butt of some of the people who've got some of that responsibility—the *official* kind we didn't talk about." Paul came close to Jake's big globe and turned it slowly. "Beautiful detail...too bad we can't see all of it this clearly."

"It'll never get done until they start dropping along Wilshire, wondering where'n hell the air went."

"We'll have missed the boat then, Jake. What time's the next swan? Hell, they'll all be dead, too." Paul pushed himself away from the globe and walked toward Jake.

"Listen, Jake. I'm an Iowa cornball who's just sweated three years at one of the best technical joints in the world. I want a couple swings at the windmill before they take me away." He started pacing again. "I'll find the dough for this thing. I'll get people to look at it—I'll scare the piss out of a lot of 'em *before* I go back to wiping shit off a cow's tail."

"Don't pick out the most expensive God damn corner lot you can find," Jake finally said, as Paul was staring out of one of Jake's big windows. When he turned to Jake, damned if Jake hadn't built something of a smile and was reaching for a big checkbook. Paul told him that this was probably the worst investment he (Jake) had ever made. Jake replied that *he* would worry about the investment and then he told Paul to get t'hell out of there. Actually, Jake thought that Paul had shown a good instinct for money. His contribution might have been another concession to a charitable nature he tried to hide...but it also had the drive of a complex intuition behind it. For extra impetus on this occasion of Paul's petition, Jake also had had some recent return flow on a presumably bad investment.

To put it mildly, Russ was absolutely dumbfounded that Paul had surmounted what should have been instant defeat for their drama of contrition.

"And you say you want me to supply the detectors and display equipment for your madness?" John asked Paul on the veranda the next evening. He was glad to see the young rebel lousing up his Scotch supply again.

"My associates and I will pay your usually outrageous prices for them... of course." Paul was also glad to have this man in front of him again under better circumstances. Paul glanced at Carla, who wouldn't be denied this conversation. Martha had also shown an unsubtle nosiness and was witness to the proceedings.

"I guess we *do* have enough off-the-shelf equipment to make a fair set-up...even to satisfying your mania for ostentation. What about construction, maintenance—all the rest in that entrepreneur's bag you seemed determined to pick up?"

"We'll worry about that...it just adds a little to an impressive pile." If Paul was worried, that company couldn't find a trace of it on him.

If John had his own doubts about the practicality, and other facets a seasoned entrepreneur would think about, he had good camouflage, too. Apparently, Paul had achieved a minor miracle of coincidence between his professional crisis and a temporary relaxation of Jake's usually severe economics. The fact that Paul was bringing Drake equipment perilously close to Jake's purview also added some fillip to his thoughts.

"If we have more luck than we're entitled to, we just might get some precedence for a little business activity." Paul used his own version of reflection.

"There's a hell of a lot of competition for attention right now. Crusading has tended to bring smiles mostly to philosophers and...well, you've seen *my* library."

"Sure have, John—one of the best collections of adventure I've ever seen."

"Where are you and Russ going to put this..." Martha contended with conciseness and decorum.

"Cry of conscience?" Paul supplied. "Some low rent area, with reasonably good advertising potential."

Martha knew about the fragility of friendship and had given field demonstrations of its principles. She was not unappreciative of the forces that argued against a further conjunction of their lives. But she could find little depression in Paul's presence, and this was the topic of their silent speech...what they'd been able to accomplish this time. Both she and John, however, experienced some negative perturbation with Paul's next announcement.

"I...I've received an application for part-time employment." He turned to Carla, and this tended to fill out his words. No one but him seemed inclined to conversation, so he moved ahead. "This thing...we haven't *any* idea how it'll turn out. There's really not much to it yet...perhaps some provocation to future action. If Carla finds some interest in this area, maybe some homework on what's being done elsewhere would be something for her to think about." There was no place for his eyes after this quiet suggestion except among the lambent light transients decorating the flagstone. This bundle of his words was Carla's child. It ran counter to his recognition and resolves concerning this family—now close to him actually, and in other dimensions to which everyone there had given, was giving, appraisal. The thought suddenly occurred to him that he—his big mouth—had just trespassed certain perimeters of John's hospitality, again.

Fortunately, unlike Tom, Carla was not talented in leaving raw nerves ascending. The present situation called for a converse ability, and she had the capacity for it.

"When you characters can take some time to point out a few directions for me, maybe that *would* be something to think about—a way to use some of that expensive education of mine." Her bag of emotion at that moment had few ingredients for a smile, but she managed to find enough. And she minimized her acting chore by stating that she was late for a tennis date. Her performance concluded with a good imitation of a favored one running off to claim more of the treasure.

16

The management of the project was moving satisfactorily. All they needed now was a place to put it. This remainder was looming prominently when Paul tracked Russ to his lair in Chemistry.

"Sorry, Russ, didn't mean to barge," he said, when he saw that someone else occasionally had access to Russ' ears.

"Come in, Paul. Stilt, meet Doctor Paul Sanger. Paul...Jason Jones. Jason—Stilt—is a graduate student of mine...God help him."

"By God...*Stilt* is right," Paul said, when the black student finally uncoiled all of himself from a chair near Russ' desk and stood, extending a hand to Paul.

"Until—if—I get my sheepskin, Stilt is okay." The grin persisted and it was contagious.

Paul claimed another chair. After some discussion of Stilt's more immediate scholastic objectives, Paul turned to Russ. "We've got a small extracurricular problem of location to chew on...maybe later on." He started to rise, but Russ waved him back to the chair.

"Great minds find food for each other." Russ turned to his student. "Stilt...we're looking for some cheap real estate for a project." Then, with some addition from Paul, Russ outlined their little arrogance for Stilt.

"Jeese...it looks like somebody's left a couple rope ladders dangling from the ivory tower." Stilt's private thoughts had more scope than his remark.

"Like we were saying, Stilt, we pay scale for any suggestions," Paul said. The first impressions here were entirely satisfactory.

"Well, I know a place that's got plenty of cheap real estate," Stilt said after they had flooded the room with silence for a few seconds. He'd lost a small piece of his grin with that remark. "You also said something about an *advertising potential*...not wanting to be too coy about your good intentions." He could have lathered that with more cynicism but these guys were asking for *his* suggestions. "East LA...lots of nice land there with plenty of advertising spots—but you might not like some of the customers."

"We don't know just who we *will* reach with this thing, Stilt." Paul shot a quick glance to Russ.

"I can give you about any shade of black, brown, white...yellow...a God damn *rainbow* of customers, within a few blocks of anyplace there. What kind of customer are you designing for?" Stilt had just made a very good point, and then he made another one. "This symbol wouldn't be good for that place without embellishment...too sophisticated. If you could make it edible—maybe a 100 foot long hot dog—you'd have *real* good advertising potential and you could find a spot for it damn near anyplace in that part of LA." Stilt turned out a good laugh, a booming laugh, with his downing of his own suggestion. He had the equipment for a fine professional athlete in several sports. But CIT had scratched him deeper and he was looking for his opportunities beyond the playing fields. Before Russ, or Paul, could respond to him, he pushed another chewing piece toward them.

"Maybe some local involvement in a project like that...don't quite see how you could play that. But you might find a way to build some interest... and pride. They sure as hell could use a shot of that in *that* part of Eden." Stilt uncoiled again and extended his big hand in Paul's direction.

"Great to meet you, Doctor Sanger. This thing sounds kind of wild, but if you ever need an extra two cents..."

"We'll sure as hell call you, Stilt." Paul strained to hold up his end of the handshake, but his smile came without any strain at all.

Stilt had left the room, but a big piece of him remained.

"Good man, there. He showed an estimable perception of our frailties." Paul started stoking his pipe.

"His analytical powers are also promising." Russ started to bring his own pipe into the fray.

"That's right. Those poor bastards wouldn't appreciate a sophisticated gesture like this. It ought to be kept deep in the bowels of PAG...surrounded by PhDs. It's..."

"Irrelevant to them is a phrase that comes easily," Russ said.

"Irrelevant to their condition is maybe a better phrase," Paul suggested.

"*Touché.* About the only thing we have in common with them is the...air."

"Yeah. Water is close, but it usually requires conduits...that would be an awkward stage for us."

"The battleground of our present concern is the...air." Russ repeated himself.

"But this isn't *near* enough of a bridge to excuse sticking our..." Paul struggled for the excusing words.

"Rigid finger of protest into a pot that already overflows with it," Russ concluded.

"Right," Paul also concluded.

So, it wasn't logical that they should look for a site within the area of East LA where Stilt's customers prevailed. And when they made the arrangement that actually nailed down a bare piece of land for them, the bad logic of it still assailed them. But it had a slight advantage of elevation. And if one wanted to take a good sniff of bad LA air, they were in one of the best corridors for it.

They contacted an engineering firm in Pasadena about construction. The owner finally had to get into the act when Paul and Russ found themselves defending their location in front of his staff. There had even been use of such pleasantries as *crazy bastards* during the dialogue among these entrepreneurs. Finally, they agreed to help Paul and Russ perpetrate their penetration into Stilt's Eden. The draftsmen were told to get on it, with the objective of starting construction ASAP. The word *permanence* sometimes intrudes new construction, but in this arena neither Paul and Russ, nor the other side, put themselves in the saddle of this word.

Before they left for their homes that afternoon, Paul made Russ take a detour to a private detective and guard outfit he knew of near Pasadena. Russ was still somewhat in the dark when they accosted the manager.

"What can I do for you, gentlemen?"

"We'd like a guard for a property we're building," Paul said.

"Fine...just a few details." The manager pulled a form from his desk drawer. When Paul told him about the type of property, there was no reaction. When he told him about the hours of protection, there was no reaction. When he told him about the location, there was a reaction.

"Well, okay...we'll try it. I'll see if I can get a gorilla—with an expert marksman's badge."

"That's just exactly what we *don't* want." Paul glanced at Russ, who was a genuine bystander. "We're looking for an older man, with a kind face...who likes kids." Paul let this monstrous inadequacy sink in for a moment.

"For Christ's sake!—and you also want this guy on the verge of suicide!"

"I don't think it'll be anything like that. We've seen some of those people. We expect to see a lot more before we're done. There were quite a few teenaged kids near the site. I think the right man could inspire a little awe, maybe enough respect to recruit a few of them for guard duty. One man—or a company—couldn't hold that place under the wrong circumstances. I think a bunch of interested—involved—kids might do the job, with some inspiration." The manager needed a little more convincing, but he finally conceded to Paul, telling him that he would do what he could, and would call him the next day. On the way out of the office, Russ turned to Paul.

"You didn't tell me you minored in psychology."

"That guy Stilt has a way of sticking to your ribs." Paul crossed his fingers where he hoped Russ couldn't see them—he had suddenly lathered science and technology with a dose of sociology.

The manager did call the next day and asked Paul if he could come to the office. He had one man, in his fifties, who did part-time guard duty and who might fill Paul's bill.

Mike was a gray haired man, medium height, well built, with eyes that looked like they knew their way around rifles, pistols and machine guns and he had a cigar box full of medals to prove it. He also had the kind of face that doesn't inspire instant panic in kids, although there had been recruits, and some veteran platoon men, who could argue that point. Paul knew he had his man as soon as he looked into that face, and gripped the powerful hand.

After two days on the site, Mike had several kids hanging around him, listening to stories of the Corps. Paul had carefully briefed him on his strategy and the old boy was all for it. Within two weeks, Mike had acquired a cadre of youngsters, of a spectrum of colors and personalities that would make a DI lick his lips. It was also a group that could hold the fort against vandalism, if the older folks didn't get too rough. Paul felt pretty good about this part of the engineering.

The steel elements quickly assumed the shape of a tower. It would be about a hundred feet tall, with several intermediate levels, and a top platform for the array of detector inlets. The building had also come up quickly under the contractor's promotion of simplicity and that implicit impermanence. Finally, everything but John's stuff was there. There had been a slow diffusion of knowledge about the project throughout the area. In the later stages, there had been considerable observation and even some questions. Paul and Russ had told the men to be cooperative with the visitors and, even at the cost of adding to the tab, to bend a lot in satisfying curiosity. And to avoid provocation—and to use their *best* gymnastic ability for that one.

When it was done, except for the instrumentation, everyone stood off and watched the sun make little stars in the unpainted steel. Some of them knew that there were other towers, not far from there, that had been erected by an Italian dreamer who also saw stars in his steel.

John made good on his promise. A small trickle of his equipment roughly coincided with completion of construction and within several weeks it had built into a stream that kept them busy enough. Russ and Paul and Stilt worked on the instrumentation and calibration of the detectors, with the help of some of John's people. After they had scrambled up and down that tower a hundred times, and had cussed and pleaded with the nerve center of electronic paraphernalia, everything gave them the response they had expected in the beginning—but not with much conviction.

John saw the completed system and he had some trouble keeping his smile modest. Paul had driven Martha and Carla to the site several times during construction, limiting his discussion to the vantage of the car. But when it was nearly done, they wanted to get closer and he had to give them a crash course on the physical chemistry of gases that included close on-site inspection, and a climb up to the top of the tower.

"I've never seen...this part of town...like *this*," Martha said. Paul was standing between her and Carla on the top platform, close enough to perform the protective gentleman if needed. From their perspective, Martha saw that *this part of town* was embedded in the whole panorama of Los Angeles...and that the general pride of this part of California couldn't avoid it much longer. Carla also exclaimed over several landmarks of Los Angeles that had now entered their perspective. Paul and Russ's tower gave new perspectives at the top—and at the bottom where the detectors talked with the recorders and annunciators.

They were ready for the first trial of detection, and display of detection. This particular technical exercise wouldn't bring the colors that five thousand degrees of Herr Fahrenheit can do and hopefully there would be no exhaust clouds—but it was building an excitement that was a close relative of another time in that control room at PAG.

17

On the day the detectors were going to throw their intelligence to the scopes and recorders that were catching, Russ and Paul and Stilt would be watching. Also, a reporter from the Times, and his photographer, would be there. Shortly after the on-site work had started, a reporter had been there. How he knew about the project was a good question. But John had always been a bit gabby around the nineteenth hole at Annandale. John would be there, too, as soon as he could sneak away from the formal part of his business. Carla and Martha were sensitive to this event, but they let the excitement have a strictly male bias for reasons of unconstrained pleasure—or cussing—if things went the other way.

After Paul had chatted with Mike for a few moments, he went into the building to warm up its temperamental occupants. Then he climbed the tower for a last minute inspection of the inlet system, and returned to the building for a few trials with display ensembles to check their humor. He had few illusions about electronics. It was wonderful stuff—when it worked—and if you had a top notch crew to keep it that way. He'd fought more with instrumentation at PAG than with the propellants. Once, they'd lost an important run because somebody at IC forgot to turn on the chart drives for the chamber pressure recorders. Their reward for success was a bunch of ink blots where the pens had quivered in frustration for several minutes waiting for a stage. But this was human error, and that was another thing to mix into the rising complication that was in the exploding sunrise of electronics.

Now they looked like they would behave themselves. Paul finally settled back in a chair and laid a smoke cloud with his pipe. Mike would poke his head into the place from time to time and sometimes Paul would put some technical words on him and Mike would leave, muttering and shaking his head.

Russ and Stilt showed up, almost together about an hour later. Stilt had not reneged on his interest in the work, and his share of the present status of it was considerable. He was working with Russ on a new technique in kinetics using shock tubes and during the gaps in his on-site services, he and Paul found plenty to talk about.

"Maybe we ring some bells today?" Russ said to Paul, after inspecting most of the system himself.

"Yup." Seeing Russ was about to swing, Paul followed up with, "And we might just get some hateful publicity while we're doing it."

"Oh...that man from the Times coming over is he?" Russ' expression confirmed Paul's ugly suspicion that media people were welcomed into the Temple precincts. In fact, those tricky priests even had a make-up room tucked behind that statue of Archimedes.

They'd been sampling the air of Los Angeles for about an hour. The oscilloscopes and recording instruments were showing traces—and more than traces—of almost *every* gas they'd set up for. By changing the sensitivity of their detector-recording couplings, they could make the lines dance over the papers and the screens. John had loaned them one of his latest experimental scopes that could display four traces, in as many different colors. It had a 4x4 foot screen and it made a wonderfully spectacular display against the green grids that could be varied at will by changing the scale spans of the instrument. By adjusting arbitrary critical limits for the detected gases, they could make lights flash, bells ring, and Stilt had even rigged up a lugubrious sounding horn for the ultimate occasions.

There was flashing, ringing, indicating, and recording when the reporter and his photographer arrived. He didn't say anything, just stared, and told his man to shoot...shoot everything in black and white and color, He got one wide angle shot from the top of the tower that picked up parts of the project and some of the Watts Towers of the Italian dreamer. That one made Life and Time a little later.

John came by early in the afternoon, after the pit crew had returned from lunch and they had everything steamed up again. They could have looked for more mature intelligence, but right now they were playing with their new toy and seeing how high it could bounce. To give the system more semblance of the scientific approach, they had installed transducers for wind direction and velocity, barometric pressure and atmospheric temperature on the tower. By imposing these real time signatures on their records, they had about all of the single point fix they could get on some of the gaseous properties of Los Angeles.

Inside the display room, Paul challenged John and Russ: "Can you guys see what an array of these things around Southern California could do? Fed into a central computer set-up, we could get virtually instantaneous displays and records of the concentration fields that covered the whole damn country here. You could set up detectors along the main arteries, specialized for auto emissions, and get a good handle on what our little indispensables are doing to us...the tailpipe part, at least." Paul hadn't moved his eyes away from the physical chemical playground plastered all over the wall in front of him.

"It would scare hell out of 'em," Russ said.

"Damn you characters! Just when I was settling down for a nice milking of the defense situation you have to open the window for me—I'm not sure I like all this fresh air." At that time John wasn't looking at the perpetrators when he said this. He was standing on the first platform of the tower and a local patch of rare blue sky had just complicated his loud complaint, pointed between up and down.

It *is* heady, ain't it, boss man," Paul shouted upward. The afterward grin felt good.

Before they shut it down, Paul called Jake and asked him to come down to the site. Jake's Rolls pulled up in front of the project about forty minutes later. His chauffeur didn't look comfortable. When Jake finally unscrambled from the rear seat, he didn't look like he'd just had his best dividend, either. At the moment Jake entered the building, the warning horn decided to speak and the light consoles played an impressive colored tune.

"What'n hell *is* this?" Jake asked anyone. They told him, and when they got to some of the critical stuff, and the fact that an array of these things could make a much more significant and impressive showing, Jake held up his hands—Jake threw up his hands.

"God help me! What have I done? You bastards have opened Pandora's box—I've *helped* you open it! My friends—the bankers—are going to be damn unhappy." Jake sat down, his face matching his acceleration.

"How so, Jake?" Jake's dramatic distress didn't do a thing to Paul's grin.

"Before *you* came to my place, I was picking up a few coupons now and then. Now, I got to look at these God damn coupons to see if they got *contamination* on 'em!" Jake's glare at Paul spread to other people about in time with *contamination*, but all he picked up was more grins.

They finally shut it down for that day. Paul told Jake that they would be seeing him about an other million, or so, and then everybody, except Mike and his crew, left. They had agreed to do a repeat the next day on a less flamboyant scale. They wanted a closer look at their sensitivities and the changes in the gas concentrations with time and atmospheric parameters. That evening, they made a minor item in the Times and a local radio station.

But they had chosen a site where there were restless customers, as Stilt had implied. They were components of an unstable equilibrium that could be broken by trivial local action. There had been some incidents during construction that didn't disabuse the opinion that they'd chosen the wrong theatre for their play. Unscheduled lines had occasionally intruded, and there had been some good pantomime tending to confirm the prediction of irrelevance. And sometimes, without either words or pantomime, there'd been a silent presence, a travesty of observation, enforced by crueler agents than air pollution.

That night, Paul called the site to check on status. It was okay, Mike assured him. He'd even picked up a new recruit that afternoon. For the overnight watch, Paul had insisted that Mike leave the site in the hands of the senior members of his platoon. Mike hadn't liked this in the later stages of construction, but Paul had insisted and told him that he would give an extra fiver to the boys selected for night duty. Mike finally agreed and organized a roster the boys went for. It *was* amazing how far some delegated authority and pride could go.

The six o'clock news gave him the first warning. It had mentioned fires in East LA and the possibility of a general police alert. The image of those fires, thrown against a low cloud cover, verified this for him. And from the vantage where he first saw it, he also saw the face of a wasting storm that was just starting to feed on the resident energy. The site could be unaffected but he didn't really believe this as he drove toward it. His track intersected increasing pulses of the action whose epicenter lay somewhere ahead of him. There were occasional pieces of official action suggesting more confused disbelieve, than authority. Somehow he made the right detours and he found a path to the site.

There was fire and noise in the neighborhood. But these were only the trailing peripherals of a storm that had passed. Paul left his car in the street, figuring he could do better with legs. It wasn't much of a run to the site, but his emotions had already taken a big draught of his energy and they now made unreasonable demands on him.

There were several others at the site who had spent more than emotion. When Paul reached it, the first target for his eyes was one of Mike's crew. He was sitting on the ground, head cradled in his arms, and there was blood on his neck and shoulders. This was pitiful, but there were more personal targets for him. Mike was also on the ground, his back supported by the building. His head was down on his chest, his chin pushed into a massive blood smear that was the gravest signal Paul had ever seen.

"Mike...my God..." It began as a loud cry and ended almost a whisper into ears that also showed blood. "Oh...Jesus...Jesus...*Jesus*..." His groans, like words, were only the tip of a berg that tried to freeze his heart. A faint moan came from underneath the panoply of shock, and then a louder one called him to the building. The door had been ripped off, so his staggering entrance was easy. Their careful display of their civilization was now a souvenir of anger with ancient precedents. He tried to study the scene, but the light was poor, and his eyes couldn't focus. The moan came again and this time it vectored him to a shadowy corner, where Stilt had been dumped along with more garbage from the storm.

"Stilt...Stilt...who?" Mike had left him a little concern and he spent the rest of it on Stilt. Stilt was hurt, but he was now enjoying one of the advantages of an uncommon body. Before the blackness claimed him, he found some fragments of a voice, and he almost made a grin. "Damn rainbow of 'em..." he said. Stilt had had earlier warning of the trouble than Paul from one of his relatives in that area, and his ties to the project had pulled him into a leading edge of the storm.

This double pounding had been almost enough excuse for a collapse. But a louder, if not more palpable blow sounded from the roof of the building. It was caused by a piece of pipe thrown from the tower. Paul ran from the building, looked up, and shouted, "Get down—you dirty son of a bitch!" There wasn't much left to give, but that noise on the roof opened his last gate of emotion and it needed to pass a better vehicle than grief. As he started up the tower, the rattle of equipment against the roof continued. When he reached the second deck, about forty feet above the roof of the building, he stumbled and caught himself with his hands against the platform. Somebody stomped on one of his hands and a pulse of unique pain shot through every fiber of his body. He staggered up to the platform and a fist smashed into the center of his face before he could identify a target of opportunity. This made a rainbow against the shadow of a customer he could barely see. He swung in that direction with his good hand and felt the impact against a face. This gave him some orientation...so he followed with a low hooking blow with his other fist aimed at his estimation of a genital target—putting Francisco kind of strength into it. A guttural expletive confirmed his target. The injured hand shouldn't have done this, but it wasn't talking to Paul and he wasn't listening anyway. He had one blow left. He drove his good fist into the face that still was no more than a shadow. He heard a body strike the far side of the framework, and then he staggered backwards toward his side of the structure, his arms spread wide in a wild grab for some part of the lattice of the tower that was probably available to him. But Herr Gauss constrained him to a far part of the tail of his damn probability distribution and Paul found only air. Then he had the short vertical acceleration that Mr. Newton had promised before he crashed through the roof of the building. During his fall, alternating images of the sky and the earth flashed in his vision and he knew he was close to the door of the infinite dream.

Russ' own presentment of crisis that night had been no less than Paul's. When he'd been unable to reach Paul, he called the police and then he fought his own battle of progress to the site. The youngster had gone when help arrived, but there was more than enough for Russ. Somehow Russ and the police vanguard found an ambulance for Paul and Stilt and Mike and a reasonably quick passage to LA General Hospital.

"He won't be doing any climbing for a long time," the white gowned gentleman said to Russ and the Drakes in the hall. "He's got a skull fracture... his nose and some teeth are broken...and his leg wasn't designed for what he did to his. It's fractured in three places, one right at the hip...I forgot a couple broken ribs and a smashed hand."

Russ had called John, and John, Martha and Carla had arrived within a half hour after they brought Paul, Stilt, and Mike in.

They let his friends take a quick look at Paul, but all they could see was a big pile of bandages. When Martha and Carla started to cry, the men got them out of there, being careful to avert their faces from the women.

They had put Stilt in a room a few doors away from Paul's. But Mike didn't need this accommodation. The knife had found a target that had been very elusive to enemies of his country, and he had left them shortly after arriving at the hospital. Paul and Russ' presentment had had company, so Mike had overstayed his own schedule for the watch. He'd done what he could do with fists. And when the thought occurred to him that Paul's limits no longer applied to him...it was too late. Paul had muttered something about Mike when they brought him in. But they couldn't tell him of the end. Even if he could have heard them, the dolmen of his grief had plenty of stones already.

Martha called Paul's parents and Mary in New York. They would all arrive that evening, or in the morning. Martha tried to invoke calm, but she didn't fool anybody, least of all Paul's mother. They all came directly to the hospital and John and Martha met them when the desk announced their arrival.

Paul's mother and father insisted on seeing their son and nobody was going to deny them...especially that man with the bushy eyebrows and the drooping mustache. They couldn't see any more than the others had seen. His mother cried, and his father laid a hand on him and squeezed it just a little. If his eyes were wet, he was damn careful to hide it. They talked with the doctors and got the same message. Mary responded to the heap of bandages like Martha and Carla had done. John took her hand, whispering something to her that was everybody's business...and something that probably wasn't.

After a few hours, John and Martha took the Sangers home with them. That evening, John showed some of the grounds to them. Later the men spent a long time in John's den looking over the equipment. Paul's father asked about the big wooden sword and John recounted most of that adventure with Paul and Francisco. Martha talked with Paul's mother before the fireplace, while Mary was with Carla, in Carla's room. His mother had known of the Drakes, of course, through Paul's letters, in-person descriptions, and had met them at Paul's CIT graduation. This one had also never believed that Paul's enthusiasm had been limited to the architecture and paintings of this house. Martha's portrait, that had captured Paul and Mary, didn't escape her, either. Before she left for Iowa, Paul's mother came to know the mistress of this house very well. If there was some censure in her, now there was also some qualification of it.

Stilt would have several interesting scars for his concern. But that compaction of bone and muscle had shown remarkable recuperation. As soon as he could bring *his* bandages to Paul's room, he came. At first, he sat in silence. And then, when Paul's receiver was better tuned, he bent Paul's ear plenty. The Drakes, his family, and Russ had been to the hospital almost every day since he'd entered it and they were beginning to bug the harried staff with their questions. Paul's mother and father had to leave soon. His crisis period was over, but hands had been pressed white when the coma from his skull fracture had lasted longer than expected.

Paul was in good enough shape for a more formal reception of guests. He was sitting up. His head was still swathed in bandages; his leg was in a heavy cast supported by an interesting pulley arrangement; one of his hands was bandaged; he had a tape across his nose and both of his eyes were still montages of the darker shades of the spectrum. And there was a fascinating scab that ran from one corner of his mouth to the cleft in his chin. All in all, he gave a classical reflection of a fractional second's obliteration of robust health. He made as good a grin as he could when his visitors arrived. The nurse had tried to shave him that morning and he did show some improvement from her effort.

"It doesn't take much to get you characters down to the hospital," he said to the faces clustered around him. These faces were all trying hard to be casual. They'd worried about him, but that crack signified that Dr. Sanger would be messing around again, any day now. They chatted about everything they could think of, trying hard not to make Paul smile...but he wouldn't cooperate. Finally, they had to leave. The women kissed him on various places which, to each, seemed farthest from a bandage. Maybe Mary's *was* closest to his lips.

The men took his one good paw in a careful squeeze, and then they all left, over his protests. Later in the day, when Paul was getting much needed rest, a gentleman arrived at the hospital in a Rolls. He was unhappy about them not letting him in Paul's room. But after he *had* taken a good look, he left, sharing a portion of his thoughts with those in his vicinity.

After three more weeks, that saw a gradual return of the horseplay component of this particular patient-visitor group, the hospital had to let him go. John and Martha insisted on taking the cast that was Paul Sanger to their home for recuperation. This decision had been bolstered by several long phone conversations with an Iowa number.

This was the second time Paul had entered this house in the capacity of a patient. This time he had better credentials and his resistance was lower. Martha installed him in her largest guest room. Apart from the progress inspections by his doctor, about the only vestige of his accident now was the leg cast. He would need this for a few more weeks, and then a cane would come in handy for a long time. He tried to get out of bed for more extensive maneuvers than the bathroom kinds, but Martha and Carla wouldn't let him. They played checkers and chess with him, and read to him. He didn't know there was that much poetry in existence, but Carla made him like it. Martha had a good library to draw on for non poetical phases. Jake brought a few volumes over. The old boy from Bel Air had seen him a few times at the hospital. At the Drake house, he didn't have much to say. He mostly gave Paul those eyes again, now couched in his version of softness. Hetty also made contact with Paul. Once, she gave him a good shot of Mid-Eastern erotica from a niche in Jake's den that hadn't been Jake's secret for a long time.

When the cast finally came off, there were anxious moments when Paul tried a few steps with a cane and he gradually put weight on the leg. John thought he would have to catch him, but Paul waved him off and was soon hobbling around in unstable equilibrium. He tried a little jig that brought small screams from the ladies, and a cry of pain from him when the leg protested. Soon, he was bothering all of them. Martha had to make the kitchen off-limits because he was using too much of her Mary's time, and laughter. John took him for long rides all over Southern California when he had to have a change of scene. Carla made him exercise for long hours in the pool before she'd let him back to the peace and quiet of John's den. No man ever had more attention than this—but that was just his opinion.

He was in John's den, reading some more sporting material and looking—again—at the pictures he and John had taken on their South American jaunt. His eyes kept drifting to Francisco's sword and the memories flooded him without his control. John came in, followed by Martha and Carla. John looked rather peculiar. Martha and Carla seemed to be carrying something extra, too.

"You want the rent."

"You've come to throw me out for another tenant—an MIT man."

"You've come to complain about the wine stain I made on the carpet last night."

"You've..."

"Shut up!" John ordered. Paul noticed that one of John's hands was behind him.

"Something's up. " Paul scanned all the faces again.

"Yup." John used Paul's own eloquence.

"You don't mean those guys from Sacramento got into the act?"

"Nope."

"For God's sake, John—stop teasing him." Martha snatched the thing from John's hand and thrust it into Paul's hand.

He saw his name on the address part of it. And then he saw the name of the place where Harry Truman had said that the buck stopped. Paul stared at the envelope and then looked up at the three postmen. He had some trouble opening it and John was about to help when a female hand stopped him.

"He wants me to come to Washington." Paul handed the letter to John, who was slow in sliding his look off Paul, toward the letter. Once, hereabouts, a man had contended with a dream. Now the eyes in his vicinity were giving him various pieces of continuity of it...and he didn't know if he could handle it.

He couldn't nail down all of his thoughts the morning he left the Mayflower for the White House. The cabby had given him an odd look when he'd casually announced his destination, but there were plenty in this town who could do this to a cabby. He thought about Russ and Mike. They deserved to be here as much as he. He thought about the great beginning they'd made on the symbol and what would become of it now. Jake had shown a generosity that couldn't be imposed on again. The fragile bulwarks John had imputed to crusades were tumbling around in his perspective again—but Martha and Carla, alongside him, looking at new perspectives, was a persistent counter image that helped put more of a proper White House visitor into him.

"Doctor Sanger...the President will see you now. Please follow me," the young man said to him a few minutes after his arrival. Paul had visited the White House as a tourist many years before, but this was new country. He was ushered into a large famous office and immediately he saw a familiar face. At that moment, it was wearing a smile that nearly overmatched the office. This man was no stranger to battles and that smile would have complimented most of the world's warriors from various arenas. They had called him beyond the uniform into this office with the interesting crest of arms and a present significance no other room in the world could match. He was contending with the course of more tracks leading to more unfriendly wildernesses than the ones Paul and Carla knew about. He'd succeeded in curving a few of them, and he'd bend some more before he was through.

"Doctor Sanger, I *am* pleased to meet you."

"Thank you, sir."

And then they talked, longer than Paul had expected for the preliminaries...largely generalizations that slipped into some specifics of sports and science projects. Then, after a short sojourn to a beautiful clipper ship model, this man turned to Paul, "And *now*, Paul?" This was one time when those words made him try to respond to them.

"Mr. President, I must presume that you've heard about our little adventure in symbolism...in LA."

"Indeed...and your leg looks like it's mending well."

"It is, thank you, sir. Well...it was just that, a symbol of the fact that some of us technical people *are* looking once in a while toward the folks who eventually pay all the bills."

"Some of your thoughts, intentions, on that subject have come to me... from a few of my associates." A topgallant sail competed for a moment with Paul.

"I think we impressed a few people out there...before East LA got tangled up with the other business."

"Your impression jumped out farther than you might suspect." The President made a slight hand motion to keep the show rolling.

"Before the...accident, we succeeded in showing that this could be more than a symbol. To be specific: a network of similar, or improved, detection stations placed in strategic areas of the country, and serviced by an adequate computer coupling, could give an excellent handle on air pollution. Similar surveillance for water pollution, with suitable instrumentation modifications, might also be a possibility. I think that comprehensive, *continuous*, monitoring is a prerequisite for getting *any* control of this pollution thing. After sufficient control *had* been exercised—probably intercontinental in scope—the network could be relaxed...consistent with the eagle's eye." The President's study of him had been sober up to the *eagle*. At that point—like a good Kansas plainsman's—that smile sprouted again.

"What about the stuff from automobiles?"

"I think we should go after the other pollution that can be handled right now. With detectors specialized to auto emissions, and suitably located, we could keep good tabs on what Detroit says they're doing to help from their side. They need time and some prodding. I suggest that the laws affecting them, and the sensible technology, should come out about together—good surveillance could move things in that direction...and make a more cooperative audience for both ends of those laws."

They talked a little more. The President was also a fly rod nut, and they got tangled up on that for a couple minutes...even bringing the Test and the Itchen into it, classic English chalk streams where this man had gone to relieve some of the tension of command. Just as Paul was leaving the oval office, he asked Paul how his golf game was coming. How'n hell did *he* know about that? Paul recovered enough to say that he might give him some competition some day—figuratively speaking, of course. The President replied that if they could overlap their schedules enough some day—it might not be so damn figurative.

Two weeks later, after Paul had assumed his own diggings again, a special delivery letter came to him. It bore the same embellishment as the previous one from WDC. He was alone this time, and his hands didn't tremble when he opened it. It was a copy of a note the president had sent to his cabinet officer who dealt with matters of health and welfare. Near the end of it, there was a list of proposals for action in the area of this officer's competence and relevance. And near the end of *that* list, there was a sentence that qualified for a hit between Paul's eyes.

"*And I recommend that consideration be given to a surveillance net-work incorporating units such as exemplified by the Sanger Tower in Los Angeles, and that...*"

Paul had to sit down. After a while he called Russ. And then he went to Arden road and showed it to Martha and Carla. When John came home he shoved it in John's face. John said that if anything ever called for a party—*this* was it.

When Paul arrived for his dinner the next evening, he gave the griffin head a good twist and then another one. Then he went in, without waiting for the maid. He felt he could indulge this effrontery—just once. It brought him to the entrance of the room with the central fireplace. He stopped at the entrance, leaning slightly on the cane he'd bought from the little man in WDC who added pieces of dapper to various officials, mostly those from State.

Martha and Carla were giving the fireplace the best frame it ever had. They saw him, and he certainly saw them. He looked at John, who was standing some distance away from the ladies, and then he concentrated his eye power on the ladies. Certainly not twins in beauty...each of them would have made Reynolds and Gainsborough happy with their contributions to the nuances of womanhood...playful and otherwise, that keep a great artist on his toes.

Before anyone could say anything, a slight motion near the entrance to the dining room caught his eye and Mary stepped into the room, once again coupling the words *beauty* and *redundancy* in the best way. John and Martha had made her come to Pasadena. After all, how many times has *your* brother talked with the President—in the White House? Paul tried to say something and then he gave it up and walked to Mary. Her last view of him had been plastered with assorted vestiges of his accident. Now, the burgeoning image of his Washington vestiges was a better sight, and when he kissed her she had to be cooperative.

Then there was a minor explosion of laughter and talk and the first of some bottles from France made their entrance and exit. Paul had drifted close to John's study in the course of playful action with the ladies. John had preceded him and when he caught Paul's eye he made a discreet hand signal for him to stop, and Paul did...right in mid-flight, so to speak. John stepped toward him and handed him a small, flat case, with the quiet statement that this was some unfinished business. John tried to reinforce the discretion by gently pressing Paul's fingers over the edge of the case and then he rejoined the ladies himself. Paul played along with John and he tried to hide it someplace in his jacket. No man has ever had much success in work of this sort within the scope of multiple female auras. The ladies were soon—two, or three seconds—clustered around him, and they made him open the case. Nearly simultaneously, everyone saw the silver chain with the amulet bearing rare latticed turquoise. Paul recognized Zuni craftsmanship of another age. He stared at it, and then he found John, who was now standing some distance away. These two made a piece of their encyclopedia again, and then Paul set the case down and fought emotion by the device of grabbing and tickling as many luscious waists as he could catch. And he did well, for a guy with a slightly game leg. The ladies had never understood the Indian nonsense that had erupted in this house—now, and once before, according to their accounting, and the insolent attitude of the men didn't encourage them.

Considering the sound and light that flowed into the palette of conversation from five directions, and the successive ornaments of Martha's repast that put in some restraint from time to time, the dinner was a success. Near its end, Mary said that *she* had something to puff up the drama of the evening a bit. Pulling at a fine gold chain, whose end had enjoyed the marvelous hospitality of her bosom all evening, she brought forth an engagement ring of impressive proportions. The rest of the company was inflicted with the blessed malady of speechlessness for a moment. And then, between their questions, and some moistened sparkle in Mary's eyes, they found that she'd finally decided to show mercy to one of the poor devils who'd come under her spell. Paul knew of it. John, too. And now another would. He was one of the Journal ones. Paul called her traitor to her face. John complimented her on her choice of man. Martha and Carla's enthusiasm was less biased. It was a totally unexpected facet of an evening that already had gem quality. So much so, that Martha made Paul and Mary spend the night, in that house of friends with various credentials.

Sleep made a hard entrance for Paul that night. *Mary's engagement announcement triggered an avalanche of memories of her. More of her would be taken from him now...but this was a natural phenomenon he could accommodate. He'd had plenty of practice for accommodation. Martha's toast...so long ago. His service to her regimen hadn't offended the graces too much, but it had been part of the stressful components of the years since her. That damn conscience of his had put its tentacles into every part of his life—Mike had died with a piece of it stuck in his throat. That Marine had put up another flag on a mountain he couldn't back away from now. And he'd pulled some more good men up there with him who now wouldn't let him relax the quality of his dreams. He'd used the words put-up or shut-up with Carla. This young one sure as hell wouldn't let him coast very far on a couple looks from a Kansas eagle. Carla...Martha and Mary's presences in him were mostly in time that had flowed past him...she was in what was buffeting him now and would be coming. She was a partial reincarnation of a dream he had, with help, relinquished. She hadn't been helpful in defining the forbidden perimeters of her. She had entangled consciences with him—a collision he'd worked on by parading his too close to hers, by insinuating other parts of him close to susceptibilities that John and Martha had made too damn much like his own. His construction wouldn't let him avoid her, deny her—go to other paths that could help work that disentanglement that had had various endorsements in this house, in himself...but they had been changeable—no really finished point of resolve had come at him and he could crowd both Martha and John into this deficiency.*

That voice from New England that started in that tangle of oaks near PAG...an insistence made for him from the softest pieces of breath. He'd stood up to it. It had been sustenance for some of the bravado he'd paraded in front of Jake...but where would the voices be for what was coming at him?

18

During the two months following Paul's White House attention, there were three events of significance:

There was Mary's wedding in Mason City. This took almost a week, and another talent of the Czechs showed during that time. They knew how to join a man and a woman in a bond that—generally—stayed well glued for life. They knew how to give solemnity, beauty, joyful madness to an occasion whose anticipation had given Mary some apprehension about her sheltered New Yorker. However, following an acclimation period that lasted about five minutes, this stockbroker showed a splendid susceptibility to the proceedings and a talent for giving—and receiving—that jumped the fence of her prior appraisal of him. Finally, they had to go to the train, and he went more reluctantly than she might have wished. Paul and her mother and father and a hundred, or so, others bade them Godspeed into matrimony.

When the newlyweds returned to their apartment in Manhattan, among many gifts was a silver service from John and Martha that made Mary gasp. Included in this equipment was a simple fruit bowl, about two feet across the top diameter. On the bottom surface that could be read from above, there was some fine, and to Mary, completely unintelligible engraving. The letters and groups made Mary's lips form words that sounded like, *"Min neep ne chek."* Her husband got a different bunch of sounds. He advised her to keep it in delightful mystery...it probably being too ribald for her tender ears. Mary was not so inclined. She went to the American Museum of Natural History. This was the right place, and she found the right man. He was tall, pink cheeked, blue eyed, and he looked like one who had known many of the first rank. He had, in fact, looked into the eyes of Joseph of the Nez Percé, and Red Cloud and Crazy Horse and Tecumseh, and when Mary pulled the scrap of paper from her purse that was a rubbing of the engraving, he studied it for just a moment. Then he looked at her, blue eyes dancing with her. "My dear...you *do* have friends of quality. This is from the language of the Nez Percé. It can be translated...*we will remember*." Mary thanked him and left. Once, while her husband was at his office, trying to extract more support for her extravagances of paint and canvas and film and books, several of Mary's tears struck the gleaming side of the bowl and part of them came to rest over the inscription, distorting a small part of it. But she could now read all of it...and she would also remember.

And there was Stilt coming to Paul's door one afternoon after Mary's wedding. Paul hadn't visited the site since his accident. Hell, a little more wreckage over there wouldn't be noticed...but it was Jake's investment, what was left of it, and they'd take care of it. Stilt insisted they see it that afternoon. When they pulled up in front of the site, Paul first noticed that the grounds had been cleaned of all debris, and that the building and tower showed no evident damage. He also noticed a miscellany of boys—some he remembered as part of Mike's crew—walking around in a businesslike way. And they appeared to be better dressed, and better scrubbed, than he remembered. He also saw a small enclosure near the building that looked like a ticket booth.

"What'n hell?" Paul exclaimed to a grinning Stilt, as they walked toward the building.

"A little entrepreneurship," Stilt replied, in shocking imitation of a Harvard.

When they entered the building, Paul was dumbfounded to discover that all of the equipment appeared to be in working order. If he *had* flipped the right switches, in the right sequence, he would've found that he could bring all the lights and scopes and charts into action again. Neither Russ, nor John was on board at the time. But they had played a little trick on Paul during his convalescence. They 'd cleaned out the wreckage, saved what they could and had gradually installed a system that was equal to the first one—Stilt said it was *better*, slyly admitting that even a CIT man can learn from experience.

A few days after the fight on the tower, some of Mike's boys had come back. A day, or so, later a few more came, and some new ones. They'd liked Mike and Paul and, finally, they had some appreciation of what was trying to happen there. They had prepared themselves in case of any trailers of the storm. There were now handy lengths of pipe, a few nasty looking things attached to long handles, and some other deterrents for unappreciative customers. These were hidden, but conveniently at hand. One of the older boys had the idea that if they got the place cleaned up, maybe some people would come to see it. And if they came, a coffee can might ring a little. It didn't take too many quarters to buy a few baseballs and a couple gloves.

Russ had called John one day and asked him if he wanted to take a look at the scene of action. When they saw what the boys were doing, they decided to make it a better deal for them. John had taken care of all the equipment refurbishment over Russ' protests that they hadn't tapped all of Jake's trove yet. Russ and Stilt had taken over the rebirth of the overall system. Stilt had matched his grin with the boys during his time there, and had also done some guide and demonstration service when they got to the ready point. There had been a fair number of quarters and everybody was fairly happy.—and then came Jake.

When Paul saw what guts and inspiration and confidence had wrought... an overlay of fresh ones over old ones...he had to call Jake and he asked him to take safari over there again. When the Rolls pulled up, the chauffeur *still* uncomfortable, Jake half stumbled out and shuffled over to the site. He stopped, a hand on his head, when he saw the condition of the place and the ticket booth and the presentable kids and a few customers. Jake had made three trips there: once during construction; this time; once shortly after Paul's accident. When he'd seen that pile of bandages, he had to see what had caused it. There was the raped inside of the building...there was blood on several of the instrument faces and the floor. He'd seen wreckage, and a challenge to lip-service. Jake was impressed by what he saw now, too. After he took a good look around, he held a seminar. Its direct participants were the boys. Paul and Russ audited. Jake told them that they would never need anything bigger than that coffee can if they didn't learn something about advertising. He said he knew a man who had some competence in that area and—if they didn't mind—he'd ask this man to help them. Anticipating some success in using his influence, Jake also told them to get a larger ticket office and to move it closer to the front of the lot so they could pack in more customers.

Not long after Jake's seminar, well designed posters appeared in conspicuous places in Beverly Hills, Pasadena and San Marino. Carla had some of the action around the Pasadena and San Marino area, even dipping into the Beverly Hills ghettos with some of her friends...and that larger ticket office soon came in handy.

The attraction would never keep Disney, or Knott up at night. But the take over a few months equipped several baseball teams, built two ball diamonds with bleachers, and some of the other amenities of the big parks on a small scale. It also accumulated a substantial fund for whatever the boys had in mind. Some people—Paul, Russ, John, for example—accused Jake of padding the take. He accused them of insulting his business sense. But it didn't insult the basic gentleman from Bel Air. Jake had, in fact, found another big piece of relevance for that project.

And there was John and Martha going to Europe for an indefinite stay. Before they left, they gave a dinner party that included Paul and Russ. During the evening, John admitted that he was thinking about retiring. He told them that some of Martha's and Carla's and Paul's descriptions had rubbed off on him and he wanted to visit some of the places where his money had gone before.

"You can't retire any more than I can," Jake said. "I expect to live to be a hundred and ten—and I expect to give a lot of guys hell *all* along the way." Hetty made a horrible grimace to Martha with that. "And speaking of hell, Paul., congratulations on your White House adventure. I'm happy that somebody else has been exposed to your damn responsibility and contamination." The aura of Jake's grin was large.

"It was quite an experience, Jake. They want me to help out on that monitoring network the president recommended. Remember what I said about those *other streams*, John? Man, if this thing has the potential I think it has, it'll take your company and a lot more to handle the business. We've just been looking at air, so far. I told the President that some of his damn water doesn't taste like ambrosia, either, and that's another kettle—of fish, hopefully." His soliloquy finished with a laugh aimed at his compadre of Cabo Blanco.

"This character has opened my window to more fresh air than I knew existed...damned if he isn't making me like it. But just lying on my butt for a while sounds awfully good to me...let the youngsters do some driving."

"I think that decision crap isn't cast in concrete, by a long shot," Paul said.

"We'll see. By the way, Paul, I got a letter from Francisco the other day... been meaning to show it to you." John was about to excuse himself for the letter, when Martha suggested a more general move elsewhere for the ladies.

The men drifted into John's study and the ladies decorated the room of the big fireplace. Almost as much laughter came from that quarter as from John's. Carla had her mother's itinerary all laid out...over Martha's laughing protests. Martha could have supplemented Carla's agenda in ways she hoped Carla hadn't thought of yet.

While the men were inspecting John's treasures, and laying down a heady aroma derived from vintage Havanas lubricated by vintage cognac, John handed Paul a piece of paper. It was written in black ink with a poor pen and worse penmanship. The paper wasn't bond, and it had several finger smudges on it, and a stain that suggested tequila origins. Paul thought he detected a lipstick smear near one corner. When they all studied it under a lamp, they agreed that it was a tequila stain and that smear sure as hell was lipstick. Correcting some interesting spelling and punctuation, it read:

Compadre,

It has been too long for you and the young one. I hope he has not found the big head. This would slow him down in the chair dance and make him less resolute. I have seen one like we saw before. Maybe he is the one. He looks very mean and I think I need two more pairs of legs on my boat before I go to him.

(signed) *Francisco Gomez*

Paul looked up at John after reading it, and he grinned...maybe ruefully, maybe like Pizarro grinned, if he ever did. "It brings back much tiredness just thinking about it, compadre." The other men understood that grin, having seen the sword and listened to John's story about how it came to his den.

"We'll talk about it. We'll probably let him try to kill us again." John's own grin was complicated. "But not, by God, until I've soaked up some peace—and strength—in Europe."

Later, after the ladies were distributed about the house, the men were camped around the big fire pit. It was active again, giving intriguing life to Martha's portrait.

"You said you were probably going to work for the government." Jake didn't bother to camouflage his disgust with that prospect. And he was looking in Paul's direction.

"With it, Jake...*with* it." Paul replied.

"You're too traitorous to make a good government man."

"Jake! You're my guest—I'll not have you..." John's dismay was phony, but Jake liked his props close to him.

"Crap!" Jake interjected sweetly. He turned to Paul, who was very relaxed and calm about everything. "You come to my fireplace. You tell me how businessmen and engineers should act. You're an engineer. With a little help from your shouting friend here...we could make a passable businessman out of you. You would then be in an excellent position to *put up—or shut up*. When you tell me you're turning to the government, then I call you traitor—to yourself." Jake leaned back, relighting his stogy, and then laid down some puffs whose totality had parts of a genii with a dirty smirk.

"*Damn* you, Jake." Paul was sitting straighter now. Jake's remarks, as a lot of his had a tendency to do, had struck a nerve. "Like I said...I'm not going to marry 'em—I'm *just* going to help out a little."

"Good," Jake grunted.

"Splendid," John stated.

"They got so damn many bastards back there now...another marriage wouldn't make any difference, anyway," Russ said.

"And now, my critical, long-memory friend, I think I got you in the vicinity of the family jewels." Paul's version of wickedness in a grin wasn't in Jake's league, and Hetty would have disputed that statement, but she was in a different part of the house. Jake just waited. He had lots of time...hell, the New York markets didn't open for a few hours yet.

"You'll make me an entrepreneur. I've heard this takes money...*carloads* of it. I wouldn't think of turning to your hated government for subsidy. I don't like a lot of your bankers—present company excepted, of course, John."

"*Naturellement,*" John murmured.

"John has already stuck his neck out farther than some of his stockholders like. This tends to suppress my inclination to lean on him some more. My acquaintances among the very affluent are damned limited. This happy situation makes my resources—for the kind of business you have in mind—damn thin...I can't even see 'em, for Christ's sake—if *you'll* pardon a word." Paul nailed Jake with his eyes, or thought he did.

"You used the words, *damn thin*, instead of *none*. This would imply that there are a few suckers—investors—who might stick their neck out for you...a little way." Jake's eyes played around on Paul's face, picking up Paul's eyes a couple times *en passant*.

"I have an interesting definition of that word, *few*."

"I don't want to hear it."

"Ah...we've got an inevitability here, John. Few equals one, Jake—few equals one. My teachers at Caltech wouldn't go into ecstasy over that, but it makes me happy. That takes us right to the little equation, *one equals who*. Want to explore the fascinating equality around *who*, Jake?"

"No."

"You equal who, Jake. You equal who...it's got a nice ring to it, eh, John?"

"It's a little owly—but it's also a little catchy," John said. Now *his* grin had a definite nuance that some nuns abhor, publicly.

"I think I'll get out of here." Jake actually started to get up.

"Like hell you will," Paul stated.

"I got to go to the john."

"You can hold it, damn it, until *you* put up—or shut up," Paul concluded.

And so, after this particular discourse among gentlemen of business and science had finally come to the room where many such talks *should* find oblivion among their own kind, the company that came to be known as Civilians, Unltd, had its genesis. Jake would be in contamination up to some extremities of his checkbook. And this also gave Paul the interest and multifaceted talent of a man who could help it along, if anybody could. If he could bring John and Russ into it—it *would* go.

About a week before John and Martha were scheduled to leave for Europe, everyone, including Carla, decided that a staff meeting was in order. The veranda of the Drake house did service, again.

"It looks like you're set with Jake, Paul. Believe me, you couldn't find a better man in your corner...and I'm not limiting myself to the buck. If I've got misgivings about Jake's gimlet eyes...I'll try to sublimate them toward a *higher* cause." John's smile was moving toward the encyclopedic again.

"I know about those eyes, John." That night at Jake's place, when nosey firelight leaked through hot iron into Jake's eyes and Martha's too, came at him. "I hope I can reach his expectations." Paul wiped a hand across his face. "You certainly weren't serious about retirement...the fun's just beginning. I don't expect my involvement with the GI boys will amount to much—I'll *keep* it that way."

"I like your attitude on that...seems like I'm liking your attitude on too damn much lately. I think real progress on this front will come from local and state efforts. They'll bring the impetus that puts the meat into this thing. You've intimated that the Feds have had a good chance to play with this ball and it's *still* a long way from the goal posts..."

"On the sidelines," Paul suggested.

"In the water bucket." John *was* getting caught up in it. "It may be a poor simile, but I know of several major breakthroughs that came from one lonely little bastard plugging away at his desk and a dinky lab, while the associated R&D complex, spending more money on toilet paper, puts out nothing but proposals and progress reports. Maybe this thing needs a few of us lonely little bastards."

"And Jake," Paul added, swinging his eyes toward the ladies who had been interested auditors of this philosophical exchange.

"God help us, yes—*and* Jake," John sighed. He turned to Carla, "Won't you change your mind and give us a break on this trip?"

"Daddy, you *know* you and Mother will have more scope without a chaperone. Besides...I happen to have a few plans of my own." In announcing this conflict of interest, Carla had used her soft voice, particularly for the last two words...but the softness didn't cover that company's reaction to her.

"Plans?" Martha asked. Maybe she could hear the rustle of an encyclopedia's pages.

"This...*entrepreneur*...made the mistake of telling me he thought there might be a place for me in this crusade of his—I mean to hold him to his word." Carla looked at Paul with just the smallest smile tantalizing him, her parents. Carla had put in enough finality, that when Paul looked at her, and then took his look to John and Martha, he didn't carry, or run into, a smile.

After the silence had become almost touchable, Paul said, "I guess that's my cue, if I'll ever hear one. I'm guilty of Carla's charge...I said something like that during a moment of weakness...admiration, for a kid who tends to weigh that *well enough* status too lightly."

"Explain that," Carla ordered. The voice was still in that mature vein that disputed Paul's charge, and the physical ensemble of her posed the strongest possible refutation of his 'kid' label. She had just placed some attributes of Huntington's aristocrats in his face again and this almost untracked his train.

"You should be thinking about bright young men at the country club, such as sleep a' night—but not too much."

"Ouch! You can do *much* better than that after all the poetry I've pushed into your stubborn hide—I must presume you're suggesting that *you* have insomnia." The tiniest lift of eyebrows, still that smile that could incapacitate a man, and that voice that could deny a man irrelevancies decorated by any voice he could pull out in front of her.

"This guy's insomnia may get him killed one day—it damn near has already," John said.

"You see, my little disciple, your parents know that I would tend to rub off some of the laughter that's your..."

"My *right?*"

"Absolutely. If you can't have a shot of it now, your bank for later years may let you down—and you'll make some withdrawals, I *can* promise that."

"In one of your less weak moments, you also made the mistake of telling me that Russ—and the others—had shown you that laughter and responsibility can be intertwined quite well...this coupling almost a prerequisite for sanity, I believe you said—in another weak moment, of course." She hadn't looked away from him. No smile now. Just blue eyes nailing him. Her father and mother were content to stay away from this chat—it had moved out of their range anyway, and they both knew it.

Paul knew that this young one had put his foot—both feet—farther in his mouth and he would have to do some extraction before he choked. He scratched his head, looked at Carla, looked at Martha, then at John...who were *no* help. The classical endowments of the Drake's landscape panorama that nudged close to him had no inspiration for him now. Finally, he came back to Carla, having just tripped over footprints that might lead to an extraction.

"In *stronger* moments, I've read a little about some of the European work on pollution. As a red-blooded American boy, I'm ashamed to say that there's more honest to God work on air and water pollution over there—right now—than anything in this country. Lip-service...we don't take a back seat to anybody. We've fed, and grown fat, on all kinds of streams from Europe. It's my two cents that it'll be this way on the pollution control front, too." He hadn't touched the modest Scotch John had provided in deference to Carla. He did so now, scanning the carefully neutral faces of John and Martha before coming back to his beautiful protagonist. "The Dutch and French...Germans and Swiss are cooperating in a large scale attack on air and water pollution. And I think that *that* happy thought might just provide my out with you." Paul's smile at his conscience wasn't nearly as good as the one he gave Carla. If he had just laid an offering on his *out*, her face was not cooperative...tending toward an explorer's assessing a very ambiguous paradise. "I don't like that word *out*...but let's kick it around a little—*before* I slap your face." Her smile was back, but it was a version he'd seen on canvas at Henry and Arabella Huntington's San Marino place...that knife edge business again between satisfaction and penalty.

"You could combine a European venture—God knows, you don't *need* another one right now—with some honest to Betsy survey and contact work for me, while I try to get a few things rolling over here." Paul's satisfaction with his sudden inspiration was definitely on an ascending trajectory. He'd also just demonstrated that venerable coupling between crisis and invention, this time flavored by the resurrection of a lady's happy excitement.

"Mother...Daddy—do you think I *could*?" The little Stanford innocent had pulsed the proceedings with an exuberance it needed.

"Don't look at me," John said, looking at Martha.

"You people have the damnedest faculty for putting me on *your* spots," Martha said. She was forceful, but she might have put a tad too much shading of irritation into it. In those moments, she'd experienced a flux of emotion whose amplitude and kind closely matched Carla's. Carla's maturing interest in Paul was certainly known to her, and John. Neither had vocalized any part of *that* complication, but there had been some silent conversation over the years when this interest showed itself in various ways. They knew their daughter would abide no regimentation and they hoped...as Carla hoped...that Time would dispense some grace in this respect. A professional involvement might be a way to at least defer, possibly diffuse, a confrontation of forces to which all of them had given life. "If I *must* say something then I'll say that I think it's a splendid suggestion. Paul has indicated that it would be important to him, probably to you, too, Carla. And now John..." Martha made the motion of a ball being hit to the side of the net that was her husband's.

"Thank you, *dear*. Well...if I must say something, I'll say that Paul may have something here. I know a little about that foreign work and a good knowledge of it could give him valuable perspective for his own efforts—God help him—in entrepreneurship. If you could tear yourself away from those handsome Dutchmen, Frenchmen, Germans...*and* Swiss, long enough, you might even make a few good *business* contacts, too." There, he'd said it. He thought he was glad he'd said it and where'n hell was a drink?

Paul negotiated with Carla for a millisecond, or two, and then it was over. She would have to do some homework before she left. She and Paul could huddle on that...what she was to try to see, whom she was to try to see. But these were details. The decision was all and Carla didn't let her sophistication override her delight. The rest of them, over a very wide range of variance with Carla's, shared her joy.

Carla decided not to go over with her parents. And then Paul told her that she would have six and three-quarter days to pack, and one quarter for business, and that proportion should allow her parents the pleasure of her company on that delightful boat ride between New York and Southampton. That suggestion fastened everything down.

Actually, Carla used only a small fraction of her packing time allotment. She called Paul at his place several days later and suggested he take her to lunch at the Ship Room because it was convenient to the Huntington Library that was displaying some newly found illustrated manuscripts she wanted to see and she would expect to be picked up at ten o'clock AM—and to be on time. He told her he wasn't sure the Ship Room could accommodate them at that unseemly hour. She replied that *somebody* would feed them, and then she hung up without spending hardly any of the subtleties she was capable of pushing into an *adieu*.

They were at the contemplative coffee stage of their lunch at the Ship Room. She had been pestering him about her guide-lines for the action she would be taking on his behalf. He'd been noncommittal up to that point. He had smiled a lot, and made a very poor effort at hiding his appreciation of the young beauty in front of him. This annoyed her, a little...he could be *very* exasperating.

"I've tried to anticipate your unladylike eagerness," he finally said. "I've got some clippings and reprints from magazines and journals on the subjects you seemed determined to add to your affection. There's enough mention of places and people in these that they should give you some good clues as to your approach—attack. And I should prepare letters of commis- eration and inspiration for some of those poor guys."

"I haven't even *been* there, yet." Her eyes' capacity for servicing the vari- ous emotions continued to intrigue him...to prick deeper places of his memory.

"They'll doubtless need as much preparation for their coming trials as they can get." He tried to use some of Russ' own severity.

After their lunch, he took her to the great estate that Huntington had built in San Marino, now dedicated to art and literature and history in a way that drew scholars from all the world. Before they went to the library for the manuscripts, he made her go to the art gallery, and there they spent more than an hour in that place of Reynolds and Gainsborough and Paine...and Madame Ligonier. Except for the bronze of the bacchante near the entrance to the gallery, and those of the full-sized boar and the deer in travail against dogs on the front veranda, Paul couldn't say much for Huntington's statuary. Most of his pictures were, however, a different matter. In the main gallery, he looked at Madame Ligonier again...and long enough that Carla noticed this attention. She came to him, and then she joined their eyes in fixation on the life-sized oil painting of the other time aristocrat.

"She reminds me of mother...maybe not the huntress in the painting at our place, but *this* woman could easily assimilate there...and Mother could here, too...change places with Madame Ligonier and frustrate that husband who's standing a few feet away." Carla nodded toward the impressive gentleman who *was* looking at them from the wall on the other side of Blue Boy who sepa- rated him from his wife. During the soft soliloquy, Carla hadn't looked at Paul. "I don't know why, the similarities are subtle...if she could speak...it would help." The last words had been almost whispered to the painting. If she'd happened to notice Paul's face in those moments, she would've seen an interesting amalgam of wonder and sadness. Thought may be a powerful surrogate of sight. When Carla did look at him, she placed her hand very gently on his shoulder, and not until he looked at *her*, did she suggest that it was time to go to the manuscripts.

Afterward, they went to Paul's apartment, where he gave her the literature he'd promised. They were seated on a couch, fronted by a large coffee table and Paul had it covered with articles and pictures. They discussed the material for a long time. Carla found the information fascinating and she promised to study it...and take good notes. Paul packaged it into more transportable form, then he settled back, looking at her. Intercepting this, Carla smiled and also assumed a more relaxed position. After a few seconds of mutual appraisal, Paul said, "If you dig up anything really interesting over there I just might join you guys for a little while, later on."

"That would be wonderful, Paul. Now I *shall* take good notes." She made a new smile for him, more complicated than the ones she'd used in that room before. In all their time together, he'd never been forward with her...to her amusement at first, to her annoyance on several occasions, and once—by the pool of the pavilion—almost to her anger. Now, she had an appreciation for his situation that probably neither Paul, nor Martha, understood. A much larger component of her now was patience in all...most...things. She sustained this new smile and the target of her eyes alternated between Paul and the pile of inspiration on the table in front of her.

Paul *needed* some contact with her. He'd never kissed her beyond the playful license permitted in full view at parties and occasional celebrations of a personal, or seasonal, nature, he'd shared with her parents. He very much wanted to kiss her now—but he took her hand, and held it tightly in the action of a handshake.

"Okay, partner—we'll give 'em hell. Now will you *please* take that package and get out of here. I told your parents, I *promised* your parents, that I wouldn't put you in any danger you couldn't handle." He laughed after this speech. She did too. And if there had been some tension there, they'd released it, harmlessly. But then she spoiled the fine equilibrium of emotions.

"You worry about the contamination—let *me* worry about the danger." Then she put some more into his ears and his open mouth, "—And you're still taking me home, *partner*," she said, finally disconnecting from his conservative hand-shake as he tried to untangle their eyes.

19

There had been letters to Paul from Washington bearing on the subject of a Kansas eagle getting ready to test his eyes on terrain Paul had publicized, if not discovered. After seeing John and Martha and Carla off to Europe, he went to Washington.

He was outside direct presidential attention now, but some of the people he would meet were not, and he was surprised at the level in the hierarchy of his first meetings. There was some capacity for buck transfer here, but the buckets still tended to smaller sizes.

He tried to explain, more fully, the perspective he'd outlined for the president. They listened to him, and the compliment of smiles had about the right proportion of respect and amusement. Hell, he never really expected any more than the use of a few ears, qualified encouragement, and carefully constructed ambiguity on commitment. They listened to him rave, and then they sent him down to where an occasional drafting board, and a handbook of chemistry and physics, could be seen crouching among the encyclopedias of guide-lines and regulations. A few of the compliments were more effusive, and some of the amusement was less expertly concealed. But he gave it the best he could, and he got a big kick out of all of it. Several times, he called Russ for advice. Russ had his own problems of guiding grad students through the quagmire. But he listened patiently and, as per usual, gave advice and unsolicited encouragement.

Paul had insisted that his consultation be on a *gratis* basis, intimating that he didn't want such future adventure as he might engage to be tainted by a conflict of interest. This had been done before around here, but there was still enough novelty to make a few smiles of the right kind. He finally exceeded the intimation about future plans and told them that he, and his associates, were planning an organization that would regard environmental monitoring and cooperative control to be a frank—and major—target of opportunity.

After three weeks that had taken him around Washington, and several laboratory and office complexes within fifty miles of that city, he returned to

Pasadena. He hadn't seen Jake since that gentleman had shuffled away from the Drake house muttering about tricky hosts and trickier guests.

"Jake, I *am* glad to see you." Paul's announcement was too loud, and his handshake too firm for Jake.

"You should have brought objects of penitence...like caviar, maybe those sesame crackers I also like. But I see nothing...nothing but that damn *expectant* grin." Jake had already planted himself in soft leather, and he waved Paul to his.

Paul finally brought Jake to a point of sensible conversation. He told him about his Washington trip and his insistence on protecting future susceptibility to government contracts.

"Good," the old boy huffed. "You—*we*, damn you—can't overlook the mother load that looms before us even if it *is* the government." Jake reached for one of his big stogies, offering one to Paul.

"There'll be other veins, Jake...coming more directly from the people." Paul's cigar was up and coming.

"That might cut down on some of that traffic in Washington." Jake sent a smoke puff that traveled a long way.

"It *would* be a shame if the Defense Department had to stand in line behind Health, Education and Welfare."

"Not too much welfare."

"I tend to emphasize the health and education bits myself." Paul thought about Russ' prejudices in these respects. "I've a hunch that those two can take care of a lot of the welfare."

"What are your plans, Paul?" Jake had inadvertently slipped around Paul's venerable dogging question.

Paul told him a few things off the top of his head...the type of equipment they might target at first, possibly some involvement with the computer people, a lot of involvement with city, county and state people...maybe a trial at getting some of the industrialists to take more looks out of their windows. He also told Jake about Carla's planned survey of some of the foreign activity.

"That *kid*?" Jake snorted.

"That kid has plenty, Jake. Some of those guys may be in for surprise when intelligence takes no back seat to beauty." Paul's frank admiration wasn't lost on the perceptive one.

"She'll get her nose in your affairs."

"I can't find much trouble in that prospect." Paul leaned back in his chair, smiling. That was too much for Jake. He was damn near ready to blurt out something about Martha—and then, a couple seconds later, he was glad he hadn't.

"She's been trying to make a mark on the social scene, the one that isn't played out in the country clubs—but it hasn't worked for her...mostly token, ineffectual stuff that bothers her. I'd like to help her get a start that's more satisfying." Some of Jake's artifacts...the twilight caressing his big globe, an intriguing swirl of color in his big oriental rug...caught Paul for a moment. "Her conscience isn't a good match for her situation. It's too damn restless, but I think it's also rare. You've given me a taste for rare things, Jake."

"And expensive things—and maybe some things that might be more than you can handle."

Paul had to look at Jake and this took away most of his smile. Then he had to look away. "I guess Martha and I didn't fool many people." It was almost a private voice, but it had used the *past* tense and this improved his prospects with Jake.

"*Damn* few—not including John, I'm sure."

"If it's any consolation, he nailed me good when he found out about us." The voice was bigger than a whisper, but he stayed away from Jake's eyes until just the end.

"What else did he give you?" For this guest, Jake had fashioned a voice of special soft attributes that blended well into a moment that had touched both of them long ago.

After some more time of sanctuary in the oriental's colors, Paul looked at Jake. "He gave me a guest card for a gentleman's club." That seemed to satisfy one of the entrepreneurs of a prospective triumvirate. Jake, with updates from Hetty, knew Martha very well. That this affair could have ended with solid friendship all around certainly bore her mark as much as John's, but Jake had just received enough from Paul to close that book without thumbing any more pages. They talked about some of the details of setting up an organization. Jake told him, and Paul didn't argue, that he (Paul) knew virtually nothing about these things. Jake said that he was too busy to do this education himself, but he would recommend several gentlemen to Paul who happened to have their offices in the LA financial quarter. Jake also recommended that Paul take damn good notes or he would find his ass in a ringer that he (Jake) would cheerfully furnish. He also told Paul that he was glad that John had been approached about coming on board. He more than intimated that Paul would need all the help he could get to become a smiling entrepreneur...and Jake was smiling when he said that.

Just as Paul was leaving, Jake poked a stubby finger into Paul's stomach.

"You think they'll buy this"

"Buy *what*, Jake?"

"This goddamn pollution crusade—those pricks we're going to be sticking up everybody's ass!" This was a question of big scope that Jake had just laid on Paul and, in his optimistic mesmerism, Paul hadn't built an adequate answer to it...but he tried.

"I think it'll be a few stones building into a big rolling that nobody can ignore. I think we're going to be in the first trickle of stones...on our side of the Atlantic. They're already starting to roll on the other side. They're starting to equate some inconvenience, and a little loss of prerogative, with ultimate survival over there—I think that some of that music is starting to be heard here. We've put more bad notes into the general air than anybody—it's time for some of our own conductors to put their batons into this while we've still got time to make some sweet tunes out of our mess. And Jake..."

"Yeah?" Jake's own question had begun to depress him...and he'd also started to look for sanctuary in his rug, following some of Paul's footprints.

"We're going to leave some room for those rhodium-plated condoms— just in case we have to fall back a little."

"Beat it—Mr. Executive Vice President!" Jake ordered, pointing a grinning Paul to the door with that same busy finger.

Between his studies with Jake's gentlemen, Paul tried to think about staff, location, equipment, facilities, programs...and the other paraphernalia of the entrepreneur. Jake had suggested that there would be plenty of time to start moving dirt after he and John had talked it over. He just assumed that it would be Sanger-Drake, or Drake-Sanger Enterprises, and no nonsense about that. Jake put him on the payroll one day. Paul had a few bucks salted away, but Jake probably knew more about that than Paul thought. He told Paul about a good bank in Pasadena and suggested that sending checks directly to the bank was a good idea, and that was where the ones he would be sending were going. Paul couldn't in good conscience make the Porsche people happy yet, but he had a toehold in that vastly tolerant stratum of the business world, called *Junior Executives.* He would need a few new rags to show this, or hint this.

20

Carla had stayed with her parents just long enough to satisfy decent filial obligations. John and Martha had let her go with some of the feelings they'd had when she entered that other sink of iniquity, Stanford. But they had confidence in her multifaceted talent. The guys she would be contacting were, however, another matter.

After she had picked Paris as her base—a decision not entirely driven by business objectivity, she studied her clippings and notes again and planned an itinerary that would take her to Amsterdam and Rotterdam and Bonn and several of the industrial and university centers of France and Germany and the Netherlands. John had made phone calls to friends and associates, and this had opened some doors for her. A certain gentleman from Bel Air had also made some calls and he'd even instructed his secretary to pound out some inspiration for help on the teletype...help for a young associate of his who would be looking after some of his interests abroad. Carla took shameless advantage of these considerations. She saw much, talked much, and she added substantially to her inventory of notes and thoughts. This one, with the good French, overcame prejudices that her beauty and background engendered in many males, some females, coming within a scope that *technical person* couldn't contain. But, between requests for dinner engagements, and other engagements, they started a dialogue with her about possibilities, problems, and realities that actually included some of the technology of air and water quality management, and she had the faculty for improving the spectrum of what they talked about and showed her, the more they gave her. She was delighted, both with the technical enlightenment, and the hospitality. She accepted much of the latter and was careful to keep it inside *her* limits.

She wrote frequently to Paul. It didn't take the imagination of Veblin to glean that she was happy, that she was doing some good work over there. He had to talk to John about his involvement and, if he succeeded in that mission—a lot more. It had been almost two months since he'd seen John.

John had sent him several letters, mostly about what he and Martha were seeing. He mentioned Francisco again, and reminded that that ornery bastard wouldn't wait forever. In his last letter, John had hinted that some alpine air, or acceptable alternative, might be good for him (Paul) at that time. Martha's postscript to that letter was no discouragement to his coming over to their side.

Three weeks after Paul had come over, he joined them in Madrid. Carla was safely back in the fold again. They were sitting in a street cafe, sipping black coffee and chatting about their itinerary before the men took up the cudgel of toil again. John had teased Paul about coming back...but this time his acting didn't keep Paul on tenterhooks overly long. Paul told him about Jake's course, and that he thought he'd passed it. With appropriate facial adjectives, John told him that Jake had kept him very well informed about that progress. And Jake had finally admitted that they might have a businessman there—but to keep the whips handy.

Carla gradually favored them with stories about her recent safari into the technical wilderness that didn't seem like that to her, now. Between their laughs—and they couldn't squeeze *all* the tears out of them—she told them things that made John and Martha and Paul know their faith in her had been true. She'd left a precocious trail for Paul and John that they couldn't deny. She had acquired valuable information, and established contacts for them that bore the unique authority and imperatives of a beautiful woman's touch.

"We've created a monster," Paul said to John.

"We'll have to extend the executive wing beyond the two cubby holes we'd planned for ourselves," John replied, reflectively.

"You'll give her space—and a salary—commensurate with her worth, or you'll both hear from me...rather *directly*, I'll add." But Martha couldn't sustain honest gravity for long, either.

"Shakespeare should have something I could use right now...something about flattery and beguiling. But I'll take the flattery—no reservations...you make me so happy," the object of this play exclaimed sincerely, testing the nonchalance of her observers again.

"I'd like to see the Parthenon again," Paul said, after they had all gone to their coffee in silence for a while. "And someday, I'd like Russ to see it...preferably under his own power. He dug into the Greeks for me...without having been there—I want to repay some of that."

"We'll have your scholar in our little group, of course, as a consultant—and at their usually outrageous rates," John said. "He should be able to make it under his own power very shortly."

"If we make his rates outrageous enough," Paul concluded.

"I think Greece and some of the islands would be lovely now," Martha said. "I've seen some of them...but you never get enough. How shall we go... train, plane, car or donkey?"

"No donkeys, please, Martha," Paul said. "I remember one we had on the farm who had a taste for flowers...and my mother's flowers *were* beautiful that year."

"To his detriment, I'm sure," Martha said.

"You've met my mother."

They went by car to Italy, and then took a boat to Piraeus, traveling through the Corinthian canal. After several detours to lesser antiquities, early one evening they stood before the principal Greek objective. Even with the depredations of the Turks, and the touches of thousands more from various ages with various tempers of mercy, the Parthenon still showed enough of what the Greeks had put into it to make them all gasp as the golden light caressed it, and this almost insolent obeisance to the gods still presented most of its important particulars. Maybe those guys had built this miraculous persistence into it that could conjure the whole from the bones.

Finally, Carla couldn't stand it any longer and she left them, running up the steps of the several levels to the temple. The twilight caught her form in different attitudes of discovery, with only occasional backward encouragement to follow her. This vision of revelation argued against further passive commitment to it, so the laggard remainder started upward. Under Paul's impetus, what had begun as a single file procession quickly evolved into a near parallel advance of three pilgrims, hands linked, Martha the center. Her laughter was sufficient protest to the running and walking combination forced on her by Paul and John. This was a moment. And Paul Sanger's total acknowledgement of it barely stayed inside a proper silence. His wasn't the only encyclopedia that went up those steps and he and Martha managed to brush several looks on each other that tended to confirm this.

Then they went down to the Peloponnesus and Paul made them scramble around the valley where Sparta had stood. There was virtually nothing but history books now. But the vestiges of these men and women didn't need souvenirs to keep them in bright memory. As he savored the soft breeze that moved the leaves of the grapes and the figs of this land, Paul knew that John and Francisco and Mike and Russ would be comfortable in these precincts.

They were gradually assuming the dress and manners indigenous to this place of Greeks. The ladies bought blouses and skirts and scarves and shawls and ribbons, and some bold earrings and bracelets. The men wouldn't be shamed by this bold embrace of the land. They found pants with sashes for belts, and shirts of white softness needing bands of silk in bold colors about the throat to complete them. And they got broad-brimmed straw hats and sandals the ladies copied in their own style. When they started out for the islands, they were ready.

They took a little steamer to Melos and from there they went where impulse pushed them and by whatever means was open to them. One day, off Paros, they took a sailboat into water that was too blue, under a sky that was too bright. The women screamed and laughed, and everyone had taken plenty of water, before the men could master the thing and they could cruise in some dignity. They pulled into a small harbor that afternoon. A village was near enough, so they piled themselves with grapes and figs and goat cheese and dark bread and wine and then they went to an old abandoned olive grove near where they'd left the boat. Carla found a remnant of ancient stonework and vines that made them a grotto.

"My God...*is* there a real world?" Paul asked, after they'd made serious inroads on their feast. John was lying on his back, his head on Martha's lap. Paul was sitting against the remnant wall, flipping grapes to Carla who managed to catch a few, eat a few, and throw some back at him. A wild flower decorated Carla's hair...a splash of yellow against an unordered black cascade...and the whole of her that could justify any Greek excursion into the unfathomable provocations of woman.

"I think there is...I think that contrail we saw from the boat says there is. But I don't want to find it...for a while yet." John was looking up at blue eyes that had caught some of the light bounced from water and sand and was now threatening the shade of their sanctuary. Martha's finger traced part of John's lips. As she did this, her smile and her hair assimilated, emboldened, the subtler complexions of their grotto and made a strong evocation of the other women who had preceded her to this, or such a place, by these waters.

And then Paul became bolder. He gradually assumed a position next to Carla and made her accept grapes from the bunch without benefit of hands. She did well, only a little of the juice spilling from a corner of her mouth. When Paul laughed at her, she pushed him hard enough that he fell backwards on the sand and small flora carpeting their arena. At that moment, some aspect of John's indolence triggered Martha, and she flipped him and he rolled close to where Paul was contemplating his next maneuver. If this was invitation to saturnalia, then, under the circum-stances, it had to be limited. But with an introduction of screams and coarse laughter, they made a race into the farthest reaches of the grove. After a while, there was the best silence that the voice of sea birds, the breeze in the olived ancients, and the soft intercourse of the water with sand and rocks, could allow.

Long after Paul and Carla had decided to let walking succeed running, they saw two figures against a tree. Rather, two figures were very close to the trunk of a tree and the more beautiful one was pinned to it by the more resolute one. They had evidently intruded the end of a little play of passion.

"I will *not*...and you're hurting me," the pinned one said, placing a finger gently on the lips of the one who had just commanded.

"Faith John...is this gentleness...and patience?" Paul and Carla had decided that the circumstances of John's command were now invalid and that they might as well complete their intrusion.

"She's the most damnable woman I've ever known," John muttered, his captive unreleased, and not helping his humor by the several ways she seemed to cooperate in her capture.

"If *this* is damnation—I must kill my dictionary" Carla exclaimed. With that, she laughed at them and then at Paul, and then she went to the one bottle of wine left to them and waited for them to acknowledge that it *was* getting late and to accept her invitation to salute their departure.

On Ios they swam in water that was blue crystal and rested on sand that was white crystal. And on Ios, the women garlanded their hair with seaweed. On Thira, faces were pushed into sea water during interstices between their explorations.

Now, they were on Crete, and had satisfied themselves with some of the haunting wonders of that place. It was another evening of beguiling twilight when they came to a hill overlooking a tapestry of new and ancient parts. Paul and Carla had lingered over a minor ruin and John and Martha had gone on to the crest. Paul finally started to walk toward them, but he was held back by a gentle hand.

"I love you," John said to the one who no longer resisted his arms. Their faces were close, but not enough to keep some soft light from fluxing between them. Carla and Paul saw this, and then they saw that light extinguished.

They had all they could take of the islands, and the Greeks, for a little while. As Martha had said, it was heady stuff...you had to creep up on it in easy stages. When they returned to Athens, Paul took his leave of them.

21

"Consultant?" Russ was in Paul's apartment. He stirred a look into his bourbon.

"That's right. You're bringing up the veneer of scientific objectivity that glorifies our little venture." Paul's reply had come over Scotch.

"Veneer...that's the right word." Russ rubbed a hand across his face, thinking about the pile of problems that was always at the elbow of a senior man at Chemistry. "You say you guys will make it possible for me to see the place of the Greeks?" That grin was on now.

"If you husband your resources carefully, you may find yourself going up the temple steps on the backs of your own maidens."

"I'll take it! I'll take it!" After some talk about Europe and the Drakes, Russ forced himself toward objectivity. "And you say that the young one actually took notes...and met people who..."

"You've always had a talent for understatement. That *young one* will keep our noses to the goddamn grindstone with her enthusiasm, intelligence... eagle eyes."

"You said you used part of that line before...the Kansas eagle, remember?" That hand was back on that face again. "Did *you* manage to sneak in a little look at any of that foreign stuff...scientifically speaking?"

"Insulting implications aside...yes...I did notice that the Dutchmen have started a damn interesting survey and monitoring network for air pollution. They're using some of their own stuff, some French, German and Swiss. By the way, I saw French detectors compact enough for very modest airborne carriers. I think we can work some cooperation over there that could pull in French talent, too...I didn't run into as much arrogant chauvinism as I'd expected."

"They're reputed to have some tendency in that direction. So far, my perspective says that, overall, they're charming bastards and I think we can work with them." Russ' *we* had slipped in quietly, he'd already taken a step beyond Paul's invitation. "What'n hell are you showoffs going to call this evolution in our symbolism? I think you said that Jake had already christened it a *proliferation of impudent pricks.*"

"John and Martha and Carla and I kicked that around a little on a beach at Paros one day." Paul's vision of a special brightness flashed into him again at that moment.

"And?"

"We thought that Civilians Unltd. might be okay." An answer...but Paul's voice told that his trip to Paros hadn't stopped.

"Not Civeltek, or Technociv, or Civiloniks, or..."

"None of your *onic* or *tek* bits. Just a plain statement of the field of our objectives...the principal players."

"Unimaginative...but I guess the bank will accept it on my checks."

"They have accepted much worse, my friend. Now...speaking of your checks. Over the next few weeks, I'm expected by my authorities to get a little something rolling over here...plans, et cetera. Maybe you and I can kick it around for a couple weeks, and then we'll kick it around with John when he returns—no, by God, we'll send it to him. We need all the help we can get from his fishing trip." Paul collapsed into his chair with that massive entrepreneurial effort.

"Splendid. You whip up a little something, bring it to me here—I'll grade it."

"You *have* been digging my bourbon garden, haven't you. We will construct this thing together and *we* will evolve such a document as would make each particular..."

"You used *that* line before, too."

They got together. They agreed on certain objectives: comprehensiveness in detection and analytical ability; compactness in equipment, permitting the broadest possible application, airborne included; the types of computer couplings needed to service partial, and complete, delineation of the concentration fields they wanted. They thought of an area of a size like Southern California's. But they dreamed of a grid and display network that could pull in much more. When they got to staffing, they stopped.

"We've got enough here for a hundred—five hundred—people," Russ said one day in his office. "Christ, when you put in the sales and advertising, marketing, and all the other crap that keeps us in this tower of ivory—it gets impressive."

"*Impossible* is another word we might use. Maybe it'll challenge us—maybe it'll screw us." Paul just had another confrontation with reality, his first good one in a long time.

"It *will* be fun." The smile, and a word, from this guy with PAG and CIT credentials, had just goosed Paul in the right direction, again.

They finally put it together in a proposal they felt wouldn't insult John's intelligence, or the discipline that Princeton and Harvard—and experience—had wetted to a fine edge. Paul wanted to show it to Jake.

"Not yet. John will have contributions...corrections. This will lesson Jake's tendency to cast us forth from his place to the dogs that prowl Bel Air."

"Mobs of dogs in *Bel Air*?"

"Poodles—vicious, snarling poodles. They can rip a five hundred dollar suit to shreds, or at least pee on it...and I'm going to cherish my five hundred dollar suits." Russ allowed his smile to be reflective, and Paul was shocked at how far his friend's eyes seemed to rove beyond the constraints of that office in Chemistry.

Paul had extracted a forwarding address from John, and he used it. John reviewed the script. He had, as Russ had predicted, some suggestions, and some alterations...the latter tending to contraction of initial scope.

Before he left for Europe, John had dissolved his connection with Drake Instruments to the extent of no more involvement that what a big block of stock would entail. And bucks had changed hands before he let another crowd assume reins he'd held proudly for many years. He was now free to exercise his options of other involvement. Presently, these concerned a rendezvous with the salmon called *Atlantic*. So, he let the mails carry back the plans with his fingerprints on them.

"Not bad, not bad. It shouldn't take more than twenty—thirty—million to get you bastards off to a *slow* start. You must think my name is *Croesus*!" Jake had just made a humble acknowledgement of the plans laid out on the massive rosewood playing field of his desk.

"No...just Sternglas, Jake." Paul said. Russ didn't feel that his area of relevance overlapped this dialogue enough to justify more than his intrusion of Jake's bourbon.

"Well—if you don't *mind*, I'll talk this over with a couple friends before I give you the God damn support my dumb big mouth has gotten me into. And staff—you were saying that maybe *five thousand* would let you put a few erections?"

"Oh, nothing like that, Jake. Hell...if we go easy on the advertising, promotion, and the entertainment—and we're counting on you for some help on the entertainment—that makes..."

"My connections in the Middle East ain't so good right now."

"We'll even take the secondhand houris," Paul admitted.

"And you'll *like* 'em—you clean bastard!" Jake exploded.

A few days later, they met with Jake again, and several other gentlemen, in an office in downtown LA. At that time, Jake made his commitment to those characters who'd challenged him in that put up—or shut up game. They made plans for life blood to get started, and there would be some reservoir capacity in case a transfusion was needed for a young patient. Hands were shaken, and everybody tried to keep the affair as inspirational as possible. And they succeeded...except for Jake...right at the end. He muttered something about *water, yet*, just as he left the room, trying to fend off several sets of hands that persisted in touching his shoulders.

Carla had insisted on a more leisurely culmination of the journey with her parents. After a series of drives and flights to residues of mutual interest, they had come to Grenada and, inevitably, to that derivative of pain and inspiration that is called the Alhambra. In a courtyard that yielded a marvelous replication of water sounds by mosaics and stones and plantings, John said, "There's too much distraction for the devotion needed to run a business properly."

"You've managed to fight it." An Andalusian light, tempered by the soft nuances of the courtyard, caressed Martha's eyes. The mantilla she'd been wearing in a token draping around her shoulders sought some conjunction with mostly unfettered hair that had found its own caress of light.

"I was—am—a giant among men." John's correlative laugh couldn't be private to Martha under the circumstances. But she felt no present inclination to dispute him, and her look to him tried to be exclusive.

"Carla, dear...what are *your* plans?" Martha asked the other beauty who was also complimenting Spain at that moment...in her instance, a smaller intricacy of black lace gathered on her neck and throat.

"Daddy...you were mumbling something about those salmon in Norway before you go home. I was...thinking." Carla turned her head away from the brightness of the small plaza for a moment, toward a tiny water jewel decorating a tile piece. The Alhambra also gave her some orchestration with inimitable soft complexities of water sounds.

"Oh God...here we go again, she's *thinking*!" John's trepidation wasn't entirely playful. "In one of my less strong moments, I remember *saying* something about that—your father never mumbles." His smile, and his rebuke, got tangled. But he hadn't made any interruption for his daughter.

"I have *all* those notes...Paul has *all* those other things to think about... and get started. I...I'd like to stay in Paris for a while...digest my stuff—maybe condense it into a minor treatise." She shot a quickie look to Martha with that. She might have just forced Martha to think about other conjunctions at that moment. Unpredictable—sometimes uncontrollable—memory suddenly made Carla think about the one she'd had with Paul and Mary when they first met... she had said that his work sounded *fascinating*...at that time, in front of her, he'd found another use for that word, silently. She hadn't known about this... but in those same moments some of him had fluxed to her, silently, and he hadn't known about this.

"And pick up a lot of expensive ideas from those Frenchmen."

"She has all the tutoring she'll ever need in that respect," Carla's chief tutor stated.

"I'll stay in Paris, while you and Mother take after your salmon in..."

"Alta." For this one of his loins, at this time, John had to use his biggest grin.

"And when you've had your fill—when Mother has had her fill—we'll all come back to see what a few weeks of quiet devotion to business has wrought." Carla looked at Martha, who seemed to support her daughter's agenda. It was, therefore, decided. The debaters of Westminster could do nothing more with it. Carla hadn't even looked at John, who was resting his head against a wall of tile, feeling the exhilarating breath of unassailable logic course about him. But those damned antique conjunctions had been assaulting John, too...they wouldn't let him lean too far into those seductive tiles...his question was inevitable.

"And then?" John finally presumed to ask her. He didn't look at Carla, and Martha nearly surrendered to the same impulse. Both of them were clutched by different parts of an encyclopedia...their, Paul's, collaboration, that had left other parts of itself to Carla.

"And then we'll see how *Carla* Drake fits into things," Carla said, her eyes finally nailing John and Martha to the tiles of that courtyard in Grenada, a city on the continent of Europe, in the country of Spain...where there had been a habit of looking at new worlds.

www.ingramcontent.com/pod-product-compliance
Lightning Source LLC
Chambersburg PA
CBHW031101020726
47495CB00007B/1985